MW01602046

Sowing Chaos

The Collapse Book 1

John Babb

and

William Alan Webb

δ

Dingbat Publishing
Humble, Texas

SOWING CHAOS
Copyright © 2021 by John Babb
Primary Print ISBN 979-87-07278440

Published by Dingbat Publishing
Humble, Texas

All rights reserved. No part of this book may be reproduced in any form or by any means without written consent, excepting brief quotes used in reviews.

eBooks cannot be sold, shared, uploaded to Torrent sites, or given away because that's an infringement on the copyright of this work.

This book is licensed to the original purchaser only. Duplication or distribution via any means is illegal and a violation of International Copyright Law, subject to criminal prosecution and upon conviction, fines and/or imprisonment. No part of this e-book can be reproduced or sold by any person or business without the express permission of the publisher.

Thank you for respecting the hard work of this author.

This is a work of fiction. Names, places, characters, and events are entirely the produce of the author's imagination or are used fictitiously, and any resemblance to persons living or dead, actual locations, events, or organizations is coincidental.

This book is dedicated to the men and women of this country who stand the watch: members of our nation's uniformed services, law enforcement, firefighters, EMTs, medical personnel, those who safeguard our public health at the state and local levels, employees of the Department of Homeland Security, Department of Agriculture, Department of Health and Human Services, Department of Energy, Environmental Protection Agency, U.S. Customs and Border Patrol, the Bureau of Alcohol, Tobacco, Firearms, and Explosives, the Federal Bureau of Investigation, the Central Intelligence Agency, the Secret Service, our federal family of intelligence agencies, and business people who work very hard to keep their portion of our critical infrastructure safe and secure. Thank you for all you do for the rest of us.

Foreword

William Alan Webb

It feels strange writing a series introduction for the sixth book to be published. Regular readers already know that *Sowing Chaos* is the long-promised prequel to the Last Brigade Universe, as written by my friend John Babb. This is the story of what happened in the 15 months leading up to The Collapse, and... well, let's not mention that. Spoilers, you know? Anyway, John was my guy to tell this story, hand-picked by me because he visualized the events better even than I did.

All kidding aside, to those for whom this is your first introduction to the Last Brigade Universe, please accept my gratitude to you for entrusting us with the most precious thing in your life—your time. I firmly believe you will find the commitment worth it.

The series has proven to be popular with thousands of readers. From the standpoint of its creator, me, this imposes an ever-increasing burden to maintain the quality of the books. I've spent 50 years working on my craft, and try very hard to show improvement in everything I write. But there are also many, many stories left to tell of America's fall and rise, too many for me to ever write them all. That's where John Babb came in.

As you might expect, I've been picky about who gets to write in the LBU. The last thing I want to do is disappoint my loyal readers. John was the author of three excellent novels prior to writing this one, all of which I read and thoroughly enjoyed. His style is quite different from mine, so for readers coming to this book already familiar with the adventures of the 7th Cavalry, be advised. I happen to love the way he writes, and hope you do too. It is more like Tom Clancy than it is my style, but most would argue that's a good thing. More to the point, if John had not written this book, I'm not sure the story would ever have been told. I just don't have that much bandwidth, and I sure don't have John's technical background The people, meetings, protocols, and references in this book are all straight from John's life. He required no research other than searching his own memory.

This is Book 1 of The Collapse. John has begun writing Book 2, and it is a damned lie that I'm standing behind him holding a blunt object and yelling for him to write faster... I prefer edged weapons. John has also finished a story-arc set more or less simultaneous to *Standing Among The Tombstones,* The Last Brigade Book 6. His book, titled *Hell's Hip Pocket*, takes place east of the Mississippi River. You can read the first chapter at the end of this book. The sequel to that is *A Reservation in Hell* and both should be out in 2021.

For me, the guy who sat down on September 1, 2014, and began typing a bit of fiction on a lark, this is all quite exciting. See, these stories are all new to me as I read them, just as they are for you. That writers with the talent of John Babb are motivated to spend hundreds of hours in an imaginary (although *how* imaginary seems to be up for debate these days) world I created, is truly humbling.

Even as I type these words, I'm working on my own novel of The Collapse, *Hallowed Ground,* and *Standing Fast, Stories in the Last Brigade Universe* is also galloping toward publication. I couldn't be more stoked about that book. For those keeping count, that's six books planned for 2021, but there will likely be a second anthology built around *Fantastic Stories in the Last Brigade Universe,* maybe *Standing Awash In Tears, The Last Brigade Book 7,* along with *Task Force Zombie 2, Out for Blood* and a full length novel, *Task Force Zombie 3: Not Enough Bullets.* So hang on, my dear friends, buy the ticket and take the ride. It's gonna be a blast!

Bill Webb
Eads, TN
9 February 2021

A Note from the Author

I consider myself very fortunate to have the opportunity to write in Bill Webb's *Last Brigade Universe*. For those of you who don't know me, I come from a background in pharmacy and public health. For several years, I was an assistant surgeon general, working in the Office of the Surgeon General. A good portion of my responsibilities was to think about various threats to our country from the CBRNE (Chemical, Biological, Radiological, Nuclear, and Explosives) point of view, and then consider how my service, the U.S. Public Health Service, would respond. *Sowing Chaos* is my attempt to tell a story that is packed with scenarios which hopefully will make the reader realize that these threats are unfortunately not only completely feasible, but absolutely possible. Indeed, it could be the accumulation of these exact kinds of events which would require that the Last Brigade Universe come to life if we are to survive.

John Babb

TABLE OF CONTENTS

Main Characters

Dr. Angela Martinelli—CIA operative/nurse/linguist

Bob Williams—CIA Division Chief for North Korea

Abel Adams—Department of Homeland Security, Assistant Secretary

Colonel Early Johnson—Director of DHS Bio-Watch Program

RADM Hope Sheffield – Director, Centers for Disease Control and Prevention

Kim Jong-Un—Chairman of the DPRK /Excellency/Wonsu/The Fat Man

Kim Yo-jong—Sister of DPRK Chairman and Director of Propaganda & Agitation Department

Colonel-General Moo-sung—Minister of State Security in DPRK

Colonel Ho-young—Operations Officer in the Bio-Warfare Center in DPRK

Xerxes Abbasi—Iranian terrorist

Yoo Ki-hong—Shepherd and deep cover South Korean National Intelligence Service agent

Hiroko Arita—Captured Japanese girl

Daniel Won-shik—CIA operative, South Korean by birth

Chapter 1

The Taking
Aikawa, Japan July 1, 2021

On the dock, the teenagers of the small fishing village talked and laughed among themselves, all the while keeping a sharp, hopeful eye on the sea. It was almost ten o'clock in the evening, but they were far enough north in July that it was not yet dark. Unfortunately, the incoming fog had quickly obscured everything within a meter of the water's surface, and shrank visibility to not much more than the length of the dock.

The six girls and two boys, all between the ages of twelve and sixteen, were waiting on the return of four fishing boats to their harbor on the west side of Sado Island. Finally, they identified the sound of an approaching boat motor, and after a few minutes, one of the girls spied the bow of a boat slowly emerging from beneath the fog bank. It was strange that the vessel showed no light, but the young people paid little attention. They all knew the process of docking a boat, retrieving its catch from the hold, and packing the fish in baskets to carry up to one of the communal freezers would take at least a half hour, so they continued their banter.

The realization that the boatmen did not belong to Aikawa was sudden. Three men leaped from the boat, all armed with automatic weapons. One of them spoke broken Japanese. "You make sound, you will be shot. Get on boat."

When one of the girls began to cry, she was soundly slapped, followed by a rifle held against her head. There would be no more noise. The eight village youngsters were rapidly loaded on the boat, then pushed quickly down a lad-

13

der into the hold. One of the men held out a sack. "Cell phones." They all stepped forward and surrendered their devices. Less than two minutes after arriving, the boat reversed its motor, turned about, and headed west across the Sea of Japan, completely disappearing into the fog within thirty seconds.

In less than an hour, and some twenty miles out to sea, two of the boatmen entered the ship's hold, each grabbing one of the teenage boys. By pushing, shoving, and other gesturing, they made it clear the youngsters were to go up on deck. The girls started to climb the ladder as well, but were waved back down by a crew member with a machine pistol, and the hatch was closed.

On deck, the boys carefully gauged the four-to-two odds, factored in the weapons, and decided to follow directions. They rapidly had oily rags stuffed in their mouths so they couldn't cry out, then their hands were tied behind their backs. Finally, a small concrete block was tied around their ankles before they were positioned on the starboard side of the vessel. The boatman who could speak their language grinned maliciously before simply saying, "We find out how well you Nips swim," and they were pushed overboard, along with the bag of cell phones.

When the boys didn't come back to the hold in a half-hour, the girls began to call out to them. There was no response. They finally decided to try and get some sleep. The hold smelled of decades of long-dead fish, and the longer they were confined, the more fetid it became. As the night wore on, it was somewhat difficult for each of them to get adequate oxygen. Their eyes were irritated and burning, and all began to experience headaches. Two of the girls banged on the hull, shouting at the men above to at least open the hatch and allow some air to flow. It seemed like hours passed before the hatch was finally propped open. All of the girls gathered as close as they could to the opening in hopes of finally being able to breathe.

The next morning the captives were advised the boys had been turned loose when the ship passed close to a nearby island. For the remainder of the voyage, the crew turned their full and unrestrained attention toward the girls. The smallest of them retreated to a corner, declaring she was only nine years old.

CHAPTER 2

The Test
East Coast of North Korea August 1, 2023

The fat man, who was often said to be the only fat man in his entire country, was perched in the back seat of the specially constructed limousine, along with two other men of considerably less girth. The vehicle was parked two hundred meters from an isolated section of beach, and one hundred kilometers south of Hamhung on the Sea of Japan. The sound-proofed section of the automobile was filled with acrid smoke, the remains of at least a half pack of cigarettes consumed by the fat man in their journey from Pyongyang.

His dress, as always, was black from head to toe, which at times in the colder months was contrasted with a snow white scarf wound around his thick neck. The only ornamentation on his clothing was a small red pin on his left breast, which was imprinted with images of his father and grandfather. His hair had been cut in one of the 28 government-approved styles. To describe it as 'high and tight' was an understatement. His hair was shaved from his neck to exactly eight centimeters above his ears, then allowed to flourish in a gravity-defying pompadour.

The men accompanying him were in the olive drab uniform of the DPRK Army. Like every military officer who found themselves accompanying the fat man, both men held small black notebooks. On this, they were expected to be ready to transcribe every interesting utterance or command of their leader.

As always, he had insisted that the day's event be conducted during a time of low cloud cover. Too often, his generals had warned of how easily spy satellites could view and interpret his comings and goings; and once sighted, it would be a simple thing for his enemies to deploy an armed drone with the mission of erasing his limousine from the face of the earth. Hence, the cloudy day.

On the sand below were six young women, clothed in shorts and tank tops, all in a bit of shock at their unexpected temporary freedom. When they spied the men in white making their way down the dunes, they instinctively all retreated into the surf, putting as much distance as possible between themselves and the newcomers. They were too well acquainted with what unspeakable actions might come next in this God-forsaken land. Five of the girls huddled together, pointing and weeping. A sixth stood knee-deep in the frigid water, her thin arms crossed, glaring toward the intruders.

The entire area, for five hundred meters in each direction, was enclosed by a three-meter-tall cyclone fence. Signs on the enclosure proclaimed "Danger! No admittance. Property of the Democratic People's Republic of Korea." Inside the fence, and standing between the women and the limo, three large industrial fans were spread out in a semi-circle, all facing the beach. The fans were similar to those found at construction sites and outdoor venues to combat hot and humid environments. Beside each fan stood a technician, clothed in brilliant white bio-safety level four laboratory gear, which covered them from head to toe. Included in each of their suits was an internal cooling system, as well as a self-contained breathing apparatus.

The three lab techs apparently realized they were being observed by a greater power, and immediately brought themselves to attention, all focusing on the black Zil 4112R limousine on the bluff above them. The bullet-proof rear window lowered, a hand emerged, awaited a curt verbal command from the interior, and immediately followed with a quick chopping motion. In unison, the technicians took two steps forward, turning on their generator-powered fans. The white-clad men then unlocked three metal briefcases and removed identical air-tight containers. Each man then carefully unscrewed the seal on their container, held it directly above the front of the fan, and gradually shook the one-ounce contents into the windstream of the three fans.

The almost invisible powdery substance from the containers was instantly propelled toward the beach, as well as its six young targets. Once emptied, the containers were returned to the metal cases, after which each technician activated a device on their individual briefcase, set them on the ground, and moved quickly away from the beach. Within ten seconds, the briefcases were consumed in the white-hot heat of magnesium fires.

As the technicians retreated further to a decontamination truck, Dr. Min-shik turned to the fat man. "Brilliant Comrade, we will know within five days if the particle size of the powder is such that it can be propelled one hundred meters by the wind of the fans, and still be airborne enough to be inhaled by the test subjects."

The fat man turned to the high-ranking officer, smiling to himself at the sight, or the lack thereof, of the man's ears. They appeared to be barely visible bumps on the sides of his head. "Senior Colonel Min-shik, can you draw similar conclusions if the distance is significantly greater, perhaps a full kilometer?"

"Alas, Brilliant Comrade, this will require additional testing." He turned briefly to acknowledge his fellow scientist, Major Ho-young. "Also, it may be somewhat difficult for us to duplicate the safety of today's test with one requiring ten times the distance, and the resulting much greater spread of the bacteria over undoubtedly hundreds of acres, without further particle size testing."

Ho-young had sat silently throughout the drive and test, in deference to his senior officer, but it was now or never, and he decided to seize the opportunity, however brief it might be. "Excellency, our research has allowed us to find what I believe is a perfect weapon-grade product." Both the fat man and the colonel looked in his direction in surprise. Ho-young decided to plow forward. "That is to say, we are using a very virulent form of the bacteria, which has undergone repetitive animal testing. In the preparation used today, we have a high concentration of the required spores. They are of uniform particle size, all between 1.5 and 3 microns in diameter. The preparation has a low electrostatic charge, and thus should not be tied up and lost by any accidental charged matter downwind. Also, we have mixed in a small amount of graphite in order to avoid clumping of the spores, which could otherwise make them difficult to inhale deeply into the lungs."

The fat man sat back in his seat, for the first time peering at the younger officer. Frankly, he much preferred the honorific of Excellency over all the other titles bestowed on him, but had never mentioned it to anyone. "Major, tell me how you arrived at the particle size you mentioned."

"Excellency, we have tested particles between a half micron and twelve microns. We found that particles less than one micron are easily exhaled by the target subject. Particles over five microns lodge in the upper airway. This often leads to infection, but it is not nearly as deadly as particles able to reach the lowest level of the lungs. In fact, particles of twelve or more microns are not deposited in the lungs at all, but rather cause a gastrointestinal infection, which also has a relatively low death rate. So our target particle size must be between one and five microns. And those less than three microns are best of all in being deposited in the alveoli of the lungs. The infection rate, as well as the death rate, are extremely high in our animal tests with that size range."

"Let me understand you, Major. Are you saying that further experiments related to particle size are not necessary?"

"As I said, Excellency, we have the perfect product already in hand. Colonel Min-shik is exactly right when he warns of safety concerns with more long-range or widespread testing. We will be able to sterilize the small amount of territory involved in today's testing by this time tomorrow, but it is very cumbersome, as well as dangerous, and can only be accomplished in Level Four protective clothing. In a larger test involving distances of a kilometer, duplicating that sterilization over at least four million square meters would be extremely difficult, if not impossible. The spores of the bacteria are able to survive in the environment for long periods of time, and they can be re-aerosolized by the wind, with the ability to kill for years after the testing."

"This is new information, Major. So if we attack an enemy with this agent, it could continue to disrupt and kill far beyond the actual time of the event."

Ho-young decided this was the time to stop talking. He slightly bowed his head forward. "Yes, Excellency, but as its concentration will be reduced, so will its effectiveness."

The fat man didn't speak for several minutes, pondering what he had just heard. Finally he faced the beach again, peering intently at the young women in the surf. "Senior Colonel Min-shik, the smallest girl—the one on the left—it seems a waste to sacrifice such a young maiden in your experiment. Separate her from the others immediately, give her your antibiotics, and when she is proven to be free of infection, install her in my compound in Sep'o County in Kangwon Province."

Despite his thirty years of military service, the scientist genuflected. "Brilliant Comrade, I should perhaps mention that all of the test subjects are only Japs."

The fat man paused in his brief moment of anticipation and turned his frozen smile toward the colonel. "Do I need to find someone else to carry out my orders, Dr. Min-shik?"

"Of course I will tend to the matter immediately, Brilliant Comrade."

The fat man spent another full minute staring out the window at the scene below. "If this test today is successful, how long will it take to produce one hundred kilograms of the weaponized bacteria?"

"With the addition of two hundred more laboratory personnel, triple our scientific equipment, and at least ten thousand additional doses of vaccine from our friends in Iran to protect everyone engaged in its manufacture, storage, and transport, we estimate between four and five months, Brilliant Comrade."

The fat man produced a smile which had the effect of lowering the temperature in the backseat of the limo (a gift from the Russian president) by a good ten degrees. "I'm sure you know better than to disappoint me, Senior Colonel."

CHAPTER 3

What If
Washington, D.C. September 15, 2023

The tap on his office door in the Health Threats Resilience Division of Bio-Watch at the Department of Homeland Security brought a gruff "Come" from Colonel Early Johnson, but when he spied the almost bald gray stubble of Assistant Secretary Abel Adams poking around the door frame, Johnson quickly rose to his feet. "Good morning, sir."

Adams smiled. "Guess I'll never get used to that response, Early. Homeland Security is a long way from your last duty station at Fort Detrick, at least as far as military protocol goes."

"A twenty-year habit is hard to break, sir."

"Just the same, most of the time I feel like I'm the one who should be standing up for you." Adams crossed the room and sat heavily in an office chair, taking the load off his six-nine NBA frame. "The secretary wants a briefing before we go over to the White House this afternoon. Talk to me about what we think we know concerning North Korea's bacterial agent program."

Johnson came around from behind his workstation and sat in the other chair in the space designated for visitors. He didn't like talking across a desk to his boss. "We believe they have at least a working stock of plague, tularemia, African swine fever, and highly pathogenic avian influenza. However, it's anthrax which has us most worried. Until recently, we were working strictly on supposition. But when one of their soldiers fled across the DMZ to South Korea, and it was dis-

20

covered that he had anthrax antibodies in his bloodstream, it was pretty clear that they were actively working on something."

"What does the presence of antibodies tell us?"

"There are only two possible conclusions—one, that at some time in the past he had the disease, but received antibiotics early enough to cure the infection—or two, that he has been vaccinated against anthrax. We think the second is the more likely scenario, but both possibilities lead us to believe that the North is actively experimenting with the bacteria. Either they were careless, he was infected, and had to be treated, or he and presumably a number of others have been vaccinated so they can work with anthrax without too much risk of contracting the disease."

"If someone is exposed to the bacteria without being vaccinated, what is their likelihood of survival? And calm down with the technical stuff, but help me understand. Can you do that?"

"I can, sir. First of all, there are three distinctly different kinds of infection: cutaneous anthrax, gastrointestinal anthrax, and inhalational anthrax. The form which keeps our planners awake at night is inhalational anthrax." Early reached for an old briefing book, fumbled with it for a minute or so, and showed his boss a picture diagram of a diseased set of lungs. "This occurs when *Bacillus anthracis* is inhaled deeply into the lungs. Those symptoms are generally sore throat, mild fever, and muscle aches, followed by severe breathing problems like pneumonia. And if inhalational anthrax is not treated before those symptoms begin, the expected death rate can be as high as ninety-nine percent."

"You mean it almost always results in death, no matter what we do or how sophisticated our medical systems might be?"

"If someone has not been vaccinated against anthrax, or they aren't treated before they get sick, then the answer, unfortunately, is yes."

"How many Americans are vaccinated against anthrax?"

"Far less than one percent, and a majority of those were military members vaccinated years ago, soon after 9/11, when we thought Saddam Hussein possessed biological weapons. So it's highly likely even they are minimally protected, if at all over twenty years later."

Adams vigorously rubbed his scalp. "Jesus, Mary, and Joseph!"

"Back in 2001, when a number of anthrax letters were mailed to members of the media and two sitting members of the Senate, this was our first time being confronted with anthrax as a weapon. Perhaps the sender expected the addressee to be the only one exposed to the disease when the letter was opened, and the individual would supposedly inhale the powder which puffed out of the envelope. But that's not what happened.

"One of the first letters was opened by a secretary in the Dirksen Senate office building, and the area was one which was frequented by a number of staff. It was then rationalized that perhaps the powder had made its way into the HVAC system and thus spread throughout the complex. Beyond that, there was speculation that the powder had even been spread outside the building."

"I recollect something about that. Remind me what happened?"

"In something like three hours, the U.S. Public Health Service received a load of drugs from the Centers for Disease Control's National Pharmaceutical Stockpile, and they began dispensing antibiotics to some six thousand politicians, staffers, lobbyists, and anybody else who had been in or near the building.

"Then three days later, the U.S. Postal Service started wondering about whether or not any of their employees could have been exposed when the envelopes went through their mail processing center here in D.C. The CDC went in and performed biological monitoring inside the mail center. They determined almost the entire workspace in a building the size of a football field was contaminated with aerosolized anthrax. So then the Public Health Service started prophylaxing not only postal workers, but anybody who had been in the processing center during the previous five-day period. I seem to remember another six or seven thousand who were treated there."

"How many people died from the exposure?"

"Hard to believe, but not a single death from those two groups. There were other locations also: Florida, Connecticut, New York City, and four mail rooms in Federal buildings here in Washington and in Maryland. All told, about eighteen thousand people were treated. There were five deaths, but only among people who opened letters and didn't know, or didn't pay immediate attention, to the fact that they'd been exposed. The conclusion was that giving rapid antibiotic prophylaxis was what saved the lives of anybody who had been exposed."

"So let's get back to North Korea. What are they up to?"

"Admittedly, we've got limited intelligence in North Korea. So all I can tell you is what we think, not necessarily what we know."

"Fair enough."

"There's good evidence they obtained three hundred and fifty doses of anthrax vaccine back in 2015 from Iran. We've heard they're seeking additional doses in the range of several thousand from the same source. So that indicates they have plans to ramp up their supply and/or their experimentation."

"What are they trying to accomplish?"

Early Johnson was a cautious man, honed by twenty years of work in military intelligence, so he generally did not like to speculate without concrete evidence, but predicting North Korea's motives often lacked hard data. "It stands to reason they know we can provide antibiotic prophylaxis to a large group of people if we know they've been exposed to anthrax. So if that's the case, why not expose people in such a way that we don't know it's happened? . If they are able to accomplish production of the correct particle size, then there are several ways to distribute anthrax to fairly large groups of Americans, perhaps in the realm of tens of thousands at a time, and we might not find out about it until people start dying."

"Wouldn't we know what was happening via those Bio-Watch collectors of yours?"

"Sir, we've only got thirty-two cities where those collectors are located. For sure, they're placed in what we believe are high-risk areas, and the filters are collected and analyzed every twenty-four hours, but the effectiveness of those air collection systems are dependent on several things happening in our favor. First of all, any biological threat agent would have to be distributed fairly close to a collection system. Next, the wind would have to be blowing in the right direction.

"For example, if we've got a Bio-Watch system sitting on the roof of a building inside The Loop in Chicago, and the prevailing wind is from the northwest, but the biological agent is disbursed at a large public gathering on the southeastern side of the city, the filter won't reveal any evidence of the threat."

"Damn! I've seen the budget on that program, many millions per year. So you're telling me Bio-Watch is not foolproof?"

"That's true. But it can be extremely valuable in the early discovery of a surreptitious attack."

"So if the attack is directed in a location where there won't be a hit on Bio-Watch, what do we do, just wait on people to start dying? After all, you said once people had symptoms of inhalational anthrax, their chance of dying was ninety-nine percent. Is that what we're looking at?"

"Yes and no. It's true that people who are already symptomatic will probably not survive, but everybody who is exposed is not going to get sick at the same time. What we hope is that some very observant physician is curious enough to pay a lot of attention to a patient's X-ray, then he or she raises the alarm."

Early once more referred to his briefing book, this time comparing an X-ray of healthy lungs with one of an anthrax patient. "The problem is that ninety-nine percent of American doctors have never seen a patient with inhalational anthrax. However, if they see mediastinal widening or pleural effusion on a chest X-ray, then we hope they would immediately order a confirmatory test by either measuring antibodies in the patient's blood or testing for the bacteria in blood, spinal fluid, respiratory secretions, or skin lesions. But these lab tests would likely be initiated before that first patient started receiving antibiotics.

"Once we've got confirmation, it's dependent on us to get the word out to local hospitals, clinics, and medical societies. So when patients number two and three are identified, we can figure out what all of them have in common."

"You mean did all three of them work at the same place, or attend the same football game, or concert, or something like that where they all could have been exposed?"

"Exactly. Then we could alert everybody who had been at that workplace or event, and get them in to receive antibiotics."

"Speaking of antibiotics, where would they come from and how many people could be treated?"

Colonel Johnson looked at his watch. "Let me call the folks at the National Pharmaceutical Stockpile and we'll get an up-to-the minute answer." Johnson scrolled through his phone list, then selected a number in Atlanta. "Captain Burke, glad you picked up so quickly. Early Johnson here at DHS. Have you got time for a SCIF call in the next few minutes? Great, I'll call you."

Johnson stood up. "Let's go downstairs to the secure communications room. I didn't want to ask your questions on an unsecured line—too many bad guys out there trying to hack in to our business."

The two men made their way to the Sensitive Compartmentalized Information Facility, left their cell phones in a cabinet outside, and Johnson used his thumbprint to access the room. The facility contained individual phone lines, a secure FAX, and eight laptops, all of which contained decoding and encoding software, as well as a small conference table with ten chairs which faced three different TV screens.

Colonel Johnson turned to his boss. "No one is authorized to be in this room who doesn't have top-secret compartmentalized clearance, so you can speak freely to Captain Burke." Johnson then used the secure conference line to reach his counterpart in Atlanta, who appeared on one of the screens. "Captain, I've got my Assistant Secretary, Abel Adams, here with me. He's got some questions about the Stockpile."

Burke briefly studied his own video feed. "I thought I recognized the name, Mr. Secretary. You spent some ten years as a power forward with the Celtics." Captain Burke smiled. "Do you mind me asking where you got your nickname, sir?"

"You mean Socko?' I try not to use that moniker here at DHS. Assistant Secretary Socko sort of clashes with the culture around here. Apparently the nickname had to do with somebody blaming me for a tussle or two on the basketball court."

"A tussle or two?" Burke chuckled. "Yes, sir, I'm sure it was only two. I also remember you set the NBA record one year for the number of games with double-doubles. And you were playing for the Celtics during at least two of their seventeen championships."

"That was quite a while ago, Captain. It was an honor to play for them, but I think my rebounding days, let alone my tussling days, are long past. At any rate, thanks for remembering. Early and I were just talking about what might be available from your shop in case of an anthrax attack."

"Anything concrete, gentlemen, or are we talking about a what-if situation?"

Johnson cleared his throat. "At this point, it's just what if, Captain. Can you tell us what antibiotics are available and in what quantity?"

"I believe our total capability, spread among multiple warehouses, is to treat one hundred thousand patients with a thirty-day supply of doxycycline. We've also got about five thousand treatment regimens each of ciprofloxacin and ampicillin for people who can't tolerate doxycycline, or for pregnant women."

"What kind of time requirement do you have for delivery?"

"Any airport in the United States which can accommodate a medium-sized jet, within a maximum of four hours from notification to touch down, then whatever amount of time is required for site delivery by truck. The Stockpile would send a team of four people to coordinate the movement and assist in set-up of the Stockpile, as well as a plug-and-play patient tracking system.

"The jurisdiction would be responsible for identifying the distribution site, security, parking, a suitable temperature-controlled building, bathroom access and hand-washing for perhaps thousands of people, drinking water, all medical personnel, plus feeding of not only those personnel, but probably a goodly number of patients. The jurisdiction will also need some plan to separate and hospitalize patients who may already be ill."

"In case of a large attack, or repetitive attacks, what about your supply line?"

"The first source of additional antibiotics would come from wholesale drug companies across the U.S. We estimate the ability to replicate the available treatment courses via that source with only a single day's delay or less. But beyond that, resupply is certainly not as rapid nor robust as in the past. Many generic drugs, such as doxycycline, are no longer manufactured in the United States. So we rely on other countries to manufacture and ship more antibiotics on demand. That time-line will likely be more on the order of three days to a week."

"Captain Burke, have there been any discussions at CDC

about expanding your antibiotic inventory?"

"I'm guessing this is about the North Korean soldier who had anthrax antibodies. Unfortunately, this news hit us in the middle of a fiscal year. I'm told we have no funds available to purchase more drugs."

Adams leaned toward the monitor. "I'll try and work on the money factor here in D.C." He thought a bit. "What are your thoughts, Captain, about sending out a reminder message to your state counterparts, asking them to take a fresh look at their site plans as well as their volunteer lists?"

"We do that every year, Mr. Secretary, but I see no problem in communicating with them now rather than several months down the road. For several years, most jurisdictions held live practice scenarios to be sure they were ready for a large event."

"That sounded like the past tense. Are you saying that's no longer occurring, Captain?"

Early sagged back in his chair. "Since about 2010, there's been a dramatic reduction in DHS funding for local preparedness efforts, Mr. Secretary."

"That could come back to bite us." He faced the TV screen. "Thank you, Captain. We'll be in touch."

Chapter 4

The Promotion
Sep'o County, North Korea October 1, 2023

A camouflaged Mi-17 HIP military helicopter, bearing an encircled red star on either side of the fuselage, had taken off from Pyongyang some forty minutes earlier, and was traveling to the southeast on its 220-kilometer flight between the capital city and Sep'o County. The aircraft would make the trip in 75 minutes, barring any problems with weather. The full complement of the Mi-17 was twelve passengers, two pilots, and a stewardess, but on this day only two travelers were on board along with the pilots.

The fat man sat on the right side of the helicopter to enjoy the optimal view of Kangwon Province, which was just coming into view. The landscape had changed dramatically during the flight, and they now flew over the confluence of two mountain ranges. Summer was already in the past, and almost all of the peaks already wore a dressing of snow. Three separate mountain streams were surging within his field of vision below. The province was almost entirely covered by what reminded the fat man of alpine forest. In fact, this was the reason behind his purchase in Sep'o of a rustic retreat, one portion of which he had quickly turned into large pastures surrounding an elegant five-bedroom log cabin.

Having spent much of their childhood in a private school in Switzerland, he and his younger sister, Kim Yo-jong, had lived in that country under the supervision of their aunt. The siblings had used assumed names, and told everyone their mother and father were the maid and gardener at the DPRK embassy in Geneva. Only their aunt knew the true identity of her charges. His friends at school were continually surprised that a youngster of apparently humble background was able to come to class regularly displaying such a wide variety of collectible, and rare, sneakers.

He had retained a great appreciation for the geography of his temporary country of residence, looking long and hard when he came back home for similar surroundings. After his father died and he assumed the mantle of leadership for his country, he didn't delay his acquisition of the property he saw below. His retreat indeed looked as though it had been plucked from a setting in the Swiss or Austrian Alps.

Not a word had been spoken between the two passengers since their initial greeting when they found their seats on the aircraft. The fat man finally pulled himself away from the view outside his window. "Have you traveled to Kangwon before?"

His passenger almost released an audible sigh of relief that the ongoing silence was not the result of his having committed some unknown faux pas. "No, Excellency. It appears to be a great change from the lands around Pyongyang."

The fat man pulled a black box from his jacket pocket, one emblazoned with the signature of Yves St. Laurent. He extracted yet another cigarette, lit it, and inhaled deeply. It didn't enter his mind that one hard box of his elegant smokes was worth approximately what a North Korean family earned in a week. "Indeed it is, as you will see when we come closer to our destination. Tell me, what progress has been made on your project?"

"Excellency, all of our goals were realized in the test you observed. Four of the five test subjects became symptomatic with a pneumonia within four days."

"Only four? But there were five young girls being tested."

"Yes, Excellency. We used what we perceived to be the LD-50. That is to say, the amount of powdered bacterium used was projected to be the lethal dose in fifty percent of those exposed. Our results were eighty percent."

The chairman's look was still somewhat dubious. "So if this same dose were to be used in the future, we could expect similar results?"

"Not necessarily, Excellency. Our test was set up under ideal conditions. If this formulation is used in the future in an uncontrolled environment, we must consider variables such as crowd size, distance from the source of air movement, wind speed and direction, humidity, any mechanically created wind involved, medical status of the target population, and the length of time each person remains within the exposure area. Also, our five test subjects were admittedly not in the best of health prior to testing. It would be very doubtful if we could meet an eighty percent infection rate with all those unpredictable variables in a field setting."

He nodded impatiently. The chairman had very little appreciation for something as mundane as statistics. "So how are you progressing in building a stockpile of one hundred kilograms?"

"We are making slow progress, Excellency. It is my understanding that Senior Colonel Min-shik is attempting to obtain new staff, equipment, and vaccine. With our current limitations, it takes us a full five days to create one kilogram of weapons-grade anthrax."

"How would you recommend those shortfalls be addressed?"

"Forgive my being forward, Excellency. In my opinion, obtaining anything from the Iranians is a slow process, as both our countries suffer from United Nations meddling in our commerce, not to mention the distance involved and the borders to be crossed. Perhaps we could shorten the time frame for equipment as well as vaccine by going to the Russians with our request?"

The fat man looked briefly out of his window as the sounds of the helicopter indicated a significant slowing of its forward progress. His herd of sheep grazed in one of the pastures near the landing site, and his old shepherd stood among them. He folded his fat hands over his large belly, appreciating the view of his property below. "In my experience, I have found that the Iranians always want something more valuable in return for the item they supply, and they think that creating delays will increase the item's value to us. The Russians, however, are usually willing to accommodate us, as long as we continue to poke a stick in the eye of the evil empire! Let's proceed with your suggestion, Colonel Ho-young."

Ho-young genuflected slightly. "Excellency, I fear you have been misinformed. I am only a major."

"I do not make errors, Colonel. You are receiving what is usually referred to as a field promotion of two grades. This is based not only on your performance to date, but your assumption of new, more complex responsibilities in the immediate future."

Ho-young could not erase the smile from his face. "Thank you, Excellency, for your confidence in me. How may I contribute?"

"You will be assuming Min-shik's responsibilities, Colonel. You will now report directly to Lieutenant General Byung-soo, the director of our Bio-Warfare Center."

Ho-young genuflected again, this time in a more exaggerated manner. "Thank you, Excellency."

The fat man extracted a bottle of Glenfiddich fifty-year-old Scotch whiskey from a compartment and poured substantial portions into two glasses. "Your promotion is deserving of a celebration, Colonel."

Ho-young had never consumed any alcohol other than homemade rice wine. He had no idea that a single bottle of Glenfiddich cost approximately four times as much as his new colonel's annual salary, nor that it contained two and a half times the concentration of ethanol as the rice wine with which he was familiar. He raised his glass. "To the success of the DPRK, Excellency."

Ho-young struggled to mask his reaction to the Glenfiddich as the chopper settled onto its landing pad. The fat man turned to his new colonel with a genuine smile for once. "I understand you play basketball, Colonel. Perhaps you'll join me before dinner in the gym."

Chapter 5

The Girl
Sep'o County, North Korea October 1, 2023

When Ho-young reported to the gymnasium in warm-ups, he was immediately supplied with a pair of Air Max Lunar-90 tennis shoes in his exact size, and was surprised to see both helicopter pilots and two others, possibly guards at the facility, along with the fat man, all warming up on a beautifully maintained regulation-sized basketball court. The Wonsu, a military term referring to a five-star general, wore a pair of Louis Vuitton red high tops. The only individuals who had ever held a higher rank in the entire history of North Korea, that of Taewonsu, were Kim Il-sung and Kim Jong-Il, the fat man's father and grandfather.

The colonel immediately noticed the large picture on the wall of His Excellency sitting beside the comedic figure of Dennis Rodman, who towered over him even in a seated position. Also displayed in elaborate frames were signed Chicago Bull jerseys from Michael Jordan, Scottie Pippen, and Rodman. Ho-young was familiar with the well-circulated rumor that the fat man had been a Bulls fan for some twenty years.

It had been at least a year since Ho-young had played, so his shots were rusty. Alas, it appeared from their shooting prowess that the others were regular players, and apparently all had been specifically recruited previously for this activity. They also had obviously played together many times.

Ho-young reminded himself that North Korean basketball rules varied a bit from those used elsewhere around the globe. For example, three points were awarded for a dunk, four points for a normal three-point shot as long as the ball did not touch the rim, and eight points for any shot made in the last three seconds of the game. Moreover, for every missed free throw, a point was subtracted from a team's score.

His Excellency made a quick challenge. "Let's see if your basketball compares with your biology skills, Colonel." They then divided into three-on-three teams, and it was decided they would only play half-court ball. Ho-young was more than pleased to hear this, as he was not in great physical condition. He found himself guarding the fat man, and was astonished to observe the foot work and ball-handling skills of the Wonsu.

Ho-young saw there was a great deal of competitive spirit among the players, but also took note that the other members of his team were careful not to foul the Wonsu. He decided that was the expected course of action, although he did try to guard the fat man as closely as possible under the circumstances. He realized his opponent actually moved very little. The Wonsu generally played at the head of the key, and though he dribbled well and moved deceptively, he never strayed more than a couple of meters from his spot. His lack of movement might possibly have been due to his weight gain of almost forty kilos in the years since he had become his country's leader. Ho–young looked at the Wonsu, trying very hard not to reveal his gut-reaction to seeing a very rotund man, wearing red tennis shoes, dribbling a basketball, all the while with a cigarette hanging from his lip.

Ho-young also noticed his opponent was not as tall as he had seemed in his other shoes, and decided he couldn't be more than 165 centimeters in height. His best guess was that the man had sacrificed his elevator footwear for the sake of shoes which allowed for optimal movement on the basketball court. They took a water break in about a half hour, but among the six of them, only Ho-young seemed to be gassed.

The Wonsu was a competent long-ball shooter, almost daring Ho-young to guard him more closely, but when he did, one of the other players inevitably drove for the basket, receiving a quick pass. It also became obvious that the official scorer interpreted almost all of the fat man's shots from beyond the three-point line as being worthy of four points, while the colonel's team seldom received that bonus. The opposing team gradually pulled away, despite Ho-young finally beginning to hit his own share of shots. After a second half-hour, they called it quits.

At the conclusion of a two hour sumptuous four-course meal highlighted by feather-light Swiss Emmental cheese, thick, perfectly marbled Wagyu Kobe rib-eyes, and supplemented by three bottles of appropriate wine the Wonsu poured Remy Martin cognac into two wide-mouthed goblets. Rather than confuse the young colonel, he gave him directions. "Hold the glass in the palm of your hand for a few minutes. The warmth of your hand expands the full flavors of the cognac." He paused, saying nothing and lost in his own anticipation. "Now, Colonel, we are done."

Ho-young was finally escorted to his Spartan sleeping quarters in the rear of the cabin, while the fat man ascended to his opulent bedroom on the second floor. Knowing after the rigorous afternoon workout he would be very sore in the morning, Ho-young took yet another hot shower before climbing into bed.

Upstairs, the fat man changed into a finely embroidered silk dressing gown and seated himself behind a gargantuan, intricately carved mahogany desk. He was impatient for the evening to proceed, lit his fortieth cigarette of the day, poured himself a glass of Cristal champagne, pushed a white button on the desktop, then settled down to wait. In exactly five minutes, the door to his quarters opened, and he heard the unmistakable whisper of silk slippers on the teak floor. He forced himself not to look up, spending several additional minutes studying various papers on his desk.

When he finally raised his head, the fat man spent longer than was necessary in evaluating his visitor. True to his directive, the housekeeper had explicitly followed a formula which had its roots many hundreds of years in the past. Ancient Japanese and Chinese Buddhist legends, as well as some from Korea itself, celebrated the presence of the tennin or tenyo, which usually were interpreted as 'heavenly messenger'. In Western terms, the messenger might compare to an angel, or perhaps a nymph.

The figure standing demurely before the fat man was dressed in an ornate kimono of five colors. She wore beautiful jewelry, perfectly applied makeup, and multiple diaphanous scarves which were wrapped around her. In her left hand, she held a small bouquet of perfect white lotus blossoms. By the look of her flowing raiment, it seemed almost possible that she, like the tenyo of olden days, could fly. The fat man allowed himself the luxury of an unguarded smile of approval at the perfection displayed before him.

He was unsure of how he might communicate with the girl. He spoke no Japanese, and had absolutely no desire for a translator to play a part in their evening discussion. He doubted seriously that the girl would know French. Finally, he decided to simply speak Korean. Perhaps they could find some common ground. "Have you been treated well?"

Although she had been thoroughly counseled to speak very little and only with most humble respect, she was not of that temperament and had more important questions on her mind. "What have you done with my big sister, Hitomi?"

Although he did not know how long she had been held in Korea, he was surprised that she did indeed speak his language, and appeared to be rather fluent. "I know nothing of your sister. When did you see her last?"

"We were taken with a few other girls to the ocean about two months ago. They told us we could go swimming, but the water was far too cold. Several people in white suits took the rest of them away, and I was separated from my sister. I haven't seen her since."

"Alas, I am so sorry. I was told I could only rescue one of your group. I chose you."

The girl started to cry, but with significant will forced herself not to break down. "What happened to my sister?"

"I am told she became ill and did not survive."

Her despair turned to resignation. "What of the other girls, my friends?"

"I am told they all became ill, like your sister. There was only enough medicine to save one of you."

"I don't believe you. Why has the old auntie been telling me how to behave around you? Why am I dressed as though I was a supernatural tenyo from the olden days?" She brushed one hand along the billowing scarves. "Surely no one expects me to fly!" She had the effrontery to toss the lotus blossoms on his desk and stamp her foot. "Who are you? What gives you the right to decide who lives and who dies?"

Even as a boy, the fat man had not been spoken to in such a manner. Indeed, other than his father, the only person who ever had dared to speak up to him was his younger sis-

ter. His first inclination was to let loose his well-known temper. Then he chuckled. Perhaps this little Nippon was worth
suspending his legendary anger. Might this girl be a welcome
distraction from the great pressures of his daily life? "You haven't told me your name or where you come from."

Her thoughts briefly returned to her home in Aikawa, and
the historic five-storied pagoda which soared above the
houses, such a source of pride for her village. She could almost see the many gardens close to her home, the nearby
mountain peaks, and even the caves and worn out gold mines
which she and her friends had once explored.

The girl sniffed twice and drew a silk scarf across her
face to wipe away any evidence of her tears. Although shy of
150 centimeters in height, she visibly stood a little taller before she spoke. "I am Hiroko, the daughter of Fujino Arita, the
greatest fisherman on Sado Island. Over two years ago, my
sister and I were at the docks, waiting on our father and his
boat to return from three days at sea. Four men came out of
the night and took us, along with six others from our small
town. They tied us up and stowed us in the hold of their vessel. In two days we were taken off the boat, apparently somewhere in Korea."

"How were you treated when you arrived in this country?"

"The other girls were all physically attacked many times
by the sailors. I was left alone, maybe because I was only
fourteen years old at the time." She paused. "Maybe because I
told them I was only nine."

He didn't bother trying to formulate an apology. They
were sailors, and after all, the girls were mere Nipponese.
What could one expect? "Where were you taken?"

She shook her head. "I have no idea, a large building.
There were other girls there, perhaps forty or fifty. Most wcre
Japanese and a few others were Korean. But even the Korean
girls were treated poorly. The building was heated by wood
stoves at either end. It was often very cold. I think our guards
were too lazy to cut enough firewood.

"There were no beds, only a concrete floor to lie on. They
supplied us fewer blankets than there were girls. We had to
sleep all together to stay warm. There was little food. We decided we were fed only what was left over from the guard's
meals. Several girls became very ill, and we never saw them
again."

"What can I do to make your stay here a happier one?"

Hiroko didn't answer immediately. Apparently he was going to let her live, at least for a while. She tended to believe
him regarding the death of her sister. She was not entirely
sure of his plans for her, but in view of the hints the old
auntie had been dropping, and the way the other Japanese
girls had been treated, it appeared that she was expected to
become some sort of comfort girl. She could only imagine
what her father would do if he knew her circumstances. But
then she reflected on just how impossible it would be for him
to even find her.

Like a small percentage of women, Hiroko somehow understood, even at her young age, that she possessed a sort of
undefined power over men. Under her current circumstances,
she resolved to better understand this power and use it to the
fullest advantage.

She looked appraisingly at the man behind the desk, trying to gauge what his response might be. "Was it your intention to have your men here making vile comments toward me
every time I'm in their presence?" He started to respond but
she shook her head, waving him off. "Am I to be the object of
their nasty jokes every single day? Is it my sentence to be
treated as someone who has no dignity? Perhaps they assume
I cannot understand their comments because of a language
barrier. It may be true that they are too stupid to understand
my language, but I assure you I can understand theirs."

The fat man's face was beet red. Even his ears changed
color. He slammed his fist on the desk. "Who has done this?"

"Everyone here except the auntie and the old shepherd."

"These insults will stop immediately! What else can I do
for you?"

She determined he might at least correct the men's behavior, if not their thoughts, and decided to go for broke. "It
would be nice to have someone who could prepare Japanese
food. I have little appetite for what is offered. Are all blankets
in this country so thin that they provide no warmth? Some
modern clothes would be nice. Unfortunately, mine were ruined during the first year I was here. What about some sham-
poo? Or is everyone expected to only use harsh soap? Also,
someone my own age who I can talk to, a friend. How about
some music besides the atrocious songs your men play on the
loudspeakers three times a day? What about some books to

read, and a television? And the internet! How does one find out what is happening in the rest of the world?"

He stood up and paced from his desk to the window, then finally faced her. "The internet will not be possible in this location."

"It's terribly slow, but what about using a phone line as the connection?"

"So sorry, the internet will not be possible here. I'll see what I can do related to your other requests." He would definitely have to make a decision as to whether this girl was worth the trouble. At the moment, that was debatable.

Realizing the evening had come to a close without further risk to herself, Hiroko carefully rearranged the kitchen implement wrapped in the scarf around her waist before retreating to her room. She had spent two weeks turning the dull table knife into a razor-edged weapon by painstakingly rubbing the blade against the concrete floor in her bathroom. She certainly didn't want it to fall out of her clothing as she left the room.

At any rate, Hiroko was fairly sure the knife would become necessary in a future encounter. Her situation might be hopeless, but she would not hesitate to avenge her sister and her friends. After all, she had spent much of her young life helping her father in his vocation. If this man tried to force himself on her, she had every intention of gutting him just like she would a halibut.

CHAPTER 6

The Coup of the Century
Airborne, North Korea October 2, 2023

As a nonsmoker, it was extremely unpleasant for Ho-young to be in a confined space, such as the rear seat of a helicopter, with the Wonsu, who continued to light his next cigarette before the previous one was finished. He looked across the aisle at the fat man, who seemed to be lost in thought. "Did you have a nice evening, Excellency?"

The initial response was little more than a snort. "It's safe to say the basketball game was the only satisfying thing about this trip."

The colonel was astute enough to make his face a mask, let alone comment, on what he assumed was a boudoir problem. However, he was not to be dissuaded. "If I may, Excellency, can we discuss some concerns I have regarding my assignment?"

There was no acknowledgment of his request from the other side of the helicopter for a long minute. Then finally, and without much enthusiasm, "Of course."

"I know that Senior Colonel Min-shik was a proponent of using ICBM missiles to deliver our weaponized bacterium, but to me, that seems a wasted and extremely risky approach."

The Wonsu was finally paying attention. "Explain, Colonel."

"If we launch missiles which are projected to touch down in U.S. territory, would not the Americans immediately put their own response plans into place, most probably concluding that our incoming missiles contain a nuclear warhead? If that is so, then the impact of our attack is immediately to their benefit. Not only is it unknown whether or not the bacterium in our own missiles can survive the heat of re-entry into the atmosphere, but even if it is successful, that would undoubtedly only result in depositing anthrax in a relatively small area."

"Min-shik seemed to believe that delivery method was the easiest."

"Easy? Perhaps so, but at what cost? We kill a few hundred, or at most a few thousand of them, yet in response, they destroy our entire country. What if we explore methods to spread the disease in ways that would not direct American suspicion to the DPRK?"

The fat man paused long enough to light another cigarette. "Of course, that would be ideal. What do you suggest?"

"A plan that requires intricate planning, the use of non-Koreans in the delivery of the bacteria, and most important of all, shifting blame to a believable enemy of the United States."

The fat man pursed his lips. "Do you refer to Al Qaeda? That is too predictable a target. Why not one of their internal right-wing groups? The Americans are always thinking the world is out to get them, when in reality, most of the time they're out to get themselves! Or even better, one of their immigrant rights groups. Perhaps we can make them go to war with each other!"

"That's genius, Excellency."

"What do you need from me, Colonel?"

"The addition of a half-dozen civil engineers to my team to assist with development of an anthrax disbursement system, and the employment of perhaps a dozen play-for-pay saboteurs who appear to be Anglo-Saxons, or Muslims, or perhaps Hispanics, as well as the additional laboratory personnel to greatly increase our inventory of weaponized anthrax, plus more vaccine, like we have already discussed."

"Surely the vaccine problem can be resolved with the Russians, as you suggested."

"Yes, Excellency, but even with the addition of laboratory personnel and saboteurs, I am reminded that anthrax vaccination is not accomplished with a single dose. To provide adequate coverage, each individual may need as many as five or six separate doses to keep them immunized long enough for us to prepare for and then complete your attack."

The two men discussed the initiative for a few minutes until the Wonsu fell silent. Ho-young paused also, giving the man time to flesh out his own acceptance of the proposal.

"Colonel, we may be missing a far greater opportunity. It's true that a number of bacterial attacks in a short period of time will make it unpleasant for the Americans, particularly if they come from an unknown origin. However, what if, at the same time, we expanded the types of attacks?"

Ho-young felt as if the helicopter had shifted beneath him. "I'm not sure I understand, Excellency."

"Consider for a moment the way the great United States dealt with the coronavirus epidemic in 2020 and 2021. Despite telling everyone how advanced their medical system is, they failed miserably. Our poverty-stricken country did ten times better.

"I'm thinking we could easily overcome their capability to respond, plus add to their confusion, if we deliver multiple attacks, using various scenarios, and spread them across the U.S. For example, in addition to anthrax, we also attack their food supply, set wildfires in every area threatened by drought, bomb public events, attack the transportation system, target chemical plants, pipelines, and water treatment facilities, maybe even give them another new disease to deal with. Not via missiles and soldiers, but by the infiltrators on the ground which you mentioned. Even if the United States does not completely crumble, we might weaken their economy to the point that recovery could be difficult. Even more important, weaken their citizens' confidence in their own government."

To say that Ho-young was struck numb would be an understatement. He gave himself a few moments to think. "It sounds like you have described declaring war, but without their ability to identify where the attacks are coming from. Excellency, your idea is supremely advanced, far beyond anything ever discussed before. In reality, it would be guerrilla warfare, but our task is to convince them that the attackers are from within their own borders, or from other countries entirely.

"It would require coordination across several offices in your government, in addition to the Bio-Warfare Center. Rather than just a handful of undercover agents, this calls for perhaps twenty or thirty mercenaries, all of whom should be of non-Korean heritage. Coordinating the training, the timing, and the geography of such a war would require several months." Ho-young paused to see if he had gauged the Wonsu correctly. "It would be an honor to participate in the planning for such a war."

The fat man smirked at the praise. "I shall create a small inner circle of planners who possess my full trust. Only this group will have the full picture. The majority will only have knowledge of one particular segment of the attacks. This way, if there is betrayal, as there has been in the past, only a small portion of our plans will be at risk.

"I'm sorry to say, Colonel, that there are still some remaining in our military who would like nothing better than to see me assassinated. I first learned that lesson the hard way soon after my father's death, when I was shot twice at a range of eight feet by a senior officer in the Army." He paused, opened his jacket, and thumped his chest. "Thankfully, the bullet-proof vest I wear absorbed much of the impact, although I did earn a broken rib that day." He laughed suddenly. "I suppose an American president would expect one of their Purple Hearts for such an injury.

"At any rate, I have now developed multiple layers of intelligence and security. I never sleep in the same location two nights in a row. I use a body double on some occasions, such as parades, when it is assumed I will appear. Almost all public appearances are unannounced, particularly near the DMZ. The Americans would like nothing better than to take me out with a drone strike, or even with one of their long-range snipers, as long as they could do it anonymously. It's hard to believe that they, the Canadians, and the Israelis have carried out sniper assassinations at a distance of three kilometers— that is, if we can believe their bragging." He peered at the colonel. "Perhaps we need to obtain similar weaponry to be used when the time is right.

"My father warned me before he died that I must always retain a high level of suspicion for those who surround me. Over the years, I have been forced to dispose of a small number of people who were conspiring against me, including traitorous members of my own family." He looked at the young officer with a strange expression. "I hope that group does not include you, Colonel."

"Your goals for our country are my goals, Excellency."

They discussed the ambitious plan over the next half

hour, identifying candidates for the inner circle as well as subject matter experts in relative fields, before the Wonsu glanced out the window and saw the skyline of Pyongyang just off to the northwest. "Look down below us, Colonel. Are you familiar with the ship moored there in the Potong River?"

"Isn't that the American spy ship, the *Pueblo*, Excellency? It is part of the Victorious Fatherland Liberation War Museum, is it not?"

The Wonsu smiled at the memory. "That ship, the USS *Pueblo*, represents one of the great moments in our nation's history. Over fifty years ago, my grandfather Kim Il-sung made a laughingstock of America when he captured that ship and her entire crew. The Americans claimed they were operating in international waters. Can you imagine attempting to justify spying on the Fatherland by arguing about the location of their ship? It didn't take long to convince the ship's captain to admit their crimes for all the world to hear.

"The Americans have been begging to get their ship back ever since. I want every Korean to see that ship and never forget our victory." The Wonsu shook his fist at the sight beyond his window. "It is my greatest wish to bring the United States to its knees, just as my grandfather did, not only by capturing the *Pueblo*, but also when he vanquished the Americans in the War of Liberation in 1953. Make no mistake, my lifelong goal is to put an end to them for all time, so that they cease to be a nation!"

"It would represent the coup of the century, Excellency."

The Wonsu rubbed his hands together. "I will not rest until I have accomplished deeds which would make my grandfather proud. If we can accomplish this broad-scale set of coordinated attacks without revealing the true source behind it, I'm sure even our hesitant friends in China and Russia will be pleased."

The Wonsu, his sister Kim Yo-jong, Colonel-General Moosung, Minister of State Security, and Colonel Ho-young boarded the chairman's private train at the Ryongsung Complex following a long phone call with the president of China. Their overnight trip to Beijing would take a daunting 24 hours. While it was a long distance between the two capitols, much of the blame for the length of the journey was due to the poor condition of rail tracks in both countries. The maximum safe rail speed in China was 80 kilometers per hour (50 mph), while in North Korea it was a mere 45 kilometers per hour (28 mph).

The slow travel was definitely not due to the chairman's train itself. The modern bottle-green armored train contained 21 cars. The cars designated for dining, sleeping, and conferences were all decorated in blinding white, while the accouterments were pink leather chairs shaded by ivory curtains. Most cars contained more than ample supplies of fine liquors and big screen televisions, while the final car carried one of the Wonsu's private limousines.

During their phone call, the Wonsu had briefly sketched his proposal for attacks on America. The Chinese leader had not been willing to discuss it at any length on the phone, and had invited both Kim and his sister to Beijing for a summit.

It was a snug fit in the Chinese version of a SCIF, as the meeting attendees not only included the North Korean delegation and the Chinese president, but also the Chinese Minister of National Defense I.P. Liang, the Iranian Minster of Defense Amir Najjar, plus the Russian Minister of Defense General Konstantin Kuzmich. The Chinese president opened the meeting, but quickly turned to the Wonsu so that he might describe his proposal.

After an entire morning of discussion and lots of questions—many of which could not be answered yet—the meeting came to a close with the decision that North Korea should take the lead in coordinating the events discussed, and that Colonel-General Moo-sung's ministry should be operationally in charge. Also, there would be no further discussion back and forth on the subject unless they met face to face. Their respect for American counter-intelligence was such that they had no desire to risk penetration of their electronic communications.

For his part, General Kuzmich left the meeting early, pleading an emergency back in Moscow. His quick departure was noted by all. As to the general, he had much to think about. Not only was he the Russian Minister of Defense, he was also the chief military officer over all of Russia's armed services. These kinds of titles tended to cause a man to think about his next logical step in life. In fact, Kuzmich's overriding concern for the last eight years had been 'what steps can I take in order to make it a reality that I am the next president of Russia?'

He had to give this his utmost concentration. Apparently, Putin had at least partial knowledge of what would be discussed at this summit, but he had chosen not to attend—even though the Chinese president and the North Korean Chairman Kim had both been there. What could Putin's absence mean? Did he think the meeting wasn't important? Did he not want to be seen as a party to that kind of initiative? After all, he had proven himself to be capable of all sorts of acts condemned by the international community. Or was he trying to simply put the general into a compromising position?

Surely when he returned to Moscow, Putin would ask for a full report. How should he handle such a request? Might it be advisable to secretly record such a meeting? But then, if he was discovered, what would be his defense? Yet if the objective was to put him in a compromising position, how could he afford not to have some proof that he was simply doing Putin's bidding? Perhaps if he took another senior Cabinet official with him? This would require much thought.

Chapter 7

How Dangerous Can You Get?
Langley, Virginia October 20, 2023

Assistant Secretary Adams secured a department vehicle and driver from DHS for his and Colonel Johnson's trip across the Potomac then west on the George Washington Parkway. Arriving at the George H.W. Bush Center for Intelligence in Langley, Virginia, Adams remembered the humorous, widely circulated quote from the former first lady, Barbara Bush, when she first saw the sign before the building's dedication ceremony. "It doesn't seem right that George Bush and Intelligence are on the same sign."

Adams and Johnson made their way through security, deposited their cell phones in lockers, and were met by a dark-haired, petite female who introduced herself as Angela Martinelli. Her smile revealed a pair of deep, and appealing, dimples. The threesome made quite the stair-stepped picture as they proceeded through the labyrinth of interconnecting hallways. Adams was almost a foot taller than the colonel, while Martinelli was no more than a couple of inches over five feet in height. As he followed along behind their escort, Early Johnson found his attention drawn to her backside. He kept telling himself to look away, but had to confess he was mesmerized.

They arrived at a locked doorway, which Martinelli accessed with the iris of her left eye. The secure communications room was three times larger than their own SCIF, and was currently occupied by a nondescript balding fellow of around fifty years of age. Even to Johnson's discerning eye, the man possessed not a single physical characteristic that might be used to readily identify him in a crowd of people. In short, he was an ideal agent for the Central Intelligence Agency.

He came forward to greet them, extending his hand. "Welcome to The Agency, Secretary Adams—Colonel Johnson. I'm Bob Williams, the Division Chief for Korea. I see you've already met our Dr. Martinelli."

The visitors glanced quickly at their escort. Adams cleared his throat. "We met all but the doctor part." Martinelli turned aside to hide her grin. "Mr. Williams, thanks for meeting with us on short notice this morning. We're trying to be as ready as possible over at DHS regarding North Korea. What can you tell us related to their capability and planning for biological attacks?"

Williams shook his head slightly. "In 2010, we discovered that the Iranians had broken in to what we thought was an impenetrable, secure internet messaging system between our Central Office here at Langley, our agents in the field, and many of their informants. We thought we'd adequately repaired the breach prior to any damage, but by 2011, the Iranians had eliminated thirty of our agents and their contacts operating in and around Iran.

"To make it worse, the Iranians sold the same sort of extremely damaging information to the Chinese as well as the Russians for something in the neighborhood of a billion dollars apiece. Between this information and the fact that we uncovered a mole in our midst here at Langley, who had been feeding the Chinese the names of our agents operating in their country in a matter of a few months, eighteen more agents, plus their assets in China, were either killed or imprisoned. The small remainder had to flee for their lives. It was one of the most devastating acts of espionage we've ever suffered. As a result, we are currently almost operating blind in China."

"What about North Korea?"

"I'm coming to that. We've never had much success placing agents in the DPRK. Almost everything we know about the North has come to us via our agents in China, or infrequently by North Koreans who defect to South Korea. Unfortunately, the G-2 derived from escapees is usually not very helpful. The defectors we have interviewed are almost always low-level soldiers or political activists, and have virtually no worthwhile strategic information to share. Worse, the ones who appear to be knowledgeable we sometimes believe are plants, sent south by DPRK authorities with the express intent of sowing disinformation."

"Do you have assets in North Korea who are reliable?"

"Almost every time we think we've got someone on the inside, they end up disappearing. We do have a team of medical experts here who analyze visual data, as well as incident reports, and they then put their heads together to advise us on the health status of literally every world leader. According to our physicians, Kim Jong-Il is not simply extremely suspicious, but rather is clinically paranoid. He is also undoubtedly hypertensive, probably diabetic, and given his lifestyle, is almost surely in danger of having vascular heart disease, as well as apparently being a functional alcoholic and a three or four-pack a day smoker. He will not live to be an old man."

"It sounds as though you're telling us that what you know is almost accidental."

"I wouldn't categorize it that way, but it's true that our intelligence is not something we can count on to warn us of events in the near future, particularly related to biological or chemical weapons. We know they have them, but lack good specifics. We do have a well-placed asset in their ballistic missile program, but hesitate to set up regular communication in case we inadvertently put him at risk. However, even working independently, he has been remarkably successful in undermining some of their high-profile ballistic missile launches."

Williams waved at Martinelli. "Angela has a unique history. She is an operating room nurse, a bio-statistician, and a linguist. For several years, she's gone undercover and volunteered with various international medical outreach organizations, which frequently sent her to areas of conflict. Tell us about those experiences, Angela."

"I served with Operation Smile, Project Hope, and Medecines san Frontieres. I've been to Indonesia, Thailand, Yemen, Syria, Afghanistan, Pakistan, Bangladesh, Burma, Djibouti, South Korea, and various Pacific Island nations. Most of those deployments were actually undercover ops, which were undertaken to investigate human trafficking, whether for sex or labor. Maybe the assignment most applicable to this conversation was with a humanitarian team which went to Iran in 2004, after their big earthquake. I just happened to find myself in the midst of a sex trafficking operation, which was involved in running girls from Afghanistan and Burma to India."

"What she didn't mention is her linguistic abilities. She was able to pick up the language on most of those assignments. And I don't believe she mentioned surviving a bomb attack on a Syrian hospital, let alone being responsible for evacuating half the survivors."

Adams and Johnson looked at the woman with a new level of respect. "Very impressive, Doctor."

For her part, Dr. Martinelli was trying to simultaneously conceal her interest in Colonel Johnson, while also making a veiled assessment: about forty years old, hair mostly brown and still full, eyes green, height about five feet ten, weight maybe 175, engaging smile, no wedding ring. It was difficult to describe, but his bearing seemed to evidence full control of himself. She also thought she noted a bit of mutual interest on his part.

Williams managed the difficult job of not moving but reclaiming everyone's attention. "One of her assignments was with an intergovernmental health clinic at the 2018 Winter Olympics in PyeongChang, South Korea. She passed herself off an Iranian nurse volunteer, and had some exposure to both South and North Korean participants, particularly to a small contingent of DPRK security forces who were attending with their athletes. It obviously helps that she has a working knowledge of the Korean language. She repeated that same assignment as a nurse during the 2022 Winter Olympics in Beijing, and was able to renew some of those same contacts."

Martinelli smiled. "Apparently the North Koreans felt very comfortable talking with someone who they thought was Iranian. One of their security officers assumed we were all on the same team with America as the common enemy. I played into that, and made some statements which would leave no doubt in their minds as to where I stood."

"Were you able to learn anything about war plans?"

"No, and I didn't expect to. However, just a month ago, I received a call via a telephone number in Iran, which was answered by one of our agents. The call came from one of the North Koreans I had met previously. After I returned his call, he told me they were putting out feelers to recruit medical personnel for some undefined program at some point in the near future. I got the idea they were particularly seeking non-Koreans. They implied when their plans were in place I should come to Pyongyang, supposedly for an interview."

Johnson couldn't help but gasp. "Good grief, I can't think of anything more dangerous."

Williams nodded. "I think we're all in agreement with that, Colonel."

Martinelli shrugged. "They have my contact information, or at least, they have a telephone number and email address for our safe-house in Tabriz, Iran. This might not turn out to be anything we can profit from, but it presents possibilities which may not come our way again, and my thoughts are that we might gain access to important information."

Williams nodded in her direction. "Yes, but until we can come up with a way to communicate with you, let alone extract you from that madhouse of a country, it's a no-go."

CHAPTER 8

The Palace
Pyongyang, North Korea October 22, 2023

The big Zil limousine headed north into Pyongyang's Central City, toward its eventual destination, the Ryongsong Residence, the principal palace of the Wonsu. The few traffic signals which were visible almost never functioned properly. At a few of the larger intersections, a member of the military stood on an elevated dais in the middle, going through the motions of regulating the meager traffic flow. Only the major roadways in North Korea's largest cities would be considered modern by western standards. Lesser streets, even in the capital, as well as all of the roadways in the countryside and smaller towns, were either poorly maintained pavement, graveled, or even dirt-surfaced.

As was the case at almost every hour of the day, vehicle traffic was extremely light. Even on the main thoroughfares in the city, it was almost unheard of to see as many as a dozen automobiles at one time. At night, the roads were virtually empty of all traffic. Typically, only senior military officers, federal officials, and special friends of the Wonsu either owned, or more likely were assigned, government automobiles. The government's control even extended to the maintenance of vehicles, with all state-owned autos required to be clean at all times, or subject to a fine, or even the loss of privileges.

The fat man had spent the night at one of his eleven alternate palaces, which were located both within and outside the capital city. He had stopped briefly to pick up his two passengers. Colonel Ho-young sat on his left, while on the right was a man who strongly resembled a wharf rat. He was small, wiry, and owned a pair of small black eyes set so close together there was little space for a nose. If the Wonsu was a chain smoker, this passenger had to belong to some higher designation of nicotine enthusiast. The air in the Zil was barely fit to sustain life.

Ho-young would have recognized Colonel-General Moo-sung anywhere. He was a legend, having occupied his position as the Minister of State Security for the remarkable span of six years. Few senior officials had lasted so long during the Wonsu's reign, particularly one in such a high-profile assignment. Every military man was acutely aware of this longevity, and begrudgingly had to recognize—and fear—his enduring, close relationship with the fat man. Consequently, the military, including Ho-young, gave Moo-sung a wide berth.

The Wonsu snickered at the sight of the general's bald pate and pretended to shield his eyes. "The glare from the top of your head is blinding, General Moo-sung."

The man rubbed the top of his head, letting slip an extremely rare display of his sense of humor. "Everybody knows grass does not grow on a busy roadway, Wonsu."

The fat man started to respond with a snide remark, but even he had to respect the power and connections of General Moo-sung. Just in his own brief reign, he had already found it necessary to put down three separate attempts by senior officers to undermine his administration, in addition to the thwarted assassination. In each of those instances, the man on his right had warned him in advance. He needed Moo-sung in his corner.

There were others in the government who had a totally different opinion of Moo-sung. For them, he was a man who got rid of his detractors by developing a story about some plot in which they were involved. The Wonsu, who saw real or imagined enemies behind every bush, was quick to believe any tale which reinforced his suspicious nature. General Moo-sung exploited this weakness whenever it benefited him.

Colonel Ho-young knew he would have to be extremely careful if he expected to emerge in one piece after working closely with the three-star general on this new and highly complex assignment. The general had been very resilient when there was blame to be placed. Somehow, there had always been someone else found to be at fault, and that individual had always taken the brunt of the Wonsu's displeasure.

As the limo passed into Kim Il-sung Square, the central square of the city, the Wonsu pointed out the ten-meter-high banners. The gigantic pictures of his father and grandfather occupied a prominent place in public squares and arenas throughout the capital. The fat man had so far resisted adding his own visage, saying that he would only agree to be included when he had accomplished deeds equivalent to those of his forebears. Those who worked directly with the Wonsu were fully aware of this mindset, and tried to regularly assure their leader that, without a doubt, he had made equal contributions to his country.

The limo passed by an imposing structure, which the Wonsu pointed out to Ho-young. "I built this magnificent mausoleum immediately after my father's death. His body lies in state in a large glass display case, where all Koreans can visit and celebrate his accomplishments."

Most of the fat man's reverence, however, was saved for his grandfather, Kim Il-sung, who had led the DPRK for 46 years, beginning with the country's founding in 1948, and held the position of chairman until 1966, then general secretary and president until his death in 1994. At that point, his son, Kim Jong-Il, then held a number of titles, leading the country until his own death in 2011. At Jong-Il's funeral, his own son, Kim Jong-un, had been proclaimed supreme leader.

The national obsession with Kim Il-sung was overwhelming. In fact, the DPRK observed his birth year of 1912 as the starting date of their calendar. Hence, as the rest of the world observed 2023, North Korea's calendars were emblazoned with the year 111. As far as Koreans were concerned, there was no worthwhile measured time prior to the birth of Kim Il-sung—no such thing as before the Year One.

The Wonsu himself was, according to some, desperate to be compared favorably to his grandfather. He had even changed his own birthday to match Kim Il-sung's. This muddied the water just a bit in calculating exactly how old the Wonsu was.

There were those in his inner circle, including Colonel-General Moo-sung, who were quick to tell the Wonsu that the advances in his nuclear and ballistic missile programs were more than enough to qualify him for an equivalent level of recognition compared to his father and grandfather. But despite the flattery, for once he would not be swayed. He believed that nothing short of a great victory in war, either over the jackals in Japan, or preferably the United States, or perhaps the long-dreamed reunification of the Korean Peninsula under his leadership, would be justifiably worthy of his ascension to true greatness.

Those who secretly hoped that one day he would place a similar premium on improving the standard of living for his impoverished people had been disappointed to date. Electricity was turned on for only a few hours a day, while after dark, the view of North Korea from space revealed only the country's capital city had any visible illumination. There was only a single television station available for the entire country, and that was regulated by the state. Worse, there was an absolute and total blockade of the internet.

A third of the DPRK's income was spent on the military, while at the same time, a third of all children in the country were classified as malnourished by UNICEF. A telling measurement was that since the two Koreas were separated after the Korean War cease fire, North Koreans averaged two inches less in height than their properly nourished kinsmen in South Korea.

Most North Korean children bore parasites in their intestinal tract, which was actually an accurate predictor of malnourishment. School children in the North were required to furnish their own chairs and desks, let alone books and supplies; teachers often required financial bribes in order to teach; and many schools were barely disguised state-owned work camps and sweat shops for any children over ten years of age.

After an appropriate minute of admiring the portraits of his forebears, the Wonsu glanced at his passengers. "Gentlemen, we need to discuss strategies for Operation Chaos."

Without a word, the colonel-general reached forward, hitting a button and closing the sound-proof glass panel between the back seat and the driver.

The Wonsu continued, but with a slight edge to his voice. "Of course you are right, General. Now, tell me your concerns about hiring non-Koreans to carry out our attack. For example, I suggest hiring entities who have a reputation for cruelty, which the United States would readily accept with minimal evidence as their enemies. I'm thinking of the MS-13 gang from Central America, which their leaders seem to obsess about, perhaps a remnant of ISIS or Al Qaeda, Cubans or Venezuelans who are dark enough to obviously be considered Hispanic, a band of Chechen terrorists, and maybe a group of Black Nationalists or neo-Nazis to carry out attacks on their opposites in urban settings."

The general carefully did not sigh. "I would place no trust in any of those groups. If captured, they would likely spill everything they know. We, and by that I mean your government, Wonsu, should not have any contact with them. We'll need to identify at least two layers of middlemen to actually recruit, train, launch, and pay such people."

By that time, they had arrived at the Central Luxury Mansion in the Ryongsong District. From all appearances, the huge complex of some twelve square kilometers looked, from the perimeter at least, like a small military base. It had been built by the DPRK Army and completed in 1983. The facility possessed an underground war headquarters, secured with walls of iron rods, concrete, and even thick layers of lead to provide protection against significant nuclear radiation. Several military units were stationed around and within the fenced enclosure, and their security included an electrified fence, minefields, trained attack dogs, and multiple security checkpoints.

The Mansion, as well as a few other residences on the base, were connected by underground tunnels. Even an underground train station was under the main residence, which would allow VIPs to exit and enter the area while completely unobserved from the air, and travel via the Wonsu's bulletproof train. The grounds included large residences, elaborate gardens, man-made lakes, and recreational facilities including outdoor and indoor basketball courts, a large swimming pool complete with a water slide, running track, soccer field, sauna, stables with a riding arena, and a five-hundred-meter shooting range.

As Colonel Ho-young was ushered inside the Mansion, he was overwhelmed with the extravagant furnishings, plush carpets, rare rugs, black marble floors which seemed to extend to every room, crystal chandeliers some two meters in diameter, marble and bronze statuary, valuable paintings displayed in every room, and gold brocade wallpaper. He had not imagined that such a level of extravagant wealth existed in his poor country. His own parents had been considered to be well-off, at least in comparison to 95% of their country-men; but that simply meant the family owned a television. The colonel had not dreamed anyone, even the Wonsu him-self, could afford such luxury.

Chapter 9

Taking a Chance
Falls Church, Virginia October 23, 2023

Colonel Johnson mustered his courage and dialed the number. "Dr. Martinelli? We met in your offices earlier this week."

She recognized his voice immediately, but decided to make him work for it. "Who am I speaking with?"

"This is Early Johnson, from DHS. I was wondering if we might meet for dinner before you disappear into the hinterlands."

"Is this dinner work-related, Colonel?"

"Oh, yes. I wanted to talk to you about your linguistic abilities."

"Is that so?"

"Actually, no. It's only related in that I met you while working."

"Should I ask how you found my number?"

"That information comes under the heading of top secret."

"Are you romantically entangled, Colonel—married, engaged, promised?"

"None of the above, Doctor."

"I suppose your top secret research found the same to be true of me. Where and when do you propose this dinner take place?"

"Why don't I come over to your neighborhood? What's your opinion of the Duangrat's Thai Restaurant in Falls Church?"

"I'm surprised. I know the place well. When would you like to connect?"

"As often as possible before you start traveling. How about tomorrow evening around seven for starters?"

"I pegged you for the slow, cautious type, Colonel."

"If I hadn't been cautious, I would have said tonight. My caution depends entirely on how appealing my objective might be. I'll pick you up at your place."

"Do you need directions, Colonel?"

"Once again, top secret information, Doctor. I'll see you at seven."

Johnson departed his office on Nebraska Avenue an hour earlier than usual, dropping by his place for a quick shower and to change out of his uniform before heading south across the river into Virginia. The traffic wasn't as impossible as he'd expected, and he ended up arriving twenty minutes early, so he pulled into the parking lot of a fast-food joint to wait out the clock. Sitting there, he felt like a high school kid, and resolved not to appear obviously overeager, although he had to admit he was.

At the appointed time, he parked in front of an attractive brick town home in a nice neighborhood. Obviously, the doctor was doing pretty well. His knock on the door was quickly answered and he was invited inside. She was dressed in a form-fitting dress the color of champagne, and he was more than impressed by what he saw. Johnson handed her a chilled bottle of chardonnay, and she asked if he'd like a glass. "Only if you do."

The wine was good, at least according to his limited experience, and he spent several minutes wandering around the living room, studying its eclectic furnishings. "It looks like you've kept something memorable from all your foreign assignments. They're very intriguing."

"I doubt I'll find anything in North Korea to add to my collection."

"Does that mean the decision has been made as to whether or not you're going?"

"I'm sure you understand, but if I go, we won't be able to talk about it." She held up her hand to halt his response. "I've checked you out also, Colonel. Your security clearance is just as good as mine, but you have no need to know."

Duangrat's had started as a small grocery before branching out to the restaurant trade. It had been a fixture in the neighborhood for thirty years, and claimed to be the first authentic Thai eatery in the entire D.C. area. The dining room was lit by faux-crystal chandeliers and the tables were graced by immaculate white linen coverings. As they took up the menus, Angela noticed the perplexed look on her date's face. "Do you mind if I order for us, Colonel? I've tried just about everything on the menu."

"As long as it's in the two basic food groups—meat and potatoes."

She snickered. "That might be a stretch. You're not allergic to peanuts, are you?"

"No."

"Good. It would be difficult to avoid exposure in this place. And would you like to try a nice lager?"

"Probably more to my taste than wine."

She turned to the waitress. "Two chilled glasses of Devil's Backbone Lager."

After they had sampled their drinks, the waitress returned, looking expectantly at Angela. "Chicken and basil fried rice and Beef Satay skewers for the gentleman. I'll have Bhram chicken, plus crab and shrimp wontons. And would you bring two extra plates so we can share, please?" She turned to Johnson. "Now, Colonel..."

He held up a hand. "Can we dispense with the rank? Please call me Early."

"Only if you stop calling me Doctor."

"Anybody ever call you Angie?"

"Not for a long, long time." She couldn't keep the wistful look off her face. "My grandfather is the only one who ever called me that."

"I'd like to, at least if you don't mind. It seems to fit."

"I don't mind. It might be nice to hear it again. By the way, tell me how you got your first name."

"I come from a small town in Missouri. I was born eight months and one week after my folks' wedding day. A couple of old biddies in the church were apparently using their advanced trigonometry skills, and started making snide statements about my birthdate, as compared to the wedding day. The way I hear it, my mother was mortified. My dad, on the other hand, just laughed and named me Early. His philosophy was to try and find something humorous in everything, no matter how temporarily distressing it might be."

"Do you see them often?"

"My mother, yes. My dad passed away five years ago—Agent Orange. I still miss talking to him."

"I'm sorry. He sounds like somebody worth knowing."

Johnson looked away for a few seconds. He was always somewhat surprised to be reminded that the memory of his father was still fresh in his thoughts. "Thanks. He was all of that. How about your family?"

"They're both alive and well in Connecticut. I think they believe there's something wrong with their only daughter, given my long spells of travel and inability to communicate with them, sometimes for months."

"Where did you get all your schooling?"

"Oh, various places, a BS and MS from the University of Connecticut, and a PhD in nursing administration from U. Mass several years later. How about you?"

"When I finally graduated at the Point, you'd be surprised to hear only three of my professors took early retirement."

CHAPTER 10

Mr. Han-gil
Langley, Virginia October 27, 2023

Doctor Martinelli was not comfortable with the arrangement. As her coach, the Agency had chosen to utilize an asylum-seeker who had fled North Korea some five years previously. Woo Han-gil had been not much more than skeletal when he'd crossed the Yalu River into China as the first stop in his escape. However, after exposure to five years of the American diet, he was now a skeleton with hypertension and a pot-belly.

Angela wasn't sure about his age, but guessed it to be well beyond forty. His black hair was filled with gray and beginning to creep back on his forehead. His right leg was withered to the point that walking was a struggle, a result of polio contracted when he was a child. North Korea had delayed vaccinating her citizens against polio for almost as long as the most resistant of countries. If anything, it would be normal to expect that the man would hold a grudge for his deformity against his birth nation.

Despite his physical damage, Angela's concern with anyone fleeing a foreign government was the chance that they could be a plant—an agent, trained to do and say the right things by handlers in their home country so as to position themselves where they might do the most damage when the time was right. Although as many as three thousand people were able to escape from North Korea every year, most of them were of the working class. Needless to say, their intelligence was worth very little to the Agency.

It was difficult to understand how a common worker could afford to escape. Once they crossed the border into China, they had to hire a smuggler to transport them via automobile or truck on a multi-day journey through that country, followed by a hike across Laos, then usually into Thailand, and finally a flight from Bangkok to South Korea. The smugglers' fees had gone up dramatically in the past few years. Now the average price was said to be in the neighborhood of 30,000.

Unfortunately, the Agency lacked human resources who had any recent exposure to the inner workings of the DPRK, and had decided to rely on Han-gil. Angela found herself watching every day for any indication that the man might betray her once she was deployed. So far she'd seen nothing, except for an undefined hunch of mistrust. She told herself this was normal on her part.

Han-gil and Angela had agreed that all of their conversations would be conducted in Korean. He was definitely more comfortable in his native language, and she welcomed all the exposure she could get prior to her potential assignment. The linguistic barrier made a few of their interactions slow going, but her trainer seemed to be a patient man.

"Doctor, there are three possible paths out of the North. The only reason I was successful was because I could pass as native Chinese. Obviously, you won't be able to do that. Defectors attempt to flee by crossing the Yalu or the Tuman Rivers into China. By the way, best time to cross Yalu is in summer, well after spring rains and snowmelt. In July and August water only knee-deep. Early in year, they both dangerous without boat.

"When escapees are caught, unless there is large payment made through brokers, the Chinese always hand them right back to DPRK. There are only two possible punishments, labor camp or execution. The DPRK is fanatical when it comes to Korean exceptionalism. They will not allow any foreign blood to foul their population. Women repatriated from China who are pregnant are forced to have an abortion.

"Another point of escape is the Sea of Japan, but the DPRK possesses excellent coastal defense systems. They know the identity of every boat, even every rickety junk, which departs their shores. It might be possible to stow away, but everybody on the boat would be arrested and sent to prison if you are caught."

"Are there groups of freedom fighters, or perhaps Christians, who might be willing to help?"

"The DPRK says that they allow freedom of religion. Out of a total population of twenty-five million, there are probably five hundred thousand North Koreans who are Christian, but they only celebrate their faith in absolute secrecy. It would be very difficult to gain their trust enough for them to risk their lives for you. The Bowibu, the North Korean secret police, employ a network of spies in virtually all communities to report on citizens who might conspire against the government. This spy network is every bit as developed as the Nazi SD and Gestapo were during the 1930s and 40s.

"Execution is something the chairman uses to regularly remind his people that they have no choice but to submit to his power. He has become quite imaginative in his murdering. Most of the killings are done in public venues, ensuring that a large audience witnesses the outcome. People are lined up and shot in public squares, in school yards, along the banks of the River Taedong in Pyongyang, or standing before pre-dug mass graves.

"He once executed eleven band members who were accused of making a pornographic video. Each of the musicians was lashed to the front of the barrel of anti-aircraft guns. The guns were fired one at a time, instantly disintegrating the victims. Then army tanks were brought in to run over the remains. This performance was done in front of an audience of ten thousand citizens. The rumor is that the chairman kept the offending video for his own library.

"In the DPRK, there are over one hundred and twenty thousand men, women, and children in prison camps. But it's the Kaechon Prison which holds special terror for the population. It holds some fifteen thousand political prisoners. They are referred to as enemies of the state, and their number includes everybody who conspires against the government, those who try to defect, and everybody who helps them. Do not expect to rely on a fair trial if you are caught. Most of the time, the Bowibu simply locks people away. Only rarely is there a court proceeding, and it is one you Americans would call a kangaroo court. Being presumed innocent before a finding of guilty is the last thing on their minds.

"The worst thing is that they observe three generations of

punishment. In other words, not only is the guilty party sent to prison, but all the members of their family, three generations of them. It is this practice which prevents almost every North Korean from becoming involved in escape attempts."

"Surely you don't mean grandmothers and babies."

"Indeed. Everyone. There is much torture, cruelty, and rape in the prison. A common prison sentence is fifteen to twenty years. The food is barely adequate to support life. The winters are very cold, with little attempt to provide scarce coal or firewood to prisoners. Grandmothers and babies are almost always the first to weaken. Many people expire in Kaechon. Dead babies are commonly fed to the guard dogs."

Angela couldn't help her look of disgust. "Then asking for help, or even paying bribes for help, is out of the question. Nobody would risk their entire family."

"Yes, Doctor. The other way out is to try to cross the DMZ. But with recent escapes, I would imagine security is increased at present. It's very likely you would be shot without hesitation. If you attempt it out in the countryside, the DPRK has mined their side of the DMZ. I do not know about the South Korean side."

"Is there any language difference between North and South Korea?"

"Not too much, Doctor, just a little bit of difference in sounds. Some say pitch can be slightly higher in North. Have to remember that the last time North and South were together was over seventy years ago. Lots of new words in language since then. People in the South usually use the English version of new terms, while those in North rely on the Russian language for new words. You and I, we only practice the North Korean voice. Just remember that if you speak to a South Korean, he will usually know within a few minutes that you come from the North."

"What difference would that make?"

"Zero trust. Probably get you put in jail."

CHAPTER 11

Sister Dear
Pyongyang, North Korea November 4, 2023

The Wonsu smiled broadly when Kim Yo-jong entered his office. When he was having a good day, she was treated as a comrade. On one of his bad days, she often felt like a mental health counselor. Her commute had been rather short, as she and her husband, Choe Song, lived in a mansion of their own no more than a hundred meters from the Central Palace and well within the protection of the larger compound.

There were some twenty large homes located on the grounds of the Ryongsung Complex. At least half were still occupied by elderly beneficiaries of the Songbun class. This system was almost as old as the DPRK itself, rewarding political loyalty and the family history of those who were close confidants of the country's first ruler, Kim Il-sung. The group had once made up the highest ranking members of the military, Workers' Party officials, and senior bureaucrats. Even the father-in-law of the Wonsu's sister, a left-over member of his grandfather's cabinet, lived within the compound.

The Wonsu was working, not only to gradually move the old guard out of positions of power, but also to get them out of the Ryongsung mansions. In this, he was finally seeing some success, and most of the power positions were now occupied by his new appointees, leaders who were fifty years old and less. Seeing the eighty- and ninety-year-old has-beens finally vacating the compound was gratifying.

His sister was what only a few would describe as an attractive young woman. In her early thirties, she wore her hair

65

long, but pulled back behind her ears. She seldom wore make-up, despite her extremely pale coloring, and did nothing to hide her unusually high forehead, let alone the continuous smirk of superiority she wore. As always, she approached her brother with complete confidence. "I have some ideas regarding public pronouncements before and during your proposed attacks."

"As the Director of the Propaganda and Agitation Department, I knew you would, sister dear."

She took one of his cigarettes from the pack lying on his desk and picked up his gold lighter. Undoubtedly, she was the only person in the entire nation who could do such a thing without fear of retribution, but she had been bumming his cigarettes since she was ten years old when they lived in Switzerland. "Correct me if I'm wrong, but in this situation, rather than draw attention to ourselves, you wish to divert it elsewhere."

"Exactly."

"Why not utilize what the Russians do in advance of the American elections, but make it more difficult to trace? I see no problem in setting up a server on American soil as you have mentioned, but why not use multiple servers in other countries to feed the propaganda we decide to use? For example, if you wish to direct suspicion to El Salvadorans, place a secondary server there or in Mexico, create some convincing bots, and start a media campaign which would make sense coming from MS-13 sympathizers. Likewise, place other servers in places like Somalia, Iran, Syria, Pakistan, Venezuela, or Vietnam, with messaging having to do with entirely different threats."

"So you're saying we could begin sowing the seeds of suspicion and distrust weeks or months before the actual events are carried out?"

"America is nothing but suspicions. Maybe start a protest campaign against the way corporate farms in California treat their migrant workers, which could eventually be traced to a server in Central America. Transmit bots which create sympathy for families being separated by immigration authorities. Then the event might be to spread some kind of bacteria on fruits and vegetables which had been picked by migrant workers in California, but sold in venues across areas where illegal immigrants are prevalent. To make it more convincing, we could counter our messages with anti-Hispanic racist threats from their right-wing nationalist groups."

"You mean we take both sides of an argument? How does that make sense?"

"That is exactly what I'm getting at. This is very important, brother. We've got to stop worrying about trying to win the argument. We don't care who wins. We're just trying to agitate both sides against the other. The Russians always transmit messaging on both sides of an issue. The whole purpose is agitation. They became so accomplished that many times messages which they originated were circulated by the two opposing political parties."

The Wonsu was slowly nodding in understanding. "We could use the same procedure for all of the attack venues we've discussed, changing the location of the server and the media campaign each time, plus matching it with a population to be blamed and a population deserving sympathy."

"Actually, we can operationalize multiple servers for the same attacks. If you agree, we'll begin preparing the appropriate messaging, plus a timeline for release. The Russians aren't the only ones who can manipulate the Americans. We'll have them threatening and killing each other before a week is out, let alone what they might do when the attacks actually begin. For some reason, the Americans now believe that every single concern is a political issue, with groups only too happy to embrace one side or the other, and giving them yet another reason to hate their neighbors.

"In fact, remember we've got three partners who will be doing much the same thing we are. So the Americans are going to be overwhelmed with electronic messaging on both sides of every argument. What we need from Moo-sung and Ho-young is a good idea of the schedule for each of the attacks. Once we have that information, all the partners will focus their social media arguments on the next event."

The fat man clapped his hands in enthusiasm. "This kind of thinking is exactly why you were selected for your senior position. Some did not believe you were ready, but this only confirms my confidence in you."

For once she bowed slightly. "Thank you, brother." She stole another cigarette. "There's one more thing which absolutely must be implemented in order to throw suspicion in another direction."

"It sounds like you've got everything in hand."

"That's just the problem. What I don't have in hand is you." She waited for him to focus on what she was saying. "From now until all this is done, you've got to stop any further blustering, let alone more threatening moves."

"You expect me to remain silent when the U.S. ramps up their economic attacks against us? They accuse us of violating their blockade against shipping. And what about their own electronic messaging? What about the helium balloons they and their friends in the South float over our borders containing all kinds of vicious propaganda?"

"Do you honestly believe you can continue to keep up what you've been doing—the missile tests, the missile threats toward Japan and South Korea, receiving fuel from embargoed ships at sea, sending missile components to Iran, being unwilling to negotiate, selling weapons to African militias—and not have the Americans suspect we've got a hand in all you've got planned? No, you have to remember how you used to play poker with your classmates in Switzerland. Say nothing. Show no reaction whatsoever. That's the way to win at poker, and that's the way to beat the United States."

"But what of our promises to General Soleimani in Tehran?"

"Face it, brother. General Soleimani is dead. The Americans killed him in 2020. We only need to worry about his replacement. Major General Hossein Salami is now the commander-in-chief of the Islamic Revolutionary Guard in Iran, and that makes him an invaluable ally. His responsibilities in missile development and covert operations make him a perfect customer for us, and now that they have created adequate weapons-grade plutonium, he'll be seeking expertise in creating their own nuclear weapon. However, Operation Chaos takes temporary precedence over his requests. That is, unless he's willing to spend several billions of his oil money.

"Let the Americans assume that you are continuing to rethink our relationship with them. Since Japan's prime minister resigned, we need to make efforts to create a relationship with his replacement. Take advantage of the gestures from South Korea; let them wonder about your strategy after our meetings with presidents Xi and Putin; make them believe we actually want to continue to negotiate, play into their foolish desire to believe that our nuclear threat is somehow less than it was.

"Follow the examples of our father and grandfather. Delay, confuse, make promises, sign agreements, lie, cheat, be contrite, tell them our people are suffering because of the sanctions, smile at the United Nations, and do whatever it takes to win international friends. But never lose sight of the final goal. Remember the economic benefits we derived from the treaty we signed in 2012. Once we received the imported food and goods, and they released the hold on our bank holdings in Singapore, it was a simple thing to resume our nuclear program.

"There's no reason to believe we can't pull off the same thing again, only on a much more significant scale now. After all, you have bona fide nuclear weapons in your arsenal now. What can they do? It may seem hard to believe, but the more the Americans strut and promise, the more beneficial it is to us in terms of world opinion. In reality, all they want to do is make a deal, any deal, anything at all to save face, anything to use in the next political campaign. For the last twenty-five years, it's made little difference which party has been in power. Only a few of their hawks insist on true and verifiable progress. The truth is, the politicians in control in America are smart enough not to insist on obtaining real proof that you are willing to abandon your nuclear capability.

She grabbed at his box of cigarettes, lighting the next one from the still burning stub of the one in her mouth. "What is more, we should not conduct missile launches or nuclear tests of any description. After all, there is no test right now which would prove to the rest of the world that we have the capacity to launch a large, two-phase nuclear weapon on one of our ICBMs, at least one we could keep secret. Furthermore, do not be tempted to use sarin on the Americans in this new campaign. They know very well what countries possess that chemical weapon, and we would immediately rise to the top of their short list of suspects. They would not believe that a small group of terrorists was responsible for using sarin.

"So do nothing to provoke their suspicion, and nothing to restart the war of insults. Let things settle down. They will soon return to complacency if we play them correctly. And above all, take a lesson from the Japanese mistake in 1941."

"And what is that, sister dear?"

"Don't unnecessarily awaken a sleeping giant. Besides, if

things go as planned, the Americans are going to be busy trying to figure out just who is behind all these various attacks,
then discovering the terrorists have no army to pursue. The
more we stay silent, the more confused they will be. The more
we talk, the greater their focus on us."

The fat man withdrew two glasses from behind his desk,
filling them both with Cristal Brut champagne. "I believe this
is worthy of a toast, sister dear."

Kim Yo-jong smirked at her ability to manipulate this
foolish brother of hers. Where would this country be without
her analytical abilities and firm guidance? She had always
known, even when they were children, that she was the one
who had inherited her grandfather's shrewdness and cun-
ning. It was she who really deserved the title of Wonsu. As she
contemplated such an eventual outcome, it was difficult to
keep from rubbing her hands together and smiling.

Chapter 12

Recalling Benjamin Tallmadge
Langley, Virginia November 10, 2023

At the CIA, Robert Williams and Angela Martinelli had reserved a SCIF for the entire morning so they could thoroughly and securely discuss their plan.

"Apparently, your hunch was correct. Our safe house in Tabriz was finally contacted by a Lee Ki-hong, requesting that Nurse Amaya Lajani contact him as soon as possible. I'm thinking we can patch you in to our guys in Tabriz so he'll interpret the call as originating from there."

"Before we go any further with this, what does Han-gil know about this mission and about me?"

"Why do you ask?"

Despite the confined space of the SCIF, she got up and paced. Williams had never seen her physically express any emotion before, so he let her vent. "Nothing I can put my finger on, but I don't trust him. In our conversations, I never gave him any name except doctor and no information about what we suspect, nor what any trip to North Korea might possibly entail."

"He's been vetted about as well as possible, considering he fled North Korea, but we never disclose mission information to a defector. You won't have any more contact with him, nor will anyone in our offices confer with him regarding anything to do with you or your mission."

"So the only information he could provide to a contact would be my physical description, and the probability that I would be a doctor. He would not know that my cover will be as an Iranian. The North Koreans I met at the two Winter Olympics knew me only as an Iranian nurse. I never use my PhD title on deployments. My hair was completely covered with a hijab during the entire time, but never anything extreme like a burka or a veil. So about all the Koreans at those games know is that I have brown eyes and I'm short. That's a pretty vague description. I think I can live with that."

"If we decide to do this, we've got some work ahead of us in providing you with a legitimate backstory. Also, you'll need a passport doctored up with arrivals and departures to include the events they know about—the Olympics in South Korea is 2018 and the Olympics in China last year until you supposedly arrived back in Iran." He paused, looking her in the eye. "If you don't feel comfortable with this, I don't want you to feel like you have to do it."

"No. I just want to be sure every base is covered. I'll need the document boys upstairs to do some work on my Iranian passport. It's too much trouble to actually physically get me into Iran. I'm thinking I need to depart from Mosul, Iraq, so I'll also need a recent departure on my passport from Tabriz and arrival in Mosul. From there I'll catch a flight to Mumbai, then use the Indian Railroad to switch cities in India, in case somebody is curious enough to watch for me, then arrange additional flights from that point.

"Han-gil said that attempting to escape from North Korea has only bad outcomes. I think we'd better concentrate on an extraction that is accomplished with their approval."

"Have you got something in mind?"

"In that backstory you're creating, be sure to give me a set of elderly parents. Then when it comes time to pull me out, the safe house in Iran will have to contact them with some sort of trumped-up family emergency and ask that I come home for a few days."

"And what happens if they won't allow you to leave in order to accommodate this family emergency?"

"I suppose the family emergency will have to get really serious, but I guess we'll cross that bridge when we come to it. You may have to tie the emergency story to someone who is really a patient in the hospital. They just might check behind me."

"Understood. We'll be prepared for that."

"Han-gil made it clear that bribing a regular citizen was

not an option because of the punishment possibilities. What are your thoughts on that?"

"I think it's doable, but the reward will have to be substantial. However, you'll obviously need to pick someone who has no family which might be endangered."

"When you say a substantial reward, what are you thinking of? What's the economic status of the average North Korean?" She picked up her laptop and added to her notes as he responded.

"There's no such thing as the average North Korean. Too many divisions in society to easily answer your question. What we know is based on information from recent defectors. We can't put much faith in Han-gil's story about the economy because it's at least five years old. The DPRK stopped publishing anything other than trumped-up economic data back during the rule of Kim Il-sung.

"When we talk about money in the North, there's a huge difference in two separate groups of people. Members of the military, the police, government workers, people employed by some special industries which are favored by the chairman, plus a majority of the populations of the largest cities—Pyongyang, Hamhung, Chongjin, Nampo, Wonson, and four or five others—all of them have monthly salaries which range from one thousand seven hundred to seven thousand won. Just for comparison's sake, seven thousand North Korean won are equal to just over seven U.S. dollars.

"You add all these people together, along with their families, and the figure is somewhere around eight million citizens. But for this special group, in addition to their salaries, they also receive rations and subsidies from the state for food, coal oil, electricity, housing, and health care. So the monetary earnings of seven thousand won is actually irrelevant for their needs. Moreover, many of those who have most-favored status have been able to make a great deal more money by managing large businesses. So there is emerging a small number of the nouveau riche in the cities."

"What about the rest of the population, somewhere around sixteen million plus people, who live in the small towns and in the countryside? How much money do they have?"

"Yeah. These are the people who end up starving to death during food shortages. They receive no rations or subsidies, but rather rely on an off-market economy to survive."

"Are they all farmers?"

Williams noticed she was pacing again, but picked up her laptop as he began to fill in some blanks. "A majority of them try to be at least part of the time, but North Korea is geographically only about the size of Pennsylvania, and to complicate matters, because so much of the country is mountainous, only twenty percent of the land is actually capable of being farmed. Then when the weather is too cold, too dry, or too wet to raise a decent crop, the government sweeps in and takes whatever the poor have been able to grow in order to feed the eight million people in the favored class. Those comprising the sixteen million are then always the first people to do without—to starve—despite having grown the crops that end up feeding the people in the cities.

"Fortunately, the majority of these sixteen million folks have gardens and farm plots which are hidden away from government officials, and they judiciously guard their secret production in order to feed their families. While technically no private enterprise is allowed in North Korea, many of these disenfranchised sixteen million set up small businesses like snack shops, greengrocers, garment-makers, repair shops, carpentry, black marketeers, and just about anything to earn a subsistence living. They call these black market operations 'grasshopper markets'.

"One of their primary problems is the lack of electricity. The Koreans refer to it as their alternative current. That is, the electric power is turned on for one side of a street for several hours, then the alternate side has power for several hours. It must be difficult to run a business which is dependent on a sewing machine or a grill without electricity half the time.

"The smaller operations, such as push carts where food is sold, are called 'jangmadang' markets. The authorities are apparently beginning to ignore these businesses, probably because they recognize their value in addressing national food shortages.

"Quite a few people sell marijuana. They call it yoksam and believe it or not, it's legal in North Korea. Hundreds of thousands more dig for ginseng and mushrooms. Sometimes they can trade a cartload of ginseng to a Chinese broker who might help them escape. A few have managed to expand their snack shops into restaurants, or their single machine sewing shop into a small three- or four-worker factory. So there actually is a tiny fraction of the sixteen million who are doing fairly well."

"Their own version of the one percent."

"You could say that."

Angela nodded finally at this subset of the population. "Sounds like I'll have to find someone among the sixteen million, who has no viable side business and no family, in order to successfully offer a bribe. I'm thinking a hundred thousand won should get their attention."

"Just remember that the secret police have people embedded in every geographic area. Whatever you do, don't proposition one of them!"

"What about the reverse?"

"No, not that either."

"That sounds like just my luck!"

"Have you got any ideas regarding how we can communicate with each other?"

"I'm guessing they won't allow me to keep a phone, let alone a computer."

"I suppose Kim and his inner circle have access to the internet, but as far as everybody else goes, the only internet they can access in the DPRK is truly an inTRAnet. The government tightly controls anything and everything online. Even if you were able to get a device into the country, you couldn't get a signal beyond anything except what they control."

"Can you log into their intranet? For example, can you sit in South Korea, or even on one of our ships off the coast, and enter their system?"

Williams picked up a phone. "Marissa, can you come down to the SCIF in the basement and answer a question for me? Thanks."

Marissa Hoelting was there in less than three minutes. She was all blond curly hair, pale blue eyes, and a dimpled smile that would light up a morgue. "What can I do for you, Mr. Williams?"

He posed his question.

"Sure. But it sounds like you're dubious that our people in the field will have access to their own computer. What if an agent was able to smuggle in a small thumb drive which could be downloaded into one of their computers in order to allow us access?"

Angela thought for a moment. "What if the agent had no time to download anything? What would be the intercept's capability?"

"We could rig up a GPS signature for the device. But we could only pick it up when the computer was actively connected to the web—not their inTRAnet."

"Would you know what was being communicated back and forth?"

Marissa shook her head. "Only if the agent made that connection. Otherwise, the intercept only verifies that messaging is occurring, rather than transmitting it to us."

"How large is the drive?"

"About the size of a dime, and the thickness of two of them. It could easily be concealed in someone's hair."

"Thanks, Marissa. I'll get back with you in an hour to firm this up."

The door closed behind the computer expert and Angela turned to Williams. She tried to stretch out a kink in her back. "We'll have to work out a pretty slick code that will not only provide you with the information you need, but also give me a defensible position if the message is intercepted."

"We'll have something for you by this afternoon."

"Where do you think all of this activity is going to take place? Will I be located near or within their Bio-Terrorism Center, or maybe in another place entirely that can accommodate numerous participants?"

Although he had no real idea, the location seemed obvious to Williams. "I'm betting they'll involve a fairly good-sized group of trainees. The first place that comes to mind is the Ryongsung Complex, where the chairman's main quarters are found. It's just twelve miles north of the center of Pyongyang. We believe there are some four thousand military personnel located on the grounds to provide security. Therefore, it's reasonable to expect there would be plenty of lodging and all the logistics needed to support you.

"Another possibility is the Wonsan Palace on the east coast. It would be particularly convenient if they plan to launch their initiative via the sea. There are a number of mansions and villas on the grounds, and there's a private jet landing strip adjacent to the property. Kim keeps a two-hundred-foot yacht in the bay near the palace, which is designed to hold and transport a large number of people. He's also got a ninety-five-foot luxury yacht in the same location, so that provides even more flexibility."

She waggled her forefinger and touched her lips with its red-polished nail, noting that would have to be removed. "So he's got two yachts and his people only have electricity part of the time? And he's got two palaces?"

"No. I've mentioned only two of the twelve palaces he uses. It's just about impossible keeping up with where he is on any given day or night. A third possibility is his world-class ski resort which he built in 2014. Lots of housing in that location. However, transportation in and out of there would be a big negative factor, particularly during the winter."

"So what's your best guess?"

Williams shrugged at the difficulty in such a request. "Who knows what goes through that man's mind. Logically, it should be the Ryongsung Complex. But if there's adequate housing and logistics available, the Bio-Terrorism Center would be my second guess."

She pecked on her laptop again. "Let's go back to communication. What do we do if I have no access to a computer? We've got to have some sort of back-up if you're going to be assured of getting information. I've heard the country has huge shortages of electricity. This is going to sound strange, but would you think when the bedding and clothing of the participants are washed, would they use clothes dryers, which use a relatively large amount of electricity, or might they go old-school and hang the laundry outside to dry?"

"I've no idea. What in the world are you thinking about?"

Angela responded, "Have you ever heard of Benjamin Tallmadge and his Culper spy ring during the American Revolution?"

"Everybody who works in this building knows that story. The man is a legend."

"So as long as a satellite can find me, maybe we can communicate anyway, even without modern communication devices."

"Old school. I like Angela."

"Not simply old school, *very* old school."

Chapter 13

Brave or Just Plain Stupid?
Langley, Virginia November 13, 2023

"May I speak to Lee Ki-hong please? Tell him it's Nurse Lajani returning his call from Iran."

"Yes, Nurse. We met at the last two Winter Olympics in 2018 and 2022. As I recall, you spoke both Farsi and Korean, yes? We are interested in employing you on an important program."

"Who would I be working for, Mr. Ki-hong?"

"That individual wishes to remain anonymous, Nurse."

"You hinted that the project was something medically based?"

"Let's not get into that right now. You will first travel to North Korea, before relocating to another country where the work will actually occur. It might be wise if your travel between Iran and North Korea is somewhat circuitous. After all, there are those who wish our two countries harm, and sometimes those people watch for direct travel to and from. Now then, how soon might you be able to arrive in Pyongyang?"

"Well, I need to resolve some matters here with my elderly parents. I should be able to begin my travel within three days, then the trip will take at least two days, depending on how circuitous I make it. But Mr. Ki-hong, we have not spoken about the financial arrangements, nor the actual length of the employment."

"Those are minor issues, Nurse Lajani. I'm sure we can come to an agreement when you arrive."

Angela looked up at Bob Williams before answering. "I'm

sorry, Mr. Ki-hong. I will be incurring large expenses just to travel to and from your country. I am not a wealthy person. I have responsibilities here with my parents. I won't be able to travel without a firm financial commitment, as well as the number of weeks you'll want me there."

"I give you my word, Nurse Lajani, that your payment will be more than satisfactory. You should set up a Bitcoin account at the Bank of the Caribbean Sea in the Cayman Islands. We'll transmit your funds there."

Angela winked at Williams. "I'm just a poor nurse, Mr. Ki-hong. My family relies entirely on me for support. I'm in no hurry to travel. Please call me back when you can provide a written contract which describes the time involved, whether or not you will provide housing and meals, and a price to include reimbursement for my travel. If it's helpful, I also speak fluent Spanish and some English. If you are still interested, the contract can be emailed to me. Thank you, Mr. Ki-hong."

She turned to Williams after hanging up. "I didn't want to sound too interested. I hope I didn't ruin our chances."

"You certainly had me convinced. This Ki-hong character probably figures you could care less. We'll look into recent or upcoming deposits at the Bank of the Caribbean Sea. Maybe we can interfere in some way with any linked to North Korea. In the meantime, I'll contact the guys in Iran right now to set up one Amaya Lajani with an email account on their server, and I'll be sure your documents are ready for travel."

"Don't forget the thumb drive from Marissa Hoelting, as well as the code we talked about."

He waited while the phone continued to ring, finally giving up for the third time. Early Johnson did not want to believe it, but was gradually coming to the conclusion that either Angela Martinelli didn't want to talk to him, or she had already departed on her mission. The latter scared the crap out of him.

After work, he drove by her townhouse in Virginia. As his father would have said, it was dark as a pocket. She certainly didn't owe him a phone call, let alone an explanation. Still, he had hoped for at least some kind of communication from her.

He ate a hurried supper in a Mexican restaurant before driving by her place again. No sign of life. He was sure of it.

She was gone. From what he had been able to assume regarding her mission, she was out there, completely on her own, headed to one of the most dangerous places on earth. All of a sudden, the pimiento relleno didn't set very well.

❀

Martinelli gazed out the window of the airliner as they slowly began the descent. The mountainous terrain below had been the site of numerous battles and skirmishes over these many years. She, along with every American man and woman in uniform, wondered when the fighting might actually be over. Was it getting better? Definitely, but it had been proven many times over that northern Iraq and the neighboring Golden Crescent were no places to make assumptions.

The landing in Mosul was quick and uneventful. At least there were no more RPGs fired at aircraft near the airport. Dressed as an American citizen, she successfully made her way through customs with her Martinelli passport. Fifteen minutes later, she had handed off everything which identified her as such, along with a small travel bag containing her American clothing and cosmetics, to an Agency contact, and emerged from the restroom wearing the clothing and assuming the identity of Amaya Lajani, Iranian nurse.

She happened to pass by a glass storefront in the terminal, and couldn't help but notice the figure reflected back at her. She wouldn't even have recognized herself had she not just gotten dressed in the outfit. Thinking about what might happen in the next couple of months, she suffered an involuntary shiver. She knew this response was to be expected before she actually settled into the mission. In previous years, there had been a time when she looked forward to it with a bit of enthusiasm. After too many close calls in the past, who was she kidding? She was getting too old for this.

It was just after seven in the morning, local time, on Tuesday, and she had been traveling for over sixteen hours. She stood in line at the Indian West Coast Airlines desk, purchasing an economy ticket to Mumbai for the price of 210 U.S.

When she arrived in Mumbai, she couldn't help but notice the extra scrutiny she and her passport received by Indian customs officials. Undoubtedly it was because she was being assessed as an Iranian, passing through Iraq, on her way to their country. All she could do was appear to be an honest, reasonable traveler with absolutely nothing to hide.

After being asked questions by three different levels of officials, she was finally passed through, and caught a taxi to the Indian Railways Station. There she was able to secure a Level II-A ticket on the 1330 train to Jabalpur. Indian Railways was the primary means of travel in the country, serving over eight billion passenger trips every year. The system was surprisingly predictable, with a high probability of being on time. What a unique concept.

Thankfully, her ticket would allow her at least enough space to occupy a four-foot-wide bench by herself, sharing an enclosed space with another woman. The rail trip would take another sixteen hours to complete. She had to reflect that it certainly was painful to travel in such a way that one's identity was not compromised.

She gave quite a bit of attention to the woman sitting across from her in the compartment. Given the vermilion bindi in the middle of her forehead, she appeared to be Hindu, was well beyond seventy years of age, and suffered such a dowager's hump that, when she stood up, she was actually looking down at the floor. Surely the DPRK wouldn't deploy such a person as an asset of their spy network.

Arriving in Jabalpur before daylight on Wednesday morning, Angela admitted to herself that she had to find a real bed and get some sleep before tackling the last two legs of her journey. She caught a cab to the Jabali Palace Hotel, soaked for a half hour in the bath, and fell into bed.

Late that afternoon, she boarded an Air India flight to Bangkok, with a stop in New Delhi. Once again, she checked into a hotel for the day, then back to the airport for a flight on China Air, with a stop-over in Hanoi. Once she had her ticket in hand, she called Mr. Ki-hong, telling him her arrival time at Sunni International Airport in Pyongyang, some ten hours distant. He simply responded that they had expected her earlier.

A young lieutenant was waiting for her just at the entrance to the DPRK customs office. "You are Nurse Amaya Lajani?"

"Yes. Are you Mr. Ki-hong?"

"Not hardly, Nurse. Come, I will accompany you through customs. Perhaps we can expedite the review of you and your baggage."

The customs officer looked at the markings on the lieutenant's uniform, immediately identifying him as being a
member of the DPRK's Reconnaissance General Bureau (the
intelligence bureau), and spent no more than thirty seconds
with Nurse Lajani's papers and baggage. "Free to go."

He was surprised to hear the response from an obvious
foreigner in his own language. "Thank you very much for your
trouble." She smiled and pushed a five-hundred won note toward him on the countertop.

The lieutenant grabbed it up quickly, handing it back to
her. "We do not do this in North Korea."

The nurse smiled at the lieutenant and placed the money
back on the counter in front of the customs officer. "Please do
not do that again, Lieutenant."

He quickly grabbed her bag and stalked off toward his
automobile. She stood at the back door while he stowed her
suitcase in the trunk. He started to head toward the driver's
seat, then noticed her waiting on his manners to show up. He
grimaced before coming back to where she stood and not so
graciously opened the door for her.

"Thank you, Lieutenant."

CHAPTER 14

The Work
Pyongyang, North Korea November 24, 2023

Her immediate impression was that it was colder than she'd expected in late November. She had no idea what to expect regarding the trip from the airport to wherever she might be assigned. Although the city was somewhat similar to several capitals in the Far East, as well as Eastern Europe, the air pollution was even more stifling than what she'd previously experienced. Apparently the entire city used coal or coal oil. Several pedestrians were wearing masks or shielding their nose and mouth with a scarf. What was starkly different from almost every other capital city in the world was the shortage of automobiles.

Their travel remained within the confines of the northern edge of Pyongyang, and they arrived at their destination in less than thirty minutes. Remembering Bob Williams' guess that she might be working near the Ryongsong Palace, she was not particularly surprised to recognize his general description of a small military base, with multiple armed checkpoints and then quite a number of large living quarters, all co-existing within the compound.

The lieutenant stopped in front of what was immediately recognizable among the world's militaries as an enlisted men's barracks. She apparently would not be housed in the opulent mansions which stood no more than four hundred meters away. He retrieved her bag while she sat in the car, then finally came around and opened her door. She thanked him and walked quickly into the wooden building, the cold wind hurrying her step.

The lieutenant returned to his car wearing a rather sour look on his face and happened to glance at the front passenger seat. There was a five hundred won bill lying there. He picked it up and started to go charging back into the barracks, thought a minute, then laughed out loud in spite of himself, before finally putting the money in his pocket.

Her billeting, along with that for two other women, was on the left side of the barracks, and had been temporarily separated by a flimsy partition from the men's quarters on the right side. Thankfully, the women had separate bathroom facilities as well.

After introductions, Nurse Lajani spoke to her new roommates, attempting to break the ice. "Have you been here long?"

"We both arrived yesterday. They told us we were waiting on you to arrive before beginning."

"Have they disclosed what they expect us to do?"

"Nothing to me." The older of the two girls, Dinh Bi'nh, looked at the other, Tran Dung, for confirmation and received a shake of the head in agreement. "I suppose we'll find out something tomorrow." In Vietnam, the family name was used first, thus the roommates' first names were Bi'nh and Dung.

Bi'nh was rather plump, and possessed very short black hair. Oddly, Dung's name was translated as 'beautiful' in Vietnamese, which she most definitely was not. Her face was significantly marked with acne scars and her left eye wandered, to the point that it was not only difficult to avoid staring at the girl, but unsettling to wonder if she was actually looking back at you.

Nurse Lajani was suspicious that at least one of them had been planted as a spy, or at the very least that their quarters were bugged. They both appeared to be of Vietnamese descent, which made sense if they each had foreign language skills. She would need to be on her guard 24 hours a day. It might be a good idea to set a bit of a trap in her luggage to see just how inquisitive one of them might be.

The next morning they and the four men who were housed on the opposite side of the barracks were awakened at six o'clock. Apparently showering was not high on the agenda, as ten minutes after waking, all were outside and on their way to a large dining hall some hundred meters distant.

Breakfast consisted of tea, a small bowl of cold noodles with a fish sauce of some unknown origin poured over them, and an even smaller container of kimchi—which in this case was cabbage fermented in a brine of ginger, garlic, and onions. Watching her fellow trainers pitch into their meal with a degree of relish, Nurse Lajani decided not to request two scrambled with a side order of biscuits and gravy, plus an extra-large cup of coffee.

The seven of them were soon escorted to yet another building, this one with an armed guard stationed out front. Before they entered, a strange synthesized music filled the air, undoubtedly via a widespread outdoor speaker system.

Nurse Lajani turned to Dung. "What in the world is that ungodly music?"

Dung shrugged. "They play it early every morning all over the city. The Koreans call it their morning exercise music. Maybe it's their idea of an alarm clock."

The nurse shook her head. "More likely they're trying to wake the dead."

By the time they were seated, two officers entered the building, the younger one taking his position at the podium while a general officer sat at the front, facing them. The general motioned to his subordinate and they conferred for a moment in low voices. Nurse Lajani would swear she heard the older man say 'female CIA agent' and 'doctor'. As far as she was concerned, it was confirmation that Woo Han-gil had indeed made contact. She hoped to have an opportunity to report that as soon as possible before he might have a chance to undermine other operations. Unless, of course, he had also provided a good description of her. In that case, she would have no future opportunity.

The younger of the two looked over the audience, then turned to the general and shook his head before finally returning to the podium. "I am Colonel Ho-young, and this is Colonel-General Moo-sung, the director of this program. This will be the only time you will be in class with each other, and from this time forward, you will not discuss your part in the program with any one of your peers, or with anyone else. Likewise, you will not disclose to the people you are about to train that you have been in North Korea, nor that any members of our armed forces were involved in any way whatsoever. To do so will be considered a serious violation of our national security and will be dealt with accordingly. Is this clear?"

Although uneasy with the tone of his remarks, each of them responded affirmatively. One of the men in the audience raised his hand. "When will we learn what is expected of us?"

"As soon as you leave this room for your individual assignments. Now, with your various skills, you will discuss your assignment with someone on the general's staff who has a similar skill set, with the goal of improving on our strategy with your input. Next, the two of you will develop a portion of the training plans for implementing that strategy. Finally, you will be asked to translate those plans into a language, of which you each have indicated you have familiarity."

Another hand shot up in the audience. "What do you mean by a portion of the training plans? Will we develop the rest of those plans later?"

"No, you will not. No one except the general and I will have visibility of the entire plan for all participants. In fact, neither will each individual, until the very last moment. Your knowledge of anything other than what you will translate is unnecessary." He turned to the general, who had just completed his second cigarette in the short time he'd been in the room. "Sir, do you have further words of direction for us?"

The general pulled himself to his feet. He was short, rail thin, and undoubtedly well into his sixties. "Regard what you are doing as extremely important. Heed the colonel's warning regarding sharing any information you will receive from this moment forward. I can assure you, we will not be lenient if such a thing is discovered." With that heavy remark hanging in the air, he stepped gingerly off the stage and strolled out the door.

As soon as the general had left, four men and two women in army uniforms entered the building. Each of them briefly studied the group, then quickly walked over to their individual assignees, spoke briefly to them, and six pairs exited the door.

Angela continued to sit, her radar on high alert, wondering if this was an indication her identity had been compromised. But as soon as they were alone in the room, the colonel turned to her. "Nurse Amaya Lajani, you and I will be working together for the next few days. Because of your medical background, as well as your multiple language skills, you are particularly important to our success."

"I assumed I would be working with Mr. Lee Ki-hong."

"Mr. Ki-hong is only an intermediary. You will not hear from him while you are here."

"I must tell you before we begin, Colonel, that my skills in your language may not be adequate to translate medical terminology from Korean."

"Just tell me when you are uncertain, and we can seek another opinion for a word here and there, as long as we can conceal any knowledge of the program itself from the third party. I've been told that you speak several languages."

"Yes, Colonel. Some better than others. Of course, I am fluent in Farsi, but also Spanish, and to a lesser extent English, Korean, and Pashto."

"Impressive. What about Tamil or Sanskrit?"

"No, Colonel. Enough Indians speak English that I am able to find my way in their country."

He handed her a black folder. "Please review these documents and we will talk again tomorrow."

She opened the folder. "I'm sorry, Colonel. Although I can speak and understand your language, I have never learned your alphabet, let alone how to read or write it. I will need someone to read this aloud to me. That's the only way I can comprehend it."

Colonel Ho-young was definitely not pleased. He thought for a full five minutes. "I have a shortage of people who I would trust to read this material. There is no option but that I will read to you. When you need to make notes, write them in Farsi, as that will be the language you will use for the end product. At the end of our work sessions, all materials will be locked in my safe."

"Do you have a computer I can use for this translation?"

"No access to computers. You may use a word processor to prepare the final materials."

"I understand, Colonel. Are we traveling, or are these agents traveling?"

"All of you will be traveling to Ho Chi Minh City for meetings and training. The agents will then have their own final destination. So the document you will be providing in Farsi will direct the agents as to how they should handle anthrax in a field setting in order to protect themselves."

The longer he talked, the more Nurse Lajani's mind

swirled. Apparently she would not be able to see information related to traveling to the geographic area of their assignment, what their actual assignment might be, or even whether or not they would have to seek employment as a cover.

She was finding it difficult to keep up with the colonel's directive, simply because all she could think about were the repercussions of such a heinous act. *What can I do?* she thought. Another thought struck her. If this was her assignment, what might the other six translators be involved in? How could she contact Langley with so much new information, let alone so many unknowns? Should she stick around and try to figure out what other assignments were being developed? Would there be an opportunity to discover how and where those assignments might be carried out? How might the CIA be able to respond?

Chapter 15

A Plea for Help
Pyongyang, North Korea November 25, 2023

The following message began to pop up in social media feeds, particularly in accounts based in Arizona, New Mexico, Texas, and Utah:

Local sheriffs have alerted residents of California's Central Valley to be on the lookout for criminal activity in their area. The annual influx of illegal immigrants, attracted by the harvesting season in the valley, is regularly followed by a peak in home invasions, robberies, assaults, rapes, and petty theft.

This was followed by messaging in similar accounts in California, Oregon, Washington, and Colorado:

ICE agents are interfering with peaceful migrant farm workers in California. Immigrants are being arrested by federal agents in the San Joaquin and Sacramento River valleys. Farmers say these arrests will severely reduce their ability to harvest a bumper crop of vegetables, fruits, nuts, and other crops, thus leading to millions of dollars in farm losses, a possible nationwide shortage of some foodstuffs, and much higher prices for consumers.

Milk out of stock? A shortage of migrant workers has resulted in a severe hardship on dairy farmers. New Mexico sheriffs are aggressively arresting peaceful immigrants working on dairy farms in the San Juan and Rio Grande River Valleys. Without replacement laborers, farmers may be forced to sell large numbers of their dairy cattle.

And then the following:

Beaten to a pulp! Two illegal immigrants were suspected

of kidnapping and raping a local sixteen-year-old high school girl in the area just east of Farmington, New Mexico. A group of citizens chased them down. When sheriff's deputies arrived, the two El Salvadorans were unconscious, and had suffered numerous lacerations and broken bones. Neither man has regained consciousness as of this morning. Doctors report brain bleeds on both men.

Followed two days later by:

If You Want War, We Will Give You War! MS-13 gang vows revenge on the cowardly dogs who attempted to murder our two innocent countrymen in Farmington, New Mexico. Is this the way you mete out justice in your country?

And the very next day with:

The Sons of the Republic would be more than happy to accommodate the MS-13 gang. We will meet you anywhere you like. It will be our pleasure to rid our country of you vermin.

These last three posts quickly spread from one end of the country to the other. Cybersecurity units at the Department of Homeland Security, the National Security Agency, and the Federal Bureau of Investigation had become alerted to all of them. After fact-checking with law enforcement and various news organizations, the unanimous opinion of the agencies was that there was no valid information to support the posts, and so they began to try to identify the actual sources. Unfortunately, much of the public accepted the messages as the gospel truth.

⚛

She decided to awaken very early the next morning, as she had a housekeeping task to accomplish. At that hour, the sun was nothing more than a reddening on the eastern horizon, but the sky was clear, with a slight wind blowing, so Nurse Lajani washed and rinsed her bedding and some personal items before the team relocated to Vietnam. This task made it obvious why none of her fellow translators had opted for a shower. There was no hot water.

Not knowing what kind of accommodations awaited her in North Korea, it made sense that she'd brought along her own bedsheets, as well as a clothesline, which she tied to a couple of trees. Both of her sheets were white, with one possessing a large, dark blue square in the middle, and the other a similar square but red in color.

As she worked at the clothesline, she was surprised to see at least two hundred occupants from three nearby barracks outside at the same early hour. All of them appeared to be rather attractive, and very young women, perhaps even teenagers. This was strange in that she had not seen a single female in uniform up to this point anywhere on the base. The thought then struck her that these could possibly be a group of comfort women, possibly designated for the male personnel on base.

The nurse did not realize she was witnessing one portion of the 2,000 North Korean girls whose function was adult entertainment for the chairman and his friends. Referred to as the pleasure squad, the girls were divided into three groups: singers/dancers, massage therapists, and sex services. They had all been promised at the end of their seven-year assignment that they would receive money, gifts, and marriage to a military officer.

Angela shook her head at the thought of what their function might be, and completed her laundry. She took care to hang the red-squared sheet on the south end of the clothesline, followed by a white blouse, then a red scarf, two more white blouses, then the blue-squared sheet, and finally another red scarf. She left them hanging on the line behind the barracks for almost the entire day.

Bob Williams, the Korean Bureau Chief at the CIA, was leading a meeting in the SCIF. Seated around the table were Marissa Hoelting from Communications, Bill Webb from Coding, and Special Agent Daniel Won-shik, a South Korean native who had successfully been back and forth into North Korea two times over the previous three years.

"Marissa, have you seen any indication that Angela was able to use the thumb drive you prepared?"

"Still no sign of it, Mr. Williams. We're watching for some kind of messaging twenty-four-seven. Of course, we don't know if she's even able to access a computer, let alone open it up for us."

"Bill, what can you tell us from the satellite?"

Webb had the appearance of an unmade bed. His long white hair and scruffy beard lacked any recent familiarity with a barber's shears. If anything, he looked like a deranged science fiction novelist rather than a brilliant CIA coder. Thankfully, his hairdo did not interfere with his deciphering abilities. "She's definitely in Pyongyang, and apparently housed near the Central Palace. The coded message with her laundry would have made those Revolutionary War spies, Benjamin Tallmadge and Anna Strong, proud."

"What could you interpret from that?"

"According to what we agreed upon before she departed, she's either trying to tell us that something is going to happen in two days, or, most likely, in two weeks, but perhaps even out as far as two months. More importantly, she's already asking to be pulled out."

"What do you make of that?"

"Either she believes she's in danger, or she's got something really important we need to hear about."

Williams turned to Daniel Won-shik. "Let's consider an assumption. If she's truly not in immediate danger, how difficult would it be to get into the compound and find out what's going on?"

If Webb didn't resemble a coder, Won-shik's appearance was certainly far removed from any preconceived vision of an undercover agent. His chubby physique, ill-fitting suit, and prematurely balding pate were certainly not going to get him a starring role in a James Bond movie. "It's a challenge just to get into the country, but to get inside the Ryongsong Compound would be next to impossible. You're talking about a scenario that would probably require taking out a member of their military in order to gain access to a legitimate uniform and identification, then penetrating or avoiding multiple layers of security within the compound, finding where Angela is located, and then figuring out a way to communicate with her without placing her in danger. If she's at risk of being discovered, we would both have to find a way out. If she's not, I have to find a way out so that I can let you know what's going on. There are lots of moving parts and plenty of unpredictability in such a plan—far too many obstacles, if you ask me."

"The last thing I want to do is lose an agent, but I sure as hell don't want to lose two agents!" Williams settled back into his chair. "Let's meet again tomorrow. Hopefully, Marissa will get a hit from a computer. We'll of course look to the satellite for another message. But whatever happens, we have to make a go or no-go decision tomorrow."

❋

Colonel Ho-young and Colonel-General Moo-sung were sitting in the library of the Ryongsung Palace. It was just after nine PM, and they had been waiting for the Wonsu for almost an hour. The general looked at his subordinate. "Have you seen or heard anything of this CIA doctor who was supposedly coming our way?"

"No, General. It's very likely that someone inexperienced in spycraft, like a doctor, would never be able to penetrate our border security."

Moo-sung nodded. "Very likely indeed. Keep me informed in case this female doctor shows up. We'll have a very special penalty awaiting."

Ho-young was acutely aware of his precarious situation, trying to maintain a positive relationship with both Moo-sung and the chairman while working on a long list of complex issues. Both of the men were dangerous as cobras, and would not hesitate to strike if they felt the plan was not being pursued properly, let alone that a spy might penetrate their security. He resolved to be extremely careful.

Finally the fat man made his entry, nursing a tumbler of golden liquid. Ho-young immediately realized he was under the influence. His gait was unsteady and his speech a bit slurred as he looked from one to the other. "Gentlemen, what do you have for me at this late hour?"

Moo-sung nodded toward the younger officer. "Ho-young has important news, Excellency."

"We have completed translating our training documents, Excellency. Tomorrow morning the translators and I will travel to Vietnam. They will be meeting with the people we have hired to carry out your attacks. They are from El Salvador, Mexico, Cuba, Venezuela, Chechnya, and Iran, as well as a group of black Africans."

"Are you certain you will be able to control such a group? The Republic of Chechnya is a tiny country, but filled with merciless cutthroats. Likewise, MS-13 gang members will likely engage in whatever gets their attention."

"As long as they have no idea we are behind this initiative, Excellency, I don't think we need to worry if they decide to create even more chaos."

"I suppose that is logical. Neither of you will be seen by these people, correct? How long will the training take?"

"I can assure you, the actual terrorists will only have contact with the trainers. As far as they are concerned, no North Koreans are involved. Each of their training sessions will be recorded and reviewed by me to ensure that level of information is not disclosed, but otherwise I will be out of sight. If anything related to the DPRK is transmitted, those individuals will be permanently silenced. The training itself is not complicated, Excellency. Two days at the most."

"How have they been paid? Is there any hint that a North Korean has been involved in the payment?"

"No, Excellency. They were all told to establish a Bitcoin account. Their fees, ranging from two to four Bitcoins, will be deposited in those accounts through a Caribbean bank. The amount of their payment depends on the complexity and duration of their activity. Most have been promised a second payment after they finish an assignment. By the way, the two Iranians and three Africans will need to receive a second dose of vaccine before they can begin their activities."

"I thought multiple doses were required."

"You possess a remarkable memory, Excellency. These two doses are just enough to get them through their assignments. It's very likely they will be victims of their own attacks."

The Wonsu smiled. "That is certainly one way to eliminate problematic witnesses."

"Speaking of problems, Excellency, as the trainers are the only ones who have any knowledge of DPRK involvement, I recommend that we eliminate all of them as soon as the saboteurs depart. What are your orders related to the trainers?"

"Elimination is always the safest policy. Proceed as you have suggested. Now, how soon can the attacks begin? We need to provide our partners with a description of the attacks, their general location, and an estimated time for the events. They will then be sending out all sorts of social media posts to inflame the many suspicions and weaknesses of the American people."

"All of the attackers are facing a nine -or ten-day sea voyage on a Vietnam-flagged vessel. They will be smuggled ashore on the west coast of the U.S., perhaps twelve days from today. Only when they make landfall will the ship's captain hand each of them their separate missions in a sealed envelope. That way, none of them will know what assignments the others will be pursuing.

"Some will have to find employment so they will have access to job sites where they can do the most damage. That may take several weeks. Others can begin immediately after they land and reach their assigned location. Although we have specific dates for many of the attacks, quite a few will depend upon the terrorists finding employment in the right environment. Therefore, predicting those events will only be approximate. At any rate, it will all begin just as soon as you say the word, Excellency."

The Wonsu plopped down in the chair behind his desk, almost falling when he did so. He raised his glass. "This is a very comical situation, gentlemen. On the one hand, we are extending the olive branch to the Americans, consulting, and promising, and offering to meet, while at the same time, we are about to unleash multiple attacks." He chortled. "As to approving the initiation of our attacks, consider the word said, gentlemen." He gulped down the remainder of his brandy and smacked the lead crystal glass on his desktop.

Chapter 16

You're Going With Us
Vietnam November 28, 2023

"May I speak to Mr. Ki-hong please?"

"Mr. Ki-hong is not available at this time. Who is calling?"

"My name is FarjAd Lajani, in Tabriz, Iran. Mr. Ki-hong hired my daughter, Amaya Lajani, some ten days ago. She left this number for me to reach her in case of an emergency."

"Is something the matter?"

"My husband Farideh has been hospitalized with a heart attack. The doctor tells me to contact our daughter, that his time may be brief."

"What hospital is your husband in?"

"Alzahra Hospital, in Baghe Shomal."

"And what is the hospital's phone number, madam?"

"Just a moment, I'll need to look it up—98-41-3553-9161. When can I speak to my daughter?"

"She is traveling today. I will pass your message along."

"But my husband..."

The line was dead.

❀

On her way to the first training class, Nurse Lajani had a fleeting opportunity to take a look at a group of Hispanics, ten men and two women, who were apparently part of the mission. If the strategy was for them to find specific employment once they reached the United States, at least half of them would need a significant makeover, particularly any who were supposed to interact with the public. Three of the men had large tattoos climbing up the side of their necks, and two of them sported jailhouse black teardrop tats just below the corner of their left eyes, which usually signified they had either successfully murdered someone in prison, or had received particularly long sentences. As these two were just in their early twenties, the former was the logical conclusion. Worse, one of the men had three teardrops displayed, which probably indicated he had killed three times.

Of course, she decided to say nothing to Colonel Hoyoung about their lack of suitability, as her hope was that they would end up being a wasted resource due to their poor appearance and poor English language skills, hence an inability to find employment. Two of the students were surely Eastern European, and with their thousand-yard stares, definitely looked the part of paid killers.

She'd been surprised to discover she was expected to train a total of five men, two Iranians and three from Niger, all of whom were undoubtedly Al Qaeda enthusiasts or instigators. The three from Niger were very thin, all over six feet in height, their complexions intensely black, and all had shaved heads. Unfortunately, these five were the individuals who would be using anthrax in their particular missions.

She realized it would be necessary to be extremely cautious when speaking to the Iranians. Although she had been in their country five times, she was concerned that a misstep on her part would lead to the men realizing she was an imposter.

The two Iranian men were handsome in the extreme. Xerxes Abbasi possessed sky-blue eyes, while the other, Javad Mokri, had brown eyes which were nearly black. They were both helpful, in that their three counterparts from Niger mixed French and the purely African tongue of Hausa along with a smattering of English in their verbal communications.

Nurse Lajani was also aware the two Iranians were unabashedly flirting with her. She paid no attention to this, but both were persistent. Javad leaned toward her during a break in the training. "What is a Kurdish girl doing involved in this thing? I thought your people were bosom buddies with the Americans."

"It's true that Lajani is a name popular among the Kurds, but that was my father's name, and his father before him. It has nothing to do with my opinion of the Americans."

"So that is not your husband's name?"

"I have no need for a husband."

"But Nurse, do you have a need? That is the real question."

She couldn't help but smile slightly at his remark. "What I need is to hammer this training into five very thick heads."

She couldn't believe she was actually training people to enter her country carrying anthrax. Although she had no specifics, she could certainly imagine the methods they might use to disperse it, and that was terrifying to contemplate. Nevertheless, she had to go through the motions, and then do everything in her power to ensure she would be able to alert Langley once she was released from her training responsibilities.

She had given the five of them their first dose of anthrax vaccine that very morning. They were all needle-averse, but Javad Mokri keeled over, pretending to faint from an allergic reaction. It was only when she reacted by grabbing a syringe of epinephrine and made ready to deliver a rescue dose that he opened his eyes and laughed at her. "I was hoping for mouth-to-mouth resuscitation, Nurse Lajani."

After the laughter died away, she advised them that this dose would need to be repeated in two weeks.

There was considerable conversation among her students related to receiving a second vaccination. Xerxes cocked his head. "How are we going to get that shot?"

"You can give it to each other before you leave the ship."

"So you're saying we have to get that shot to keep from catching this anthrax?"

"That's right. One dose is definitely not enough to give you immunity."

Javad frowned. "We don't know anything about giving no shot. There's no nurse or doctor on the ship?"

"I don't think so, no."

Xerxes leaned toward her. "You're a nurse, aren't you? How come you aren't going with us?"

"Yes, I'm a nurse. But I don't have any authority to go with you."

There was more conversation among the group, with the men from Niger becoming particularly animated. "If you aren't going, then we aren't going."

That statement was all it took. The five of them agreed.

⚛

Nurse Lajani repeated their conversation to Colonel Ho-young later that afternoon. He was furious that the recruited Iranians and Africans would have the gall to stand up to his authority. His first inclination was to threaten them himself, but knew he had been ordered not to reveal the role of North Korea in the training nor the attacks to come. His next approach was to tell Nurse Lajani to threaten them.

"They all know I'm only a nurse, Colonel. The way I see it, you can recruit more trainees, you can offer them more money, or you can cancel this portion of your plan."

"I don't think you appreciate what my future would be if I were to cancel. Those in my chain of command are not prone to understanding when someone fails to carry out their orders. As to more money, this group has already received a significant down payment. If I had not been ordered to keep my nationality a secret from these fools, I would walk in the training room right now and simply shoot one of them." He slapped his baton against his pant leg. "There is no honesty among thieves."

Nurse Lajani did not comment on the irony of his statement.

He paced from one side of the training room to the other, continuing to slap his leg. Finally he stopped in front of her. "The most logical solution is for you to accompany these jackasses."

She feigned alarm. "That wasn't part of our arrangement, let alone part of the financial agreement."

"The voyage will involve an additional ten days, plus a return trip." He paused for a quick calculation. "We will triple your payment." He slapped the baton against a desk. "I apologize for this, but there seems to be no other way."

He neglected to mention two things. There was indeed a nurse aboard the ship, but he had no desire for that individual, who had not been vetted, to wonder why she was asked to administer anthrax vaccine to five passengers. He also had no intention of telling Nurse Lajani about the message he had received that morning from Ki-hong. It would be pointless to upset the nurse, and she certainly was not going back to Iran at this point, no matter what was happening with her damned father. He smiled to himself.

In fact, none of the trainers were going to survive. Nurse Lajani's demise would simply be delayed for three weeks when she eventually returned to Vietnam.

Back in their quarters, she attempted to draw her fellow translator-trainers into a conversation, hoping it would lead to them revealing the attack methods which their groups were going to use. However, she was unsuccessful. The threats from Colonel Ho-young had been very effective. None of them had any intention of finding out what he meant by severe consequences.

All of the trainers accompanied their students the third day on the seventy-kilometer bus ride to the harbor at Haiphong. They stood together and watched the 24 trainees board a large cargo vessel bearing the name *VNL Emerald*. All of them were shocked to see Nurse Lajani, with two travel bags in tow, trooping up the gangway. And right behind her was Tran Dung, who was being sent along as an interpreter between the trainees and the ship's Vietnamese captain.

As the trainees, Dung, and Lajani got settled on board, the other trainers were quickly escorted back to their bus. All of them, including the driver, would meet with an untimely accident. The horrific explosion on the bus would be investigated, unsuccessfully, by Vietnamese law enforcement.

The deck of the *VNL Emerald* was stacked high with freight containers, while above the bridge waved the flag of the Republic of Vietnam. At the top-most horizontal surface of the ship, immediately next to the flag, was a silver dome-shaped object. Nurse Lajani had seen similar devices at sea and recognized it as a misshapen seagoing satellite dish. She concentrated on studying every characteristic of the ship, hoping she would have an opportunity to describe it to her associates at the Agency before it arrived at its destination.

She and a few of the trainees stood near the bow of the ship, watching as it was towed away from its mooring by a half-dozen tugboats, then as they cast off lines, heard the mighty power of the engines as they picked up speed toward the southeast, before finally departing the Gulf of Tonkin two hours later. Nurse Lajani knew the ship would soon be coming around to an easterly heading as it reached the South China Sea and the Pacific Ocean beyond.

She glanced to her right and left, wondering at the motivation behind each of the trainees. Was it just a matter of money, or did they all really hate her country enough to carry out mass murders? Reflecting on previous attacks all over the globe, she sadly acknowledged the latter was the more probable of the two.

Her plan, if she had one at all, could only be described as a work in progress. She definitely couldn't eliminate all 24 of the trainees on board, nor would she be able to keep up with all of them as they separately went in multiple directions after they left the ship. Certainly the satellite dish provided at least a chance to communicate with Langley, but gaining access to an on-board computer was an entirely different matter.

Also, there were satellite internet systems powerful enough to provide access to communications at any point on the globe, and then there were others which were not. The most powerful systems were quite expensive. If Nurse Lajani's Spartan living quarters were any indication of other luxuries or the lack thereof on board, perhaps she would have to wait until the ship was near land again before she attempted to use the thumb drive. Nothing like waiting until the last moment to call for help.

⚛

At the same hour Nurse Lajani was departing the South China Sea, Agent Daniel Won-shik was preparing to cross the Yalu River from China into North Korea by clinging to a log. In early spring the water was absolutely frigid, and his wet suit did little to preserve his body heat. When he finally arrived on the river's eastern bank sometime after ten PM, he wished for a warm fire, but had to settle for the protection of a small barn as he quickly donned the clothing of a villager. His journey to Pyongyang should be fairly simple if he could find a train headed toward the capital.

His concocted background story was well known to him, as he had used it successfully on two previous occasions when he entered the country. Once he was away from the Yalu, he was confident of his ability to avoid detection, at least until he tried to penetrate the security around the Central Palace. That was an entirely different matter.

Chapter 17

The Attack
Pacific Ocean December 5, 2023

The huge container ship had no sooner reached the waters of the Pacific than the vessel began to roll in fifteen-foot swells from the southeast. In less than a half hour, the skies opened in protest and proceeded to dump buckets of rain on them. Nurse Lajani went from one set of quarters to another, checking on her charges. Of the 25, fourteen, including Tran Dung, were already prostrate in their bunks. The sound and reek of vomit permeated almost every space.

She'd already discovered the ship had its own nurse and sickbay, so was able to finagle a couple of dozen scopolamine patches for motion sickness, although they were far more effective as prevention rather than treatment after the fact. The patches were affixed behind 26 ears, including her own. She had considered trying to gain access to a computer while they were still somewhat close to land, but the world was spinning far too fast for her to do anything other than retreat to her own quarters and hold on to her bed while they all waited out the storm.

Thirty hours later, as the wind and waves died down, it was a bedraggled group which met her in the dining hall. None of them had escaped the personal torment which accompanied the storm, and most were unsure if they could keep down the ship's chow. The crew thought the passengers' appearance and complaints were hilarious, and didn't hesitate to eat extra portions of the breakfast meal, which most of the still queasy trainees could not accommodate.

It was three days later when the real trouble started.

Apparently the ship's Vietnamese crew had smuggled aboard quite a store of alcohol. Sometime after nine o'clock in the evening on their sixth day out, they felt generous enough to share their stash with the El Salvadorans and the Iranians. Perhaps some money exchanged hands, who knows. Although both Xerxes and Javad were supposedly constrained by their religion from alcohol, they both seemed more than willing to participate.

They each had previous exposure, but it had only been with wine. They had no experience whatsoever with 100-proof vodka mixed three parts to one with fresh-squeezed limes. After four drinks, Xerxes was trying to decide if his seasickness had returned, and was strategically positioned within three feet of a garbage can. Javad, on the other hand, had simply become loud and boorish.

Unfortunately, Lajani chose that moment to pass by the group, all of whom were well under the influence. Javad watched her pass. "Hey, Nurse, how about having a little drink with us?"

She looked from one to the other, quickly assessing what was going on. "I don't drink." She looked directly at Javad, then glanced at Xerxes. "I didn't think you would either."

"Nobody is looking over your shoulder out here in the middle of the ocean. Why don't you join our little group?"

Xerxes temporarily left the safety of his garbage can. "Leave her alone, Javad. The nurse is just doing what we should be doing."

"Mind your own business, Xerxes. Me and the nurse are gonna get a lot better acquainted."

"You mind your manners, Javad. This is a nice girl here."

Lajani straightened. "Thank you, Mr. Abbasi. I'm calling it a night, gentlemen." On the way out of the recreation room, she picked up one of the now empty liquor bottles. "I'll just throw this in the trash."

Oddly, she passed by two trash containers on the way to her bed without discarding the bottle. When she arrived in her room, she noted a couple of teaspoonfuls remaining in the bottle and turned it up. It only left her wishing for a couple of additional shots. She turned to her task and carefully broke the bottom of the bottle off, exposing several sharp, jagged edges, then placed what was now a weapon under her pillow, undressed to a degree, and got into bed.

Thank goodness her intuition's warning bells were going off, and she decided to stay awake for a while. In twenty minutes, she heard someone jimmying her door lock. She reached under her pillow and located the bottle. The next sound she heard was the door opening. Then Javad was standing over her. "Why don't we make this voyage a bit more enjoyable?"

"Javad, don't come near me. If you do, I'll scream loud enough to wake everybody on the ship."

Before she could react, he quickly put a hand over her mouth and hit her in the stomach. "I'd rather be rough anyway."

He had knocked the breath out of her and she was gasping, trying to refill her lungs. It was almost impossible to accomplish with his hand still clamped over her mouth. When he jumped on the bed, straddling her, she realized she had to get a breath and tried to bite him. He removed his hand just long enough to slap her on the side of the head. It temporarily stunned her, and he took advantage of her apparent lack of resistance.

She got a good grip on the bottle, and when he leaned forward to strike her again, the bottle came out, thrusting toward his face. Even in the darkness, he reacted, jerking his head backward. Nurse Lajani missed her intended target, but not by much. When she felt the bottle strike something, she twisted it as hard as she could. Then there was blood. Lots of it. On her face, her arm, and soaking her sheets.

She tried to push him off so she could turn on the light, but he was too heavy, and between him and the restrictive bedding, she could get no leverage. Suddenly the weight was much less, and finally she was able to extricate herself. Then the light came on.

"How in the world did you accomplish this, Nurse?" Xerxes whispered. "He was highly trained in martial arts. Nobody ever got the best of Javad in a fight." He knelt down and felt for a pulse. There was one, but it was growing fainter as the blood spilled from the sliced carotid artery in his neck. He looked up at her. "He won't live another thirty seconds."

Xerxes thought while Lajani hurriedly pulled on her clothes. "There's only one thing to do."

She looked around for the discarded weapon, thinking she would need it a second time. "You didn't come here to finish what he started, did you?"

"I followed him because I was afraid of what he might do. We're going to bundle him up in your bedding, take him up on the deck, and pitch him over the side."

"Do you really think we can get away with that?"

Xerxes pointed at the gore in the room. "Do you think you can get away with this?"

"I'm sorry. I didn't mean to kill him. I was just trying to hurt him enough so he would leave me alone." She looked at Xerxes. "I guess he was your friend."

"I've known him for three years, but he's never been my friend. He made it far too difficult to be a friend."

After they accomplished the deed without being discovered, Xerxes wiped his hands on a damp cloth. "As far as I'm concerned, the last time I saw him he was falling-down drunk. Let them assume he fell overboard. Now you've got to go back to your room and clean up whatever mess remains so no one finds anything to connect you to Javad."

The nurse wiped down the mattress once more, then turned it upside down on her bunk and made up the bed, using her message bedding. She then mopped up any additional blood with a towel and rinsed it, as well as her pajamas, multiple times in the sink. She completed her task with liberal applications of cologne, and finally went to sleep sometime after two AM.

The next morning, when Javad was missing, all of the witnesses agreed he had been staggering drunk when he left them. After a quick search of the ship, the captain declared him lost overboard, and that was the end of it.

Lajani took Xerxes aside. "I appreciate what you did for me."

"It was obviously Javad's foolish ego which cost him his life. You bear no blame for what happened. Hopefully, his wife in Tehran will be able to get to his Bitcoin payment." He ran his hand through his hair. "I hope we can still be friends."

"Of course, Xerxes. Thank you for your understanding."

Understanding or not, Xerxes continued to reflect on what had happened. He couldn't erase the question from his mind. How had this small woman, this nurse, for Allah's sake, not only fought off Javad in close quarters, but dealt him a fatal blow? Not only that, she hadn't shown any emotion whatsoever when she'd discovered he was dead. No hysterics, no tears, no shakes, not even a quiver to her voice. Could it be possible that she was part of Savama? (Iran's Ministry of Intelligence and National Security) He certainly would not duplicate Javad's mistake of underestimating Nurse Lajani.

The voyage continued without further incident. She administered what she claimed was the second anthrax immunization to the men from Niger, as well as Xerxes, and realized they couldn't be far from the American west coast.

She found Tran Dung and the two of them went hunting Captain Dao Hung. He was a slender fellow who sported a sparse goatee and mustache. The only thing not slender about him were his forearms. They were twice the diameter that might be expected compared to the rest of his frame, accented by ropey muscle and sinew. Along with the rest of the crew, he wore blue coveralls. His only visible separation from them was the white naval officer's cap he wore, complete with the gold braid on the brim signifying senior rank. He stood by the rail smoking a thin cigar, or at least he had been. The cigar was extinguished, but he was chewing on it for all he was worth.

Tran Dung paused as a discreet distance. "Captain Dao, we understand you are the only person on board who is aware of your passengers' circumstances."

"I'm not sure what you are referring to."

"That they are to be taken ashore in a small boat, but not in an area that is near a usual port of call."

"I might have heard something like that."

"Can you tell us when we will be close enough to land for that to happen? We'd like to be sure our people are ready to depart."

"That will happen tonight, sometime around two o'clock."

"Thank you, Captain. We'll be ready." She started to walk away, then remembered the favor asked of her by the nurse. "Captain Dao, Nurse Lajani's father is in very poor health. Do you suppose she could use a computer to find out from her mother how he is doing? In the rush to leave Haiphong, she was unable to contact her."

"I'm so sorry. Part of my instructions were to prohibit all ship-to-shore communications from the passengers."

When Dung translated his response for the nurse, she asked her to make an amended request. "She's not really one of the passengers, sir. She is only a nurse who was sent along with them."

"I'm sorry. You're all passengers as far as I'm concerned."

"Then she asks if you could at least send her mother a quick note right before they are taken ashore?"

"If you will give me the message and her email address, I will send it myself."

Chapter 18

Landfall
Schoolhouse Beach, California December 17, 2023

Tran Dung was not particularly happy to be rousted out of her bunk at one AM, but she accompanied Nurse Lajani to see Captain Dao. He was just returning to the bridge after distributing envelopes containing their specific orders to the 23 trainees. "Captain, as we discussed this evening, the nurse has a short message for you to transmit to her mother."

Dao hated speaking to Dung, as her amblyopia was so distracting, he kept glancing to his right to see what in the world the woman was looking at. "Let me see it." Dung handed him the note, and he added, "Please translate this for me."

To FarjAd Lajani—Mother dear, I have heard nothing from you, and am wondering about Father's health. I am far from home, on a ship with 23 others, and have not been able to contact you. I will try to call you tomorrow. Amaya

The captain thought for a moment. "Tell the nurse I will transmit this as soon as she and her group have left my ship."

When Nurse Lajani received this response, she smiled politely. "Would the captain please send the message now, so I might receive an answer about my father?"

The captain stared at the nurse before turning to the translator and speaking in Vietnamese. "Tell me, Dung, do you have any reservations about this woman? This request makes me somewhat uncomfortable."

Dung did not look at the nurse. "Maybe, Captain. I do not

understand why she is on the ship to begin with. You already have a nurse on board."

"Tell her I will send the message as I said, when she has left my ship."

Angela tried to look nonchalant, but realized the conversation which had just taken place was more complicated than a simple yes or no. Although she did not speak Vietnamese, in listening to the tone of speech, she believed the captain had asked a question during the interchange, which didn't make much sense. She was uneasy, and wondered if her message would be transmitted after all. When she and Dung left the bridge, she purposely left her pen on the desk beside the captain's computer before departing.

The two of them had reached the next level on the ship when she snapped her fingers. "I left my ballpoint up there. I'll run back and get it."

"Shall I go with you?"

"You've already missed enough sleep because of me. Just tell me the Vietnamese words for ballpoint pen."

"It's simple, *bút bi.*"

"Thanks. I'll be right back." Angela hurried back up the ladder, retrieved the miniature thumb drive from her hair, concealed it in her hand, and entered the bridge after tapping on the door. Captain Dao turned at the sound, saw it was the nurse, and frowned.

Angela made a motion in the air as though she was writing. "*Bút bi.*" The captain glanced questioningly around the room, and the nurse pointed to the desktop. "Ah-ha!"

Before the captain could cross the room, she quickly stepped in front of him, grabbed the pen, dropped it by mistake, and knelt by the computer to pick it up. She turned and smiled at the captain, who had briefly turned his attention to a camera shot of the top deck, port side, where the launch was being lowered. Mission accomplished.

In ten minutes, Angela was boarding the small boat with one piece of luggage along with the 23 remaining trainees (her other suitcase, filled with bloody bedding, had been thrown overboard a week earlier). The twin outboards fired up, and the boatman immediately maneuvered the small vessel toward the northern California coastline. The fog was not terribly thick, but certainly enough to obscure any lights from the shoreline some ten miles distant.

On the bridge, the captain sent an email, not to the nurse's mother, but to an address in Vietnam, which was automatically re-routed to Colonel Joo Ho-young. Dao was uneasy about the nurse's message, and chose to send a copy of it to the unknown individual who had paid for the passage of this strange group of people.

The afternoon was almost complete in Pyongyang due to the sixteen-hour time differential with California, and Ho-young responded to Captain Dao as quickly as the message could be translated. "No one in the group you have aboard is to be allowed to communicate with anyone, whether it's a sick family member or otherwise. Do not send this message to the nurse's mother. Repeat. Do not send."

"Understood. I am destroying the message."

In less than three minutes, another email came through. The colonel did not speak Vietnamese, and the captain spoke no Korean, so translation interfered with the speed of response. All communications back and forth were in Vietnamese. "Please tell Nurse Lajani to make no more requests like this."

"Your group has already left the ship via our motor launch. They will probably be arriving on the coast in the next few minutes."

"Good. Thank you for your contribution. The second half of your generous payment will be deposited in your account. I will speak to the nurse and the translator when your ship returns. We have some final business to transact."

Again, there was at least a two-minute delay for translation in between messages.

"The nurse will not be returning. She went with the rest of the group. Only the translator, Dung, remains on board."

"What are you telling me? Why did you allow the nurse to depart the ship?"

"She said it was expected that she go with the group. Something about giving them their shots. The scuttlebutt among my crew figures she and the Iranian have something romantic going on."

"Damn it! Do you have visual contact with the launch?"

"No. They have been gone now for almost fifteen minutes, and the fog is quite thick."

"Do you have voice contact with the launch?"

"A two-way radio, yes."

"Immediately contact the launch. Tell your men not to allow the nurse to disembark. She must be brought back to the ship and placed under arrest."

On board the launch, the pilot had greatly reduced his speed for the past minute, and was maneuvering to unload his passengers in the surf. It was a delicate maneuver, trying to get to water shallow enough that his charges could safely make it to shore, yet not so shallow that the props on his motors would strike rock and gravel. He was raising the motors some fifteen centimeters to avoid that very thing when his two-way buzzed at him.

If he turned his attention away from the maneuver long enough to pick up the radio, it was quite likely a wave would push his boat into nearby boulders and he would be stranded. "Everybody out." He motioned with his hand for emphasis.

Angela and the others assumed his directions in Vietnamese were to go overboard and wade ashore. People began going over the side into very cold waist-deep water. While this was occurring under the watchful eye of the boatman, she picked up the buzzing radio and dropped it overboard.

With the last passenger out, the launch reversed course and carefully turned about to run back to the ship. Angela and her charges did not hesitate. They, along with the baggage which had been assigned to them as part of their various missions, headed for dry land. All of them had long journeys ahead. The water was cold, but the northern California air temperature at night in mid-December was frigid. They were determined to quickly find cover.

Along with the specific items they would need to carry out their assignments, each of them had three changes of clothing, a script in English to ask for a hotel room, a wallet or purse with a forged driver's license, Social Security card, credit card, and automobile insurance card, plus a couple of "family" pictures and three thousand dollars of real American currency. They each had another forty thousand in counterfeit twenties, which was stuffed into a false bottom in their luggage. Their instructions encouraged them to spread it around whenever the opportunity presented.

Although the North Korean planners were not aware of it, several years ago the U.S. had stopped requiring that immigrants carry proof of their legality, as issued by ICE. Nevertheless, each of the 23 people carried a forged Form 1-551 (green card), and had been told they should be prepared to show it if requested.

Their instructions had been to separate as soon as they reached land, as nobody could deny the suspicious scenario of two dozen people of various races and origins, all soaking wet up to their waists, walking away from the California coast in the middle of the night. Angela tried to argue that they should all remain together, at least until they found a town and could arrange for transportation.

She, of course, was hoping they all would be scooped up by law enforcement, particularly if someone at Langley was paying attention and was able to pinpoint the location of the computer on board the ship. Perhaps she would have a chance to get a look at their orders. Failing that, she needed to find a telephone before they were all separated to hell and back. She glanced at the bluff above the beach. The good old U.S. of A. At more than one point in her journey, she had been doubtful of ever seeing her country again. She was so glad to be back, it took all her willpower to keep from kneeling down and kissing the ground.

Chapter 19

A Pair of Shoes
Schoolhouse Beach, California December 18, 2023

Marissa Hoelting's phone began to beep at 4:24 AM Eastern Time. "Slow down, Louis. Let me get waked up enough to concentrate on what you're saying. All right, tell me what you've got."

"You asked us to call you the minute we got a hit on your intercept chip. You assumed the location was going to be somewhere in North Korea. You only missed it by almost six thousand miles. We just got a transmission about ten miles off the coast of California, straight west of a remote area called Schoolhouse Beach."

"I've got no idea where that is, Louis. Give me five minutes and I'll be on my way to the office. I'll call Bob Williams from my car. Do you know what military aircraft are in the area?"

"The beach is west of Santa Rosa. There's a Coast Guard base near Petaluma, about sixty miles away. Then there's Travis Air Force Base about one hundred fifty miles east, and a second Coast Guard facility in San Francisco, one hundred twenty-five miles south."

"I'm guessing the Coast Guard has rotary wing assets. Call them and get them on standby. We'll wait for Williams before turning them loose. While you're at it, call Santa Rosa PD and ask about their chopper as well."

✵

"Mr. Williams—Marissa Hoelting. The office reports a hit on the intercept thumb drive that was issued to Angela Martinelli. They say it was located ten miles off the California coast. Yes, sir. Apparently our folks are sure of that. I'm on my way in. We've got no assets anywhere close. Shall I call Homeland Security and Santa Rosa Police to see if they'll each put a helicopter up? That way they'll be en route by the time we figure out what's going on."

"Bill Webb—Marissa Hoelting. I'm on my way to the office. We finally have a connection with Angela Martinelli's intercept. We may need you to decipher any messages that she may be sending in the code you developed. Thanks."

With his team finally gathered in the SCIF at Langley, Bob Williams leaned on the table. "Marissa, what information have you got from the intercept thumb drive?"

"Only that the first location we identified was ten miles west of Schoolhouse Beach, and the thumb drive remained in that location for some twenty minutes." She looked at her watch. "Twenty-two minutes ago, the drive began traveling in a northerly direction, staying fairly close to the coastline, but still about fifteen miles out to sea."

"Was Angela able to transmit any information?"

"No. She may not have had an opportunity."

Williams looked from one to the other. "What do you think might be happening?"

As was his habit, Webb pushed away from the table and paced around the room as he puzzled things out. As usual, he was wearing his black cowboy hat. "We know they spent almost a half hour near this Schoolhouse Beach. That could mean the delay was to get a landing party to shore. Then again, maybe they couldn't land safely at that location, so they headed north seeking a better site."

Louis tapped the table like a snare drum. "Maybe they're depositing a nuclear device near the shoreline."

Williams tried not to roll his eyes. Louis was always looking for the most dramatic solution to a question. "Why would they do that in a desolate area? Why not make port in San Diego, or L.A., or Long Beach, or San Francisco, where they could deliver maximum damage?"

Marissa didn't hide her eye roll. "If that was true, why is

Angela with them? Wasn't her role connected to some sort of medical issue?"

"We don't know that for sure, but I agree. What would be the purpose of her being along if it's a nuclear attack?" Williams turned back to Marissa. "Do we know anything about the ship she's on?"

"It's a Vietnamese freighter, sir."

"Vietnamese? What the hell?"

Raines leaned between them, making eye contact with Williams. "We've got helicopters about to lift off, coming from the Petaluma Coast Guard Base and the Santa Rosa Police Department."

Williams nodded. "Let's get both of them over that beach area, as well as any nearby housing or businesses. Hopefully they'll have infrared body heat detection equipment on board. If they've landed anybody, maybe we can locate them. If so, we'll grab them up. If that ship makes for land, one of the choppers needs to break away and chase it down."

Marissa glanced up from the SCIF laptop in front of her. "Google Map shows no towns near Schoolhouse Beach, just golf communities and ocean-side residences along Highway One. They could be using Martinelli as a hostage. How about putting roadblocks up on the highways between the beach and Santa Rosa?"

Williams looked exasperated. "What do we tell them they're looking for?" He suddenly slapped his forehead. "Good Lord, I forgot about Daniel Won-shik! We sent him off to infiltrate North Korea in search of Angela. We've got to call him back before he enters the country."

Angela and the others had already crossed the beautiful, secluded beach, then climbed a steep wooden staircase up the cliff, hoping to figure out where they might go next. On the bluff above the ocean, there was little fog, and they could clearly see the lights of various residences straight in front of them, as well as in small groups to the north and south along the seaside highway. Maybe she could get some idea of where or what the potential terrorists would all be doing. "Where are all of you going?"

Xerxes shook his head. "Don't ask us what you don't need to know, Nurse. If you get caught, you will undoubtedly be tortured. We've all heard about their CIA interrogators. You'll be forced to tell what you know."

Angela kept a straight face. "Yes, I've heard terrible stories about their torture techniques. But how are we supposed to link up after this is over if we don't all know where everybody is headed?"

Xerxes simply shook his head again and kept walking. The group was hell-bent on separating, despite her arguments to the contrary. Four of the Latin Americans opted to head north along the highway, ultimately in the general direction of Oregon, while their counterparts from El Salvador and Cuba walked toward the south, knowing that somewhere down there sat San Francisco. The remaining thirteen, including Angela, crossed Highway One and entered the neighborhood beyond. The terrorists were determined to find transportation and travel toward their ultimate assignments, getting away from the landing area as quickly as possible. Given the number of homes in the distance, finding vehicles likely wouldn't be a problem.

It was only by chance that the five men from Niger and Somalia united with Xerxes and Angela. The group didn't hesitate when they spied the late model Buick SUV and the Lexus sedan in the driveway of the second home on the street. They signaled to their Chechen and Mexican counterparts on the opposite side of the roadway, who were also seeking transportation, that they were breaking into that particular house.

The men from Somalia squatted on their haunches in the shadows of the garage, while the three from Niger, Xerxes, and Angela looked for an easy entrance into the home. The doors were well secured with bolt locks. However, two large windows on the west side of the residence, which afforded a beautiful panoramic view of the Pacific, had been left unlatched.

Jimmy and Marilyn Aaron had spent forty years saving enough money to purchase an elegant ocean-side villa just off Highway One. They lived in a community of similar homes, many of them unoccupied except on weekends or during the summer. Probably less than twenty residences in their development were lived in on a full-time basis. The Aarons had an excellent alarm system which they engaged on the rare occasions when they were away on a trip, but the rest of the time, and as long as at least one car was parked in the drive, they had no fear of burglars. After all, Santa Rosa and its crime was almost an hour away.

When their silver Maine Coon cat, Festus, jumped up on the bed and began mewing and pawing at Marilyn, she tried to ignore him, but he was insistent. It was unusual behavior for the middle of the night, and the only times he had acted that way before, a neighbor's cat had been in heat. Marilyn assumed that was again the case, and wasn't about to let Festus go outside for an evening of hide and seek. However, she decided to get up anyway, as she didn't want her husband awakened by the cat. After all, a decent night's sleep was a rare thing for him since his diagnosis.

Marilyn shut the bedroom door behind her as she and Festus went into the den. She flipped the light switch, but for some reason the bulb chose that particular moment to not work. She then fumbled for a lamp and was able to get it turned on. Festus continued his mewing. She thought perhaps she could sit with him for a while and get him calmed down.

She turned to pick up a magazine and noticed the oddest thing. Apparently, Jimmy had left a pair of his shoes up against the drapes in the den. How many times would she have to clean up after that man? When she bent down to pick them up, only then did she realize there was a black man standing in them.

Before she could make a sound, an arm wrapped around her shoulder and covered her mouth. Then a woman in Middle Eastern dress stepped in front of her, speaking perfect English. "If you cooperate with us, you won't get hurt. We need the keys to both of your cars, any guns you have in the house, and I need a change of clothes."

A man who looked Arabic whispered something to the woman and gestured toward the bedroom. She spoke again, this time in a language Marilyn didn't understand. "Don't wake him up. Just keep an eye on him. We'll only deal with the woman."

When the woman explained this, Marilyn Aaron nodded her head in understanding. The black man cautiously removed his hand and she spoke in a low voice. "We don't have any guns. My husband doesn't hunt any more." He turned her loose and followed along behind her as she collected the car keys.

Angela then accompanied her into a closet, where she changed clothes and dropped her voice to a whisper. "Ma'am, don't open this door yet. I'm trying to save your lives, as well as a lot of others. Can I borrow your cell phone?"

When she emerged from the closet, dressed in jeans and a pull-over top, Angela went straight to Xerxes. "Let's tie them up. By the time someone finds them, we'll be long gone."

"Why not just get rid of them?"

"Why start your escape with two murder charges? If you just steal their cars, the police will stop looking for you in a day or so. Cars get stolen all the time. Two elderly people murdered in their home will draw all kinds of attention from law enforcement."

✦

Williams quickly re-gathered his team. "Believe it or not, I just spoke to Angela. She says she landed with a group of twenty-three terrorists at Schoolhouse and that the group has separated into five or six smaller teams. All of them are trying to steal automobiles near where they came ashore. Her group is about to take off in a white Buick SUV and a red Lexus sedan. The others have gone off in different directions. Everybody was still on foot fifteen minutes ago, but she doesn't know their current status. They may head in different directions, but she doesn't know at this point. She intends to be in one of the vehicles. Apparently, at least some of them have specific destinations where they are supposed to carry out a variety of attacks."

"What kind of attacks?"

"She was whispering and didn't have time to discuss anything, but said to send somebody out to 135 El Camino Bella Drive, which is apparently near this Schoolhouse Beach. The occupants are in their seventies and will hopefully be tied up and alive. Angela says she hopes to convince the terrorists not to kill them."

He paused. "Louis, get back with those choppers and tell them what we know. Marissa, contact Santa Rosa and San Francisco to set up roadblocks. Give them the info on the Buick and the Lexus, but make sure they know there are other unknown vehicles. Tell them to detain anybody that looks the least bit suspicious."

✦

Xerxes was driving, Angela was in the passenger seat, and the three men from Niger were in the back, while the two Somalis had taken the Lexus. They continued up Highway 1 until they reached the intersection with 116, where both vehicles turned eastward. Angela had high hopes that all of them would be stopped by law enforcement. In fact, the more she observed their poor driving skills, the more likely it seemed that they all would be arrested for a traffic violation the first time they passed a patrol car.

The road was curvy and narrow, and Angela wondered more than once if they might run off the highway. In less than an hour, they arrived at the resort community of Guerneville, along the Russian River. At the first major intersection, the Lexus continued easterly on Highway 116, quickly disappearing from sight. The SUV turned off to the left, and Xerxes stopped in front of the West Sonoma Inn.

Angela turned to him, surprised that he would stop so close to their landing site. "Are you planning on spending the night here?"

"Not exactly." He reached into his jacket, retrieved a wad of bills, and handed her several. "We're not stopping, but you are."

"Why are you doing this? I thought we were a team."

"We're going to be traveling all over the place, and you have a pretty good idea about the kinds of things we're planning on doing. There's no guarantee we're not going to get caught and perhaps executed. You need to get out while you can."

"But I wanted to stay with you."

"That's not going to happen."

"Does this mean I won't see you again?"

Xerxes pondered this, then extracted his envelope from an inside pocket and glanced over the instructions. "If you're still in the country, maybe you could meet me someplace called Memphis, on May nineteenth."

She smiled at that and nodded. "I've heard of Memphis. There's a famous place there, I think it's called the Peabody Hotel. I'll meet you in the hotel lobby when they bring the ducks down to the fountain."

Xerxes nodded back with a somewhat bewildered look on his face. "Sounds more like a farm than a Western hotel." He reached across her and opened the door. "You need to get out of the car now." And with that serving as a goodbye, the SUV pulled out, following the roadway to the northeast.

Angela noticed a sign that indicated they were headed for The Redwoods Reserve. She had been relying on staying with the four men in the SUV long enough to find a way to get them arrested. After all, as far as she was concerned, they were the most dangerous of the entire group, as it was these four who obviously had one or more anthrax missions.

She woke up the night clerk, checked into the West Sonoma Inn, and asked for a pay phone. The clerk groggily pointed toward one on the wall and retreated to his easy chair. Angela dialed zero. When the operator picked up, she simply said "Ma'am, this is a federal government priority call number two seven two two seven."

The operator, startled at hearing that request for the first time in her career, quickly confirmed the code in her policy manual. "Understood."

Angela gave her a Northern Virginia number and Williams picked up on the second ring. "This is an unsecured call, Bob, but you need this information right now." After briefing him regarding a description of the trainees, the two vehicles, and what she knew about the routes taken by them, he told her to sit tight, that someone would be there the next morning at the latest.

For a reason she couldn't exactly explain, Angela wanted very badly at that moment to call Early Johnson. The emotional response when she reminded herself that calling him was totally against protocol, and she wouldn't be able to do it, surprised her.

※

Williams was frustrated when he updated his team later that day. "There were six separate groups who found vehicles and fled the Schoolhouse Beach area, and we have complete descriptions of the cars and their license plates. Two of the owners were killed by the foreign agents, and the remainder were left alive. Despite that, and setting up four separate roadblocks within an hour and ten minutes of receiving the first message from the ship, we caught none of them. We found one of the stolen vehicles dumped just north of San Francisco and another in Santa Rosa.

"A few minutes ago, local law enforcement arrested a

couple of skin-heads driving one of the cars in Sacramento. But Angela confirmed there was nobody in the bunch who would fit the description of those two. I think it's fair to say that they are all loose and headed who knows where. If they're smart, they'll have split up even more. They could be using different cars, trains, buses, or just holed up somewhere.

"Angela has spent the whole day with a sketch-artist from the San Francisco Police Department. At last count, they had six completed, and they're being circulated in a five-state area. She says she can probably help with two more, but the other faces she's just not sure of."

"What do we know about the ship they were on?"

"Homeland Security tracked the ship to the Port of Eureka. That's in northwest California, and is the least utilized of all California ports. Customs and Port Authority personnel, along with two FBI agents, went aboard the *VNL Emerald* as soon as the ship docked. It's a Vietnam-flagged vessel, and apparently the captain, as well as all the crew, are Vietnamese. The intercept thumb drive was still plugged into the computer on the bridge. When the Bureau guy waved it in front of the ship's captain, he acknowledged allowing twenty-four stowaways to go ashore. At least stowaways is what he called them."

"Does he realize he's going to jail for that?"

"That's just the beginning of his problems. It was raining the entire time Customs was on board. Apparently it rains a great deal in Eureka, but they didn't let that interfere with their investigation. The ship and its cargo were searched by two separate teams, including dogs. They even brought a couple of experts out from UCSF to inspect some of the merchandise. They had shipping manifests which accurately listed the contents of every single container—with a couple of exceptions."

"Did they mention where the goods came from? Nothing from North Korea, I suppose."

"Everything originated in either China or Vietnam. There were a hundred and twenty containers of clothing, two containers full of several hundred thousand gaudy plastic-beaded necklaces, all in clear plastic bags, and get this, two containers full of thousands of Elvis, Rolling Stones, and Beatles albums. Customs assured me they opened everything and examined every box within the containers. Those shipping containers are eight feet wide, eight and a half feet tall, and twenty-four feet long. You can put a heck of a lot of stuff in there.

"A couple of drug dogs hit on the back of one of the ship's containers. It took a while, but they figured out there was a false wall at the back of the unit. When they ripped it out, the floor was covered in charcoal. Probably they figured it would throw off the dogs. Under the first layer of charcoal were bags of black tar heroin."

"How much are you talking about?"

"The FBI flew it down to San Francisco. If you figure a hundred milligrams of heroin per dose, then they figure over a million doses."

"Why is it called black tar heroin?"

"It's dark colored, usually sticky, like tar. Apparently their manufacturing process is pretty crude. There's no standardization between a shipment from last month and one the following month. The lab says it's almost always full of impurities. It often clogs up needles, or worse, your veins. Because of the impurities, the druggies are never sure how much of it to use to get the high they're after. That's one reason for all the opiate overdoses. Sometimes it's more concentrated than they expect.

"The worst part of it, all of the heroin was impregnated with Fentanyl. Of course, Fentanyl is somewhere around a thousand times more potent than opium. The lab figures each dose of a hundred milligrams of heroin also had five hundred micrograms of Fentanyl mixed with it. So basically every addict who used it would have overdosed. Whoever put this combination together was intent on murder, and I mean murder on a gigantic scale."

"Any idea where it came from?"

"Most black tar heroin comes out of Mexico, but we're seeing more and more shipped out of China and Vietnam. The stuff coming from China is almost always mixed with Fentanyl. Our folks upstairs say the Chinese government knows exactly what manufacturer it comes from, ignores it, and endorses it on a gigantic scale. This batch was concealed in a shipping container which was otherwise filled with clothing made in China. Of course, the ship's captain will say that anybody could have stashed it in the container."

"Did you track where the containers were going?"

"All the clothing containers were headed to distribution centers for two big-box store companies, one in Ohio and the other in Arkansas. The record albums and memorabilia were being shipped to warehouses in Murfreesboro, Tennessee and Newark, New Jersey, to somebody called The Music Man, and the necklaces were addressed to The King's Krew in Baton Rouge."

"Other than circulating the police sketches, what do we do next?"

Chapter 20

Sweet Tea
Purdy, Missouri January 6, 2024

A week passed, then another. Despite the publicized sketches being widely circulated in the western states, there had been no sightings. Local and state law enforcement began to spend less and less time on reminding their forces about the potential threat. Before long, more pressing matters took precedence.

In the offices of the FBI and DHS, they certainly didn't have the resources to canvass twenty percent of the land area of the lower 48, but they were still paying attention. They had stood up a joint task force, which was housed at Homeland Security, and included the CIA as a silent partner. The task force was overseen by Assistant Secretary Abel Adams.

They hosted a teleconference six days a week at one o'clock Eastern Time, with participation by the CIA's Robert Williams and Angela Martinelli, who had just returned to Langley, and the FBI's Special Agent in Charge for San Francisco, as well as heads of the state police forces in Washington, Oregon, California, Arizona, and Nevada. The telecon had deteriorated into little other than eight separate reports consisting of 'nothing new to report'. Dr. Thomas Chu, SAIC in San Francisco, was the first to bring up what they were all thinking. "As things stand right now, we're wasting time that none of us have. We've all got this information on our desks. Why don't we re-initiate these calls when one of us gets something to report?" And so they lapsed.

❋

Old Bob Reams and his wife Stella had been running the Happy Valley Dairy Farm two miles outside Purdy, Missouri for 47 years, ever since Stella's father, Oscar, had run off and left the family just a few months after Bob and Stella married. It was brutal work. Five years previously, and under considerable pressure from his wife, Bob had finally relented and hired Pablo Vincenza to work for him.

Was Pablo legal? Bob had decided not to pry. Besides, he didn't really want to hear the response, but whatever the reply might have been, Pablo was an answer to prayers. Now it was Pablo who awakened each morning at 4:30 AM to begin the milking. Now it was Pablo who finished cleaning up in the barn every evening at half past six, seven days a week. The cows did not take a day off, and neither did Pablo.

One day ago, on Sunday, Pablo did what he had never done before—he didn't show up for work. Bob checked the ancient travel trailer parked behind the barn which Pablo used for sleeping quarters, as it certainly made for an easy and economical commute. Pablo did not own a vehicle, but he sometimes caught a ride down to a local nightspot on Saturday evening, which was frequented by a number of people who worked at a nearby chicken processing plant.

Surely Pablo had not been dumb enough to get involved in a fracas, or even drunk enough to get the attention of the local law. If he'd been arrested, ICE might have come in and picked him up, and then what? Bob drove down to see what he could, but the honky-tonk was closed up tight, with no sign of his employee.

Reams had no choice but to go home and milk his 130 Holstein cows. The milking began almost three hours later than was the custom, and the cows were really squalling by the time the last group was relieved of their load. He then finished the evening milking well after eight o'clock, and was completely exhausted.

So when Miguel Belgodere, driving an old Chevy truck with a camper top, showed up at his barn on Monday just after seven AM, asking if there was any work available, Bob knew there was indeed a God. He explained the finer points of the operation to Miguel as they finished the morning milking together, cleaned the machines, and looked after the milk in the two cooling tanks. After that, Bob promptly adjourned to the house for a long nap. He wasn't entirely sure Miguel understood English as well as Pablo had, and the man certainly had some remarkably severe tattoos, but he was too tired to think about any shortcomings.

By Wednesday morning, Miguel had the operation well in hand, and Bob only functioned as a helper. It was Miguel who was awake and dressed at four-thirty in the morning, letting the cows into the lot, getting the first twenty into the milking barn, putting their feed concentrate in the trough, brushing and cleaning their distended udders, hooking them up to the electric milkers, then getting them unhooked and out of the barn, before bringing in the next twenty. Bob came outside during the third group of twenty cows to assist, as well as be sure his new worker was following instructions to keep everything clean.

Sometime after seven-thirty, the actual milking was done and all the cows were back out on the pasture. The farmer watched Miguel doing a final cleaning of the twenty electric milking machines before he went back to the house. The farm owned two cooling tanks, each of which was capable of holding 550 gallons of unprocessed milk. Miguel opened a port on each of the tanks to be sure the milk was circulating, and to check that the temperature in the tanks was exactly thirty-seven degrees Fahrenheit.

On this day, he spent a bit more time at Tank Two, quickly uncapping a one gallon jug of pre-packaged sweet tea, for which Miguel had already shown a preference. But rather than taking a refreshing swig, he emptied the entire contents into the cooling tank. He then disconnected the pipe from the tanks to the milking machines, and ran first a disinfectant then clean water through the pipes and hoses as part of the final clean-up.

Each of the cows provided between two and three gallons per day, so by each third day, the accumulated milk totaled somewhere between 950 and 1,000 gallons. Right on schedule at nine-thirty AM, the milk truck from Green Pasture Dairy, located seven miles away in Monett, Missouri, arrived at the farm, and the driver transferred the contents of the two cooling tanks to his truck. Once this was accomplished, Miguel then cleaned the tanks in preparation for the production from the coming afternoon's milking.

By the time Miguel's task was finished, the truck had

completed its morning route, with five more stops at area farms, combining Happy Valley's milk with that of the other farms, and then depositing the entire load into the pasteurization tank at Green Pasture Dairy. The 5,000 gallons from this truck was combined with the milk from one other truck, and the entire 10,000 gallons of raw milk began pasteurization in a machine which could accommodate over 12,000 gallons.

The standard pasteurization process is an important last step in ensuring that common diseases are not present in milk and milk products. During pasteurization, the raw milk passes between superheated stainless steel plates which rapidly reach 161.6 degrees Fahrenheit (70 degrees C.), remains at that temperature for fifteen seconds, and then is immediately cooled to 37 degrees F. The milk industry endorses this particular high temperature/short time process (also known as flash pasteurization) to not only make the milk safe for consumption, but also to avoid reducing its taste, which happens if it's heated at a higher temperature or a longer time period.

Raw milk often contains a number of pathogens which can cause disease in humans, among them tuberculosis, brucellosis, diphtheria, scarlet fever, salmonella, staphlococcus aureus, E. coli, Yersinia, and campylobacter. After flash pasteurization, these bacteria are either completely destroyed, or so drastically reduced in number that the end product, when properly refrigerated, is safe for consumption for two to three weeks.

One pathogen, however, which is not found naturally in raw milk, is extremely heat resistant and produces a lethal toxin when packaged in airtight containers of milk and other food products. The toxin can be destroyed by heating to 85 degrees C for five minutes or longer, whereas the actual spores of the pathogen must be heated to 120 degrees C for thirty minutes. Neither of these kill-temperatures or time frames are ever reached during federally approved standard pasteurization. As it happened, this particular pathogen, *Clostridium botulinum*, had been the main ingredient in Miguel's gallon bottle of sweet tea.

Green Pasture Dairy packaged their product as whole milk, 2% milk, no-fat milk, flavored milk, yogurt, cream, sour cream, cottage cheese, white salted cheese, and butter, as dictated by the day's customer orders. On that Thursday afternoon, eighty percent of the now-cooled, pasteurized product was packaged in half-gallon and one-gallon containers of various milk fat percentages for delivery to area groceries and convenience stores. The remaining 2,000 gallons went into 20,000 half-pint containers of 2% chocolate milk, and 12,000 similar sized containers of unflavored milk. All were made ready for Friday morning delivery on four trucks, whose routes included six nursing homes and all the public schools within a thirty-mile radius of Monett.

Back at Happy Valley, Miguel finished the Thursday afternoon milking as usual. After cleaning up, he checked the cooling tanks for the second time that day. Also for the second time, he dumped another bottle of sweet tea into Tank Two. It would be in the tank, along with the milk which would accumulate on Friday, and be picked up yet again by Green Pasture Dairy.

Old Bob Reams was devastated on Friday afternoon to discover that yet another farm worker had abruptly disappeared—and he hadn't even paid the man!

On Saturday morning, between the hours of five and eight AM, an ambulance was called four separate times to a local nursing home in Cassville, Missouri (twenty miles south of Monett). One patient was dead of unknown causes when the vehicle arrived. Of course, Annie Davidson had been ninety-four years old. What could one expect, after all? The other three had various symptoms which appeared to be only slightly related.

Eighty-seven-year-old Gregory Stanton had been awakened by his bladder at five o'clock, and he promptly fell, breaking his hip on the way to the bathroom. The staff on duty said they suspected he might have had an ischemic stroke, as he was having difficulty speaking. Of course, his pain with a broken hip was excruciating, so some problems with communication were to be expected. However, the only evidence of any difference in appearance on his right and left sides was that his right eyelid had a severe droop. Likewise, his blood pressure was within normal limits. Mr. Stanton seemed to be complaining most about dizziness and blurred vision, but his speech was very hard to understand. The local hospital transferred him to a regional medical center in

Springfield, Missouri. The receiving physician authorized the EMT to administer a dose of TPA on the way in the ambulance to try and reduce the effects of what he suspected was a stroke.

Patricia Antle and Dianne Jeffries had eaten almost every meal together at the same table in the nursing home for the last three years, and spent most of the time telling and re-telling the same stories until the point that either of them could have recited the other's favorite tales word for word. They had met in kindergarten, and had lived the remainder of their lives within ten miles of one another.

On Sunday morning, the women had been sitting in their wheelchairs in the dining area when they both began to complain of muscle weakness in their neck and arms. The nurse wondered if one was simply complaining because her friend was. By the time their breakfasts arrived, Trish couldn't seem to negotiate with her spoon. Each of them had difficulty in swallowing their food, despite it being nothing more substantive than cream of wheat and coffee. After sitting there for no more than ten minutes, Patricia said she felt like she couldn't hold her head up, and slumped over in her chair. Dianne promptly threw up, and regained her breathing only after a struggle. They were each admitted to the local hospital.

In the nursing home in Aurora, Missouri (fifteen miles east of Monett), three somewhat similar cases were occurring before the noon hour. All complained of weakness, particularly in their neck and shoulder areas. One was vomiting with diar-rhea. Two of them had difficulty speaking and swallowing. There was an almost constant stream of tears running down Rebecca Henningson's left cheek, and both her eyelids had be-gun to droop. All three were transported to the local hospital.

It was not until the fifth and sixth cases arrived at the small hospital in Cassville (one of whom was a nursing assis-tant from the nursing home) that the physician on call for the weekend realized all of the cases must be somehow related. She contacted the registered nurse in charge of the nursing home, asking if other residents or staff were ill in similar ways. She was told that four other patients had complaints which sort of resembled the aching muscles and joints of the flu, but that no one had fever. She also noted that one nurs-ing aide had called in sick, but she didn't know specifically what her complaints were.

Mulling this over, something caused the physician to make the unusual decision to go to the nursing home to see if she could get a better idea of patient symptoms and just how many might be ill. After touring the two wings of the facility, what she concluded was that actually sixteen people were similarly affected. She believed they weren't infectious, as none had a fever nor a cough.

However, everything pointed to an infectious agent of some kind, probably transmitted by improperly prepared food since so many had gotten sick in about the same time frame. She checked the menu for lunch and supper on the previous day, looking for potential problems that might be caused by food not properly kept hot enough, or cold enough, to prevent bacterial growth.

Her next suspicion was that someone involved in handling the food might have been infected with something which could have spread to the patients. She mentally went through a laundry list—E. coli, Salmonella, C. diff, even diphtheria—but nothing seemed to fit. She asked for access to the kitchen and literally sniffed a number of food containers, seeking any characteristic odor of spoilage. She found nothing. She noted, in fact, that it was quite clean.

To follow up on the employee angle, she telephoned the director of nursing at home, told her what was going on, and asked her to draw blood on all her staff, particularly those on duty during the previous two days, and bring the samples to the hospital as soon as possible, but no later than the next morning. Her next call was to the director of the Barry County Health Department.

On returning to the hospital, she called the medical center in Springfield to ask if they had an opinion on the diagnosis of Gregory Stanton, who she had sent to them early that morning. She was not too surprised to hear he'd been in respiratory failure when he arrived and had passed away an hour earlier.

The doctor immediately ordered blood cultures on each of the patients she had admitted to the hospital that day, then took the step of sending a nurse to the nursing home to draw blood on each of the sixteen residents she had just identified as having similar symptoms. Now all she could do was wait for the results and hope no one else came into her ER, as the small hospital was completely out of beds.

Also on Saturday, small hospitals and physicians in a four-county area in southwestern Missouri began to call the state health officer, reporting large numbers of children, as well as a few adults, who were complaining of the same kinds of symptoms as the elderly nursing home patients. As word spread, parents with children who had no symptoms at all began to panic. Emergency rooms and doctors' offices were jammed with both the sick and the well.

CHAPTER 21

Clarification?
Southwest Missouri January 12, 2024

By Sunday morning, the number of nursing home resident admissions had reached 39 and were being reported in Cassville, Monett, Aurora, Pierce City, and Neosho, all located in the southwest corner of Missouri. Twenty-two of them had been placed on mechanical ventilators in larger hospitals in Springfield, Joplin, and also in Rogers, Arkansas, while seven others were being closely monitored. Missouri's state health officer, Cindy Kunkel, had been notified, and she contacted the Centers for Disease Control in Atlanta, requesting the assistance of a team of epidemiologists as well as a shipment of ventilators. The CDC contacted the Assistant Secretary for Preparedness and Response in the Department of Health and Human Services, which had taken over the management of disaster-related equipment, while the CDC continued to manage the pharmaceuticals.

Beginning around nine on Monday morning, and continuing through early afternoon, results from a number of the blood cultures began to come back, both from state labs and from the CDC. All were positive for *Clostridium botulinum* toxin, or botulism. All the cultures had been classified by the CDC as Type E. Had it been Type A or B, perhaps the Cassville physician would indeed have detected the toxin from her smell test at the nursing home, but Type E usually exhibits no characteristic odor.

Dr. Kunkel, in collaboration with Governor Bill Shiveley, submitted a clarified request—send all the ventilators available, as well as every dose of botulism antitoxin in the National Pharmaceutical Stockpile. When asked if they had received a disaster declaration from the president, signifying that the Federal government would pay the associated costs, Governor Shiveley put the CDC director on hold and called the White House. He enjoyed telling folks that he had the president of the United States on speed dial. Although he was unable to speak to the president, he did receive verbal assurance from the chief of staff, not only for the assets of the Stockpile, but also the large and ever-expanding hospitalization costs, with a promise for signed documentation within thirty minutes. The governor was quickly back on the line with the director.

It was agreed the Stockpile would be landing a plane at each of three locations, with each one carrying ventilators as well as antitoxin. One destination was the Springfield-Branson National Airport, one at Joplin Regional Airport, and the third at Northwest Arkansas Regional, all by one PM. Along with a total of 300 ventilators and 5,000 doses of antitoxin would come three logisticians and three epidemiologists. It was agreed the assets would be shared among the three regional medical centers in the immediate area, and they would utilize Missouri's disaster declaration, even though some assets would be going to an Arkansas hospital. The CDC folks argued that all of the patients at this point were coming from Missouri, and if it got too complicated, they would make adjustments later. It undoubtedly would.

Further complicating the issue, Green Pasture Dairy had pasteurized and packaged an additional 10,000 gallons of milk on Saturday morning in various forms and sizes. This had included the contents of the second adulterated cooling tank of milk from Happy Valley Farm. Unfortunately, those containers were arriving on grocery and convenience store shelves on Monday morning and afternoon in many areas which had not received a milk shipment the previous Thursday.

Thankfully, the ventilators shipped were extremely flexible, in that they could be adjusted for all types of patients, from the elderly to neo-nates, so the state requests could be filled with a single model. However, before the ventilators and antitoxin could arrive, children were in respiratory distress. In order to keep patients alive without a ventilator, it was necessary to use a hand-operated bag valve mask. This required dedicated staff members, working on shifts, to constantly be at a single patient's bedside, manually using the bag valve twenty-four hours a day, for as long as it took.

Several discussions were held behind closed doors in hospitals, questioning whether the few automatic ventilators they had, which were already being used on the elderly, should be removed and switched instead to children. After all, the nursing home patients had a short life expectancy anyway, as well as a comparatively poor quality of life to begin with, whereas the children could logically expect another seventy-plus years of life if they could only make it through their immediate emergency. Very difficult decisions had to be made in many hospitals, and depending on one's point of view, none would be interpreted as the right one.

Also on Tuesday morning, the major networks began reporting new cases with similar symptoms in a large area surrounding Bend, Oregon, as well as a cluster of cases on First American reservations and pueblos in northwestern New Mexico, northeastern Arizona, southern Utah, and southwestern Colorado. The federal government's stockpile of antitoxin had already been severely depleted in Missouri.

Through their state health officers, the governors of these five states began contacting neighboring states to borrow resources. Other states were hesitant to lend automatic ventilators to their neighbors in case they experienced similar attacks on their own turf. Although since the coronavirus epidemic of 2020 and 2021, every hospital of any size possessed multiple ventilators, discussions occurred relative to sharing a piece of equipment which might unexpectedly be in demand in their own ER. It was a hard choice, but in almost every case, hospitals shared with their neighbors.

A main concern with botulism was that a patient's respiratory function could be impaired for weeks or even months. That meant a ventilator might be required to keep a patient alive for a significant period of time before it would be available for someone else's use. Several large medical centers in the eastern U.S. volunteered to share their own stockpiles of vents, and they were quickly shipped to both Oregon and the southwestern states.

In Missouri, teams of county health officials were collecting samples of food and beverages to be cultured from every impacted nursing home and school. They knew there had to be a common denominator, but had to determine what it might be so they could address the source. This process was immediately started in Oregon and the Four Corners area as well.

The National Pharmaceutical Stockpile contacted the manufacturer of the botulism antitoxin. The world's sole manufacturer was in Canada and produced a heptavalent antitoxin, one which was effective against all six serotypes of botulism. The company had already increased their production due to the number of cases reported in Missouri, but it would take time, too much time, to meet the new order requests. Of course they immediately shipped the 72 doses they had on hand to Oregon and the southwestern states. But too much production time was needed to quickly provide even a single, life-saving additional dose to the children and adults who were already ill.

⚛

DHS Assistant Secretary Abel Adams was speaking on a secure teleconference with Rear Admiral Hope Sheffield, director of the Centers for Disease Control, and Rear Admiral William Harrison, Assistant Secretary for Preparedness and Response at HHS. "I think we should all consider not disclosing to the media what our limitations are related to the botulism antitoxin."

Harrison snorted. "Don't you think that will come back to bite us in the butt if we don't make it plain that we have literally done all we can to provide treatment to all patients?"

Adams turned away, shook his head, and turned back again. "If we're fighting a war, do you think it wise that we tell the enemy when we've run out of ammunition? Because according to the CIA, this could possibly be linked to a group of terrorists sent here with a variety of weapons."

"Can I include that in my remarks?"

"Hell, no!"

"Then what do I say when reporters ask me why we sent so many resources to Missouri and less than half of that to Oregon, New Mexico, Arizona, and Colorado? How do I explain that governors' requests are going unfilled? Even worse, what do I say to the First American tribes who are watching their people die and asking me why all the antitoxin is going to whites?"

"Tell them we are working night and day with our state partners, as well as neighboring countries, to expedite and fill shipment requests, *in the order in which we receive them.*"

"Just refer those questions to me, Bill," Admiral Sheffield said. "Tell them it's a fluid situation, and I'll have the most up-to-date information on product availability." She neglected to mention what she really thought of her counterpart, let alone his crisis management abilities.

❀

By late Monday afternoon, they believed the source had been identified in Missouri. As additional laboratory reports came in, there was no doubt in anyone's mind. A teleconference chaired by the Federal Bureau of Investigation, which had overarching law enforcement authority for attacks related to food products, had just under a hundred participants, with county health officials, hospital authorities, the Food and Drug Administration, USDA, CDC, FBI, CIA, DHS, state health officers in Oregon, Arizona, New Mexico, Colorado, Missouri, and Arkansas, and Tribal officials from New Mexico, Colorado, Utah and Arizona.

"We identified a single milk plant as the source of all these cases in southwest Missouri. Thank goodness they keep excellent records as to what farms supplied a given truckload of milk, and then how that particular lot of milk was packaged and where it was sold. The milk plant is currently picking up all stock from two particular lots right now, and hopes to have the last of it in hand by tomorrow morning. We've put out a public service announcement on TV, radio, and social media, telling people not to consume those products, and to bring them back for refund or exchange at the point of purchase."

"Have you been able to identify the farm which supplied the bad milk?"

"We've narrowed the suspected farms down to ten. All of them are being checked as we speak. We hope to have an answer to that by mid-morning tomorrow when the laboratory cultures are completed."

"Do you feel like this was accidental or done on purpose?"

"CDC, do you want to take that?"

"If we were only talking about the cases in Missouri, then we might consider withholding judgment. But with the same situation occurring in Oregon and in the Four Corners area, the chances of an extremely rare event happening at three different places at the same time is so remote that it's not worth considering. Without a doubt, these events were acts of terrorism, coordinated in such a way that we would be depleted of necessary response resources."

"Thank you, ma'am. So it's safe to say that the other states that have been affected should begin their searches at a milk plant which supplies the areas that were stricken."

Angela Martinelli waved at Bob Williams. He nodded for her to go ahead. "We don't know for sure that these same three terrorists don't have additional supplies of botulism at their disposal. For all we know, they could be heading to new locations in the coming days to repeat their attacks. After all, we haven't identified or caught the perpetrators. We have no reason to believe they won't act again."

Williams paused. "Allow me to amend that. Nor do we have reason to believe that they will act again."

"We've notified the National Association of City and County Health Officials and the Association of State and Territorial Health Officers," said the CDC director, "to send out an alert to their memberships in the event they see similar patients in their jurisdictions. My staff is telling me that we should also contact the Dairy Farmers of America and the American Dairy Association. Everybody in the chain needs to be hyper-vigilant."

The Deputy Commissioner of the FDA coughed. "This is for the state health officers on the line whose jurisdictions were affected: If you will contact our regional offices in Kansas City, Seattle, San Francisco, Denver, and Dallas, our food safety officers will be glad to assist in your site inspections and investigation."

At the close of the meeting, Angela leaned toward Bob Williams. "When I was in North Korea, I specifically overheard General Moo-sung mention a CIA agent doctor to Colonel Ho-young."

Williams jerked his head around. "Are you sure?"

"I'm thinking you either need to arrest Han-gil, or at least monitor his computer and phone traffic to see if you can't catch him red-handed. If he had sent them a sketch or a picture, I'd be dead right now."

"If we decide to just monitor him, we'll want to make sure he doesn't see you back in the office."

✵

Bob and Stella Reams had always taken comfort in the knowledge that all the intrigue and terrible incidents in Washington, D.C. and the rest of the big cities were far away from their farm and would never interrupt the tranquility of their lives. They could look out their back windows and see much of their 240 acres of pasture and hay fields, their dairy cattle, and the nearest neighbor's house some half mile to the west. Safety and security had always been something they could count on at Happy Valley.

At eight AM the following morning, the Barry County sheriff, the regional director of the Missouri Bureau of Investigation, the Special Agent in Charge for the FBI Regional Office in Springfield, and two food safety officers from the Food and Drug Administration's office in Kansas City were standing on the doorstep of the Reams house near Purdy. Stella stood behind Bob when he answered the door.

Bob looked from one to the other, his look of surprise giving way to a horrible realization. "Surely you ain't gonna tell me it was my farm."

The sheriff stepped inside. "I'm afraid so, Bob. What can you tell us about the milk that left your farm on Wednesday, April 18th?"

"To tell you the truth, I don't know much about it. I had me a new worker that week, at least 'til he left after milkin' time on Thursday afternoon. He was doin' most of the work. Oh, I was helpin' some, showing him the ropes. But it's a young man's job. I didn't do much."

"What can you tell us about this new worker? Where did he come from? How'd he come to be here? What was his name?"

"About all I know is his name, Miguel Belgodere. The man who'd worked for me for several years just disappeared the weekend before." He looked at the sheriff. "I figured you either had him locked up, or maybe handed him off to those ICE fellers."

"Are you talking about Pablo?"

"Yeah. Pablo Vencenza. Best hand I could ask for."

"I didn't arrest Pablo. So you're saying Pablo disappeared, and this Miguel fellow just shows up and you hire him?"

"That's about it."

"What did Miguel look like?"

"Not much different than most o' the Hispanics around. Fairly long hair, average height, slightly built."

"Did he have any distinguishing marks?"

"Wasn't nothin' distinguished about it. Had him some hellacious big tattoos on his neck. They stuck up above his collar."

"Could you make out what the tattoo was?"

"All I could see was a big thirteen on both sides of his neck. Had some on his right arm, too, but it was just a bunch o' curlicues."

"What kind of vehicle was he driving?"

"An old black Chevy pickup."

"Where was he living while he worked here?"

"He had a camper top on his pickup. He used that."

"Bob, I want to caution you about telling anyone that it was your farm which was the source of this botulism. Some folks are always looking for somebody to blame for the bad things that happen. Quite a few folks in this area lost family members. Between Barry, Stone, Lawrence, Newton, McDonald, and Jasper counties, the number of deaths last night was at forty-six. If word got out that it was your farm, you folks could be in danger. None of us want that to happen."

Impatient with the slow progress, the FBI agent pushed past the sheriff. "Mr. Reams, do you belong to a right-wing nationalist group?"

The old man took a half step backward. "Why, no. You don't count the American Legion, do you?" He turned to his wife with a baffled look. "I don't, do I Stella?"

The sheriff shook his head at the agent before proceeding. "Bob, I have a couple of folks with me who are going to check your milking equipment to be sure it's not still contaminated."

"I keep it awful clean, Sheriff."

One of the FDA officers cleared his throat. "We may have to use a special technique to clean your equipment, Mr. Reams. You can't just use washing and a regular disinfectant on this botulism. The spores are extremely resistant."

The FBI agent pushed past the sheriff once more. "Mr.

Reams, we're going to get a special kind of portrait artist out here this afternoon to see if you and your wife can't help him create a good likeness for this Miguel character. We need to circulate his picture all over America in case he tries this again."

❀

"It was great to hear your voice today, Angie."

"Hello, Early. There was a time when I wasn't sure whether I would ever get back." She paused for a few beats. "In fact, there were several of those times."

"Do you suppose we could take up where we left off?"

"That sounds good to me. But for the next several weeks, or maybe even months, I'm not going to have any kind of regular life, let alone a predictable schedule. It's likely that you won't either."

"Does that mean we've got more bad things to come?"

"This is not a good time to have that conversation. Maybe you could come with your boss the next time he drops by for a visit. Then we can talk."

There was a hesitation on the other end of the line. "I understand, Angie. I've been thinking about you."

There was another hesitation before she admitted, "Same here, Early." She paused, momentarily surprised at herself. Normally, she was more reserved than to say something like that. "Actually, I've thought about you quite a bit."

❀

By the next day, the same process had been completed at dairies near Farmington, New Mexico and Bend, Oregon. Angela Martinelli had looked at the three portraits, a pair of which were similar to two of the drawings which had been developed with her input. There was enough difference in them that the decision was made to circulate all five drawings.

The five portraits of the transient Hispanic employees were sent from one end of the country to the other. Instructions to local law enforcement offices included the information that at least two of the suspects had tattoos which suggested they were current or prior members of the notorious MS-13 gang. Before the week was out, a leak had occurred at a police department in Poplar Bluff, Missouri.

Headlines in various local newspapers the next day were

picked up by big city papers as well as national television news outlets. The banner running across the bottom of 300 million television screens read, *Breaking News: Missouri dairy farmer identifies botulism terrorist as member of MS-13 gang.*

A social media post had over ten million hits within twelve hours. *MS-13 Gangsters Murdering Americans in Terrorist Attacks. Click Like and Share if you want all El Salvadorans immediately removed from the United States.* Inexplicably, the posting included all five portrait drawings, which had supposedly only been distributed to law enforcement.

Another post appeared to come from a different perspective. *White House proposes punishing all for the sins of one man. There are 900,000 El Salvadorans in the United States. Are they all guilty of terrorism? That's like punishing everybody named Arnold for the treason of Benedict Arnold.*

Perhaps the one most likely to enrage was a Photoshopped picture of six small Indian children, appearing to be of pre-school or kindergarten age. They were lying in a row, bundled in blankets, and undoubtedly dead. The caption: *White House decides to withhold emergency medical care from Native American babies. Many dead children. Our sorrow did not end at Wounded Knee. When will this racism end?*

Kim Yo-jung was admiring her brother's latest acquisition. "So this porcelain is attributed to the Northern Song Dynasty? Brother, this bowl and platter may be a thousand years old!"

The fat man smiled broadly. "So I am told, sister dear. I have documentation from two Chinese scholars to substantiate the connection."

"Truly a wonderful specimen. Speaking of that, apparently the Americans are checking on specimens from one end of their country to the other."

"I like that, sister dear. I would love to tell that joke face to face to their president."

"Remember what we agreed, brother. None of that will be helpful. Besides, it appears they have no clue that we are involved."

"I'm advised by General Moo-sung that none of the people carrying out our plans can trace this operation back to the Fatherland."

"What comes next?"

"Moo-sung tells me that is dependent on how soon the people on the ground can find proper employment to allow them to proceed. Otherwise, there will be other actions taking place as opportunities present."

"Apparently, we can only sit back and be surprised, like the Americans!"

The fat man laughed until his face was red. "There you go again, sister."

Chapter 22

Connections?
Baltimore, Maryland January 25, 2024

The Fort McHenry Tunnel was the last segment of Interstate 95 completed between Maine and Florida. The submerged portion of the tunnel (referred to by the builder as the tube) is just over a mile long and runs beneath Baltimore Harbor. At its deepest point, it is 107 feet below the water's surface. Some 115,000 vehicles per day use the route. Cars pay a four-dollar toll, while trucks are billed up to thirty dollars for the privilege. The tunnel is lit by a line of lights on either side, as the tube sections would otherwise be in complete darkness, not only at night, but also during the daytime.

A sign posted at both ends of the tunnel reads: *Vehicles carrying bottled propane gas in excess of ten pounds per container (maximum of ten containers), bulk gasoline, explosives, radioactive materials, and other hazardous materials are prohibited from using the Ft. McHenry Tunnel.*

Cubans Paco Batista and Raoul Hernandez had stolen vehicles multiple times on their travel from the west coast to Baltimore. Raoul was something of an expert, as he had been a locksmith, both legally and illegally, in Santiago de Cuba, which was located just a few miles from Guantanamo. In fact, it was a favorite pastime of his to steal vehicles from the American personnel stationed there.

On this particular Monday morning, the two men were in possession of an old Ford Bronco and a white panel truck. As they entered I-95 just north of Baltimore at five-fifteen AM, Paco was in the lead, driving the Bronco, while Raoul was immediately behind him in a well-loaded panel truck. They obviously had not read the warning sign at the tunnel's entry.

Over the last two days, they had procured forty bags of ammonium nitrate from area garden shops, several five-gallon containers of kerosene, and six large canisters of propane, just for good measure. Before departing on their journey that morning, they had opened the bags of ammonium nitrate in the back of the panel truck and thoroughly saturated the contents with kerosene. Tied securely in the midst of this pile was a device which Paco had been taught to make back home in Havana. The device's wiring was attached to a cheap flip phone. The Americans referred to such a creation as an improvised explosive device, an IED. However, this was a bit more powerful than the IEDs normally encountered in the Middle East.

There was little traffic at forty minutes after five, but the rush hour would begin in earnest, both into and out of Baltimore, in about twenty minutes. The Cubans had traversed approximately 75% of the tube when Paco came to a complete stop in the far right lane, directly adjacent to the tunnel's tiled wall, and flipped on his blinkers. At that point, Raoul stopped the panel truck immediately behind the Bronco, left the truck, and jumped in Paco's vehicle. As they sped away, Raoul dialed a number.

The sound of the phone's ring was completely obliterated by the explosion. The flying debris almost caught up with the Bronco as it blew out of the tunnel, headed to the southeast toward Washington, D.C. Their hope was to not only block the tunnel, but to blast through to the harbor water above, thus flooding the tube from one end to the other and making any repair of the critical highway a very long process.

Ten vehicles traveling in both directions were immediately destroyed by the blast, with four of the propane containers exiting the rear and sides of the truck like fire-breathing missiles. Both sides of the highway were successfully blocked with a debris pile which stretched for well over fifty yards in both directions. The tile was eradicated, the tube severed, and a great tear in the earth was opened; but nothing more than a trickle of water entered the tunnel.

The Cubans would not learn the extent of the damage until much later that day. Had they used a larger conveyance for their bomb, such as the rented Ryder truck which was used to blow out the entire front of the federal building in Oklahoma City in 1995 and killed 168 people, they might have realized their goal of creating such a severe gash that the tunnel indeed might have flooded. That may have occurred despite the presence of fiber-reinforced concrete in the tunnel, which is theoretically able to dissipate the energy of such a blast. Nevertheless, their efforts caused the I-95 corridor to be closed for almost a month to remove debris, perform an assessment, and make repairs on the tunnel.

The only possible witness to the event, the driver of an eighteen-wheeler, was quoted on the news as saying a red Bronco passed him less than a mile from the tunnel, going westbound at a high rate of speed. The trucker stated it was occupied by two people. He noted there was a bit of debris from the explosion adhering to the rear of the Bronco. The only one he could see with any clarity was the male passenger, who he described as possibly Hispanic.

By six AM, Paco and Raoul had exited the interstate, heading north toward the bedroom community of Columbia, Maryland. They stopped at a Dunkin Donuts shop. Within sixty seconds, they were continuing through the city, not with a supply of pastries, but now riding in a white Chevrolet Impala. Raoul's skills were not required, as the keys had been left in the ignition by a considerate young woman seeking her morning chocolate crème-filled donut fix. They drove around the western then the northern perimeter of Baltimore, before finally re-entering I-95, this time northbound, headed toward their next destruction project.

⚛

Paco and Raoul's second assignment was at a chemical manufacturing plant just outside New York City. The company's website touted merchandise for sale such as explosives, ammunition, pyrotechnics, ordnance components, and special chemicals. Given the products one could assume were stored in the company's warehouses, it seemed like a perfect match for Paco's expertise.

They discovered, however, that the level of security surrounding the business complex was a bit more than they had bargained for. The entire area was enclosed by ten-foot-high chain link, topped with three strands of barbed wire. Cameras were visible approximately every fifty yards along the perimeter. Armed guards were posted at the employee entry gate as well as the truck entrance. From their distant surveillance, it appeared that employees were required to show identification; while at the freight entrance, the single guard was also checking papers of some kind. These precautions were undoubtedly related to the fact that a good portion of the company's products were designated for military use.

Their solution to the high security required several days to gather the components they needed. Raoul hot-wired an older model heavy duty GMC pickup in Trenton, New Jersey, switched tags with another vehicle, then picked up a nondescript automobile, a Toyota Corolla, in Elizabeth, and a Smith and Wesson .38 revolver from a punk on Palisades Avenue in Hackensack. Once again, they purchased the components for another fertilizer bomb. This time it would be a bit smaller, as they believed if they could generate one explosion and fire inside the building, several manufactured products in the warehouse would then ignite and finish the job.

Well before daybreak on Sunday morning, they drove into New York City, then out on Long Island. Raoul broke into a construction company near their target, hooking up a trailer with a big Caterpillar bulldozer on board to the hitch on their pickup. They approached to less than a half mile from the manufacturing plant before unloading the dozer, which had a large scoop attached. They quickly mixed their explosive components in the well of the scoop, and Paco rigged the IED much as before.

When he arrived at the freight gate, clanking along the pavement with the large steel treads of the dozer chewing gashes into the asphalt, the guard quickly exited his shack and waved him down, saying the facility was closed until Monday. Raoul leaned over and picked up some paperwork, attached to a clipboard, then extended it toward the guard. When the guard accepted the documents, Raoul shot him in the forehead at a distance of two feet and continued on, plowing right through the closed steel gate with the big dozer.

When he reached the large freight doors at the receiving dock, he rammed the scoop completely through the steel doors before jumping off his heavy equipment and running back toward Paco and the parked Corolla. Aware of the security cameras, he was in a bit of a hurry. As he passed through the completely destroyed gate and jumped over the body of the lifeless guard, he made sure the clipboard was safely stashed underneath the body, then dialed the required phone number.

There was the expected large explosion, followed almost simultaneously with multiple blasts that literally shook the earth. As he fled the scene, Raoul couldn't resist the opportunity to watch the ongoing destruction. He paused and turned just as an even larger explosion occurred, this time shredding the steel freight doors into bits and pieces. Unfortunately for Raoul, one fragment of shrapnel slammed into him just above his right knee, severing muscle, tendons, nerves, and blood vessels. A second fragment, this one no bigger than a dime, struck him on the left side of his forehead, and he went down in a heap.

Intermittent explosions were still occurring some three minutes after the initial blast, with black, perhaps toxic clouds of smoke and flames rising up at least two hundred yards into the still-dark sky. When Raoul didn't appear when he'd promised, Paco—a bit nervous of all the attention the fireworks would cause—assumed the worst, put the Toyota in gear, and fled west toward the big city, eventually crossing over the Long Island Sound and heading toward White Plains.

The chemical company sat along a creek leading into a bay, which lay on the south side of the Sound. There would be year-long investigations after the explosions and fire, figuring out what hazardous products had found their way into the Sound as well as into the downwind neighborhoods, in what concentrations, and at what risk to the fishery, the wildlife, and the public. Nitrate compounds, hydrochloric and sulfuric acids, nitroglycerin, ammonia, mercury, lead, arsenic, and benzoyl peroxide were all in play.

The cause of the blast was not debatable. The twisted remains of the bulldozer testified to that. The investigation revealed no evidence of a second perpetrator. Although he was not in the FBI's database, Raoul's prints were found all over the GMC pickup, the trailer, the revolver, and the door of the burglarized construction company's office in Glen Cove. The bed of the pickup also showed traces of ammonium nitrate. An open and shut case, except for the part about discovering who was really behind the event.

The clipboard, still holding the paperwork which had been handed over to the now-deceased guard, read in large lettering: *Long Live the Legitimate President of Venezuela. Death to the Pretender.*

Representatives from the Environmental Protection Agency; Alcohol, Tobacco, and Firearms; the National Transportation Safety Board; explosive experts from the Department of Defense; harbor police from New York City and Baltimore; bomb squads from both cities' police departments; governors from Maryland, Delaware, New Jersey, New York, Connecticut, Massachusetts, and Pennsylvania; mayors from Washington, D.C., Baltimore, Philadelphia, New York, Hartford, Providence, and Boston; the Agency for Toxic Substances and Disease Registry; and the Department of Homeland Security (with undisclosed participation by the Central Intelligence Agency) were all hosted on a teleconference call by the Federal Bureau of Investigation's Assistant Director for Counter-Terrorism, Lynn Jones. "I'm going to call on Special Agent in Charge David Taylor from New York City to begin this discussion."

"Good morning. I'm here with my colleague, SAIC Don Wetter from Baltimore. First order of business, this is an informational meeting. What we discuss this morning is close-hold, and absolutely not for public dissemination, but we do believe all of you should hear this recent finding by our friends at ATF. Assistant Secretary Campbell, the floor is yours."

"Thank you. After a thorough analysis of the recent explosions in the I-95 tunnel under Baltimore Harbor and the chemical plant in Glen Cove, we can say conclusively that the bombs were virtually identical, down to the addition of multiple propane tanks. The triggering mechanism utilized in Baltimore was severely damaged, but there was enough remaining for our analysis. Unfortunately, the mechanism was almost completely obliterated in New York due to the additional explosions and fire. However, based on the remaining components, as well as witness descriptions of the initial explosion, we believe they were constructed by the same individual or team of individuals."

"Thank you, Secretary Campbell. That leads to the next matter. The perpetrator, or one of the perpetrators, was severely injured in the explosion in New York. However, if we think about the circumstances in the tunnel explosion, there were obviously two vehicles involved, one to carry the bomb and the other to escape the scene. So pursuing the ATF's analysis of the two explosions being the work of the same man or team, we can only conclude that at least one other terrorist is alive, as he or she was waiting in an escape vehicle to pick up the fellow who is currently in intensive care. Therefore, we cannot assume that these attacks are over just because one of them is out of commission. I'm also going to venture the theory that the remainder of the team will continue to operate in this geographic area. That means all of us still have to be vigilant in protecting critical infrastructure in our cities and states."

"Special Agent Taylor, Abel Adams from DHS. Were you able to ascertain an identity or at least a country of origin from the injured terrorist?"

"No, Secretary Adams. He's not in anybody's database. We believe he is of Hispanic origin and more specific genetic work is being performed now, but we can't guess his nation of origin. Despite the note he left, which seems to cast suspicion on the supporters of the current president of Venezuela, we must consider that this message could be a diversion."

"Have you been able to interrogate him?"

"No, sir. Due to a brain-bleed, he's currently in a medically induced coma. His doctors have no timeline as to when they will attempt to bring him out of that."

"Could there be a link to the MS-13 attacks out west?"

"We saw no physical evidence of that at the scene, nor any obvious signs on the terrorist himself. Moreover, large scale explosions have never been an MS-13 tactic."

"Secretary Adams," said the governor of New York, "my state is full of hundreds of critical infrastructure targets, both public and private. There is no way my state and our cities can continually guard all these sites. Is Homeland Security going to deploy personnel to assist my state?" Five other governors interrupted each other with "me too" admonitions.

"Gentlemen, we have already sent additional staff to work with law enforcement in your cities. But we are also spread thin. I suggest you connect with any and all private sector targets immediately and encourage them to increase their own security. It would stand to reason that if this terrorist cell strikes again, they will be aiming for a weak link. They've already shown a willingness to attack both public and private sites. It's to everybody's benefit to do all we can to strengthen our defenses."

"Special Agent Taylor," said the mayor of Boston, "my city is one of the major points of entry to the U.S. We continue to read about the possibility of cyberattacks from abroad on our electric grid, natural gas pipelines, water and sewer systems, air-traffic control, nuclear plants, election process, the banking industry, communication systems, and personnel databases—particularly in the public sector. We hear they may have already positioned malware in some or even all of those IT systems, just waiting to flip a switch and watch us flounder around. Could these bombing attacks also be attributed to any of these enemies who have been implicated in cyberwarfare? I'm talking about Russia, China, Iran, even North Korea. Are we looking at some kind of grand plan of attack?"

"Special Agent Taylor, Abel Adams again—let me introduce Assistant Secretary Chet Hollomon to address that question. Chet runs the Cyber and Infrastructure Agency within DHS."

"Mr. Mayor, we're looking at every possibility. I'm definitely not trying to minimize your concerns. But at this point, there is no tangible evidence to suggest a link between the recent physical attacks and a cyberattack plan. That said, we are as prepared as we possibly can be here at DHS. And I would recommend that all our partners, both public and private, spend some time going over their own emergency protocols in case that very thing does occur."

"Fair enough, Secretary Hollomon. Then as a follow-up, should there be consideration of increasing the number of ICE personnel at our ports and airports?"

As guests of DHS, Angela Martinelli glanced around the table in the SCIF, past Bob Williams sitting beside her. Their hosts, Assistant Secretary Abel Adams, along with Early Johnson and Chet Hollomon, simply shook their heads. They weren't about to comment, but the mayor had just verbalized what they had all been thinking. However, this was not only the wrong audience, it was also not the time to speculate. Despite the warning at the start of the meeting that the information was not for public dissemination, with all the politicians on the phone, anything they said would, in all probability, be breaking news in the media before the day was done.

At the conclusion of the call, Adams, Hollomon, and Johnson swiveled their chairs for their own meeting. The Assistant Secretary cleared his throat. "Dr. Martinelli, regarding this fellow in the hospital, have you had an opportunity to look at any pictures to see if he was one of your twenty-three terrorists?"

"Actually, I didn't want to rely on pictures, so I took the Acela Express train to New York yesterday and spent a half hour in the ICU. It appears his injuries are severe, and his face is quite swollen, but even taking that into account, to tell you the truth, I didn't recognize the guy at all. However, I spent most of my time with the Iranians and the Africans, so I'm not willing to say that the man in the hospital was or was not a member of the group.

"When he's conscious, I'd be happy to participate in an opportunity to interrogate him. Perhaps my experience on board ship with these people can be helpful in refreshing his memory."

From social media: *I live on the south end of Long Island Sound. The explosions at the chemical plant in Glen Cove spewed all kinds of chemicals into the air and water. There's a grey-brown powder covering all the trees, the grass, and even the houses for miles around. Dead fish are floating everywhere in the Sound. All the ducks and geese are dead. The stench is overpowering. My neighbor's dog just died. Our kids are sick. Not knowing what we were being exposed to, we've had to temporarily relocate away from the Sound. What if my kids are permanently damaged? Who is going to reimburse us for this? What if we can't move back in our house for a long period of time—or maybe never?*

Why were these kinds of chemicals and explosives being produced right next to a neighborhood? Why was the facility built next to a waterway? What government entity makes those decisions? Surely they won't be allowed to rebuild their production operations in the same place.

Why is the United States getting mixed up in the politics of Venezuela? This is what happens when we decide to be the policemen of the world.

I heard about a nuke down there.

Be serious, dude, it's Venezuela.

I'm not a dude.

Chapter 23

An Attack on Basketball?
Kansas City, Missouri March 8, 2024

In the United States, approximately 100,000 train car loads of toxic chemicals travel over some 300,000 miles of rails every year, and frequently pass through densely populated urban areas. Chemicals are often transported via ninety-ton pressurized tank cars. There is always a risk of leakage or derailment, but thoughts of a terrorist attack on the transport of toxic chemicals, poisons, and highly explosive materials definitely occupy the minds of emergency planners at the Department of Homeland Security, as well as every fire chief and public health official in America's largest cities.

Some of the most lethal toxic chemicals, such as chlorine or hydrogen fluoride, could be deadly for several miles from the site of a release, depending on the velocity and direction of the wind. A standard procedure would be to evacuate people within a five-mile radius of such a release.

Thankfully, since the attacks of September 11, 2001, at least some industrial manufacturers have switched to less toxic chemicals where possible. For example, some utility companies switched from chlorine gas to either sodium hypochlorite or ultraviolet light in water treatment facilities, although chlorine remains the disinfectant of choice. Some refineries have switched from hydrogen fluoride to sulfuric acid, which is considered less dangerous, but of course, not without its own risks. Many have not made the switch simply because of the cost of sulfuric acid. Unfortunately, the chemicals manufactured by some industries specifically require hydrogen fluoride in their processes.

There are only two manufacturers of that substance located within the lower 48, and they supply industries across the nation. One is located in south Texas. That particular facility commonly uses the Union Pacific Railroad to transport hydrogen fluoride.

Manufacturers restrict sales of hydrogen fluoride only to known, vetted industries. Individuals are not allowed to purchase it. So when an industrial facility in Des Moines, Iowa, a regular customer, contacted the manufacturer with a request for two tanker cars of hydrogen fluoride on February 28th, the product was shipped seven days later via the Union Pacific, with a planned route through Ft. Worth, Wichita, Kansas City, and finally to Des Moines.

Kansas City, Missouri is considered to be the second largest rail traffic hub in the entire United States, with almost all rail lines converging at Union Station, located at Main and 22nd Streets, approximately one mile south of the city center. The hydrogen fluoride shipment arrived in the railyard of Union Station late on Friday afternoon during the second weekend of March. This coincided with a rather important weekend for the city, as the Sprint Center was hosting the Big Twelve Men's Basketball Tournament from Thursday through Sunday. The arena was eight blocks directly north of Union Station.

Fans from all over the Midwest were in town, hoping their favorite team would make a good showing in the tournament and thus be attractive to the selection committee for inclusion in the NCAA March Madness National Basketball Playoff. When their chosen team was not playing inside the Sprint Center, there was no shortage of things to do in the city.

Just one block from the 19,000-seat Sprint Center was the nine-block Power and Light District. This area was developed soon after the turn of the 21st century and offers a myriad of entertainment, dining, and retail establishments from one end to the other. On the Friday evening of tournament weekend, it was jammed with close to 70,000 revelers, many of them outside, enjoying the rare nice weather in early March.

Eighteen blocks straight south of Union Station was the nation's first shopping center, which had been designed with the architecture of the Spanish city of Seville in mind. However, just because it was now over eighty years old did not diminish the glitz and glamour of its painted tiles, intricate brick work, artistic fountains, and elegant towers. The fifteen blocks, thirty-odd buildings, and well over a hundred high-end shops, restaurants, hotels, and a movie theater attracted tens of thousands of shoppers and gawkers every evening.

Just after dark, at six PM, a man dressed in the uniform of a Union Station laborer cut through the chain link fencing on the northwest border of the railyard. A portion of the targeted train, including the two tanker cars which had originated in south Texas, sat on a siding very close to the perimeter fence. The man placed a pliable explosive charge of Semtex directly on the large valve at the rear of each tanker car, then set the timer on the embedded detonators of both for fifteen minutes.

He exited the way he had entered, leaving a placard affixed to the fence which read *Death to the American Imperialists—Long Live the Califate.* Before returning to his vehicle in a nearby restaurant parking area, the Cuban obscured his face with a black hoody, and then quickly drove to the northeast, entering eastbound I-70 six miles away, approximately twenty seconds before the tanker cars exploded and their toxic cargo headed toward the north via a light southerly wind as a colorless gas.

The cloud's first victims were patrons at three high-end restaurants on 22nd Street, immediately north of the explosion. When the effects of the gas struck, the first inclination of the diners was to run outside, seeking the safety of the open air and their vehicles. Unfortunately, that only subjected them to the full concentration of the poison, and most people never reached their cars, falling to the ground in the parking lot in desperate straits. They had no chance.

The huge crowd standing in six lines to enter the Sprint Center for an important game scheduled to start at seven PM heard two fairly large explosions toward the south, but thought nothing of it, as it surely had nothing to do with them. They all were focused on the upcoming game between Kansas State and Texas Tech, but most realized the championship game would probably feature the basketball powerhouses in the conference—Baylor and Oklahoma.

Likewise, the thousands of weekend celebrants milling around outside the bars and restaurants in the Power and

Light District ignored the whole thing, at least temporarily. Over a thousand Kansas fans in blue and white were occupied with mindlessly and repetitively screaming "Rock, Chalk, Jay-Hawk" at the top of their lungs. One of the assembled Baylor fans turned to a fellow reveler. "What exactly does that mean, anyhow?"

Since hydrogen fluoride is heavier than air, it stays close to ground level rather than floating off into the upper atmospheres, so it is more concentrated close to the ground. Unfortunately, small children are among the first to be affected, simply because of their short stature and small lung capacity, so children waiting to attend the basketball game with their parents were the first to exhibit symptoms.

As the white fog spread outward, almost everyone it encountered experienced a dramatic response. It began as a cough, then noses started to run and eyes to tear. It progressed within minutes to raw throats and bronchial tubes, then bleeding sinuses, severe eye irritation, and an extreme respiratory response. If the individual was outside, standing in a low-lying area, or exposed for several minutes, the effects quickly became more significant. The longer someone remained in an area of high concentration, the greater the chance of disabling or fatal outcomes. The victims' breathing soon became labored, while their eyes ran painfully and constantly with tears.

It seemed that nobody was hanging around for that. Hundreds then thousands of people began to run. As to which way led to safety, they had no idea. Many tried to force their way into the basketball arena, but the doors were still locked, awaiting the end of the four PM game, which was in its final minutes. The crowd outside became panic-stricken. Many crossed the road to try entering some of the restaurants in the Power and Light District. They were already filled to overflowing with people just as affected as they were. Adults and children began to run toward their parked cars.

At Power and Light, as well as the Sprint Center, if you were outside, you were in a dire condition within a few minutes of the arrival of the ground-hugging diaphanous cloud. Within five more minutes, ambulances began arriving on the scene. In that early stage of the emergency, personnel lacked information about just what they were facing, and so a few failed to don adequate personal protective gear. A small number of EMT personnel themselves were quickly affected.

Inside the Sprint Center and the Power and Light businesses, the air intake systems had begun to pull in toxic air from outside. Within a very few minutes, coughing, tearing, and runny noses became evident on the basketball players, coaches, referees, scorekeepers, and those people located on the lowest level of seating. Several of the players were standing with their hands on their knees, trying to get a decent breath.

The coaches managed to get their players off the court and into their dressing rooms. However, the dressing rooms were also at a low level, and the players' symptoms continued to worsen. As the inside air circulated, more of the crowd became affected. Within minutes, there was pandemonium inside, with people pawing all over others to reach the exits. Those people in the seats high above the arena floor also panicked and tried to hurry down the stairs to escape. What they failed to realize was that in their elevated seats, they had been in a comparatively safe spot.

Fire stations #10 on east 9th Street and #25 on Missouri Avenue got the emergency call simultaneously, four minutes after the tanker cars exploded. As the firemen loaded up, they were informed of the calls for medical assistance from the arena area. The vehicle from #10 was routed west, while #25 was routed east, with both trying to go around whatever the toxic material might be. There were three fire stations in the Kansas City Metro Area with an enhanced hazardous material response capability. The closest was eight miles to the east on Truman Road in nearby Independence. Their two special operations vehicles were rolling five minutes after those from stations #10 and #25, with Lieutenant Larry Lumpkin on board. Although Lumpkin's crew had trained once a year for a chemical spill, this would be the first time they had engaged with the real thing on a large scale, let alone with such a number of victims.

Lt Lumpkin was on the radio immediately with the other units, and they agreed to set up one operation six blocks west of Power and Light, near the convention center, and a second operation site eight blocks east of the arena in the parking lot of the federal building between Twelfth and Thirteenth Streets. All police and emergency vehicles in the area were advised to don whatever safety equipment they had on hand

and to evacuate themselves and the public toward the operations locations.

Lumpkin set up his incident command station at the federal building, parking one of his special ops vehicles beside a fire truck from station 17, which had less than a mile to travel from their location on Paseo Boulevard. They left a ten-foot-wide walkway between the two vehicles, and as victims began to arrive, the two fire department vehicles turned their spray nozzles on that walkway, spraying approximately forty people a minute as they walked through the gauntlet, to decontaminate them before further damage was done. Several emergency personnel were among those decontaminated, as they either had not been issued the appropriate level of safety gear or failed to don it in time.

Decontaminated people were then wringing wet, and although the temperature was moderate, with the wind blowing, they all became quite cold. Those at the Twelfth Street location who had been hosed down were ushered into the underground parking garage of the federal building. Entry into the garage was limited to those who had been decontaminated. A call went out for blankets for all decon operations.

The same process was established at the convention center, using Lumpkin's second vehicle and a firetruck from station #10. A third operation was established in front of the Internal Revenue Service Building immediately south, and upwind of the railyards, using a haz-mat unit from Overland Park, Kansas and a firetruck from station #25.

Lumpkin contacted his chief to ask that school buses or city buses be obtained to move decontaminated victims from each of the three operations sites to hospitals outside the affected area. Twenty-five minutes would pass before the first bus arrived.

Hospitals were jammed with people self-reporting to emergency rooms, and they immediately contaminated those ERs by off-gassing hydrogen fluoride from their clothing, skin, and hair. Each of the hospitals had procedures in place to receive contaminated patients, but it took almost ten minutes before the ERs were locked down, and decontamination of victims slowly began to occur outside the buildings.

Hydrogen fluoride is easily absorbed by body tissue and rapidly breaks down into hydrogen and fluorine. Washing the skin with water does not effectively neutralize or stop the reaction, although large amounts of water are very helpful. And so the fluorine continued to damage tissue. Within 12 to 24 hours after exposure, victims might experience chills, fever, pulmonary edema, pneumonia, permanent eye damage, perforation of the nasal septum, and perhaps uncorrectable damage to the liver and kidneys.

The antidote is to administer calcium gluconate solution intravenously, which will bind with the fluorine. However, rapidly beginning this treatment is a must. There wasn't enough calcium gluconate within a thousand miles to treat all the people who needed it.

It was after seven PM before officials at the Union Station Railyard were able to identify the contents of the exploded railcars. Only then was the antidote determined. Supplies were quickly exhausted as exposed patients were finally treated with the appropriate drug in emergency rooms. Calls went out to neighboring communities for calcium gluconate. Two local pharmaceutical supply warehouses were opened by seven-thirty PM, but only 24 dozen doses were obtained.

By sunup, there were 69 dead, with twenty times that number listed as critical. There were no beds available at any hospital within fifty miles. U.S. Army personnel from Fort Leavenworth were setting up a field hospital in the Kansas City Royals baseball stadium parking lot, on the eastern perimeter of the city, with a U.S. Public Health Service response team under the direction of Captain Jim Imholte on site, and the Missouri-1 Disaster Medical Assistance Team on their way. Supplies of calcium gluconate were placed on every commercial airliner landing in Kansas City, as well as CDC planes from Atlanta and two other Stockpile warehouses. Despite these efforts, various stages of vision impairment including blindness was the outcome for over three hundred, permanent respiratory damage affected over six hundred people, cases of kidney failure would number 32, and seventeen more deaths were reported in the next three days.

The treatment recommended for the environment by the Agency for Toxic Substances and Disease Registry (ATSDR) was to spread either quick lime or soda ash in the railyard, nearby streets, parking lots, buildings, sidewalks, medians, and even yards. Crews began to accomplish this by midmorning on Saturday. They were outfitted in extremely uncomfortable personal protective gear, including a self-contained breathing apparatus. All rail traffic was temporarily rerouted through St. Louis. A 20x20 block area in Kansas City was declared a crime scene, and all residents there were evacuated.

Remnants of the cloud, although dispersed significantly, remained potent enough in the northern portion of the city so that dead birds littered every yard and street. Cats, dogs, and rats were in distress or dying in droves. Veterinary offices were overwhelmed. Ornamental trees, forsythias, crocuses, and daffodils, some of which had been showing some signs of life in the spring warm spell, were now withering. The ATSDR advised that environmental mitigation, clean-up, and disposal would be difficult, costly, and require weeks or even months. And then they found the sign at the railyard.

⚛

Social media was on fire.

Could the "evidence" in Kansas City be a red herring? Are the real culprits still members of MS-13?

The local Mexican Consulate provides support to immigrants from not only Mexico, but a number of Central American countries. There has not been any evidence to link Hispanic people to the hydrogen fluoride attack against the city. That post was signed by the Mexican Consul of Kansas City.

If we bomb Syria when Assad uses chemical weapons, where is our response when the Caliphate uses them against us? Is there no red line where American citizens are concerned?

There is ample proof that ISIS is sponsored by extremists in Iran, Syria, Afghanistan, Iraq, and Pakistan. Shall our dead have died in vain? Where is our government? Is it too much to ask to be safe on the streets of our cities?

There are nine Islamic mosques in the Kansas City area. Our local elected leaders advised us to be tolerant while they were being built. How many of them are breeding grounds for extremism?

To the people of Kansas City: The members of the Islamic Society of Greater Kansas City wish no ill upon our brothers and sisters, friends and neighbors. We celebrate a peaceful religion. More than anyone else, we want the perpetrator(s) brought to justice. That one was signed by the imam of the society.

In the months and years immediately after 9/11 and the anthrax letters, the Department of Homeland Security handed out blocks of grant money to state and local governments to be ready for CBRNE (chemical, biological, radiological, nuclear, and explosive) attacks. Since 2010 most of those funds have disappeared. Now our EMS and haz-mat personnel don't even have the funds to replace their outdated equipment, let alone train for events such as our citizens experienced in Kansas City. Congress decided to drastically reduce funding to DHS for local preparedness. Did they think the world was no longer dangerous, or like everything else, they decide to spend money only AFTER it's needed?

Paco Batista sat in a cheap hotel room in Cumberland, Maryland. It was Wednesday at two PM Eastern time, the pre-arranged day and time his wife would be standing by at a pay phone near their home. Using his cheap throw-away phone, he dialed 011, then the country code for Cuba, 53, then the pay phone number. "Hola, bebe. Don't forget, no names."

"When are you coming home? I don't have money to pay the rent."

"I'll send you a money order."

"Just answer me, when?"

"I'm making good money, bebe. Probably a couple more weeks."

"*Probably* doesn't keep the bills paid, nor me warm at night."

"Two more weeks, bebe. I promise."

He hung up the phone, which he would discard in a trash can at a fast food drive-thru within the hour. He turned on the television, but all they were talking about was the chemical attack in Kansas City. Up until that time, he had been happily engaged in killing American adults. But the kids, that was entirely another matter.

The money was fantastic. He had received three Bitcoins in his Caribbean bank account for each of his assignments so far. He had five more locations on his list. One of the remaining assignments involved a water park in Orlando. He could only imagine the victims at such a venue. Paco resolved to find a way to limit his efforts to only American adults. After all, they deserved it. But no more kids. What kind of monster did they think he was?

Just before he turned off the TV, they mentioned an injured suspect in the New York bombing, saying that he was currently in the hospital and was being interviewed by the FBI. That came as a shock, as Paco had assumed Raoul had been killed in the explosion. Unfortunately, Raoul knew just enough about their remaining targets to make things difficult if he spilled his guts.

Not that he would have understood the implication, but Paco had no way of knowing that one of Raoul's injuries had been to the frontal lobe on the left hemisphere of his brain. Called Broca's area, that location controlled an individual's ability to speak, and thus far, Raoul's only confession to the FBI had been in the form of unintelligible squeaks and grunts.

❀

Daniel Won-shik wore the rank insignia of a North Korean corporal, which consisted of red shoulder boards with two narrow gold stripes. He had appropriated the uniform from an unfortunate soldier who had wandered into the market area not too distant from the Ryongsong Residence in Pyongyang. Unknown to the deceased soldier, who was now resting peacefully at the bottom of the Taedong River, Daniel had exchanged clothes and taken on his identity, which now identified the CIA agent as Corporal Shin Soo-gun. He then hid his original identification near the waterfront in case he needed it again.

He observed the comings and goings of other enlisted personnel at the security gate until he was satisfied every entrant was required to show an identification badge. Thank goodness the badge he inherited was held together with nothing more than two pieces of plastic, so he was able to replace his own picture for that of the now dead corporal.

He waited until what appeared to be a shift change in late afternoon and simply waltzed through security with nothing more than a wave of his identification. He sought out a private first class and started up a friendly conversation, with the result being that the PFC had indeed seen a group of outsiders in the chow hall. They were undoubtedly from a number of different countries. But they had all disappeared a couple of weeks previously.

Daniel kept his composure and grinned at the PFC. "I heard they had a good-looking woman with them."

"There were three of them. One was so covered up in one of those cursed head shawls it was hard to tell."

"Well, I guess she's gone now. No point in speculating." Daniel had seen the satellite photographs of Angela's coded laundry message, and he assumed the building where she had been housed was adjacent. He decided to check that area for any clue as to where she'd gone.

The barracks was currently not in use, so he returned later that evening. One of the windows was so loose in the frame that the lock was non-functional. He could imagine how drafty the building had been in a frigid Korean winter.

Upon entering, he used a ballpoint pen which also had a pen light function. He found no evidence whatsoever of Angela ever being there, at least until he entered one of the bathrooms. There in a corner of one of the mirrors was some very small lettering which had been applied with a lipstick. "Vietnamam" had either been written by a poor speller, or by someone who'd entered an extra 'a' and 'm' at the end of the word.

At least he thought he knew where she had gone next, but that broad location certainly was not particularly helpful. Daniel silently cursed his luck. Here he was, stuck on a military base in the capital of North Korea, and Angela Martinelli was long gone. The last time he got out of Pyongyang, it took three weeks to make it back to South Korea. And he had wondered whether he would make it back in one piece more than once. Damn it!

CHAPTER 24

I'm Gonna Pour It Down Your Throat
Dodge City, Kansas April 10, 2024

American beef is considered to be among the safest in the world. From birth to the plate, it is highly regulated by the Department of Agriculture, the Food and Drug Administration, and even the EPA. Additionally, each state government also regulates agriculture and foodstuffs. Finally, most concentrated animal feeding operations are run by very competent people.

So it was with Keeble Cattle, a huge beef feedlot operation on the south side of US Highway 400, ten miles east of Dodge City, Kansas. The operator, Will Keeble, was a knowledgeable third-generation cattleman, having graduated from Iowa State with a degree in animal science, in addition to fifteen years of apprenticeship to his father and grandfather.

Did the three generations always see eye to eye? Probably not, but a visit to Keeble Cattle provided an education in how to maximize beef production. Unlike movie cowboys, the workers on Keeble's 720 acres didn't holler, or wave their hats, or shoot guns around their animals. The rules were simple. No yelling and screaming. No litter blowing around which might spook the animals. Stay calm and quiet, move slowly and deliberately, then reap the dividends when the cattle stayed calm, moved easily, and spent a good 95% of their time eating or napping. If things were done right, a 200-day stay at Keeble's enabled stocker cattle to increase their weight by about 600 pounds, and they averaged close to 1,150 pounds when they were shipped to slaughter.

Of course, the operation was far more complex than that. A veterinarian stayed on call and was on site weekly. At the first sign of an illness, the animal was isolated, diagnosed, and treated if necessary. The 12,000 head present on the Keeble property were separated into large pens according to how long they'd been in residence, so that every month, about 2,000 were shipped to the slaughter house, and 2,000 more took their place.

There were two video cameras installed at opposite ends of each pen, and the constant feed from those devices was viewable on multiple screens in Will Keeble's office. He spent at least an hour a day watching the cameras for any sign of an animal showing signs of illness or injury. Things like sluggishness, drooling, not eating, or standing off by themselves were common warning signs. He liked to believe he could discover a sick animal just as quickly as his vet.

Keeble's father had built huge, roofed areas along one side of each pen. The animals were fed and watered in long concrete troughs located under the covered sections. This created a protected area for the food as well as the cattle in case of inclement weather. Also, each pen had a large, elevated mound or hillock constructed of compacted dirt so the animals could avoid lying down in mud after rain or snow.

The feed was a scientific mixture of corn, corn fructose, milo, corn stalks and other roughage, vitamins, and minerals. On occasion they would also administer antibiotics in the mix. The formula was designed to quickly add weight, the kind of weight that created the marbling which customers sought for quality, flavorful beef. Keeble's formulation was designed to add an average of 2.95 pounds to each animal daily. To accomplish that, the cattle were fed seven to nine pounds of feed and lots of water every day, depending on their current weight.

The average steer or heifer produced about six and a half pounds of solid and liquid waste per day, and with 2,000 animals in an individual pen of fifteen acres, that began to pile up—literally. Manure was removed from each pen weekly and transferred to an EPA-regulated waste treatment site well away from the cattle. The dried and seasoned manure was then eventually used as compost on the farm's six hundred acres of corn, milo, alfalfa, and fescue.

Keeble was acutely aware of the difficulty in keeping good

employees in this work environment. It was surprising how many workers failed to see the romance in spending ten hours a day outside in all kinds of weather, much of it moving slowly around on horseback, living under the constant admonition to be calm and quiet, no females in the vicinity to interact with all day long, smelling cow biology up close and personal, and receiving the princely sum of eleven dollars an hour.

Manuel Betances was a new hire, and so far, Keeble had found little to complain about related to his work. Despite a lack of good understanding of English, Manuel had obviously spent a great deal of time around cattle. However, the man was in a probationary period, so Keeble watched him, both in person and via his camera system.

On Betances' eighth day of employment, he was walking behind the feed truck, which dispersed cattle feed directly into the troughs via a chute system. It was Betances' responsibility to spread the feed evenly along the trough with a rake. It was not desirable to have greater amounts of food in one location than another, as the cattle would tend to bunch up, and pushing and shoving would result.

The day was hot, and Betances wore a Camel-Bak, which contained two liters of fluid. The device was worn as a backpack and included a drinking tube which the wearer could suck on as he went about his duties. It was actually a timesaver, as the worker didn't have to pause in his work to seek out water from the single drinking fountain in the feed lot.

Keeble was watching, though not with much interest, when he noticed the worker pause in his raking, withdraw his drinking tube, and apparently squirt the contents across a wide area of feed. At first, Keeble wasn't sure of what he'd seen, but as the feed operation moved another twenty or so feet along the trough, Betances did it again. Keeble quickly called the supervisor of that particular pen, and hollered at him to move the cattle away from the food.

"Boss, how in the heck am I supposed to do that? There's just three of us in this pen, and all two thousand of these animals know it's dinner time."

"Do what you can. I'll be there in just a minute."

Keeble caught up with Betances, still following the feed truck. "What's in the Camel-Bak, Manuel?"

The man turned with a look of innocence on his face.

"What, Señor Keeble?"

Keeble pointed. "The Camel-Bak."

The man produced the drinking tube, showing the label to his boss. "Is energy drink, señor."

"Good to know. Let me see you take a big drink of it, Manuel."

"I no thirsty, señor."

"If you don't drink it, I'm gonna pour it down your throat."

Manuel slowly removed the cap on the tube and prepared to take a swig, but at the last second, he squirted the mixture in Keeble's face, then turned and ran. He forgot that it might be hard to outrun someone on horseback, and he was quickly subdued by one of the cowboys.

Will Keeble had no idea what was in the energy drink, but he immediately called his veterinarian, Hugh Mainzer.

"First things first, Will. The wind is out of the northwest, so get the cattle in that pen isolated and moved to one of the pastures on the south end of your property. Then bring me that backpack and I'll see if I can make out anything under the microscope."

After a quick look in his small laboratory, Dr. Mainzer turned to Keeble. "I don't see a thing, but whatever this is, it certainly doesn't look like any energy drink I've ever seen." He paused. "I get all these alerts from the USDA when there's any kind of disease outbreak, and they've been warning everybody about those botulism incidents three months ago. They say it was terrorism."

Keeble pointed at the bottle. "You're not supposing this is botulism, are you? What would be the point of that with beef cattle?"

"No, but I am wondering if it has anything to do with terrorism."

"You just said you didn't see anything in your lab."

"Yeah, but there are some things I wouldn't be able to spot with the equipment I've got. I want to overnight this to Plum Island."

"What are they gonna do that you can't do?"

"Plum Island Animal Disease Center is the USDA's level four research facility. It's located two miles off the coast of Long Island and is the nation's premier facility for identifying animal diseases. Maybe they'll give you a clean response and you can continue without too much interruption. But if they don't, the sooner you know about it, the better."

Once he and his crew got the 2,000 head relocated, Keeble went back to his office and looked through camera film for the past three days. He finally found a run of film which showed Betances wearing the Camel-Bak two days previous. In that tape, Betances was not putting the contents on food. Instead he was squirting the liquid on his gloves, then rubbing the wet gloves on a number of animals' muzzles while they were feeding.

From a distance, it appeared he was simply petting the cattle and keeping them calm. However, with the suspicion that there was some sort of foreign substance in the backpack, it was even more intentional than simply squirting the liquid on cattle feed.

Two days later, Keeble called Dr. Mainzer. "Hugh, I was down in that south pasture first thing this morning. I don't want to make a wild guess, but you'd better come out and take a look at a half-dozen animals. I've got them penned off in a corner for you."

Hugh Mainzer was closing fast on sixty, possessing a head of disappearing grey hair and a wispy mustache. Although he practiced on large animals in Dodge City, he had spent his early career at the Centers for Disease Control in Atlanta. He would say there was nothing even remotely similar between his current life and what had gone on before, but that was about to change.

"Will, the first thing I want to tell you is that I've never seen this in my practice, so maybe I'm wrong. Lord knows, I hope I'm wrong." The vet pulled off his latex gloves and deposited them in a sealed bag. "The six animals you've shown me have a fever, and three of them have blisters and canker sores along the gum line. They're salivating heavily. Also, it looks like two of those are showing signs of developing sores between their hooves. I've taken tissue samples from the sores in their mouths and took pictures of their mouths and legs. This has got to go back to Plum Island for confirmation in their bio-containment lab, but the diagnostic evidence is pretty strong."

"Shit, Hugh! Are you saying—"

"I think it's hoof and mouth disease, Will."

"What about the rest of my herd?"

"We've got to wait on confirmation. But if I'm right, it's likely you'll have to get rid of all of them."

"But I've got ten million bucks worth of cattle on the place!"

"Have you shipped any cattle since this happened?"

"No. That was gonna happen next week."

"Have you had any trucks come onto your property since you fired that Betances fellow? If so, they could have spread the virus wherever they went next."

Keeble turned pale as skim milk. "Let me think. I'll have to check in the office."

"The wind is still out of the northwest. What farms are downwind of you?"

He pointed to the line of trees less than a hundred yards away. "The Arkansas River is right there. Only milo and wheat farms beyond the river for two or three miles."

"That may be far enough, but the USDA and the state may want to declare everything within five miles as a contaminated zone." Mainzer slapped his leg. "The river! I forgot about the deer and wild hog population around here. They're just as susceptible to hoof and mouth as cattle and pigs, and they're not penned up. Once they're infected, they can harbor the virus and spread it wherever they go." He peered closer at his friend. "Didn't you tell me that worker squirted some of the contents of the Camel-Bak in your face?"

"Not much, but yeah."

"I don't see any symptoms yet, but the incubation period is anywhere from one to twelve days. You'll need to start checking your temperature twice a day, and look over the inside of your mouth and nose, plus your eyelids, for any sign of blistering."

"I didn't realize it was transferable to humans."

"It doesn't happen often, but you can't ignore your exposure. There are plenty of other precautions you need to take. If you're infected, you could spread the virus to other herds if you leave your own farm."

"What about my family? Can I spread the infection to them?"

"There's no human-to-human transmission. But it's highly transmissible to animals. In fact, it's probably a good idea for all your workers to park their vehicles out at the highway and not drive onto your property. If their trucks are already on the property, they'll need to wash them down and decontaminate them with a diluted Clorox solution before driving back to town. And the workers are going to need spare clothing and boots which will only be worn on the farm. They'll have to change clothes when they arrive and when they leave. The clothes they wear on the farm will have to be bagged and decontaminated."

"Is it really as serious as that?"

"Will, if I'm right, this could touch every cattleman around here."

"But Hugh, we're talking ten million bucks. I couldn't come up with that kind of money if my life depended on it."

"Let's check with the USDA. I know they've got some indemnification funding prior to a Stafford Act declaration, but I don't know what restrictions are on that money. Remember though that right now we don't know for sure about a diagnosis, let alone how many other ranches might be affected."

❊

The teleconference was a gloomy affair, with USDA Assistant Secretary Willis Ames hosting. Others on the call were representatives from the FDA, FBI, DHS, EPA, and FEMA, as well as the governors and state agriculture department directors from Kansas, Colorado, Texas, South Dakota, Oklahoma, and Indiana. "Ladies and gentlemen, although this series of attacks was first discovered in Kansas, we also found evidence within a couple of days of similar attacks, undoubtedly by a group of agricultural terrorists, in your five midwestern states. Although only one of the terrorists was caught red-handed, in the other five instances FMD was found in those herds within two or three days of the departure of a newly hired worker."

Early Johnson slouched back in his chair. Such phone calls were becoming all too common, a dark moment in too many days. He glanced at the FBI agent beside him, wondering if the man felt the same way. The agent's tense face, though, showed little sign of the depression and anxiety felt by Early.

"So that we're all on an equal playing field," Ames continued, "I'd like to share some basic information about foot and mouth disease. The disease is caused by a virus and is the most highly contagious disease among cloven-footed mammals. So cattle, hogs, sheep, goats, deer, antelope, bison, javelinas, and wild hogs are all susceptible. Because wild animals can carry the disease, this adds another level of complexity to our ability to accurately determine the area of containment. Actually, it forces us to enlarge the area of containment due to wild animal movement."

A new voice broke into the conference call. "Secretary Ames, Governor Galen Goeden here from South Dakota. We've got an issue that might be different from other states. The affected feed lot in my state was located just outside Fairborn, which is approximately ten miles from our Custer State Park. The park is home to one thousand three hundred buffalo, and as far as I'm concerned, that herd is a national treasure. We simply can't afford to lose it. Your comment about wild animal movement hit home, as the park is also home to free-range deer and antelope, which could easily bring the disease ten miles to our buffalo."

Ames looked across the table at his subject matter expert and nodded for her to respond.

She leaned toward the phone mic. "Governor, Patty Sullivan here from USDA. Is the buffalo herd situated so that they can be moved another twenty miles away?"

"I suppose it's possible, but not easily accomplished."

"Then can you round them up and get them into a corral?"

"We round them up every September for branding, recordkeeping, and thinning."

"Then we would highly recommend you immediately round them up and vaccinate every one of them against FMD. It's the only way to guarantee the virus doesn't impact your herd."

"Thanks for that. We'll make that happen."

Johnson expected crosstalk after that interruption, but Ames kept control of the conversation.

"Willis Ames here again with a bit more information. By using DNA probes, and reverse transcription PCR from animal lesion specimens, our scientists at Plum Island identified the virus, and then the particular strain of FMD which all of you are dealing with. There are seven serotypes of FMD, and the one being spread by the terrorists is the Asia-1 strain. This one is not common, but was reported in Pakistan in 2000 and in China at various times from 2005 through 2010, and probably more recently, but they aren't exactly trustworthy in what they report. The Chinese tend to cover up FMD outbreaks, referring to it as canker or hoof jaundice, but the world is aware of their subterfuge, so their beef and pork is not able to be exported to very many countries."

Another voice interrupted. "Mr. Secretary, Amber Ferrell here in Colorado. We understand there is a vaccine bank somewhere, a joint operation between the U.S., Mexico, and Canada, which contains at least some of the FMD strains. Does this bank have the strain we need to vaccinate our cattle?"

"Thank you, Governor. I was about to get to that. The short answer to your question is yes. But what the vaccine bank has in storage is a highly concentrated form of the Asia-1 strain. We believe it will provide an appropriate vaccine, but the concentrate has just been sent to a contracted vaccine company, first for dilution, then addition of an adjuvant to increase the level of immunity, and finally packaging into vials and labeling. We should have a half million doses of Asia-1 vaccine available in approximately eighteen days.

"During that time frame, there is much to do. We recommend that all cloven-hoofed animals residing on the six farms where cases have been found should be put down, and their carcasses buried in concrete- or plastic-enclosed chambers to prevent virus from entering the environment."

"What about burning the corpses, Mr. Secretary?"

"There's plenty of evidence from an outbreak in England that burning doesn't always kill the virus. In fact, it can aerosolize the virus and spread it over many miles downwind."

Early grimaced again. That was all they needed.

"The feed lot which was hit in my state has twenty thousand cattle on it. How can the farmer be expected to prepare a pit large enough to contain that kind of volume?"

"A representative from FEMA is here, along with my counterpart from USDA, Dr. Bill Stokes, and they're ready to work with each of you governors to prepare a request for federal financial assistance through a Stafford Act declaration. Now, we also need to create a circle around each of the affected farms with a five-mile radius. Let's call them vaccine buffer zones. Every animal within that area must be vaccinated as soon as possible. Each animal's vaccine status needs to be recorded, and then they need to be transported to slaughter. There should be no animal still alive six weeks from now which was exposed or vaccinated."

"Even if there's no sign of FMD in the herd?"

"Unfortunately, yes."

"I thought the mortality rate from FMD was only about five percent, Secretary Ames."

"That is true, Governor Ferrell, but we have multiple concerns regarding infected animals. First, those animals infected with FMD suffer from an inability to gain weight as they should, and second, there is a high incidence of aborted births, but most importantly, the presence of those animals means the U.S. is branded as a source of FMD in every market around the world. Our estimate is that ninety-five thousand animals were directly exposed, and another four hundred thousand cattle plus fifteen thousand hogs must be vaccinated, then slaughtered."

The FBI agent finally showed a reaction. He closed his eyes, then reopened them and leaned toward the phone line with even more intensity in his expression.

"Governor Goeden again, Mr. Secretary—my guesstimate on the value of those ninety-five thousand animals is somewhere around one hundred million dollars. Six feedlot owners can't be expected to take that loss if they're not insured for this sort of disaster. That doesn't count the four hundred fifteen thousand animals on the ranches and feedlots within your vaccine buffer zones. That's close to another five hundred million dollars."

"Our FEMA and USDA reps are aware of the potential cost, Governor, and will be working with each of those ranchers and feedlot owners. Just keep in mind, if we complete this vaccination project, then the United States can eventually reapply for FMD-free status. Otherwise, your beef's access to foreign markets is stopped until that happens.

"Think about where our beef is purchased. Every nation in Europe, Canada, Japan, Australia, the Philippines, Indonesia, and about half the countries in South America are FMD-free. None of them will buy your animals."

"But what about the four hundred thousand we're going to vaccinate? Can't they be sold?"

"Yes, but only to buyers inside the U.S. And their FMD vaccination status has to be disclosed at sale. Here's the problem. Imported beef is tested around the world for FMD antibodies. However, the test can't differentiate between animals infected with FMD and animals vaccinated against FMD. So none of those animals can be exported. If we move quickly, and the disease does not spread beyond our vaccination containment zones, then this can hopefully be resolved and things will be back to normal within six months. But if we fail in this, ladies and gentlemen, an entire industry is at risk. Governor Goeden, that goes for your bison as well. You won't be able to ship any animals or meat outside the U.S."

"With the size of that circle of containment, you could be talking about a hundred thousand animals just in Kansas, Secretary Ames. Where are we going to find enough qualified people to vaccinate those cattle?"

Another voice took the microphone. "Kathleen Downs here, Governor. FEMA will be requesting that HHS deploy their VMATs—that's Veterinary Medical Assistance Teams if you're not familiar with the term. Each of your states will receive the services of one of those thirty-person teams to assist your local veterinarians and vet techs as soon as the finished vaccine is on its way. We'll also be requesting that each VMAT be supplemented by perhaps a half dozen U.S. Public Health Service vets as well.

"Also, we have mental health teams who have experience in working with farmers who are going through this kind of traumatic loss. A couple of these teams were deployed after two farmer suicides during an FMD outbreak in England some twenty years ago."

"Ms. Downs, Governor Goeden here. I certainly don't want to wait until something like that happens to our people in South Dakota. Can I request one of those teams now, rather than later?"

Governor Ferrell quickly added her voice to the request, as did several other state leaders. Early managed not to sigh. The prospect of farmer suicides, added to the dead animals, was an extra level of cruelty from the terrorists.

"I agree with the necessity to address any and all mental health issues now," Downs said, "rather than waiting for something terrible to happen. FEMA will work with HHS to fill your requests as soon as possible."

"Secretary Ames," Governor Ferrell said, "do you have a theory as to the source of this Asia-1 strain, and where these terrorists came from?"

They'd been expecting the question; after all, it was what

all of them were thinking. Early Johnson looked over at his counterpart from the FBI, and both of them silently shook their heads in the secretary's direction.

"We're joined at the hip with the FBI in this matter," Ames said, instead of answering the question. "The investigation will be ongoing, Governor. I couldn't begin to speculate at this time. We only hope that the five terrorists who haven't yet been taken into custody have neither the additional virus nor the opportunity to do this again."

※

The participants on one side of the observation glass in the Jail Unit of the Federal Penitentiary in Leavenworth, Kansas included Avery Meyer, Special Agent in Charge for the Kansas City office of the FBI, Willis Ames, USDA Assistant Secretary, Early Johnson representing DHS, and Angela Martinelli from the CIA. On the opposite side of the one-way glass sat Manuel Betances, who was speaking to FBI Interrogator Kevin Helms.

"Let's go over this again, Manuel. Who gave you the liquid in your Camel-Bak?"

"Señor, I keep telling you. He didn't have no name. He just say if I put it in cattle feed, he pay me for it."

"Where did you meet this man?"

"I don't remember. Somewhere in California."

"What did he tell you the liquid would do to the cattle?"

"He say it was experiment to stop cattle from eating. He say people should eat vegetables instead of cows and pigs."

"When was he going to pay you?"

"He say when cattle stop eating, he pay me."

"If he was somewhere in California, how were you going to get the money?"

"He say he mail me a check, señor."

"And where was he supposed to send this check, Manuel?"

"To my house, Señor."

"And where is your house?"

"Uh, in California."

"Where in California, Manuel?"

"Oh, in San Diego."

"What's the address?"

"Uh, I don't remember, señor. I just live there a little

while."

"How many other people did he hire to do this same thing, Manuel?"

"Just me, I think."

The interrogator received a signal in his earpiece, stood up, and left the room. When he entered the viewing space, SAIC Meyer stood also. "Good job, Agent Helms." He turned to his counterparts. "Do you recognize this fellow, Dr. Martinelli?"

"Yes, sir. I had no direct dealings with him, and did not know anything about his particular mission, but he was on board the ship and landed with the group in California."

"Do you have any information that would lead you to believe he or anybody else in that group were contacted by another party in California?"

"No, sir. Every individual departed the ship with a large canvas duffel bag as well as an envelope. I assumed the duffels contained any special items they might need in carrying out their missions. Also, when I asked one of them about how we might contact each other, he opened his envelope to find out just where one of his assignments was going to be so he could give me the name of the city. So I'm sure all the envelopes contained their specific mission information and location."

"So you have no inclination to believe this story of a contact in California?"

"None whatsoever. I think they each had all the information and supplies they needed when they departed the ship. I would also imagine he received training in Vietnam on how to handle the FMD virus."

Meyer considered for a moment, and looked around the table. "Would it be advantageous for Dr. Martinelli to confront the prisoner?"

"My agency thinks it best that I remain completely out of the picture. We have no desire to disclose that anyone other than the Iranian nurse I was portraying was involved."

Meyer turned back to Helms. "Why don't you let the prisoner know that the only way he doesn't spend at least thirty years in the penitentiary is if he starts telling the truth? Tell him you know he arrived on Schoolhouse Beach in California with an envelope containing his mission, and a duffel bag with the materials he needed for the attack on the feedlot. Tell him you know he and his friends stole a car to get away from the coast, and you know there were others with similar missions to his, and if he helps us find them, we might seek a lesser sentence."

"Should I bring up any reference to the training he received in Vietnam?"

Early Johnson and Meyer conferred. "Right now, we'd like to keep that close-hold. We don't want this guy knowing we have that information. He could turn around and share that little tidbit with some court-appointed attorney, who then could easily go out and blab that to a TV reporter."

Chapter 25

What Makes a Person Breathe?
Pyongyang, North Korea April 15, 2024

"Mr. Putin has inquired whether we are responsible for the recent bombings, as well as the attacks on the American food supply."

Kim Yo-jong looked hard at her brother. "What did you tell him?"

"He knows very well that those attacks were listed on the information he received so that his social media attacks could focus on those events."

"Then why would he ask such questions if we had already provided him with that information?"

"I can think of two possible reasons. First, we actually provided the list of events and the probable dates—not directly to Putin, but to his representative, General Kuzmich. Perhaps the general is withholding that information from the Russian president. Another possibility is that he may be taping our conversations so that, at a date convenient to him, he provides the tapes to the United Nations, or something like that, proving his non-involvement."

"And that, brother, is what makes him such a dangerous man to have as a so-called friend. He only is concerned for himself, and has no loyalty to those who have confided in him. Could you get any feeling as to what his true opinion on the matter might be?"

"That is the main problem with communicating on the telephone through interpreters. Neither one of us can read the other person. However, there is another problem. We obtained anthrax vaccine from our Russian contacts only a few months ago. When the anthrax poisoning occurs, it will become too obvious to Mr. Putin who is responsible."

"Perhaps you should delay that portion of the attack until some time in the future."

"And there is the third problem, sister. We have no contact with the hired people on the ground in the U.S. We have no way of knowing if the agents are still pursuing their objectives, other than what is reported in the American press. In fact, we don't even know how many of them are still alive. There's been a news report that a Hispanic male was injured during an explosion at the chemical plant, but we really don't know if he was one of ours or not."

"What about using the Vietnamese to communicate with the agents?"

"No one has a way to contact them. If that were so, then if they were caught, the Americans might be able to trace their activities back to us." He thought for a moment. "There is one man who may know something. In fact, he may know everything. Colonel Ho-young, who works for Moo-sung, is primarily responsible for developing the plans and the destinations for these attacks. Perhaps he knows where and even when the anthrax attacks will occur. Of course, if we sent him to interfere with the agents, then it could open us up to our country being discovered as the initiator.

"So then we would be in the unenviable position where the U.S. could discover who is behind these attacks, and the Russians may find it no longer in their interest to stand in our defense, particularly since there will be widespread international condemnation of a biological attack, let alone the suspicion that the chemical attack in Missouri could be related. I believe you are correct about Putin trying to position himself as an innocent party."

"Is it possible for you to contact this General Kuzmich to obtain clarification as to what is going on?" Kim Yo-jong asked.

"That would be extremely awkward."

"Do you have something you can offer Putin which might be worthy of his understanding the position we're in?"

The fat man pursed his lips in thought. "Well, he certainly has no need of our enriched uranium or our missile technology. We did get some of our much-needed critical components from him, after all. And he's the one who recommended we start manufacturing counterfeit American currency, so I doubt he would have any need for a bale of their twenty dollar bills. Do you have any ideas, sister?"

"Do you remember our conversation about information warfare, brother?"

The chairman was not in the habit of admitting he didn't have complete awareness of all critical issues. "I juggle so many problems, I find it difficult to remember everything. Remind me again, sister dear."

She smiled, realizing it would be necessary to start at the beginning. "The Russians have a saying which explains this strategy. They seek to understand 'what makes a person breathe.' In other words, they want to know everything possible about an opponent—his desires, his strengths, his weaknesses, his motivations, his finances, his family situation, his quirks, even his sexual preferences.

"The Americans pretend to be shocked that the Russians might have a dossier on their president. Whether it's truly compromising is anybody's guess. However, everybody with any sense knows they have a dossier on every American president, all important American politicians, everyone who works in the American embassy in Moscow, every known CIA agent, and even every businessman who attempts to engage in commerce with Russia. What's more, they have similar information on important people from every country in the world, including you and me, brother."

"Just how do they accumulate such information?"

"Of course they use normal intelligence gathering and spycraft, but with the introduction of social media, the depth of information they have been able to accumulate is amazing. In 2014, the Russians established the Internet Research Agency in St. Petersburg. While this is their center of operations, they also purchased server space and other internet infrastructure in Vietnam, Iran, Syria, Venezuela, Cuba, the Philippines, and even inside the United States."

"Why all over the globe?"

"They set up many thousands of fake internet accounts and began bombarding social media sites with all kinds of so-called information. Because these posts were coming from so many sites, the Americans had trouble identifying their true source. Complicating this was that both China and Iran began doing the same thing, although to a lesser degree.

"The Americans are absolutely addicted to their cell phones. They receive messages from their friends, as well as from people they never heard of, all day and half the night. Many of those messages have their true origin in St. Petersburg, but once they transmit those messages directly to American cell phones, somehow the messages take on a level of believability. The Americans have no clue this is happening, despite being warned numerous times by news commentators. The amazing thing is, as long as the posts seem to be on their side of an argument, the Americans usually believe what those messages say, no matter how outlandish, concocted, or dubious they might be. And then they turn around and forward that same message to all their friends, having no clue that it originated in St. Petersburg."

The Wonsu dug into his pocket and retrieved his own phone. "I'd love to throw this thing away. It gives me no relief and certainly no pleasure."

"That's because, brother, the messages you receive require your urgent attention. They ask you to make critical decisions, sometimes with far-reaching implications, even on life-or-death matters." She paused to assess his nod of agreement. "It's no wonder you feel that way about your phone. But the great majority of Americans have no such requirements. They waste hours every single day simply reading and responding to frivolous communications and often forwarding them to their friends. Many times their friends send those same messages to all of their friends, and then those people send them to their group of friends. Before you know it, a hundred million people have seen the same drivel."

"So how is this personality defect something we can gain from, sister?"

"What if we could send messages to a group of people who had already been identified as easily duped? Then what if those messages played into their biases? That way, we can assume they would forward those communications to their friends."

"How are those people identified?"

"This is hard to believe, brother, but the social media companies in the West serve as intermediaries for us. They often send out messages on various websites which might include a 'personality determination' or a questionnaire, or an

IQ test, or a post which they are asked to like if they agree
with it. After receiving and analyzing that information, the social media companies sell that information to international
companies which seek to communicate with a group of people
who have been pigeon-holed into a given set of opinions or
preferences. They know in advance what those people are
likely to think about a subject like gun ownership, police brutality, race relations, saving the environment, abortion, white
supremacy, immigration, taxation, or politics. Sometimes a
company who has purchased such a list of names might offer
some ridiculous prize to them if they will only share one of
those posts with all their friends. Of course, no prizes are ever
distributed. It's all part of the hoax.

"All of a sudden, they've got contact information, as well
as personal opinions, for a couple hundred million people.
This same weakness is prevalent in almost all western countries, brother."

"Don't their governments step in to stop this kind of activity?"

"No. And neither do the companies which offer these social media portals. They're supposed to self-regulate messages
which they know originated from a hate group or foreign government, but it's been an almost total failure. The so-called
boundaries they were to construct to reduce or eliminate false
and inflammatory messages are a complete joke. They commonly claim that they are defending freedom of speech or
freedom of expression, with the result that they block almost
nothing from being transmitted to their customers. The reality, though, is that those companies' stated business plans
are strictly to accumulate this data and then sell it."

"Are Americans truly so foolish? Are their personalities
and opinions really that easy to discover?"

"Apparently so, brother. It appears only a minority of
Americans engage in independent thinking. Most of them rely
exclusively on social media, or perhaps even entertainment
and sports personalities, to tell them what to think."

"How do we get our hands on information about these
people, sister?"

"What would you say if I told you we could buy the contact information for ten million people, all of whom have expressed hatred or disgust for the American president, as well
as ten million more who are in full support of that same

president?"

"How much for that kind of information?"

"Twenty million names for a half million American dollars."

The fat man rubbed his stubby hands together in anticipation. "What shall we do with that kind of information?"

"We start sending out one-sided, biased posts that are either designed to make them very angry, or cause them to feel like we understand their concerns and are on their side. This is what the Russians, Chinese, and Iranians have been doing for several years. They turn every anthill into a mountain, and blow up every crack until it's a chasm.

"The strategy is very effective in separating and manipulating people into two extremes. Half of them are convinced a particular post reveals a plot to destroy their way of life, while the other half agrees wholeheartedly with such a message. It feeds into their distrust, lack of respect, and hatred for one another.

"As a result, they either don't believe anything that a particular politician tells them, or they blindly believe anything that individual says. Most of them can be duped by a skillful piece of misinformation. It's difficult for us to understand, but many of them also apparently believe that breaking their laws is perfectly acceptable as long as they are protesting something they don't like."

"Sounds like an excellent reason for us to continue our policy of restricting the internet inside the Fatherland, sister dear."

"Absolutely, brother. Our father was extremely wise when he made that decision. He undoubtedly could see into the future. So back to your original question. I am suggesting that you contact President Putin and offer to contribute to his cyberwarfare activities. Our participation might confuse the Americans enough that they won't be able to establish a firm link to Russia. In fact, this might be the time to enroll our other friends, China, Iran, and Syria, in a multi-pronged partnership with which to launch a joint information warfare campaign against not only the United States, but many of their allies."

The chairman clasped his pudgy hands over his very round belly and smiled at Kim Yo-jong. "That could be a very appealing idea. Whoever said that women can't grasp complex issues?"

With the recurring reminders that it was she who should have been promoted after the death of their father, she smiled a self-satisfied smile. "I think it was you who said that, brother."

CHAPTER 26

All You Can Eat
Various Locations May 1, 2024

It was the beginning of the supper rush at Big Jim's All-You-Can-Eat Restaurant in the northern suburbs of Tacoma, Washington. Shortly after five PM, it was self-explanatory to see why this portion of the evening dinner was referred to as the blue-hair special. At least three-quarters of the early customers were over 75 years of age, displayed a variety of shades of dyed blonde, platinum, or steel-blue hair-dos, and were happily taking advantage of the senior discount.

Already the salad bar was a disaster, with scraps of vegetables and cheese and dollops of salad dressing strewn from one end of the 24-foot, temperature controlled salad bar to the other. A Hispanic woman in her mid-twenties was in charge of keeping the area clean, and she was utilizing a spray bottle of cleaning solution and a handful of towels to wipe up the messes.

She sprayed the cleaner on the stainless steel counters and the slanted panes of glass at eye-level, which kept customers from coughing or sneezing directly on the food, or leaning over too far and dipping their hair-dos into the salad. As she went about her task, a half-dozen times she accidentally sprayed her solution on the mound of iceberg and romaine lettuce, as well as two or three times on the cut vegetables.

As the dinner hour progressed, she repeated her cleaning activity, and continued to spray the food as it was gradually replaced with new offerings throughout the evening. Although she had not mentioned it to anyone, this would be her last day on the job. She and her cleaning bottle would leave no forwarding address.

On the same evening, that identical activity was repeated in Salt Lake City at the Salty Dog Restaurant, and in Lincoln, Nebraska at the Cornhusker Cafe. Other than the fact that in Utah the employee performing the cleaning process was male, and the one in Nebraska was female, there was one rather important difference. In Tacoma, the cleaning spray had been laced with the hepatitis A virus. In Salt Lake and Lincoln, the spray was fouled with *Escherichia coli* (E. coli) bacteria.

Not just any E. coli. This was the toxin-producing Shiga strain, which had a history of causing severe effects, like bloody diarrhea, vomiting, cramping, fever, and even kidney failure, particularly in the elderly or in those with a damaged immune system. E. coli had a relatively predictable time from exposure to the onset of symptoms, generally three to four days, but sometimes up to eight days. That made it somewhat simple to narrow down the location of where people had been infected, but to complicate tracking, E. coli can also be spread by household contact or even sexual contact.

Hepatitis A was not nearly as predictable, as symptoms don't occur until around four weeks after exposure. That makes back-tracking to the source of infection extremely difficult for public health disease detectives. It is not usually deadly. However, the elderly, pregnant women, people with other liver disease, and those with a weak immune system are at a higher risk of severe symptoms. If a patient receives hepatitis A vaccine or a dose of immune globulin within two weeks of exposure, they will likely not have an infection, or at least it will be a minor one. However, if the first person does not get sick for four weeks, the deadline for immunization or immune globulin will have already passed before anyone knows they need to take preventive action.

Within four days, two hundred people were quite ill in both Lincoln and Salt Lake City. Identification of the bacteria took an additional day before local health departments' laboratories confirmed the data and they notified their state counterparts of the outbreak. The state health officers contacted the CDC to report the infection. Eighty-four people had been hospitalized, but only six were currently classified as critical. Two of the critically ill were small children.

Accompanied by the two FBI Special Agents in Charge from Lincoln and Salt Lake City, the CDC director, Rear Admiral Hope Sheffield, was on a teleconference line with the state health officers in Nebraska and Utah, as well as local officials in the two affected cities. "Mr. Mayor, I know it sounds counterintuitive, but your health officer is absolutely correct. We don't recommend giving anti-diarrheal medicine in E. coli infections. What we want to do is flush the bacteria out of the system as quickly as possible, not stop that process. And we don't recommend antibiotics, as they can further complicate things in the GI tract."

"So, Admiral, what do you recommend?"

"For people with moderate symptoms, plenty of fluids, Mr. Mayor, and bed rest. For people with more severe problems, they should receive intravenous fluids, and rarely it's necessary to perform kidney dialysis and blood transfusions. I would probably err on the side of caution for people with complicating medical conditions. That is, I might hospitalize them and pump them full of IV fluids before they get really sick. I'm sure your physicians are inundated with sick people as well as questions from patients who aren't sick at all, but I'm also sure they will make the best medical decisions for their patients. No doctor, including me, should sit on a teleconference line and dictate how to care for a specific patient they've never seen."

"How unusual is an outbreak like this, Admiral?"

"Although each state has stringent regulations related to food safety, it is impossible to have an inspector stationed at every restaurant every day across a city or a state. Unfortunately, these outbreaks do occur every year, and they most commonly happen because an employee didn't wash their hands somewhere along the chain, and the chain is long and complex. Think of all the steps which must occur. Food is grown, fertilized, treated with chemicals, harvested, transported, sometimes treated with a preservative to prolong shelf life, packaged, transported again, displayed in a grocery or restaurant supply entity, prepared in a kitchen, and finally served. Along most steps in that process, a single individual can defeat all efforts to make the food safe, usually by simply not washing their hands after going to the bathroom."

"Admiral, I have three people who've called my office, all convinced this outbreak should be blamed on a Hispanic woman who worked at the food bar in our restaurant in Lincoln, which has been identified as the source."

"Have you interviewed her?"

"No. Apparently she disappeared after working the night people believe they were infected."

"Then it's doubtful that theory will ever be confirmed or disproven."

"Admiral, Nina Payne here in Salt Lake. I didn't want to bring it up, but I had two similar calls myself. They each implicated a male Hispanic."

"Has he been interviewed, Madam Mayor?"

"Same story, Admiral. He left town immediately afterward."

"Respectfully, Mayor Payne, with no other evidence than what you have mentioned, I think those kinds of stories have to be set aside. On top of some of the media theories of the last few weeks, these stories blaming unknown Hispanics can't lead to anything positive. After all, who do we think is performing a high percentage of the menial jobs in this country? If and when more credible information is produced, we can re-evaluate this. In the meantime, we should spend our efforts on making sure sick people receive good treatment."

FBI SAIC Kevin Meeks decided he needed that info, no matter the admiral's opinion. "Sir and ma'am, related to your suspicions of the two Hispanic workers, do you know if either of the restaurants have photographs of these two employees? Or do they have security cameras inside the food service area which might show these workers?"

"Special Agent, we'll investigate this immediately here in Lincoln."

"Same here in Salt Lake. If there are photos, we'll get them to you as soon as possible."

"Thank you for that, but my counterpart, Kim Elenberg, in Lincoln and I will pursue this further with the restaurants. Even if the businesses don't have photos, maybe one of the employees took pictures. We'll look into all possibilities."

⚛

Angela Martinelli had studied the three pictures for the last half hour. The photos had been pulled off a phone from one of the food preparation workers at the Cornhusker Cafe in Lincoln. Their regular employee, Jorge Santos, had apparently been a bit infatuated by the new girl he knew as Marta Dominguez. This had prompted him to surreptitiously photograph her as she unknowingly went about her duties in the restaurant.

The FBI crime lab had enhanced and improved the pictures as best they could, but none were of good quality. All the poses were taken from the side, and the lighting in the kitchen was not helpful. Complicating the issue was the hairnet Marta had been required to wear in each photo.

From her office in Virginia, Martinelli called Elenberg on the phone. "I'm sorry, Special Agent, I can't confirm or deny this individual was part of the group of people I traveled with from Vietnam. I really had very little interaction with more than a dozen of them, so I'm afraid I can't help with this one."

From social media posts of undetermined origin:

Democrat Mayors Playing to their Base. Who Are They Protecting? Authorities in Nebraska and Utah ignore public outcry that Hispanics are responsible for food poisoning. Eyewitnesses in both states blame Hispanic employees. Yet no one is arrested.

Stop Illegal Immigration! Build the Wall! Mayor Lester Samuels of Tucson refuses to cooperate with ICE. Sanctuary cities provide a safe haven for terrorists.

Grieving Family Calls for Action. Joseph and Kathy Anderson demand justice for their three-year-old daughter, who died as a result of food poisoning in Lincoln, Nebraska. They've set up a GoFundMe account to help pay funeral expenses.

County Health Departments in Utah Require Extra Staff! Most counties are woefully understaffed to deal with increased demands from the public for food safety inspections. Source says tripling of personnel necessary to adequately assure safe food in restaurants. County government and the state legislature says no budget for staff increases.

And in response:

Skin-Head and Neo-Nazi Forces Blame Hispanic Food-Service Workers. Try to Provoke the Nation Against Lowest Income Immigrant Group.

Running on one of the national television news stations:

Breaking News: Prominent Latino Congressman Encourages a Strike, Demands Respect! Congressman Enrique Posado of California's Sixth Congressional District calls on all Hispanic food workers in the nation to strike next Friday, for better pay and for respect.

⚛

The Wonsu had far too much to drink by the time he pushed the white button on his desk in the bedroom of his cabin retreat in Sep'o County. He had wavered back and forth all afternoon and evening regarding the decision he would have to make. What a waste!

When Hiroko entered the room, he was just finishing what he had promised himself would be his last cigarette of the day. This time, her hair was pulled away from her face and neck, coiled intricately in a French twist on the back of her head. She was wearing skin-tight jeans, a simple white silk peasant blouse, and sandals. The difference between this time and the last was striking. Gone was any attempt to pretend to be a tenyo. Nevertheless, the effect was just as mesmerizing.

Her slim, exposed neck gave the impression of vulnerability. The fat man, however, had to acknowledge that this was only a figment of his imagination. Apparently, one of his lackeys at the estate had made a similar miscalculation.

She stood there, some ten feet in front of his desk, spending some time appraising the luxurious appointments of the room. He, in turn, sat silently, his hands crossed over his stomach. Each was waiting on the other to begin the conversation.

He finally broke the silence. "The last time we spoke, you asked several favors. If I'm not mistaken, almost all of them have been granted." He held up his hand and ticked them off on his short, fat fingers. "You now have luxurious, warm bedding; a selection of DHC bath products and cosmetics, produced in your own country, I believe; a CD player and a number of discs popular in Japan; many books, written in Korean, to improve your language skills; a television; and you have even been served Japanese food."

She screwed up her face in a cute grimace. "I'm trying to teach Auntie. She is making some progress."

"I'm pleased to hear it. You even had a friend to keep you company, a young girl from your country."

"Konomi is a very nice girl. Like many others, she was raped every day by her guards for six months before coming here."

"I can do nothing about what has happened in the past. I—"

"Then by all means, let us talk about the present and what you should do about that."

"Apparently you have already addressed that issue."

"Only because there was no alternative. The other three soldiers you keep here were doing nothing, despite her pleas for help. In fact, I would imagine they were simply awaiting their turn."

"Apparently you had been planning this all along."

"Why do you say that?"

"The weapon. You didn't sharpen it in the few seconds you had between her scream and your response. And yet you cut him from his navel to his breastbone."

"That is true. I sharpened that knife in the first week of my stay here."

"For what purpose?"

"Self-defense. I believe I told you about your men saying vulgar things to me."

"Yes, but I was under the impression those actions had stopped."

"That is also true, but I still felt like I was in danger."

"From who?"

She stuck out her small chin. "From you, among others."

The fat man fumbled with his lighter, lighting yet another final cigarette. "When have I threatened you, Hiroko?"

"You threaten me by keeping me in a prison for two years. Then you threaten me by holding me here. You threaten me tonight by summoning me to your bedroom."

"And how do you propose I act so you will not feel threatened?"

"From the way you look at me when I enter this room, I doubt you would do anything to change that feeling." She paused, deciding to go for broke. "Except to let me go. Return me to my family. Only then would I believe you."

He stuck out his lower lip. "I suppose you realize the guards are asking for retribution."

"Then either let me go, or change the guards for men with a sense of honor and decency. Besides, they took their retribution out on poor Konomi."

The fat man pondered again. Perhaps that solution would be the way to resolve the situation. Not to let her go, of course, but to change out the guards. He would have to pull in a replacement for the one she attacked anyway. Once the current problem was resolved, he would find a way to change her attitude. Unfortunately, her friend had not survived her two hundred kilometer trip to the hospital in Wonsan. He decided not to mention that outcome.

Chapter 27

❋

The Biggest of Them All
Various Locations May 6, 2024

The first quarter moon provided just enough light at two AM for the pickup truck to use only its fog lights to maneuver down the county road some twenty miles northwest of Hutchinson, Kansas. A light wind from the west had held promise earlier in the day, but the weatherman now confirmed there was no rain behind it.

In fact, rainfall had been missing in the area for over three weeks, but Ted Tyrrell and his neighboring farmers were not particularly upset about it, as they were looking forward to getting heavy equipment into their fields in the next few weeks to harvest what appeared to be a bumper crop of wheat.

The passenger in the pickup gathered his gear, and as the vehicle slowed to a stop near Tyrrell's mailbox, which stood on the road some two hundred yards north of his small farmhouse, he slipped out of the cab, crossed the ditch, and paused after entering the wheat field. It took a couple of minutes to get his metal sprayer primed, then he proceeded to coat an area some twenty feet long with kerosene. He gave the liquid a minute or so to thoroughly soak into the grain crop, then used a cigarette lighter to start the fire.

He got back in the pickup. They drove two hundred yards to the midpoint of the field, then he stepped out again and repeated the process. Looking back behind them, he noted the first blaze was making significant progress in the field, propelled by the accommodating wind. The growing inferno was not only destroying the crop, but it was headed directly at Ted Tyrrell's house. He and his wife Minnie were no longer young. Running away from a fire propelled by a strong wind on the flat Kansas prairie was out of the question. The only way off their farm was to head up the dirt drive, straight into the intense heat.

Twenty minutes later, the two Somalis were on the northern side of Rice County. Having located another desirable field with the wind flowing across the length of it, the passenger lit two more fires. Within an hour, the process had been repeated a third time just north of Langley, Kansas.

The next night, they were in southwestern Iowa, this time addressing a massive corn field. Once that field was afire, they repeated their evil task three additional times by four o'clock in the morning. At the second farm, the passenger "accidentally" dropped a set of directions, which outlined their methods, at the edge of the roadway. It was written on an index card, in Spanish.

※

Assistant Secretary Willis Ames, from the Department of Agriculture, was hosting a telecon with the governors of Iowa and Kansas, Special Agent in Charge Garland Crawford from the FBI's Des Moines office, as well as law enforcement personnel from both states. "Governor, I agree that the index card you reference is at least a piece of evidence. But from that, is it possible to link the four crop fires in your state, as well as the three which occurred in Kansas, all to that Spanish-language card?"

"Secretary Ames, I'm not much of a believer in coincidence. I'll admit that we have experienced crop fires before in my state, but certainly never four in the same night, and all within easy driving distance of one another."

"Mr. Secretary, Governor Hayes here. We feel the same way here in Kansas. Three fires in the same night, and the night before the Iowa fires—it's more than coincidental. As far as my farmers are concerned, that's more than just suspicious. Besides, it's an understatement to refer to the events as just three fires. Two of them together destroyed multiple farms including over six thousand acres before we could put them out the next day."

"Same story here in Iowa, Governor. A total of eight farms

totally destroyed."

"Governor Hayes, Governor Redmon, Mr. Secretary—
Garland Crawford from the FBI office in Des Moines. Maybe
my counterpart, Special Agent in Charge of our Kansas City
office, Avery Meyer, and I can provide a little bit of information to tie these fires together. We found matching tire im-
prints on the side of the road, immediately adjacent to two of
the Iowa fires, and when we shared that information with the
Kansas Bureau of Investigation, they acknowledged their
agents had found the same tire tracks in the dirt at the side of
the first fire set on the Kansas side."

"So you didn't find those same tracks at the site of the
other fires?"

"No, sir, but that really doesn't prove anything one way or
the other. They might not have pulled completely off the
roadway at those sites, or maybe some of the local law enforcement and fire department vehicles who responded that
night simply blotted out any tracks."

"So you're confirming that all of the attacks are by the
same party?"

"I'm confirming that a vehicle with Hankook All Season
tires, which have a very distinctive tread pattern, visited at
least three of the seven fire sites sometime before we investigated the fires the following mornings. At this point, it would
only be supposition to infer that all the fires were set by the
same person or persons acting together. However, that and
the index card are all we have at the moment."

"If I understand you, Special Agent, there is also no evidence to suggest that these seven fires are *not* the fault of the
same party."

"That's also correct, Governor."

"Governor Hayes, I don't know about you, but my whole
state is up in arms over what they claim are Hispanic saboteurs who are about to burn down every farm in Iowa."

"Yes, Governor Redmon, I'm getting the same thing in
Kansas. Besides that, Ted Tyrrell and his wife, who died in
one of those fires just west of Sterling, was a friend of my father. In fact, he used to take me fishing on his place along the
Arkansas River when I was a kid. I don't intend to forget
that."

"Gentlemen, Special Agent Meyer again. Can I suggest
putting additional highway patrol vehicles out during the

night shift? Perhaps park them near likely targets for a couple of nights. If they see somebody suspicious out on those county roads in the middle of the night, pull them over."

"We can do that, Special Agent, but I'm a Kansas farm boy from way back. I'm betting we've seen the last of these fires for a couple of weeks."

"What makes you say that, Governor Hayes?"

"The moon—we're coming up on a full moon by the end of the week. I figure they were out and about while there was just barely enough moonlight to see what they were doing. By this weekend, it'll be almost bright as day from nine PM until five AM. Low-life, murdering skunks like these won't operate in that much illumination."

Ho-young had been summoned to the Central Palace, for what reason he did not know. From what he could tell by the American news reports received at the Ministry of State Security, the various attack plans were working extremely well. Also, the multi-media blitz seemed to be effective. With the relatively good progress of his planning, for the life of him he could not imagine a poor outcome to his meeting with the chairman. He also had to admit to himself that their leader could be a very volatile man. Furthermore, it was highly irregular for his boss, Colonel-General Moo-sung, not to be invited as well. So his movements were somewhat less than confident as he walked up the steps of the palace.

"Good morning, Colonel. I hope this meeting was not an inconvenience."

"Of course not, Excellency. It is my pleasure."

"Your project seems to be paying the kind of dividends we hoped for on the other side of the Pacific."

"I think so, Excellency. I've been following the news reports closely. I certainly hope you are pleased with the results."

"Yes, yes. That is what I want to talk to you about."

The colonel's warning antennae buzzed on high alert. He was prepared to defend himself, no matter what happened. At least so far he saw no armed guards at the perimeter of the room. "Yes, Excellency?"

"I have multiple tasks for you. First, I want you to identify twenty of our military personnel within the Ministry of

State Security's Bureau 121."

"I'm not familiar with that organization, Excellency."

"Bureau 121 has been carrying out information warfare, the utilization of American social media to confuse, misinform, and alienate them from one another, for some time. However, to date, their base of operations has been inside the DPRK. Once you identify your team of twenty, these individuals will leave immediately for Vietnam, Venezuela, and Mexico, where they will set up similar bases of operations. From there, they will launch an even more aggressive information warfare campaign that simulates American reactions to our attacks on both sides of the political divide."

"Do I work with the Vietnamese, Venezuelan, and Mexican governments in any of this, Excellency?"

"Absolutely not. They are to know nothing. We are simply using these three countries because they are accepting of our travel visas, and to confuse the Americans if they are somehow able to trace the source of the misinformation."

"If it meets with your approval, perhaps we should consider setting the sites up as fake businesses of some sort. The teams will most definitely need powerful servers, as well as individual workstations, and perhaps other electronic items of which I am not aware. It may be quite expensive."

The fat man waved his hands in the air. "Of course, of course. You will have adequate funds for everything required for these operations. Once established, they should work on shifts so that we are transmitting twenty-four hours a day from all locations.

"However, I expect Bureau 121 will more than pay for its expenses. Their other mission is to discover vulnerable cryptocurrency exchanges which have lapses in their security. The demand for Bitcoins, Ethereum, Litecoin, and Ripple has far outstripped some exchanges' ability to control access and security." He smiled with real enthusiasm. "Just in the last two years, Bureau 121 has found ways to relieve those exchanges of three-quarters of a billion dollars, and the fools are apparently none the wiser."

After completing his notes on the Wonsu's directives in his black notebook, Ho-young bowed as a way of showing his respect for the achievement. "Understood, Excellency. You mentioned other tasks."

"Mr. Putin has expressed his concern about any plans we

might have for anthrax. He believes the Americans will be able to trace our acquisition of anthrax vaccine back to them, and hence assume that they are involved in the use of a biological weapon against civilians. Of course, we are already on the U.N.'s shit list, so I don't know what else they might do to punish us beyond what is already in place. Unfortunately, Mr. Putin thinks they will be painted with the same brush."

"What is your decision, Excellency?"

"Do you have any means of contacting the agents who are to utilize the anthrax?"

"No, Excellency. We didn't establish any communication plan because we didn't want any of their crimes traced back to the Fatherland."

"How many agents were trained to use the anthrax they were given?"

"Only five, Excellency."

"Did you not give specific instructions about the destinations they were to use in spreading the anthrax?"

"That is true, Excellency."

"And do you know an exact date, or perhaps an approximate date, when they are to use the anthrax at those destinations?"

"The answer is yes to three of the four venues, Excellency. For the fourth, the date was at their discretion."

"If they were intercepted at one of the three places where you know they will be, might there exist a chance to stop them from visiting the fourth?"

"Yes, Excellency, but only if they don't strike the fourth destination first."

The fat man sat with his head down, hands clasped across his stomach. He didn't move for a full minute. "Then that is a chance we will have to take." He stood up and walked over to where Ho-young stood. "You realize, of course, that since you are the only one of our countrymen who has personally seen these agents, you are the only individual who can perform this mission."

The colonel started to speak, then thought better of it, and spent the next few seconds thinking about an alternative or the lack thereof. "Of course, Excellency. It would be my honor."

"I understand you speak English."

"I would describe my English skills as rudimentary, Excellency."

"Good enough." He walked back to his desk, sat down, and ruffled in the top drawer for some paperwork. "This is a perfect opportunity to initiate the boldest attack of all."

"Is this something new, Excellency?"

"Come and look over my shoulder, Colonel." He spread the paperwork out in front of him, including a detailed satellite view of the southwest shore of Lake Michigan. He pointed at the map, "See where the shoreline juts out into Lake Michigan? There is a narrow waterway which allows very large container ships to pass into the Indiana Harbor Ship Canal.

"There is a large ship, the *Indianapolis*, owned by a U.S. steamship company, which frequently visits this canal. It often transports coal and iron ore from Duluth, Minnesota to Whiting, Indiana. The ship has a self-loading boom onboard, which allows for the loading and unloading of cargo without the use of shore-side equipment. If we could arrange to have two containers on this ship to be offloaded at the dock in the canal, it has the potential to dwarf everything we have so far accomplished in America."

"What would be in those shipping containers, Excellency?"

"Two large stainless steel cylinders no more than five feet long and three feet in diameter. These two-thousand-kilogram steel containers were designed to prevent port authorities from successfully using radiation monitors to detect the material they house. Inside each cylinder will be found an atomic bomb which will utilize one hundred and fifty pounds of uranium 235. With today's technology, such an amount can produce approximately fifteen times the power of the atomic bomb dropped on Hiroshima in 1945."

Ho-young was awestruck, yet tried to keep his composure in front of the chairman. He finally nodded. "What would be your ultimate target for such weapons, Excellency? And how could we carry out your plan without implicating ourselves?"

"American intelligence was extremely worried that several containers of U-235 would be captured by our ISIS friends in Mosul, Iraq a few years ago. Of course, those fears were not realized, as the ISIS fools didn't recognize what they literally had in their hands. Since then, however, their Iranian masters have educated them. They then had a similar opportunity when they and their Syrian brothers occupied Raqqah. As of this very moment, their prizes are on an Egyptian-flagged freighter, heading north along the west coast of Africa, having just rounded the Cape of Good Hope.

"The containers will arrive at a warehouse in Duluth, Minnesota within ten days, and remain there until such a date that you provide them a final destination address. I suggest as soon as you put together the teams I mentioned for information warfare, that you go to the United States—perhaps on a Vietnamese passport—by traveling through South America, then Canada, and on to Minnesota. The final shipping addresses you will provide shall be the Western Kentucky Warehouse in Paducah, Kentucky, and the East Jersey Storage Facility in Hackensack, New Jersey."

He pulled a card from his desk drawer. "You will find this Syrian, Abbud Dweck, living in Minneapolis, who has a reputation for reliability. He will coordinate the pick-up and transport of the steel containers to Paducah and Hackensack, as well as their ultimate destinations.

"As soon as you have made contact with the Syrian, you should immediately intercept those five agents carrying anthrax. When you have the anthrax in your possession, you should eliminate those individuals. Dead men tell no tales, Colonel.

"The Syrian and his team know exactly where to place the bombs for maximum effect. A word to the wise, Colonel—do not be within five hundred miles of southeastern Missouri on next April 15th or New York City on the 17th. The Syrian will be meeting you for final payment. I would suggest you select a site at least five hundred miles from the explosion to avoid any suspicion, let alone radiation exposure. At that point, there will be no payment. You will simply eliminate him."

"How will we escape suspicion, Excellency?"

"The Americans are aware that the terrorists already on the ground are both Hispanic and Middle Eastern. They also are at least suspicious that the uranium 235 was taken by ISIS in Raqqah. Rest assured, they will jump to conclusions. Perhaps you should reinforce this belief by appearing briefly in a few small towns in southeastern Missouri and in Manhattan, prior to April 15th, dressed as a conservative Muslim woman.

Ho-young nodded. "The way I understand a fission bomb, Excellency, the uranium would be spread as far as the materials within the crater created by the bomb—dirt, rock, vegetation, water, and bomb components—will spread as far as the explosion, or the wind, can carry it. Then the entire area for perhaps hundreds of miles downwind is radioactive. And it will stay that way for far beyond our lifetimes. As I remember, the half-life of uranium 235 is eight thousand years."

"All the attacks we have planned are to accomplish one goal: to convince the Americans that their government is unable to protect them, that there is no safe place anywhere in their country, and that, because of political and social differences, it is impossible for the country to work together to solve great problems. Time is of the essence, Colonel. You will need to depart on your multiple missions as soon as you put the dis-communication plan in motion. Select three exceptional men, technical experts, to represent you in Vietnam, Venezuela and Mexico."

"Yes, Excellency."

Chapter 28

Red Cloud's Revenge
Spring Grove, Iowa May 8, 2024

The Dakota Access Pipeline stretches 1,172 miles, beginning in North Dakota, passing through South Dakota and Iowa, before ending near Patoka, Illinois, a small city some 85 miles east of St. Louis, where it's connected to a storage and terminal hub. The pipeline carries 500,000 barrels of oil per day from the Bakken and Three Forks shale formations, which cover over 200,000 square miles in North Dakota, Montana, and Saskatchewan.

There was substantial opposition to building the pipeline by environmental groups, and in particular by the Standing Rock Sioux Tribe. The holding company which built the pipeline held over 500 public meetings on the subject, obtained over 1,000 permits and approvals, and rerouted the venture multiple times in response to a multitude of objections. One significant change was to route the pipeline completely away from the Standing Rock Sioux Reservation.

Once that had been decided, the new route veered into an area that drew more opposition, this time from a mysterious group represented by the largest law firm in America. Rumors flew that hedge fund billionaire, and the driving force behind the militant group *Antikapitalista*, Gyorgi Rosos, owned a massive complex and wouldn't allow the pipeline on his property.

The holding company quickly pointed out the ten thousand jobs created during the building of the pipeline, the 55 million paid to counties in annual property taxes along its route, and the extreme safety standards of the line itself. The heavy-walled steel pipe used in construction was 50% thicker than that required by law. The pipeline lay below ground for its entire length, some two feet deep in agricultural areas, and much deeper underneath bodies of water and roadways. Where the pipeline passed under the Missouri River it was buried between 95 and 115 feet below the river bottom.

The alternatives of rail, truck, and barge transport of oil are far more likely to result in hazardous waste spills. The pipeline company cited a total of only four barrels of oil spilled during the first six months of pipeline operation as proof of their emphasis on safety. A weekly inspection by aircraft ran along its entire length, and embedded sensors and cut-off valves remotely monitored for leaks 24x7.

Hawkeye Construction Company, located on the southern end of Mt. Pleasant, Iowa, possesses heavy equipment, such as bulldozers, dump trucks, track-hoes, and trenchers. Most are stored on heavy-duty trailers for ease of movement. Everything is locked up tight every evening and weekend behind an eight-foot chain link fence.

At two AM, Joselito Garza climbed the fence, disabled the alarm, broke into the office, and found the keys he was seeking on a pegboard. Conveniently, a large Caterpillar hydraulic excavator/track-hoe was secured to a trailer, which was already hooked up to a dump truck. Garza made sure his keys matched the two vehicles, then unlocked the fence and departed. The town of 8,600 citizens and two graveyard-shift patrol cars did not stir as the rig exited the little city, headed south on US 61.

Garza left the highway just past the farming community of Spring Grove, then drove a mile to the east on a gravel road, where he unloaded the track-hoe, then disconnected the trailer from the truck to speed up his getaway. He was pleased to note that the attached bucket was only two feet wide, as he might have a significant distance to dig, depending on the accuracy of his GPS coordinates.

He began his work in Ryan Velderman's soybean field. The Des Moines River was approximately a mile and a half to the south, and the mighty Mississippi was about the same distance to the east. Velderman's 320 acres was just about the last arable land, as property any nearer the two rivers was covered with a smattering of small ox-bow lakes, sloughs, and willow thickets.

Garza shut off the vehicle lights, turned the track-hoe around on its track, and started to dig while backing up. He headed straight to the south across the bean field, digging a ditch two feet wide and three feet deep, with the result that the tracks destroyed an eight-foot-wide swath of recently-planted cropland in his wake.

He had been digging for about thirty minutes when he decided to re-check his GPS. His location appeared to be right on the spot, so he began to deepen his ditch. Perhaps it was a bit deeper than he'd been told. In five more minutes, he struck his target.

He spent the next ten minutes digging a trench along both sides of the pipeline, then switched around and struck it at a ninety degree angle. The steel bucket perforated the pipeline, but created very little damage. His next attempt was to get the bucket underneath the steel pipe and lift it. This action finally ruptured the pipeline.

Within seconds, the trench work he had created was submerged in oil. He backed up the track-hoe to higher ground, hopped off, and ran back to the dump truck. Within five minutes, he was on Highway 61. He drove at a leisurely pace to Keokuk, Iowa, where he crossed the Mississippi into Hamilton, Illinois. When Garza left the dump truck at a truck stop, he placed a piece of paper on the front seat, which read, *Remember Wounded Knee! Signed, Chief Red Cloud*, then stole an SUV, which he used to cross back into Iowa, heading further south toward Missouri.

The emergency cutoff system for the pipeline worked fairly well. The pipeline had been depressurized within ten minutes. The spill only involved an estimated 28,000 barrels of oil, which gradually made its way into the Mississippi lowlands and waterway. The pipeline operator would not speculate on a timetable for clean-up operations. One thing was certain—Ryan Velderman would never be able to plant 80% of his soybean field again.

Social media erupted.

We tried to warn you that the pipeline was a disaster just waiting to happen. How is the company going to assure us that this won't happen again and again? They tell us it involved 28,000 barrels. How do we know that is true? It could be ten times that.

Now we're fighting Indians? Surely nobody believes that so-called clue which was left near the scene of the pipeline break.

I only wish I had struck against the pipeline while it was being built. Rise up, my brothers! Red Cloud.

The white panel truck, with PEPCO painted on the front doors, was parked on New Hampshire Avenue, immediately north of DuPont Circle in Washington, D.C. The Circle was a large roundabout which accommodated the huge eight-pronged intersection of New Hampshire Avenue, Connecticut Avenue, Massachusetts Avenue, and P Street. Far below all of this ground-level chaos sat the DuPont Circle Metro Station, which saw at least a hundred thousand riders pass through every day.

During the daytime, the tony area was in constant motion between hundreds of pedestrians, bicycles, and vehicles vying for the right of way at each traffic light change. All of the small retail establishments for several blocks in every direction did a brisk business. They had to, given the exorbitant rents that were charged.

At three AM, however, there was no traffic, and the panel truck stood all alone in the middle of the street. Orange work cones were arrayed behind the truck, and a temporary fence was set up surrounding a work area. A small generator hummed in the truck, which powered a blinking caution light in front of the fence. Additionally, the open manhole revealed lighting for the benefit of the work going on beneath the surface of the street.

A police cruiser passed through the roundabout, headed southeast on Massachusetts, but that was the only sign of a vehicle. The officer paid no attention to the PEPCO work site, as this was a common occurrence in his sector of the city. By 3:30, the utility work was apparently finished, the manhole cover was replaced, and the work cones, fence, lighting, panel truck, and Paco Batista had departed, having completed preparations for his fifth attack. He had already decided he would complete number six, but there would be no seventh. He was not going to blow up a bunch of kids in Orlando, no matter what the payoff might be. Besides, there was the matter of his wife. The D.C. rush hour was just three hours away.

At 7:15 AM, a *Washington Post* assistant editor received a text, which read in part: *Your country's military continues to blow up the lives and fortunes of the innocent Muslim people of the Middle East, who only wish to be left alone to worship Allah in our own way. If your murdering ways continue, we—the courageous defenders of Islam—will bring this fight to your own shores and to your own capital, just as we will do this morning in exactly fifteen minutes.* Paco did not bother to sign the message. Yet another flip phone was discarded.

When the assistant editor showed it to his boss four minutes later, the response came from someone who had heard it all in his 24-year newspaper career, "Probably nothing at all, Dave. Just the same, follow protocol and call the police department."

The call to police headquarters was duly completed at 7:26 AM.

At 7:29 AM, at the height of rush hour, DuPont Circle, both above and below ground, was a mass of bustling pedestrians, bicycles, automobiles, buses, and metro trains. As the clock clicked over to 7:30, a connection was completed on a timer, and a large explosion blew two manhole covers fifty feet into the air, underground water lines, electrical conduit, and cable lines were fractured, a sewer line separated, store windows blew out, pedestrians were killed and maimed, three cars and a bus burst into flames, and the street itself buckled, forming a hole twenty feet wide in New Hampshire Avenue.

At the PEPCO monitoring site, a computer instantly received the information that there had been a sudden break in electrical current, and responded by shutting off power to that small area of the city. Store lighting as well as every traffic light went out for at least six blocks in both directions on New Hampshire Avenue and P Street, thus snarling traffic for at least an hour.

The emergency response was large and immediate. Police, fire, and ambulance personnel were on the scene within three minutes. The entire intersection was clogged with vehicles which had no room to maneuver in any direction. The police set up barricades on the four streets, both into and out of the roundabout, barring any additional traffic from entering the area except for emergency vehicles. The D.C. fire department struggled to put out the blaze which continued to burn over fifty feet below ground level.

At 7:45 AM, another timer connection was completed, and a second explosion, of similar capacity to the first, occurred on Connecticut Avenue. The damage was no less horrific, particularly above ground. Once again, that power trunk line was cut off, this time up and down Connecticut and Massachusetts Avenues.

Additionally, the second device had been placed so that the blast ruptured the wall which enclosed the Red Line Metro, halting subway trains in both directions. All of the electrical lighting in the underground metro station was cut off. As the station in the system which was furthest below ground, it was black as a bat's arse. People in the dark Metro tunnel were choking on the smoke and dust. Some would succumb to it.

Although asked not to publish the text message by law enforcement, the editorial staff determined it was information the American people needed to know. D.C. Police Chief Katherine Ash argued with the editor that the message could indeed have been created by the bomber, but was possibly designed to shift suspicion to ISIS sympathizers rather than perhaps the true culprit. Despite her caution to the contrary, the message was printed.

Washington Post *Receives Text Message Warning in Advance of Bombing. At 7:15 AM yesterday, the Post received the following text:* (Quoted in full.) *The newspaper immediately notified the D.C. police department at 7:23 AM. Note that there was no specific target identified in the text. At 7:30 and 7:45 AM, two bombs went off underground at DuPont Circle.*

The police warn we have no way of knowing the true source of the text message. It could have been ISIS, as is claimed, or the real culprit could be trying to shift the blame, as well as the investigation, away from them.

Social media exploded in a flurry of messages.

Pearl Harbor in our own backyard! Yet our "leaders" can't even decide who did it, let alone what to do about it.

TURN IRAN INTO GLASS! Let's end these attacks once and for all, and rid the world of a festering, malignant sore.

What about all the evidence against MS-13 over the last month? Can no one see that this is just a ploy to get them off the hook?

ISIS or MS-13? Why not simplify this and take them both

out? We all know they're both guilty as hell!

Two of my friends have been killed. Another is in the hospital. Here I live in the nation's capital, and I'm afraid to leave my house. What have we come to?

Things are not always as they seem. Do not jump to conclusions. These incidents need to be fully investigated before our country takes action against people who may or may not have been involved.

Under a picture of Democratic leaders of the House and Senate, who were gathered around a microphone: *Liberals in Congress intend to protect Hispanics at all costs from conservative Republican attacks. If these illegals didn't vote Democratic, what kind of protection would they receive? Republicans will not surrender to anarchists, despite Democrats' opposition.*

A social media post from a source described as "Patriots for America" displayed the picture of a calendar: *Our political leaders say we need to take action someday soon. Someday? There are seven days of the week. Someday is not one of them. The time to act is now.*

Chapter 29

The Country is on Fire
Various Locations May 12, 2024

Although the moon was high overhead, the night was cloudy, and very little moonlight filtered through at one AM on Sunday night in southwestern Missouri. The white pickup truck was straining a bit as it climbed the grade on the otherwise empty state highway leading away from Roaring River State Park, eventually heading in the direction of the small town of Seligman, some twelve miles distant.

As the vehicle entered the large area designated as part of the Mark Twain National Forest, a passenger exited the cab, sprayed a wide swath of underbrush with kerosene, and used his lighter to start the fire. He then crossed the road, repeating the process in the dense stand of red oaks and post oaks on that side. The pickup drove another mile, and the passenger doubled his dirty deed. One more stop, two more fires set, and they were on their way. A glance in the rear view mirror confirmed the success of their handiwork.

They then made the drive to Eureka Springs, Arkansas on one of the most dangerous roads in the state, before finally turning east for some fifty miles to Harrison, then heading south on Highway 65. About halfway to Little Rock, they approached the Buffalo National River just after four AM and duplicated their fire-setting actions in the pristine forest on either side of the waterway.

After departing the Buffalo, they eventually found their next target in southeast Texas. On Monday night, their objective was the Sam Houston National Forest. On Thursday night, they were 2,049 miles to the northwest, setting eight separate fires in the large land parcels of the Flathead National Forest in northwestern Montana.

They weren't finished. On Saturday night, the two men were in Oregon, east of the High Cascades Range with its many ancient and long-dormant volcanoes. West of the Cascades is a very wet environment, but on the eastern slopes, the average annual rainfall is only nine inches. The trees are primarily ponderosa pine, but also include an abundance of western larch and mountain hemlock. The trees, the vegetation, and the pine needles were dry as toast.

The men entered the Deschutes National Forest on Highway 97, then turned north toward Mount Bachelor, where they set a series of three fires before exiting toward Bend, Oregon. They struck Highway 20 and entered the huge Willamette National Forest, lighting four separate fires in a ten-mile stretch east of Belknap Springs, before finally departing to the west toward Eugene. The Oregon fires would eventually consume almost 200,000 acres and 87 residences, as well as claiming the lives of three volunteer firefighters.

The fact that the widely spaced fires were separated by seven days led the National Fire Service and their state counterparts to wonder if the same individual was responsible, as the timeline between the events were estimated drive-able distances. A second possibility was that copycats were simply taking advantage of the situation to satisfy their own demented pyromania. That option had actually occurred several times during previous multiple fire events. Alternatively, there could be three or four distinct teams which had coordinated their actions. The Fire Service was on high alert for additional fires.

To complicate the argument, a tire track was discovered at the Sam Houston fire and the Willamette fire which was identical to the Hankook All Season track found at the earlier crop fires in Kansas and Iowa. There was no other evidence, other than the analysis which concluded that a petroleum-based product was used in every location. None had been accidental.

※

At eighty years of age, Betsy Valenti was widely acknowledged as a saint, at least when it came to caring for her 85-

year-old husband, Ben, whose mobility was limited to a pair of quad-canes and rocking like a demon in his leather recliner. In other matters, perhaps *saintly* would not apply in her description. She was not happy, and the receptionist was well aware of the reason, because the physician's office had put her off until the next day, despite her having asked for an immediate appointment for Ben.

He had been experiencing diarrhea for the past two days, and that very morning had vomited after his breakfast. That was another thing. His usual healthy appetite had been almost nonexistent for several days, and he complained of pain and tenderness in his stomach, as well as aching in his back and shoulders. She had finally convinced him that she needed to take his temperature, and the thermometer read one hundred and one degrees. He had two more bouts of vomiting. Thus she stewed until the next morning. By then, Ben's diarrhea was more unpredictable, and he worried about having an accident at the doctor's office.

Ben's internal medicine specialist, Doctor Eugene McKenzie, had an office bordering the city of Tacoma, and had been in practice for half a century. Given his white hair and mustache, evidence of his professional experience was quite obvious. He asked a few questions, then began a systematic exam, including some poking, prodding, and pinching of the skin. When he focused on the left side of his patient's abdomen, he got a quick reaction. "Is that painful?"

"I didn't realize it until just now. It's real tender."

McKenzie palpated his liver again and got the same response, then looked closely at the sclera of his eyes. Seeing nothing particularly incriminating, he ordered a urinalysis and some blood work. "I'm not sure what's going on, but we need to do something about your fluid intake right away. Your skin shows obvious signs of dehydration, and when you're on the far side of eighty, that can be a dangerous thing."

"You're not gonna stick me in the hospital, are you, Doc?"

"If I thought you could get by with just one IV, we'd give it to you here in the office, Ben. But with your diarrhea and vomiting, as well as a tender liver, I think it's going to take a few days to get you back in the saddle." He waved his hand at his frowning patient. "I know, I know. Maybe the blood work will tell me what's really going on. But right now, you look like hell, old friend. I can't afford to lose a paying patient, and I'm determined to take care of you."

By the time Mr. Valenti's lab results were back, Dr. McKenzie had three other elderly patients with the same symptoms. Two of them were already jaundiced. Also, Betsy herself was displaying similar symptoms to those of her husband. McKenzie drew blood on each patient, despite having a strong hunch that all five of them were in the same boat.

When the doctor called the local health department, he discovered two other local physicians had also reported patients who were positive for the hepatitis A virus. The county health department was in the middle of contacting the state health officer to make what would undoubtedly be the first of several reports.

The Washington state health officer chaired a teleconference call with the governors of Washington and Oregon, the director of the CDC, the deputy commissioner of the FDA, the FBI's SAIC in Seattle, his counterpart in Portland, and at least thirty directors of city and county health departments in the area surrounding Tacoma.

"Let me bring all of you up to date on our situation. As of a few minutes ago, my office has received reports indicating thirty-nine hepatitis A infections in and around Tacoma, with most located on the northern boundary. Another eighty patients are currently being tested for the virus. I've asked the FBI's Special Agents Bill Russell and Jerry McCarson to be on this call, in view of the several food poisonings which occurred in other states earlier this spring. Can I ask the Oregon state health officer, Dr. Michael Martin, if he has cases at this time?"

"Thank you, Dr. Simms. We only have six cases confirmed as of this morning. But if the source of infection is indeed centered near northern Tacoma, that's to be expected, given the distance Oregon residents might have had to travel to be infected."

"From the standpoint of tracking," said Rear Admiral Hope Sheffield, director of the CDC, "we've found in previous outbreaks of hepatitis A that it is very difficult to identify the source. In other food poisoning cases, the length of time from exposure to the onset of symptoms of infection is short, anywhere from twelve hours to perhaps four days. So once a cohort of patients is identified, it's fairly easy to backtrack to a recent exposure source.

"With hepatitis A, however, the time between exposure and symptoms is anywhere from two to six weeks. That said, it stands to reason that these confirmed forty-one patients are going to be joined by quite a few more by the time we reach the six-week exposure-slash-symptom time limit.

"Governor Wallace and Governor Randall, the CDC will be happy to assist both Oregon and Washington in your disease investigation if that is your wish. We will detail three epidemiologists if you so decide, and they can arrive in Tacoma by tomorrow."

"The FDA will also be glad to send food safety inspectors from our Seattle regional office," said Dr. James Savage with the FDA, "but perhaps we should schedule them after you've narrowed down the site of infection."

"Governor Wallace, here, Admiral, and Regional Director Savage. The State of Washington would be very grateful for the support. Before I relinquish the line, what about the hepatitis A vaccination? Once we identify a source, can we start vaccinating potential patients?"

"I'll interrupt, then let the Admiral answer that question. Governor Randall on this end. Oregon looks forward to the assistance from both FDA and CDC, and thank you."

"Thank you both. As to the vaccine, in order to be effective, the vaccine needs to be administered within two weeks of exposure. But since the first cases don't commonly report symptoms until at least two weeks and usually closer to four weeks after that exposure, it would seem a waste of resources to start now. Of course, if you're asking about treating other adults in the same household who have no symptoms, vaccination would be a good idea, as they may not have been infected by the original source. However, if they are involved in cleaning soiled clothing, bedding, or bathrooms of the infected person, then vaccinating them immediately should be a priority."

"I notice you said adults, Admiral. What about children in the household?"

"We started recommending that children receive the hepatitis A vaccine at the age of one in 2006, Governor, so they are seldom victims nowadays. However, I must mention the fairly high percentage of anti-vaxxers in both Oregon and Washington. In those cases, particularly of having unvaccinated children in the same household with an infected person, their immediate vaccination should be strongly considered.

"Given the rash of food and milk disease outbreaks this spring, and in the name of caution, it's CDC's plan to send out an alert to all our state and local partners to be on the lookout for similar disease clusters. We would very much appreciate regular updates, preferably daily, from Washington and Oregon if that is possible, at least until the site is identified and a majority of patients are under treatment."

"Admiral, one more question. How many of these patients might be expected to not survive?"

"Governor Randall, hepatitis A is not usually fatal. With bed rest, extra fluids, and over-the-counter pain relievers for the aching and fever, the great majority of people are commonly back to their former selves within three months. However, people with pre-existing liver disease, such as cirrhosis or a hepatitis C infection, or those with a weakened immune system, are at higher risk. They need to be closely monitored by their physician."

※

The spotlight flooded the surface of the Yalu River, quickly outlining the solitary figure. The 7.62 caliber Soviet-bloc bullet entered the back of his upper right leg just below his pelvis, and left behind an ugly exit wound in front. Although it missed the femur entirely, it certainly created plenty of damage to muscle, nerves, and blood vessels, let alone pain for the recipient. The water ahead of him was sprayed with Daniel Won-shik's blood.

He was less than forty yards from the North Korean side of the river, and knew that with such an injury it was foolish to continue to try wading across to the Chinese side, some eighty yards distant. In all likelihood, if he had proceeded, the shooter would simply continue firing until he was finished. He certainly wouldn't be the first person whose escape ended in that manner. Therefore, he stood still and raised his left hand over his head. His right hand was busily trying to staunch the flow of blood.

※

There are over two and a half million miles of fuel pipe-lines in the United States. Their use is broken down into two categories—hazardous liquids, like crude oil, gasoline, diesel, jet fuel, butane, ethane, and propane; and natural gas, which is in a category by itself. In the case of natural gas, the prod-uct is carried from the well through production lines, which lead into larger gathering pipelines, which carry the product to a refinery, then away from the refinery via large transmis-sion lines, which may be three feet in diameter, until they reach a population center, where the gas arrives at a city gate.

At that point, the high pressure required to move natural gas long distances is greatly reduced, and the product then enters a system of main and service lines to bring the fuel to homes, businesses, and industry. It's also at the city gate that a scent is added to the gas, similar to rotten eggs, to allow customers a method to notice when there's a gas leak.

In the midst of an area of small warehouses on the north side of Rockville, Maryland there is a large city gate facility, owned by the Potomac Electric Power Company (PEPCO), which supplies electricity and natural gas to the fourth larg-est city in Maryland. The city gate is protected by a high chain link fence, three security cameras, and a monitoring system within the pipeline itself referred to as SCADA, a supervisory control and data acquisition system. The regulators, valves, and sensors built into SCADA allow for the constant monitor-ing of the pipeline and its pressure, which in turn enables the remote operation of the equipment which can increase pipe-line pressure or reduce it with release valves when required.

The SCADA monitoring system is housed in the PEPCO operations center on Gude Drive, less than a mile from the city gate. The operations center is manned 24 hours a day. There is generally no one physically present at the Rockville city gate, particularly at night.

Until now. The individual wore the blue coveralls and baseball cap and carried the blue tool bag of a utility com-pany employee, thus initially drawing no attention from the fellow on Gude Drive responsible for maintaining vigilance over the security cameras. Strangely, the man in coveralls did not go to the facility entrance, but rather maneuvered around to the east side of the fence line, placing himself immediately underneath the camera which was the sentinel for that por-tion of the perimeter, but had no visibility directly below it.

The man removed heavy-duty long-handled bolt cutters from his bag, and snipped a vertical hole five feet tall in the fence. Once inside, he went to the eight-inch-diameter release valve, removed a bulky item from his pack, and taped it securely to the base of the valve. He then left the way he had come, retreating three hundred yards from the facility before he paused and pulled out a flip phone. He heard a police siren in the distance and wondered if it was headed his way. Perhaps they would be distracted by the time they arrived.

He dialed a number, the Semtex detonated, the valve was sheared off at ground level, as were several other structures inside the fence, and the pressurized escaping natural gas caught fire in a purple-blue plume which reached over a hundred feet in the air and was visible 35 miles away in Baltimore.

Paco Batista hurried into a nearby wood line, which ran along the back side of a warehouse, removed his utility company coveralls, and stuffed them in the tool bag. Underneath, he was dressed in a pair of jeans and a Penn State sweatshirt. He walked away, heading to a cab stand located at the Shady Grove Metro Station. He inadvertently left a torn receipt in the pocket of the coveralls. Although it only revealed the name Embassy Suites at the Convention Center and a number in the corner of the receipt, there was also an address, 1240 Watkins Bend, scribbled on the back. This just happened to be the address of the PEPCO city gate. After a small amount of detective work, it was revealed that the hotel room in question was paid for by one Reza Sassoni, who gave a California address. An Embassy Suites clerk vaguely remembered him as a Middle-Eastern type, clean shaven and of average height.

At the SCADA site, the flow of natural gas was cut off by the automatic shutoff valve (ASV) embedded in the transmission line some four hundred yards west of the city gate. The terrorist had picked a poor target for his deed. The gas industry's argument that the huge cost of retrofitting and embedding ASVs in large transmission lines was cost-prohibitive meant that many cities had no such protection. Rockville, Maryland would later be very thankful that they had spent the 300,000 for an ASV system, thus serving to protect much of their infrastructure at the site. Their city gate would only require 72 hours to repair.

Chapter 30

A Plan?
Washington, D.C. May 15, 2024

It was a small group that gathered in the SCIF at Homeland Security headquarters, hosted by Assistant Secretary Adams, with Col. Early Johnson at his side. Visitors were Lynn Jones, Assistant Director for Counter-Terrorism at the FBI, and Special Agent in Charge for DC, Michael Seward, as well as Bob Williams and Angela Martinelli from across the Potomac at the CIA.

"Given the hair-trigger political environment," Bob Williams said after the preliminaries, "we thought it important to keep the meeting attendees to only those with a need to know." He turned to his co-worker. "Dr. Martinelli, I think we need to disclose exactly what you know, or at least what you suspect, about this raft of attacks."

Although Adams and Johnson knew some of the story, she glanced toward the two men from DHS before beginning. "I was sent to North Korea, posing as an Iranian nurse, because I had been contacted by them in that same disguise at the 2018 and 2022 Winter Olympics. They were seeking people with a medical background who could function as translators to a group they had recruited to launch a series of attacks on the United States."

"Who did you deal with in North Korea?"

"Most of the time with Colonel Ho-young, from their Bio-Terrorism Directorate. Only on the first day did we meet Colonel-General Moo-sung."

"We believe Moo-sung is the Minister of State Security,"

said Williams, "and is closely linked to Kim."

"How in the world did you manage to get in and get out?" asked Jones.

"There were times when I didn't think I would get out. But that's a tale for a different day. When I arrived in Pyongyang, there were several translators there who spoke multiple languages. We were all threatened our first day to not communicate with one another, and I think all of us realized the threats were quite real. My task was to translate directions on how to handle anthrax in the field, and I'm supposing the other translators worked on other kinds of threat agents. Once our translations were completed, we were all transported to Vietnam.

"At that point, our North Korean handlers disappeared into the background, so when the twenty-four recruited terrorists arrived, they only dealt directly with us translators."

"So you're implying that the terrorists themselves didn't actually know that North Korea was behind the whole operation?" said Jones.

"Correct. I tried repeatedly to get the other translators to disclose what they were working on, but the threats and intimidation had been enough to convince all of them to keep their mouths shut. We then spent a couple of days basically training the various groups of terrorists how to handle the agent they were to use and telling them how to use them effectively.

"The other translators worked with nineteen recruited terrorists, but I don't know what any of their assignments were. I translated material from Korean to Farsi, and trained five men who had been recruited to perform terrorist acts involving anthrax against the U.S. In my group, two were Iranian and three were from Niger. There were a large number of Hispanics and Africans, plus a couple who looked like Eastern Europeans in the second group. I was attacked by one of the Iranians on the way to the U.S., and was able to kill him and get rid of the body at sea."

"Damn!" came out before Early Johnson could help himself.

Angela stifled a smile. "Apparently, there was another Korean-Arabic speaker who translated the actual plans for distributing the bacteria. Once again, I tried to get that additional information from the terrorists as well as the woman I assumed was that translator, but no one was talking. While I supplied input to create drawings of some of the terrorists after arriving back in the U.S., I really didn't trust my recall on most of them.

"I ended up accompanying the group on a freighter in order to give five of them a second dose of anthrax vaccine, but instead of returning to Vietnam, and perhaps North Korea, I convinced the ship's captain to allow me to go with them when they reached the U.S."

"So they were vaccinated?"

"Sort of. I certainly gave them each an injection, but I'm afraid it consisted of water and a bit of alcohol to mimic the sting of the actual vaccination."

"So they're unprotected?"

"They only received the first injection, and that was before they left Vietnam. It's doubtful that will be enough to protect them once they're exposed to the bacteria. A full anthrax vaccination series consists of five separate injections, followed by an annual booster. They only received a single injection, and that was six months ago. Frankly, I don't think the North Koreans had any intention of really protecting these guys. My impression is that they would be perfectly happy if all of the terrorists died after their anthrax missions were completed.

"I was able to strike up a friendship with the remaining Iranian, and went with him and the men from Niger when they stole a car. They put me out of the car at the first town we came to after leaving the beach in California. I asked the Iranian when we could meet again, and he referred to a paper he was carrying, then told me to meet him in Memphis on May 19th."

"That's next weekend."

"Correct. But that's the only clue I've got as to anyone's assignment. All these other attacks may or may not be connected. I was able to identify the Hispanic who was taken into custody after initiating the foot and mouth disease attack in Kansas. But none of the other security photos or the fellow who was injured in an attack on a chemical plant in New York were recognizable."

"Minus the Iranian you got rid of, how many were in the group who actually landed in California?"

"Twenty-three."

"You don't have any idea where their assignments were to

take place?"

"None. I can only verify that the majority of them were Hispanic. I can't break that down into their actual country of origin, except to say I'm sure they weren't all from one country. They argued frequently about which form of government was superior. I can only speculate, but I got the impression that there were people from Mexico, Central America, Cuba, and maybe Venezuela. All were men except for two women. I did see three of them with tattoos which would indicate membership in MS-13. But I'd also bet the four men I was in a car with, as well as the Somalis, had all been radicalized."

"So these sightings of left-behind evidence from various bombings, fires, and food poisonings could very well be from this group."

"I can't say with any certainty. But it doesn't seem plausible that all these things are happening within a few months of them arriving in our country."

"Now, ladies and gentlemen," said Abel Adams, "like it or not, we are part of a huge drama here. As I see it, the real crux of our dilemma is our polarized political environment. Given that environment, what do we think happens if we share this information with our political appointees, the House and Senate Foreign Relations Committees, and the White House?"

"Unfortunately, there is a second dilemma, Secretary Adams," said Williams. "What do we think happens to us if we fail to share this information?"

"I've been thinking a lot about that," said Adams. "I keep going back to the bigger question of what are the possible actions our government will take as a result of receiving this information. Although it's true that we can't begin to know what the reaction will be, I'm worried that it will be a knee-jerk response, rather than one which keeps us out of a shooting war. After all, we've got an election in just under six months, and we can always expect a certain amount of posturing—by everybody in positions of authority. It's happened before, and it will undoubtedly happen again.

"Additionally, if our nation takes violent action against North Korea, or even announces our knowledge of their link to the attacks, might we lose any opportunity to find and get rid of the terrorists? They may simply go underground and wait for us to drop our guard.

"According to Dr. Martinelli, we may have an opportunity to take this remaining Iranian into custody in Memphis. Unless he launches an attack before that, we will have stopped at least that threat. But if we go to the politicians, an unknown or unexpected response may overtake us, the press may be drawn in, the Iranian could get spooked, and then he might bide his time to spread his anthrax another day, at a time and place completely unknown to us. Additionally, we need him to lead us to the three men from Niger. They also may have a similar plan in the near future."

That response raised the discomfort level in the room, as if the air conditioning had suddenly quit.

"But Secretary, what if we fail to apprehend the Iranian? What if he's already accomplished his mission? What if he has no idea where or when the Africans will strike? What if they've already separated from one another?"

"So how many targets can there be in Memphis?" said Adams, rather than respond to Williams' questions directly. There's the Civil Rights Museum and Beale Street and the Elvis Presley Mansion. The NBA playoffs are underway, but Memphis doesn't have a team in the mix this year, hence no crowds around their arena."

Early glanced up from a quick check of the internet. "There was a big music festival in Memphis last weekend, but it's over. There's some kind of barbecue contest there next weekend, but how big could that be?"

Secretary Adams laughed. "You obviously haven't been to Memphis. I'm from North Carolina, and we get pretty riled up over our barbecue. But in Memphis, barbecue is considered to be one of the basic food groups. They get into fights over which is better, wet or dry ribs."

"*Dry?*"

"For dry rub. No sauce."

"Huh. So maybe we need to look into that contest and see if it's big enough to be a target.."

"Trust me, it is. But let's get back to the big question. What do we tell our directors?" Williams turned to Lynn Jones. "Or what do you tell the attorney general?"

Adams nodded at Angela. "So these portrait sketches, do they include the Iranian and the three guys from Niger?"

"Yes, sir. I spent far more time with them than I did the others. I'm confident that at least those four are pretty accurate."

Adams turned to his counterpart from the FBI. "Lynn, what if you put ten agents on that barbecue event, equipped with the four sketches?"

"I could pull a couple of portable bio-detection devices for us to place at various locations in the area," added Early. "Of course, they won't give us a specific identity of a biologic agent, but at least we'll be warned that something has been released. We can also pre-identify a lab in the city which is equipped to handle anthrax, then we can perform any testing needed in the shortest time possible."

"I've got a couple of questions," said Jones. "How big is the crowd? Is the event only during the daytime, or are we also searching after dark? Will they use a disguise? Will they recognize Dr. Martinelli? But if she's not there, can we recognize them? Are we looking for a group, or just singles? What do we do if we only identify one of them, arrest him and perhaps alert the others, or do we just tail him? And finally, are they armed? Do you want a shootout in the middle of a large crowd of people?"

"Damn, Lynn! That's what I get for asking an operations guy an operations question. What do you suggest?"

"I've got three to go before I hit my thirty-year retirement. But I'm afraid if we go through with your suggestion to keep the principals in the dark, I'll never get there. And I might not be able to find gainful employment in this town ever again."

Adams nodded. "Tomorrow is Wednesday. What if we gather the two secretaries and the AG together in this room tomorrow afternoon, tell them what we know, that there is a chance we can stop the whole thing this weekend, and tell them we're worried about what the response might be if it goes any further."

Jones looked at SAIC Michael Seward for agreement, while Bob Williams did the same with Angela Martinelli, and Adams shot a look at Early Johnson. The shrugs and the nodding seemed to agree 'that's about all we can hope for,' and they proceeded with their plan.

⚛

Despite all the political intrigue in Pyongyang, the fat man spent a great deal of time thinking about his mountain cabin in Sep'o County; or more specifically, about Hiroko. The young Japanese girl managed to intrude on his thoughts four or five times a day.

Did he love his wife, Ri Sol-ju, who had borne him three female children? Although she was admittedly an attractive woman, if honest with himself, he would probably have replied perhaps or it depends. In truth, he could go for days on end without his spouse even entering his mind. Her failing to provide him with a male heir was very important, but she also no longer emotionally touched him. In fact, after a parade of a few hundred interludes with his pleasure squad, he no longer yearned for his wife at all.

There was no logical reason for him to visit the cabin retreat, but he was compelled to see Hiroko, look at her, talk to her, and simply be in her presence. It made no sense. Then again, it seemed like the most sensible thing he could possibly do.

After arriving at the cabin in mid-afternoon, he promised himself he would simply spend enough time there to see the girl for a brief period, then return to the capital that night. His schedule did not work out.

She kept him waiting for two hours, with the excuse that she had to prepare herself for their meeting. The longer he waited, the more convinced he became that the delay was because she was carefully readying herself for his visit. Perhaps this time would be the time. He caught himself licking his lips.

In order to adequately prepare himself, he asked the auntie for a bowl of shark fin soup, and he began to drink the first of several glasses of snake wine. The wine bottle contained the entire coiled body of a dead cobra. Both snake wine and shark fin were known to be of great benefit to male virility. By the time she arrived in his rooms, he'd had far too much to drink, perhaps because he wished to be fully prepared for the evening, or maybe it was simply due to his nervous anticipation. The delay was worth the wait, at least at first.

She entered wearing a sheer red blouse which she had tied in a knot above her small waist, very snug black leggings, and high-heeled sandals. Her hair was again tied up in a French braid. For the first time in his memory, he was unable to trust his voice.

The silence continued until it became embarrassing. After all, he was the chairman of all North Korea. Millions of people loved and revered him. His senior leaders all confirmed it. And yet this mere girl had taken his tongue.

Finally he cleared his throat. "You appear to be doing very well."

"I would do better in my own country with my family."

"Here you have everything you could possibly want. How could your fishing village compare with this?"

"Family and friends are the most important things in life. Clothing and jewelry are all temporary, and they certainly do not love you back."

"Spoken wisely. But perhaps love and affection are nearer than you think. They are within your grasp. All you have to do is wish it so."

"I was raised to believe that one must be free in order to make good decisions. Without freedom, one is likely to make choices only because they believe they truly have no choice."

"I hope you realize that I am trying to give you opportunities which most girls would appreciate."

"I understand very well what you are offering, as well as what you expect in return."

"Do you also understand the restraint I have exercised up to this point?"

"I think I do. My question to you is, am I worth your restraint, or will you treat me like so many who have gone before me?"

Chapter 31

The Peabody Ducks
Memphis, Tennessee May 18, 2024

Xerxes Abbasi drove the stolen Hyundai Tucson across the Mississippi River, heading west on I-40, then north for some fifteen miles on 1-55, until he reached the exit for the small private airstrip just outside Parkin, Arkansas. Two planes were parked in front of the hangar, but his attention was drawn to the one with an outsized wingspan.

The man who emerged from the office owned a head of snow-white hair, but from his brisk stride, still appeared to be in good physical condition. Xerxes noticed the small automatic pistol in a holster anchored on his belt, just above his right rear pants pocket. The old fellow nonchalantly hooked his right thumb over his belt just in front of the holster flap. He looked to be the sort who knew perfectly well how to quickly draw and fire his weapon.

"What can I do for you?"

Xerxes' English skills had improved over the last twenty-odd weeks, and he managed to throw in a hint of Spanish when he spoke, but he still struggled to understand, particularly the perplexing drawl of these Southerners. "My boss have peanuts—eighty acres—want it sprayed."

"Where's his place?"

"You got map?"

The fellow motioned for Xerxes to follow him into the office, where he pulled out a book of satellite maps for eastern Arkansas. The man looked up from the map, realizing he had forgotten his manners, despite the looks of this new customer. He extended his hand. "Van Cooper."

Xerxes used the name on his identification materials. "Miguel Cruz." He stared at the map for a few minutes until he located the spot he had discovered earlier that afternoon. It was actually planted in soybeans, but that would make no difference in what was about to happen. He pointed to a particular plot and said, "Brian Black." At least, that was the name he'd seen printed on the roadside mailbox in front of the property in question.

Cooper looked at the map and wrote down the coordinates. "When does your boss want this sprayed?"

"Quick, quick. White mold mucho bad. He say best spray at night."

"He's right about spraying after the sun goes down." Cooper glanced at his watch. "It's only about ten miles from here. I'll have to go look at it first. See what obstacles are in the way. Map out how I want to tackle it."

"Tackle?"

"Figure out the best way to spray the property without killin' myself."

"Can I see plane?"

"Sure. Come on, I'll show you." They strolled out to the bigger of the two planes. He was obviously proud of it. "This is a Model 660 Turbo Thrush. At twenty feet off the deck," he pointed to the steel nozzles under the wings, "this baby can spray four hundred square feet per second. If you've got more fungus in part of the field, it has a variable spray rate to accommodate that.

"Here's another advantage. No more scrambling out there on top of the fuselage." He indicated an opening which was reachable just behind the cockpit. "You just fill the spray tank up from here."

When Cooper climbed down, he waved Xerxes toward the office. "Come back in and we can fill out the paperwork. I'll have to ask for payment up front, since I don't know Mr. Black."

"Not problem. I got cash."

When Cooper sat down behind his computer, he was surprised when he looked up to see a snub-nosed .38 revolver pointed at his head. "Take off belt. No touch pistol." He waggled the revolver at Cooper. "Your phone." After he had collected everything he gestured for the man to sit back in his chair.

Cooper wondered briefly if he would see his family again, at least until Xerxes tied him securely to his chair, jerked the cord from the back of his office phone and the keyboard from the computer, breaking the plastic clips of the connection, before turning to the old man. "No worry about plane. I fly good."

⚛

The Memphis in May World Championship Barbecue Cooking Contest draws at least 100,000 people to the celebration on the bank of the Mississippi River. Every year, the festival is held at the thirty-acre Tom Lee Park downtown, on the east bank of the river. The park was named after a black boatman who, in 1925, rescued 32 people from a steamboat wreck on the Mississippi in his small skiff—despite not being able to swim himself.

Two hundred and fifty barbecue cookers filled the park, preparing their most competitive offerings. Some of the booths were elaborate, complete with costumes for the cooks and skits to attract crowds to their operation. The contest claimed it crowned the best of the best barbecue in the nation. The event typically ran Friday, Saturday, and Sunday; however, the weather forecast included a 70% chance of rain for the second day. While the cooking would continue despite the weather, the crowds would undoubtedly thin considerably.

At 7:15 PM on Friday, the temperature was a balmy 75 degrees and the wind blew from the southwest, directly across the river and into the Festival at just under ten miles per hour. Old weather-watchers would say they could smell a storm coming. However, it was unlikely that such a scent could be detected at that particular time and place, as the olfactory impact of over five hundred braised and glazed pork shoulders overwhelmed the senses.

As the huge crowd gathered in front of the main stage for entertainment and a preliminary VIP recognition ceremony at 7:30, the din all but drowned out the approach of a revving engine. Finally the crowd turned its collective attention toward the river as a small plane streaked down the waterway at 130 miles an hour, no more than twenty feet above the water's surface. It towed a large advertising banner, which proclaimed *Mayor Castle Eats Quiche! Sean McCreave is a BarBQ*

Man. Vote for McCreave!

The crowd laughed and pointed their cell phone cameras at the spectacle. It was widely acknowledged that candidate Castle possessed a long-standing appreciation for frilly food. As the plane passed by the main stage, it rolled on to its right side for about five seconds, before righting itself and proceeding down the river toward Presidents Island.

Perhaps only Angela Martinelli and Early Johnson noticed the crop duster's ten brass spray nozzles, which extended some eight inches below the over-sized wings. Angela wanted to draw her concealed pistol, but realized she had no hope of a successful shot, let alone any proof that a biological agent was being released.

On board the crop duster, Xerxes was fervently praying his vaccinations would protect him. He had certainly gotten a snoot full of the agent when he filled the spray tank. It was only after the fact that he began to wonder if his potential payday was worth the risk.

As Angela looked over the crowd, seeking Early's face, people began to laugh once again. The plane had returned for one more pass, this time turning on its left side, before heading back upstream in the direction from which it had come.

The pilot kept the little plane close to the water's surface, even flying underneath the Hernando Desoto Bridge to avoid detection by area radar. The plane continued north, straddling the middle of the river channel for four miles, before making an abrupt right turn—all at extremely low altitude. Within three minutes, Xerxes was on a glide path to the runway at the private DeWitt Spain Airport, which was unmanned after three PM on Fridays. He landed just as the light was disappearing in the western sky and walked casually into a nearby neighborhood, looking for a convenient car to steal as soon as it was completely dark. Van Cooper would not get his plane back anytime soon, as it would not only be tied up as part of the crime scene, but would also require significant detoxification.

Back at the barbecue contest, the crowd had no idea that two hundred grams of anthrax was contained in the totally scent-free and almost invisible gray cloud which had been released in their direction with each pass of the crop duster. They continued their celebrating as the light to moderate wind propelled those invisible particles into their mouths and nasal passages, eventually reaching the alveoli of their lungs, where they began their evil work.

When Angela finally found Early thirty minutes later, he was on the phone. She tried to keep the urgency out of her voice, but only partly succeeded. "Both of the portable bio-sensors I brought with me have alerted, Secretary Adams. I'll pull their filters and make sure they get to the St. Jude Hospital's lab immediately. They said it would take about twelve to fourteen hours after they receive the samples for us to get verification."

He stuck the phone back on his hip and rubbed his forehead. "You were right."

"I certainly didn't expect to see a crop duster doing the dirty work." She shot Early a worried look that bordered on frantic. Even for highly trained agents, dealing with reality ramped up the tension by an order of magnitude over practice runs. "I've been vaccinated. How about you?"

Early involuntarily shuddered when he thought about the possible danger. "Part of my job description at DHS. I just got my annual booster last month."

"We should both take a round of antibiotics, just to be sure we're covered."

"Agreed. Did you have a chance to recognize the pilot?"

"No, the plane turned on its side and the cabin wasn't visible on either pass."

Early shook his head. "I thought this was supposed to happen tomorrow."

"Me too. Maybe he decided to go a day early because of the rain forecast for tomorrow."

"Adams is calling the mayor and the governor as soon as he talks to our secretary. Given that this whole area is probably covered with a biological agent, they'll need to cancel the rest of this festival."

"We'll need to call the CDC to get antibiotics headed this way. There must be at least seventy or eighty thousand folks out here this evening, and that doesn't count the people who live immediately downwind up on the river bluff. The city is going to need a tremendous amount of assistance to dispense antibiotics to everybody at risk."

"If it's really anthrax," Early said, "everybody who's exposed will need to get treated within seventy-two hours, so once the word gets out, there's going to be a lot of panicked people."

"I'll bet quite a few of them are from out of town."

"Yeah, we'll have to make sure the media goes on a blitz campaign so nobody fails to get the warning."

Another thought struck Angela. "Just make sure nothing gets out to the public until after ten AM tomorrow. That's when the Iranian is supposed to contact me. If he finds out we already know what happened, he may get spooked and not show up."

"Yikes! I'll call Adams back right now."

⚛

"Governor Reese and Mayor Castle, thank you for taking this telephone call. I'm Assistant Secretary Abel Adams from Homeland Security in Washington. Everything we discuss on this call must be considered as top secret at this point, as I'll explain. As we discussed from a theoretical standpoint yesterday, we now believe the barbeque contest in Memphis has just experienced a terrorist attack with a biological weapon."

"Are you sure? I've heard nothing."

"Mr. Mayor, right now nobody is aware that there has been an attack, but my agent on the ground is reporting a hit on his two biological sensors. He's reasonably sure much of the crowd was exposed when a crop duster flew by the event just about forty-five minutes ago. We're waiting on identification of the specific biological agent right now, and have been told by the lab folks at St. Jude that they'll have verification sometime before noon tomorrow. If what we think is true, you'll need to set up multiple treatment sites to accommodate everybody who was exposed tonight."

"Do you have people who can advise on that, Secretary Adams?"

"Yes, but we have an additional problem. An undercover agent is supposed to meet with the terrorist tomorrow morning at ten o'clock. If that happens, maybe we can stop any future attacks at other sites—and we're depending on the terrorist to disclose those locations to us tomorrow. Therefore, we need complete media silence on this attack until then."

"That's impossible."

"Mayor Castle, until we get verification from St. Jude, we're only guessing. So why not put all our plans together for the treatment sites, let that meeting occur, get the laboratory's confirmation, and then immediately go to every public and social media venue to tell your citizens to come to a treatment location?"

"Clark," said Governor Jerry Reese, "I think the secretary makes a lot of sense. Mr. Secretary, given that Memphis borders both Arkansas and Mississippi, we should bring Governor Lynn Anderson and Governor Doug Herold in on this, as well as the mayors of West Memphis, Arkansas and both Southaven and Olive Branch, Mississippi. My office can contact them if that will free you up. Now, what can we do to get things moving?"

"Let's put a call together for ten PM your time, sir. We'll include your fellow governors as well as the mayors. I suggest the local emergency managers, fire chiefs, police chiefs, and health department directors be on that call as well. Given the different authorities involved, may I suggest setting up a joint command center in downtown Memphis? All of us are going to get a great lesson in collaboration before this is over. Everyone will have a tremendous amount of work to do in the next seventy-two hours. Remember, this is top secret. No external discussions before this is announced to the media."

He was having a hard time keeping his name straight. Between the fever, the beatings, and the lack of food, he was terrifically disoriented. He'd been hit in the head so much that his ears rang continuously. It had been his intention to only use Pak Dong-woo, the alias he had used previously in his forays into North Korea. At least he possessed a believable background for that name, but he was afraid during his torture sessions, he may have gotten mixed up and used the name of the dead DPRK corporal, Shin Soo-gun, or even worse, perhaps his own Daniel Won-shik.

Otherwise, why would they continue to beat the hell out of him? There were 3,000 successful escapes each year from North Korea by way of China. Between the Chinese border authorities, the DPRK Security Service, North Korean civilians who ratted out their neighbors, and lowdown "facilitators" in China who took the escapees' money and then sold them out, the number of those caught was completely unknown to the outside world. Surely they didn't apply this level of abuse to each one of them.

His leg was obviously infected, but he had only seen a medic. No physician was apparently available. The medic had administered two injections of what was supposed to be an antibiotic. All they had done otherwise for his injury was wrap it with a pressure bandage, and that was accomplished by a guard with no training, let alone a shred of human decency. Daniel had looked at it several times since. The upper leg was swollen, and the exit wound was seeping pus. But now the swelling and redness extended down toward his ankle. In fact, the interrogators were quite expert at striking the area of the gunshot wound with a baton every time he failed to answer a question the way they wanted.

He'd been taken to the Kaechon Prison, officially known as Re-Education Camp #1, the first night of his captivity. He'd been placed in a room with around eighty other inmates, all of whom were skeletal in appearance, despite being fed three times a day. Unfortunately, the meals only consisted of about a hundred grams of moldy cracked corn, a small bowl of tepid salt soup, and a tin cupful of cloudy water. He'd dislodged two fillings in his teeth trying to chew the corn.

All eighty men in the cell utilized a dozen common buckets as their toilet, which were emptied every evening. There was no running water in the cell—either to wash their hands or to drink.

The buckets stank. The rags they wore stank and were crawling with fleas. Daniel's wound had a rancid odor to it. At least half of the men had dysentery, which made its own contribution to the cell's miasma. At least a dozen prisoners in his cell were missing portions of their fingers, toes, and ears due to frostbite during the frigid winters. His formerly chubby body was nowhere to be found. In two weeks he had lost at least thirty pounds, and now looked just as malnourished as his fellow prisoners.

He realized no one at Langley would have any idea he was in prison, and it was unlikely they would independently come to that realization any time soon. If he told his captors he was an American, it was doubtful that would accomplish anything other than initiate more enthusiastic beatings, or maybe even a pistol shot to the head. However, he was not sure he could survive much longer anyway if nothing changed.

※

Angela had checked in to the Peabody Hotel, in case Xerxes Abbasi was staying there in preparation for their reunion the next morning. Early was also there, but they took the precaution of keeping their distance in and around the hotel, in case Xerxes happened to be in the area.

At nine o'clock on Saturday morning, Angela made her way to the lobby. She was quick to note that Early Johnson was sitting at a table in the corner, along with a tall and very fetching FBI agent, Sara Wood. Angela knew this was Agent Wood's first field assignment, and she fervently hoped circumstances would not require the young woman to act.

The Grand Lobby of the Peabody Hotel was ostentatious yet classy, as might be expected of one of the truly great hotels in the South. The huge room extended to two stories, with massive square pillars which supported the hand-carved, intricate woodwork on the ceiling. There were two very large crystal chandeliers overhanging elegant leather chairs which surrounded small tables. But the centerpiece of the lobby was the huge Italian marble fountain with its cherub statuary, and leading from the fountain to a nearby elevator was a carpet of brilliant scarlet.

The lobby was already filling with onlookers, all waiting for the morning festivities. Angela found a place with her back against one of the front windows. Her view of the central fountain was limited due to the standing room only crowd, but her primary mission was to find Xerxes, not watch the morning parade.

At ten AM on the dot, the official Peabody Duck Master exited the elevator to the tune of John Philip Sousa's *King Cotton March*. He carried a gold-handled cane, and was dressed in a bright red coat with gold buttons and epaulets, from every angle looking like a circus ringmaster. He followed dutifully along behind five full-grown mallards, one drake and four hens. Children on their knees lined the sides of the carpet, while adults, both old and not so old, hovered above them. Despite the crowd and the hundreds of camera flashes, the ducks were completely oblivious to their surroundings and their celebrity status, waddling straight down the red carpet per the Duck Master's direction, and then hopping into the elaborate hotel fountain, where they began to happily swim and ruffle their feathers.

There was much clapping and laughing among the

guests, and Angela noticed an olive-complexioned man headed toward her. He wore khaki slacks, a red and blue Ole Miss sweatshirt, sandals, and an old Colonel Rebel ball cap. The fellow sported a trimmed black beard, along with a pair of thick-lensed black horn-rimmed glasses. He reached for the empty chair on her right and sat down. She started to say that she was waiting for someone when the man whispered in Farsi, "Nurse Lajani, I didn't know whether you would keep our date, or if you might have given up on me and gone back to your home in Iran."

Angela's brain quickly turned a switch and she responded in his language. "Xerxes, I didn't recognize you. Where in the world did you find those birth-control glasses?"

He looked puzzled. "Birth-control?"

She snickered. "They call them birth-control glasses because nobody would have sex with someone who wears them."

He laughed out loud, despite trying to avoid attention, then glanced around at the surrounding crowd. The tourists had begun to mill about, taking more pictures of the now placidly swimming ducks, as well as the Duck Master.

"Where are your friends from Niger?"

"I have no idea. We separated the night you left us."

Angela took a deep breath. "Do you know where they were going?"

"We didn't share our mission destinations."

"How is your assignment going?"

"One down and one to go."

"Is the second one here?"

"No, the first one was here. The second is in some place called the Mall of America. It was actually Javad's mission, but I suppose it now falls to me."

"What will you do there?"

"It should be very simple. All I have to do is spray the trees, bushes, and flowers in the children's play areas."

She had a pained look on her face. "How does that make you feel, targeting children, I mean?"

"Probably the same way the American pilots felt when they bombed hospitals and schools in Iraq, Afghanistan, and Syria—nothing. I will feel nothing at all."

She badly wanted to debate his statement about American pilots targeting children by reminding him of al Qaeda and ISIS blowing up buses and markets in Iraq and Afghanistan, as well as entire apartments and hospitals in Syria, all of which included so many deaths of children. However, she was sidetracked by a low voice from the table to her immediate left.

"Nurse Lajani, we meet again." The voice spoke Korean.

She avoided jerking her head to one side, was able to muster a smile, and turned to the voice. His disguise was complete, as he had dressed as a Muslim woman, including the niqab covering. She had to lean closer for a few seconds to recognize him. "Good morning, Colonel Ho-young."

"Please don't use that name. What have you done to Xerxes Abbasi? And please tell me why you are here?"

She realized the colonel had either not recognized her companion, or perhaps had never seen him before, and turned to block Ho-young's view of her tablemate while simultaneously kicking Xerxes' foot. "I'm here to meet him. What are you doing here, Colonel? I thought you were avoiding any chance that your country would be implicated in these attacks."

He silently congratulated himself that he had made contact with his dis-information group in Vietnam that morning and told them he had not been able to find Xerxes, nor could he say for sure if the man was still working for them. He had also asked that his information be passed forward to Colonel-General Moo-sung in Pyongyang. Now if he found Xerxes, it would be interpreted back home as brilliant detective work. "My need to talk to him is more important. I must see him before he initiates his attack today."

"If I see him, I'll be sure to pass your message along. Is there something specific I should tell him about when or where to meet you?"

Ho-young glanced around the room. "This is too public. Come with me and we can better discuss the problem."

They both stood, and Angela was fairly sure she knew what he was reaching for when he slipped his hand into a pocket of his long black gown. She glanced toward Early and caught his eye, before stepping in front of Ho-young and following his gesture toward the elevator."

When the elevator door opened, Angela was painfully aware they were the only two to enter, but just as it began to close, Agent Wood slipped inside, apologizing for their inconvenience. Ho-young started to object, but the door had closed. He punched the tenth floor, while Agent Wood selected eleven.

At their destination, Ho-young and Angela exited, hurrying down the hallway to the left before the elevator door closed behind them, or at least it almost did. Agent Wood stuck her foot in the closing door, waited a few seconds before sticking her head out into the hallway, then slipped out herself.

Ho-young pulled his weapon out of the pocket far enough for Angela to see it when they stopped under an exit sign at the end of the hallway. "Let's have a little discussion, Nurse." He motioned for Angela to enter the stairwell.

When Agent Wood reached the end of the hallway, she could hear voices, but she had no knowledge of Korean, and hesitated before entering.

"Why did you leave the ship in California, Nurse Lajani?"

"Xerxes asked me to go with him. We had become close friends on the voyage."

The colonel scoffed. "Friends—I'll bet. I'm afraid that was a fatal error on your part." He raised his pistol. "We no longer have use for either one of you."

At that moment, Angela could only hope that help was in the hallway, but knew they would not understand the danger she was in. In a loud voice, she switched to English and shouted, "Shooter!"

Agent Wood shoved the door open and led with her Beretta 9mm, squeezing the trigger three times. As the first bullet struck the colonel, he fired his own weapon, before the next two relieved him of his life.

After making sure the still-twitching man was no longer a threat, the FBI agent turned to Angela, who found herself on the floor, propped against the wall. Her pasty skin color was dramatically contrasted by the growing red blotch three inches above her heart.

Agent Wood applied pressure to the wound with her left hand and called for back-up with her right. Despite her youth, her voice was unbelievably calm. "Just hold on, Martinelli. The shot was high. We'll have help here in just a minute. You're going to be all right."

"You've got to stop the other guy, the one with the beard. He's the one spreading anthrax."

Wood made another call, then turned back to her patient. "Early went after him."

Meanwhile, the forecasted rain had arrived and was bucketing down in sheets as Xerxes exited the Peabody. Early tried to stay as close to his departing quarry as he could, although he could only assume that either he or Agent Wood was chasing the true suspect. He couldn't imagine who the other man at the table had been. He tried to call Wood, but she didn't answer. He fumbled with his now wet phone, trying to find his contact with the Memphis Police Department, while still trying to stay close to Xerxes. He gave up on trying to do those two things simultaneously.

Xerxes noticed the man juggling a phone while following him. At the next intersection, he abruptly turned right on Jefferson Avenue. As soon as he was around the corner and out of the view of his pursuer, he kicked his sandals off, pulled the sweatshirt over his head, tossed it to a kid standing under a store awning, and began to run barefoot. By the time Early reached the intersection, the sweatshirt was no longer visible, but a man in a white T-shirt ran through the downpour some fifty yards ahead at a good pace. That seemed to be a fair indication that Early was indeed still tailing the right man.

For once, Early was thankful the Army required both enlisted personnel and officers to annually pass a physical fitness test, regardless of rank or age. So despite his forty years, he was confident of his ability to keep up with the fleeing man. What he did not know was that ISIS also encouraged fitness. It would indeed be a race.

Xerxes was confused. Who was chasing him? Who had Nurse Lajani left with? Why had she alerted him with the kick under the table? He glanced back over his shoulder. Whoever this man was, he could certainly run. Xerxes stretched his legs out and settled into a demanding pace. He knew from experience that he could run at that speed for at least five kilometers. Whether he could keep that up in the rain was up for debate.

Early's phone buzzed and he managed to answer it while continuing to run. "Sara?"

"Yes. You sound out of breath."

"I'm chasing this bearded fellow east on Jefferson Avenue."

"Do you need support?"

"Hell, yes. Call Memphis PD."

"Angela wanted me to tell you the fellow you're chasing is

the Iranian terrorist and he's planning another attack. She says you've got to stop him. Shoot him if you have to."

"Understood. Can I speak to her?"

"Not right now. She'll get back to you."

Early could see his target, now close to a hundred yards ahead, as he passed over a bridge which straddled a large highway. Given the phone call he had just received, he redoubled his efforts to catch up, but frankly made no progress. In the distance, the T-shirted man turned left on North Orleans Street, passing by the stately Victorian mansions before disappearing for good in Morris Park. Early ran on, hoping to spot him, but even with assistance from two squad cars, he had to admit defeat, and they eventually gave up the chase. Early was soaking wet.

"Mr. Mayor, this is Abel Adams again. Once more I need your immediate assistance on a matter of national security."

"Does this have to do with the incident at the barbecue festival last evening?"

"Yes, sir."

"I've prepared a press release. Would you like me to read it to you?"

"If it contains any information whatsoever about a suspect, or about the shootout in the Peabody Hotel this morning, you've got to remove anything related to those items."

"Can you explain why I'm not supposed to tell my citizens what happened in my city?"

"I understand, but the identities of the people involved in the anthrax attack as well as the shooting must be on closehold while our government decides exactly what our response is going to be."

"What then can I say?"

"Just as we discussed last night, we should have verification from St. Jude any minute now. At that point, you pull out all the stops to warn your citizens who were at the festival that they're in grave danger from exposure to anthrax last evening, and you can tell them about the crop duster, but you can't speculate in any way about the guilty party. It would be best if you didn't even refer to the shooting, unless you simply say the identities of the victims and the shooter are unknown at this time."

"Nothing like having your hands tied behind your back."

"Thank you for understanding, Mr. Mayor. You might be

interested to know that I oversee the DHS grants program in Washington. Let me assure you that your *full and complete* cooperation on this matter will benefit your city in a very tangible way in the near future."

"Are you saying—?"

"Let's just leave it at that, Mayor Castle. Thank you very much for your assistance in protecting the security of our country."

※

"Admiral Sheffield, Abel Adams at DHS. Thank you for your quick action in sending antibiotics to Memphis from the National Pharmaceutical Stockpile."

"Actually, that was the simplest thing I've done lately, Mr. Secretary. One of our warehouses for the Stockpile is held in a Fed-Ex hanger at the Memphis airport. All we had to do was load it on an eighteen wheeler and deliver."

"Good to know. Unfortunately, we have good information to indicate there may be three more attacks."

"When and where, Mr. Secretary?"

"We believe one will be near Minneapolis," said Adams, "but don't have any info on the other two. However, we feel our intelligence is completely reliable. I'm sure you'll be making arrangements to replace your antibiotic stock, but I would just encourage you to do that sooner rather than later, and undoubtedly at least twice the amount which you had previously stocked."

"Understood. We've got replacement stock ordered, but will increase that amount per your request. I'd appreciate something in writing so I can use that to obtain the extra funding."

"You'll have it in a few minutes, Admiral. And thank you."

CHAPTER 32

A Piss-ant Country
Memphis, Tennessee May 19, 2024

Memphis newspaper headlines, local, regional, and national television and radio broadcasts, online messaging, and thousands of social media posts published the following:

Anthrax at BarBQ Fest! Friday evening, attendees at the Memphis barbecue contest were attacked by an unknown assailant in a crop duster airplane, using anthrax in its spray apparatus. The presence of anthrax was confirmed overnight by the St. Jude Hospital Laboratory. Every person who attended the festival after 7:00 PM on Friday MUST BE GIVEN ANTIBIOTICS to prevent an anthrax infection, and that treatment must begin within 72 hours of the exposure.

Anthrax spores, when inhaled, can cause high fever, pneumonia, and death in a very high percentage of patients. Although there is a vaccine, it cannot provide immunity in time to prevent illness in this situation. The only way to protect yourself is by taking the correct antibiotic. The free clinics will dispense those antibiotics at no cost to those who were exposed.

Free clinics have been set up at the Memphis Convention Center on Front Street in Memphis, the Landers Center in Southaven, Mississippi on Venture Drive, and the West Memphis Civic Auditorium just south of the I-40/I-55 split. The clinics are open 24 hours a day through Monday evening. Clinics will be run by the Shelby County, Desoto County, and Crittenden County health departments, with assistance from local fire and police departments, the Centers for Disease Control, the

U.S. Public Health Service, The Mississippi-One and Arkansas-One Disaster Medical Assistance Teams, and the Memphis and Desoto County Medical Reserve Corps units.

Memphis BarBQ Contest Canceled! There will be NO ADMITTANCE to Tom Lee Park until further notice.

Tom Lee Park, the nearby area of Riverside Drive, and the condominiums immediately east of the park are contaminated with anthrax. The entire area has been quarantined by law enforcement until a sterilization process can be completed. The Agency for Toxic Substances and Disease Registry, as well as the National Institute of Occupational Safety and Health, estimate a minimum of fourteen days to complete the detoxification. No entry to the area will be permitted during that time frame. Traffic on the south end of Riverside Drive, Front Street, and Main Street will be blocked.

Clothing worn by those attending the BarBQ festival should be assumed to be contaminated. Simple washing will not decontaminate those clothes, and may in fact only spread the contamination. Clothes should be double-bagged in plastic and taken to any one of the free clinics, where large incinerators will be set up.

A few somewhat less supportive social media posts were circulated far beyond the boundaries of Memphis:

How are our local officials sure the anthrax exposure is limited to Tom Lee Park and the condos on Front Street? How far can the wind carry a microscopic anthrax spore? Midtown? East Memphis? Cordova? The wind was blowing from the west. How do we know the entire city hasn't been exposed? We demand answers from our elected officials!

Where did the anthrax come from? Only a few countries have a biological weapon program, let alone the technology and expertise to "weaponize" anthrax. The last time anthrax was used in attacks on the United States, the culprit was found to be a U.S. bio-scientist. Who is guilty this time? Russia? China? Iran? North Korea? Or perhaps us? Then again, was the anthrax handed off to yet another country, or maybe a pack of terrorists?

How long will our leaders do nothing in response to these attacks? Two eyewitnesses who were in Tom Lee Park swear the pilot of the crop duster, which spread anthrax in Memphis, was without question a Hispanic. The owner of the aircraft, which was stolen, says the pilot's name on his identification was Miguel Cruz. And Miguel Cruz GOT AWAY! Do we just sit and wait on him to do it again and again?

There is an anthrax VACCINE, for crying out loud! Why are we not all being vaccinated? Is it a matter of MONEY, Mr. President?

⚛

"Chairman Kim, thank you for taking my call."

"It's good to speak with you, Mr. President." The fat man swallowed. Speaking with Putin wasn't always good.

"I have a couple of concerns which I hope you can help with."

"It would be my pleasure, Mr. President."

"My people have been tracking a dis-information campaign directed at the United States. Do you know anything about such an activity?"

"I have heard similar stories, Mr. President."

"Generally, I would be supportive of a campaign like this. However, in this case it presents a problem."

"How so, Mr. President?"

"Because the entire thrust of the campaign seems to direct the blame for a large number of criminal acts, including the use of biological and chemical agents, toward one of my country's close allies, as well as two other groups which we support with arms and funding."

"I don't understand, Mr. President."

Putin was not a man to show his temper, but this idiot's obvious pretense of not knowing what he was talking about was dangerously close to putting him over the edge. His voice took on a sharp quality, which unfortunately the translator was not able to accurately transmit. "Let me be clear, Chairman. Your amateurish dis-information operations based in Vietnam, Venezuela, and Mexico are implicating Iran, ISIS, and an El Salvadoran gang for your own agents' activities in the United States. Exactly what did you hope to accomplish with this?

"Are you so foolish as to think that China will come to your rescue again? I'm sure Xi is just as sick of you as I am! More to the point, the Chinese went to great trouble to help install the present American administration, and you are now threatening that status. Furthermore, if I know it is you who is responsible for the Vietnam, Venezuela, and Mexico campaigns, as well as the attacks in the U.S, what in the world makes you think the U.S. Cyber Command at Fort Meade doesn't also know you are responsible?"

"But, Mr. President—"

"Don't interrupt me again!" Putin thundered. "I am not the American president, do you hear me? You are not my equal and I will not treat you as such. The second problem is the recent anthrax attack in the U.S. Although they will most assuredly trace it back to you, I would bet they also know we supplied you with a large shipment of anthrax vaccine just six months ago. Your sloppiness in communication security makes that very likely. And that transaction implicates my country, you damned fool!"

"You can't talk to me like—"

"Silence! Because of your actions, both your little kingdom and my country will be even more heavily sanctioned by the United Nations. To prevent that I will have to negotiate with Chairman Xi—*if* I can prevent it. The existing sanctions are stifling enough as it is, and now you have most assuredly put Russia into the same category as your little piss-ant country. It makes me sick to think that Mother Russia will be grouped with Iraq, Syria, and you as countries who will use banned biological and chemical weapons. And for what? To kill a couple of hundred civilians? Idiot!"

The phone line went dead.

At the very thought of repeating that last insult to the Fearless Leader, the Korean translator had turned pale as a ghost.

⚛

Early was happy to find Angela sitting in a chair in her hospital room. "Aren't you supposed to be in bed?"

Angela was surprised she couldn't keep the smile off her face when she saw him. "They want me to be up and around three times a day. I think they'll let me go tomorrow as long as I'm fever free."

Early pulled a sack from behind his back. "I was hoping you'd be feeling better. I thought I'd bring you something to remind you of your recent escapade."

"What have you got there?"

"Genuine Memphis pulled pork barbecue, along with a dose of barbequed beans and slaw."

"Here I was in the middle of a barbecue festival, and I was too pre-occupied to sample the merchandise." She sat up a little straighter. "That sounds a whole lot more appetizing than the tasteless K-rations I've been getting, what they call hospital food."

They sat together, enjoying their lunch. Finally Early could put it off no longer. "We've got surveillance set up at the Mall of America, including several portable bio-detectors. Agent Wood is already there, along with three other agents. So far there's been no sign of Xerxes Abbasi. What concerns some of us is whether or not he could use another disguise and slip by us again." He stood up, fidgeting with his hands. "You're the only person who might recognize him, or maybe his voice. When do you think you might be well enough to travel?"

She looked up at him. "If it was up to me, I'm ready to go today. I want this thing stopped as badly as anyone."

"You wouldn't be running up and down the Mall. What if you were set up in the mall security office to watch the video cameras around the children's play areas? Then if you were suspicious of someone, we could take him into custody long enough for you to get a closer look."

"Will you be going, too?"

"Somebody has to fetch your lunch. Might as well be me."

Social media posts in the Memphis area were not particularly positive over the next couple of days:

No wonder the "free" clinics are free. Stand in line to park. Stand in line to sign up. Stand in line for a one-minute interview. Stand in line to watch a video. Stand in line to get your antibiotic. Stand in a different line if you're pregnant. Stand in a separate line if you're allergic to the antibiotic. Stand in line for the bathroom (be sure not to wait until the last minute). My free visit took over four hours! If your small children were exposed, plan on another line for the liquid form of the antibiotic, as well as another two hours.

The free clinics are only treating people who were at Tom Lee Park, or those who live in the high-dollar condos on the bluff. If you live in the South Memphis area, you get nothing. How did they decide the African-American neighborhoods didn't deserve their services?

Are Our Lives Not Worth An Extra Fifty Bucks? Why are the free clinics handing out the cheapest antibiotic they could find to treat such a deadly infection? Why aren't we receiving ciprofloxacin instead of doxycycline?

Don't waste your time at the free clinics. Just call your doctor and have a prescription called in to your pharmacy.

Is our city being reimbursed for the use of its convention center? Its police officers? Our fire department? The parking garages which are temporarily "free"? Its health department personnel? Who pays for the drugs? Who pays for all the physicians, nurses, and pharmacists in those blue uniforms? Who pays for all the extra security when the president and the governor showed up?

Be grateful for once in your lives. The personnel manning the free clinics are working around the clock to save the lives of Memphians and those who were visiting our city. Try saying thank you instead of posting your usual whining complaints.

The call came into the Memphis NPR radio station just after noon on Monday, and the secretary immediately put her through to the program host. "Am I speaking to Kacky Walton?"

"Yes, Judy. What an honor! What can we do for you in Memphis?"

"Memphis is all over the national news, Kacky, and I understand you were right in the midst of the whole thing on Friday evening."

"I suppose I was, yes, along with about a hundred thousand of my closest friends."

"Would you be willing to be interviewed, live and on air, by me this evening?"

"Of course, but remember that I was only there as a citizen, enjoying the festivities like everybody else. I had no special insight into what was going on."

"A personal story is exactly what we're after. My producer will call you at six PM Eastern time."

⚛

"You've heard from a number of medical experts related to the anthrax attack in Memphis on Friday evening. Now we'd like to talk to someone who experienced the entire thing from beginning to end. In fact, Kacky Walton is a program host with our NPR affiliate in Memphis. Good evening, Kacky. Please tell

us if you are all right."

"I'm doing well, thank you."

"You were actually at the BarBQ event on Friday. Can you describe your experience?"

"The Memphis in May World Championship BarBQ Cooking Contest is one of the biggest events in our city, and we usually have well over a hundred thousand people attending. Just after seven PM on Friday, we were having one of those warm, humid evenings along the river, and everyone noticed a small crop-duster aircraft flying low over the river. It was towing a funny political sign, and it drew a big laugh from the crowd. As it passed us, it turned on its side, then it came by a second time and turned on its side again."

"Could you see or smell anything that might have been sprayed by the plane, Kacky?"

"Not a thing. I don't think anybody realized what had happened at the time. The plane flew off to the north, and we went about our evening. Had it not been for those bio-detectors, we would have had no idea."

"When did you learn what had actually happened?"

"About noon on Saturday, a report came back from a laboratory here at St. Jude Children's Research Hospital, confirming the whole area of the BarBQ Fest was contaminated with anthrax."

"What happened next?"

"The broadcasts on TV, radio, and social media were non-stop. Messages went out from Governors Reese in Tennessee, Anderson in Mississippi, and Herold in Arkansas, as well as all the local mayors. I received at least a half-dozen messages on my phone—all warning people who'd been at the festival that they had to receive antibiotics from one of three treatment sites—one in downtown Memphis, one just across the river in Arkansas, and one about twenty miles south in Mississippi. The announcements stated that we would all need to be treated within seventy-two hours of exposure, or it could be fatal."

"And did you go to one of the clinics?"

"I did. They were all operational on Saturday afternoon. I went to the site in Memphis about ten PM, thinking that there wouldn't be large crowds by then. Wow, was I wrong. I can't estimate how many were there when I arrived, but I'd guess something like ten thousand."

"How long did it take to go through the process?"

"Actually, I looked at my watch when I arrived and when I left, as I thought I might be there all night. I was back in my car in seventy minutes, and was given thirty days of an antibiotic."

"How would you describe the scene at the site?"

"At first, I thought it was chaotic—several people were angry, rude, scared, shouting, or antagonistic. But within a few minutes, the lines started moving. Once they realized they were making progress and would get treated, almost all that chaos stopped."

"This was such a new thing. Did any of the workers seem to know what they were doing?"

"There were obviously volunteers at the site who were trying to learn as they went along, but there was a large number of people in blue uniforms—they said they were from the U.S. Public Health Service—and several of them had actually been at some of the anthrax events back in 2001. In fact, I met one of them—a Captain Rob Tosatto—who had been at five of those responses. He was a great asset, and workers kept coming to him for direction."

"We've heard news reports that some people were very unhappy with their treatment at those clinics."

"I can only speak to my own experience. I found it extremely reassuring."

"Thank you for sharing with us, Kacky. We wish you well."

Chapter 33

The Mall
Minneapolis, Minnesota May 30, 2024

The gigantic Mall of America, located a few miles south of Minneapolis, Minnesota, with 520 retail stores and fifty dining spots, has been a popular shopping destination for over thirty years. There's something awfully appealing about a place where the temperature is always seventy degrees, particularly when compared to a typical Minnesota winter day when the thermometer hovers around seven degrees above zero.

Among the mall's most desirable features are the many places which are kid magnets. Several are free, like Lego Land and Silly Mirrors, and allow the kids to play while the parents sit on the sidelines, sipping their designer coffees. Other sites are expensive, but will certainly entertain children. There's a huge merry-go-round, a Ferris wheel, an arcade, the Sea Life Aquarium, Nickelodeon Universe, Moose Mountain Mini-Golf, Crayola Experience, and the Barbie Dream House.

Many of these areas are landscaped so as to be pleasing to the eye. Flowers are always blooming, and ornamental bushes and trees are scattered everywhere within the mall. In many spots, trees separate the play areas from the retail surroundings.

Of course, all that flora requires care, whether it be replanting, pruning, watering, or fertilizing, so a contracted landscaping crew works inside the mall at least once a week. They're easily identified by their white coveralls with a green and red patch on the front, which reads *Keeping the Mall of America Beautiful.* Their white panel trucks possess the same logo, as well as the contractor's company name, Lake Superior Landscaping.

Every Tuesday is children's day, and all of the play areas are either free or discounted. When the mall opens on Tuesday morning at ten AM, the place is quickly packed with laughing children.

On this Tuesday, Angela Martinelli was in place at the mall's security office, watching video camera feeds from all of the play areas. When she spied five men in white coveralls working in Lego Land, she asked the regular security supervisor about them. His reply was meant to mollify her concerns, but when she saw that two of the landscapers were using backpack sprayers, she asked Early and Agent Wood to escort the five of them to the office so she could get a closer look. All of them were Hispanic.

"Were any of these guys on the ship with you?" Early asked her.

"I don't recognize any of them, but I can't say for certain." She turned to the landscapers. "What is in your sprayers?"

"We fertilize today, miss."

Angela glanced at Early. "Would you spray a sample of both of these on a bio-sensor?" As he left, she turned back to the men. "How long have you been working here?"

The answers varied from three months to four years.

"Are you the only Lake Superior Landscaping employees who work here in the mall?"

"Si." He glanced at the others before adding, "Except the new guy, Miguel Cruz. He say he too sick to come inside today."

"Miguel? How long has he been working with you?"

"Just this week, miss."

"Where is this Miguel?"

"Oh, he sick in our truck."

"Do you mean he's here?"

"Si. He in truck out in parking lot."

Although Angela's left arm was still immobilized with a sling, she and Agent Wood accompanied one of the men from the landscaping company to the parking lot. Wood was worried about Angela's pale appearance, but Angela waved her off.

When they reached the truck, Angela turned to the landscaper. "This Miguel Cruz may be armed and dangerous."

"Oh no, miss. He very calm fellow."

"I want you to walk up to the truck, knock on the door, and call out his name. Then I want you to step back out of our way. Understand?"

"Yes, miss."

He followed her directions to the letter. There was no response from within the panel truck. "If this is Xerxes, and he sees you, there's no telling what he'll do," Angela whispered to Wood, "so stand back at the rear of the truck."

Angela held her pistol in her right hand, tapped on the door with the butt of the grip, and called out in a loud voice, "Xerxes, it's me, Nurse Lajani. Are you sick?"

There was still no response, although she could swear she heard some movement inside the truck. "Xerxes, wake up. It's Nurse Lajani." Still no answer. She tried the handle on the side door. It seemed to be unlocked, but she was unable to manage the door and her weapon with only her right hand. She motioned to Agent Wood to help. "Yank it open in one quick motion. I don't really know if he'll interpret me as friend or foe, so be prepared to shoot."

Wood yanked the door open. A very pale Xerxes Abbasi sprawled in the back seat. He trembled with a fever. Blood splattered the front of his shirt and his chin. He had shaved his bushy beard, gotten a haircut, and dumped the horn-rimmed glasses, but it was still Xerxes.

When he saw the familiar face, he managed a weak smile. "Nurse Lajani, you are Allah's answer to my prayers. I think I have a bad fever, and I can't seem to catch my breath. What is wrong with me?"

"I believe you have pneumonia due to anthrax infection, Xerxes."

"But that can't be. You vaccinated me."

A quick search produced a snub-nosed .38 revolver, identification papers for Miguel Cruz, and an eight-ounce steel container concealed inside his shirt, which Angela did not open.

Steel jewelry bound his wrists and he was taken into custody by the FBI, who escorted his ambulance to a local hospital, which possessed positive pressure rooms where prisoners could be kept in a safe and secure environment. Neither of the backpack sprayers used in the mall contained anything besides fertilizer. However, the steel container which Xerxes had concealed in his shirt was transported to the Minnesota State Laboratory, where it was found to yield concentrated *bacillus anthracis.*

Xerxes died during the night. His body was handled by men dressed in protective clothing, placed in a sealed body bag, and sent directly to a crematorium. There would be no embalming or autopsy. Thousands of children and adults in Minnesota had been saved from the same fate.

※

Early and Angela were finally able to have some time to themselves after the events in Tennessee and Minnesota.

"Angie, I hope you realize that, in all likelihood, you saved thousands of people from death. If you hadn't gotten this Xerxes character to tell you to meet him in Memphis, think of all the folks who were exposed to anthrax, and we wouldn't have known a thing until it was too late to help them."

"Wouldn't the Bio-Watch filter system that's permanently set up in Memphis have alerted to the anthrax?"

"That filter is located seven or eight miles from the Mississippi River, near their football stadium, and so far, that filter still hasn't indicated the presence of anthrax. So without your G-2, there would have been no alert. Then Xerxes told you he was headed to the Mall of America. Just consider how many people—not to mention how many kids—were in that place on Tuesday morning!"

"I guess we were awfully lucky."

"Lucky is one way to look at it. Brilliant work, not to mention bravery, might be another."

"Speaking of bravery, we've still got an agent in North Korea. He volunteered to go over there to find *me* and get *me* out of there. We haven't heard from him since. And don't forget, there are still three men out there with what we believe are two more anthrax missions."

"Did Xerxes give any clues about where those might be?"

"I don't think he had any idea. He claimed they split up right after we landed in California."

"We've circulated the sketches of those three guys to law enforcement from one end of the country to the other. I don't know what else we can do."

"We wait, and we hope somebody sees something, then

has sense enough to report it."

"By the way, how long do you have to wear all those bandages?"

"Another week or so." She smiled slightly. "Why do you ask?"

"Ulterior motives, Dr. Martinelli."

⚛

The mood in the Central Palace was somber, to say the least. Kim Yo-jong had spent much of the last four days sitting with her brother. The phone call with Putin had put him into a state of depression, and he had begun to rely on the numbing benefits of Scotch whiskey literally all day long.

"I can't believe our collaboration with Russia is disintegrating before our eyes. After my meetings with the South Korean leader, plus those with the U.S. president, I thought we had complete control of our destiny. Both Putin and Xi encouraged me to resist any attempts to give up our nuclear program. They agreed that once that happened, we would be at the mercy of the Americans. I was positive that they were thrilled to see the Americans keep on squirming in fear, realizing they had no options to have their own way.

"The South Koreans and Americans were so eager to have a peace agreement, they were willing to believe everything I told them. I think both of them would make any deal in order to be re-elected. That is such a weakness in their so-called democracies. Their politicians spend too much time doing and saying things to get elected, or raising money to get elected, rather than making the decisions which, though correct, might be unpopular. Thank goodness we have no such failings in the Fatherland."

"Did you have an opportunity to discuss a merging of Korean currencies?" his sister asked.

"Only a short discussion with the South Korean president. He was intrigued, but it will definitely take more manipulation on my part. Our won is worth eighty-four percent of the South Korean won. If we can get agreement to making them equal, we'll just print another couple of billion worth of ours and pocket the difference."

"Was Putin really so negative about our information warfare operations?"

"I think his anger was based upon how his own intelligence service had easily discovered what we were doing. Thus, if they uncovered the operations, then he assumed the Americans would know also."

"I recently spoke to a representative of the Namibian government who offered to set up a cyber-attack site in their country on our behalf."

"At what cost, sister dear?"

"That we would continue to supply them with weaponry, mostly anti-tank weapons and mines. Certain factions in their military continue to believe South Africa is their mortal enemy."

"As long as we can remain a silent partner, I see no problem with that."

"I'll put a plan together for your consideration. Now, what about our nuclear program?"

"The test site we destroyed was beyond repair anyway. We'll reluctantly hand it over to the United Nations inspection team after a suitable delay. In the meantime, we've already moved the majority of our missile stockpile operation to six locations further to the north, near our wonderful ski resort. We've been working on developing an underground capability there for almost five years. Besides, General Moo-sung assures me we have no more need for nuclear testing. Our engineers have perfected the systems to launch and target our intercontinental missiles.

"The Americans have no idea how much plutonium 239 and uranium 235 we have. Their estimates are all over the map, from enough for ten warheads to enough for a hundred."

"How much do we really have?"

"The general says enough for fifty-four uranium and twenty plutonium warheads. We've left fifteen of the first and five of the latter divided among the three storage facilities which we believe they already know about. We'll delay for a while, but eventually, after more negotiations and considerable economic relief from the Americans, we'll turn all twenty of those weapons over to the United Nations, as well as their storage sites.

"The Americans keep saying they want us to turn over sixty to seventy percent of our warheads as a condition of removing all the sanctions. Of course, they don't know how many we have to begin with, so it's up to us to convince them that we only have thirty. They're so anxious to sign an agreement which they can wave in front of their voters, I think they'll believe whatever we tell them, or at least they'll act like they believe it."

"Remember what our father said, brother. If you want a deal badly enough, then that's what you will get, a bad deal."

"I remember, sister dear. However, to placate Russia and China, maybe we should continue to put them off and just concentrate on an agreement with South Korea."

"What will you do with the remaining warheads?"

"They've already been relocated to six secret sites in Hamgyong-Bukto and Yanggang-Do provinces near the border with Russia. Thirty-nine of them are mounted on intermediate and long-range missiles, all of which are targeted at South Korea, Japan, and the United States. The seven intermediate-range weapons are all mounted on mobile trucks and can easily be moved around like so many chess pieces.

"The thirty-two aimed at the United States are all in fixed positions. No matter, all of them can be unleashed in a matter of ninety seconds, according to General Byung-soo.

"All our efforts in the future will be to use the twelve hundred gas centrifuges the Americans don't know about to enrich our stockpile of uranium 235, with a goal of possessing enough for a total of one hundred warheads within three years."

"Why are we focusing only on uranium?"

"The production of weapons-grade plutonium creates a great deal of heat, which the Russians warn can be detected by American satellites. Weapons-grade uranium enrichment is much more difficult to identify because it lacks that dramatic heat signature."

"How many sites are involved?"

The fat man laughed. "We have fifty-five sites spread around our country. General Byung-soo believes the Americans know the location of no more than twenty of them. Whenever we finally admit a U.N. inspection team, we'll only show them what they know about. The remaining sites we will use like a shell game, moving our assets from one location to another."

"How much space does all that nuclear material occupy, brother?"

"Both final products are extremely dense. The amount of plutonium required for a medium-sized warhead is between six and eight kilograms, and that is compressed into about the size of a softball. The uranium required for a weapon of similar potency is twenty kilograms, about the size of a liter of water. And by a medium-sized warhead, I mean weapons approximately double in potency to the atomic bomb which was dropped on Nagasaki during World War II."

"Much smaller in size than I thought, brother. How many people are working on our nuclear program?"

"Three hundred scientists and some ten thousand support staff. We'll make a great show of getting rid of half of those personnel for the Americans."

"Have you heard anything from Colonel Ho-young regarding his assignment in the United States?"

"A message from him was passed along through Vietnam. There was no word as to whether he was able to contact the Syrian in Minneapolis and give him instructions as to where our bombs should be located. However, as of the nineteenth of May, he was unable to contact any of the agents who were carrying anthrax."

"And yet at least one of them used anthrax in this place called Memphis on the eighteenth."

"Yes, and somehow the Americans knew what had happened by the next day. They started treating everybody who'd been exposed. The American media, jackals though they are, have only reported less than forty deaths as a result. I think that was one reason Putin was so angry. So much put at risk for so little result."

She looked at her brother, understanding full well his shortcomings. "Has there been news from Ho-young since then?"

"Nothing at all. He apparently knows the date and location of two more anthrax attacks, so perhaps he is remaining silent until that is resolved. His successful mission to relocate our bombs, however, is the most important of all our immediate plans. Beyond that, if he expects to have a healthy return to this country, he had better produce results related to the anthrax attacks. He may be afraid to contact us and admit any failures. I only hope he hasn't been captured and interrogated by their CIA. He knows far too much. In fact, his capture might be the explanation for why the Americans were immediately able to respond to our first anthrax attack."

"What of the other attacks?"

"Ho-young is supposed to intercept those agents before they're able to carry out their missions."

"Let us hope that is the case. I can't imagine what the American reaction might be if they're attacked three more times with a biological agent. What do you think they will do?"

"Not so much what the Americans will do. The bigger question is what will Putin do?" The fat man finished another large tumbler of Scotch. "And will he encourage President Xi in China to follow his lead? We could end up as a pariah rather than a hero."

❈

The South Korean Unification Minister told his parliament: *Our estimate on the size of North Korea's nuclear arsenal range from twenty bombs to as many as sixty.*

After much consultation, nuclear physicists based in the United States generated the following statement: *We estimate North Korea's weaponized plutonium at fifty kilograms—enough for eight bombs—and their highly enriched uranium at 250 to 500 kilograms—sufficient for twenty-five to thirty bombs.*

❈

Daniel Won-shik, a.k.a. Pak Dong-woo, vaguely remembered the trek from his large cell to the tiny interrogation room earlier that morning. Just in that short walk he had passed three corpses laid out in the corridor, waiting to be hauled off. He had no idea what had been the actual cause of death, but resigned himself to a similar outcome.

He'd been asked over and over again who helped him in his escape. He could only reply that no one had. That he had no family in the country. That he had spoken to no one about his intention to flee. That nobody was waiting for him in China. These answers, however, they refused to believe.

He tried to respond to his interrogator, but realized he could no longer hear a word the man said. That day he had been beaten simultaneously on both sides of his head with two cloth bags which held dried beans. Too many times he had been struck on or about his ears, and as a result, both eardrums had finally blown out. It was extremely painful, as well as disorienting.

Sadly, the more he failed to answer the questions posed, the more he was beaten, and hence the more severe the damage to his hearing. He tried to tell them he was now deaf, but there was no let-up in the punishment. He finally decided they were doing it solely to entertain themselves.

Chapter 34

The Music Man
Manchester, Tennessee June 10, 2024

The Bonaroo Music and Arts Festival takes place on a large farm some sixty miles south of Nashville, Tennessee, near the small town of Manchester. The event's humble beginnings no longer apply, as it currently attracts well over 100,000 rabid music fans, and offers 150 different entertainers on ten separate stages over a four-day span in early June. In addition to the music, vendors with food, arts, and crafts offer their wares from food trucks and exhibit booths.

Most attendees stay on the grounds in motor homes and campers, or they rent tents of various sizes from the organizer. The festival takes special care to warn attendees about staying hydrated, using sunscreen, avoiding drugs, and limiting their intake of alcohol. None of those warnings would prove to be particularly important this year.

Several of the vendors offered crafts which coincided with their particular culture. Among them were basket weavers from coastal North Carolina, a duck decoy carver from Arkansas, a potter from Mound Bayou, Mississippi, several oil painters, and three black gentlemen selling a huge collection of records and memorabilia from the most famous recording artists of all time. All three sported an impressive six-month growth of facial hair to accompany their thin six-foot-four-inch frames. The banner above their exhibit proclaimed *The Music Man*.

By eleven o'clock in the morning, the temperature was already rising toward ninety degrees. 'Hot as Alabama's armpit' was heard from the crowd. The booths were almost universally 10x10 tents, with the front open to the parade of attendees. A few of the more insightful vendors had paid extra for an electrical connection, offering the temporary relief of large fans. This was true of The Music Man booth, where they also blasted a steady diet of musical hits from the 1960s to the present day. Not surprising, the electric fans were a big hit.

Besides a huge offering of albums, 45s, and CDs from the likes of Elvis Presley, Michael Jackson, The Beatles, The Beach Boys, Queen, The Rolling Stones, The Allman Brothers, Lynyrd Skynyrd, and The Grateful Dead, the booth showcased unbelievably rare and valuable items for sale. There were signed albums from at least twenty artists; a signed white scarf worn by Elvis during his last performance in Las Vegas; an eight-inch-long plastic replica of a yellow submarine signed by all four Beatles; Freddie Mercury's handwritten musical score to *Bohemian Rhapsody*; a black headband signed by Jimi Hendrix; Michael Jackson's black top hat—also signed; a huge belt buckle from Elvis, with his logo TCB embedded with what was claimed to be authentic rubies; a set of Ringo Starr's drumsticks; and a pair of size 10½ black rhinoceros hide boots, complete with the initials E.P. in pink leather emblazoned on the pointed toes.

The Music Man booth also displayed Elvis Presley's original single 45, *That's All Right*, in one of three locked glass cabinets. Accompanying the record was an affidavit from the Beverly Hills Auction and Associates that a similar record had been sold for $9,000 two years previously. This particular record was on sale especially for attendees of Bonaroo for a mere $6,000.

In the second cabinet stood a gold-topped guitar, lovingly nicknamed *Layla*. It had belonged to Duane Allman, and had been played during several memorable performances, among them when he played the hit song *Layla* alongside Eric Clapton. The guitar was accompanied by a photograph of that very event, as well as a certificate of authenticity from the Allman Brothers Band Museum in Macon, Georgia. The asking price was a mere quarter of a million dollars.

In the other locked cabinet was an unblemished first-day issue of the Beatles' *Yesterday and Today* album. What made it particularly special was that the four musicians were shown on the cover wearing butcher's jackets, while casually holding bloody, decapitated dolls and recently butchered shoulders of meat. This cover had been offered for sale to the public for only a single day in June of 1966, until there was an outcry about the grotesque cover and it was pulled from record store shelves that very afternoon until it could be replaced, or at least covered over with a more palatable picture. Hence, though in unbelievably poor taste, it was extremely valuable. Again, the Beverly Hills Auction provided notarized proof that a similar pristine copy had been sold for $125,000 and used copies were going for $50,000. The special, one-time-only Bonaroo price was $35,000.

Every rare item in The Music Man booth had two things in common. They all were accompanied by a signed and notarized certificate of authenticity, and they were all fake, courtesy of our creative trading partners in China. As soon as the Elvis belt buckle was sold for three thousand bucks and the buyer departed the booth, it was replaced on the display shelf with a second identical item. Nevertheless, the attendees' enthusiasm for collectible rarities was extreme, with four copies of Elvis' scarf being sold to four different fans for the bargain price of five hundred dollars apiece, Layla fetching $60,000, and the Beatles album for an extra special $30,000.

As the crowds grew outside The Music Man tent, one of the workers adjusted the two fans to maximize the benefit of the airflow. The sweaty attendees were appreciative, although they did not notice the worker also activated a small device on each fan which dispersed fifty milligrams of a practically invisible gray powder directly into the perspiring faces of fans every five minutes. On those few occasions when the crowd thinned out in front of the booth, the worker de-activated the procedure. Each device held a total of ten grams of powder, and lasted into the evening.

On the second day of the festival, the thermometer was in very uncomfortable territory again, the crowd was just as miserable in the heat, and the procedure with the two fans was repeated multiple times, until they had exhausted their supply of powder. Toward the end of the afternoon, one of the workers in the booth lamented to the exhibitors on either side of them that they weren't selling enough merchandise to make their stay worthwhile.

The next morning, The Music Man exhibit had disappeared, having sold their entire remaining inventory to a vendor directly opposite their booth for a mere twelve thousand dollars. The purchaser, a dedicated Freddie Mercury fan, was ecstatic at the deal he had struck.

It was supposed to be a nice, romantic evening at the Army-Navy Club in Arlington, Virginia. The two parties had already agreed that any discussion of work was off limits. That agreement didn't last beyond parking the car.

"Where do you suppose something will happen next?"

Angela shot Early a glance. "I thought we promised not to talk shop tonight."

"I know, I know, but it's impossible not to wonder when and where, and we certainly can't talk about it inside the club."

"If I start worrying about it, I can't focus on anything else. I can't concentrate at work, and I sure can't sleep at night."

Early shook his head. "I'm sorry. This is just exactly why we weren't supposed to talk about work."

"I've spent the last two days putting together a list of all the large gatherings of people which will be happening in the next thirty days. There's a meeting of the U.N. Security Council in New York next week, a G-7 summit in Baltimore, over three hundred major league baseball games, possibly sixteen NBA playoff games, twenty-six musical festivals, three NASCAR races, seventy Broadway shows, the Belmont horse race, over fifty outdoor concerts, a couple of hundred college graduations, and over a hundred cities with large firework events on the Fourth of July.

"That list doesn't begin to account for all the situations every day where large numbers of people come together: Union Station in D.C., Grand Central Station in New York, airports, cruise ships, subway stations, theme parks, political rallies for the two presidential candidates, and who knows what else. It's impossible to cover all those venues."

"It's pretty inconvenient, being a free country."

Her smile was without mirth. "That's an understatement. And yet all of the people who plan to attend those events expect to have their fun and be completely protected. The expectation is that we, the government, should have everything under control. Otherwise, we must have failed in our responsibilities." She shook her head. "It's like being responsible for catching every raindrop during a thunderstorm."

There was an irritating buzz from Early's phone and he read the text. He shook his head as if to clear it of all the evil of the last several months, then handed the device to Angela. She read the message a couple of times before raising her head. "I guess we were right to worry."

"Thirty suspicious pneumonia cases being reported in Nashville, Knoxville, Chattanooga, Murfreesboro, and Atlanta hospitals. I'll call in. I suppose there'll be a teleconference either tonight or first thing in the morning."

"Where do you suppose the attack actually occurred?"

"Heck if I know. It's probably someplace on your list."

The call began at ten PM Eastern, after the first lab reports were completed, and was attended by the principals and various representatives from DHS, FBI, CIA, CDC, ASPR, and ICE, as well as state health officers from Tennessee, Alabama, Georgia, and North Carolina, their state bureaus of investigation, and their governors. The results from thirty cultures had come back in the early morning hours as positive for *Bacillus anthracis*, and a total of 107 people were hospitalized with similar symptoms. An in-depth interview of ten patients had determined they all had one common factor within the previous four days.

"Dr. Wilson," said Rear Admiral Hope Sheffield, "my office will be glad to deploy epidemiologists to assist you in trying to identify exactly where the anthrax was distributed on the Bonaroo grounds. However, as much as the attendees move from one area to another, it's unlikely that knowing the exact location will be of much benefit."

"I understand, Admiral, but folks are demanding to know at least something more definitive than somewhere on the Bonaroo property. Maybe pinning down where it came from will help our Tennessee Bureau of Investigation in identifying the guilty party."

"Understood, Dr. Wilson. However, I think the primary concern for all of us right now is to quickly get every single attendee treated with antibiotics, no matter where they spent most of their time at the festival. Unfortunately, far too much time has elapsed for us to help everybody."

"Just how much time do we have, Admiral?" asked Special Agent in Charge John Mallos of the Nashville FBI.

"Some people come down with symptoms in as few as four days, while others could take as long as four weeks. There are two stages to inhalational anthrax. The first symptoms are generally fever, sore throat, body aches, a cough, and shortness of breath. About the time this happens, a physician can look at a chest X-ray and see a bloody fluid beginning to accumulate in the chest cavity. From there, it proceeds to a second stage where the infection spreads in the lungs. Then we see extreme shortness of breath, coughing up blood, pneumonia, shock, and death.

"If we can start antibiotics before stage one, then patients have a very good probability of surviving. If we wait to start antibiotics until the patient is already in stage one, then their survival is significantly reduced."

"What about after stage two begins?" Mallos asked.

"There's very little chance of survival, certainly much less than ten percent, no matter what treatment we use at that point."

"Dr. David Rutstein from North Carolina, Admiral. What about the new monoclonal antibody for patients in stage one?"

"Raxibacumab injection may be worth trying, Dr. Rutstein. We don't carry it in the National Pharmaceutical Stockpile. If you do use it, I'd be very interested in hearing your results."

There was a competition to see who could speak next, with Assistant Secretary Abel Adams winning the contest. "You're the expert, Admiral. What do you recommend our next steps should be?"

"Whatever your thoughts on this, ladies and gentlemen, we are in the middle of a war here, and we must act as though every minute counts. There must be an all-out effort to set up at least ten prophylaxis sites so people won't have to travel a great distance to obtain treatment. Every health department in all your states, every Medical Reserve Corps unit, every Disaster Medical Assistance Team on call, and every team of the U.S. Public Health Service have got to deploy by tomorrow morning.

"Yes, I know, moving all those resources sounds impossible. But any and every delay could mean hundreds or even thousands of people who've progressed too far in the disease process for treatment to be effective. In the next hour, each state health officer needs to identify three sites to prophylax patients, and report that to my office tonight by twelve o'clock Eastern, so we can prepare to send medications overnight to those locations. Personnel need to be deployed to those sites by nine o'clock in the morning Eastern to receive antibiotics via the Stockpile. Medical personnel and other distribution personnel will need to be ready to go to work no later than eleven AM, and because so much time has passed since people were exposed, those clinics will need to be open twenty-four hours a day."

"Did you say twenty-four hours, Admiral?"

"I'm afraid so, Governor Reese. Quite a few people are likely to die, so each of us needs to be able to look our constituents in the eye and say that we did everything humanly possible to save people. Another thing—each site will need twenty-four hour law enforcement coverage. Let's face it, some people are going to be desperate, and others may even try to take a large amount of antibiotics by force. Whoever the terrorists are, they may even try to interfere with people being treated.

"And finally, every governor and every mayor will need to publicize these free treatment clinics in every media form available to them. Once you identify prophylaxis locations, my office will create a press release which can be downloaded from our website and used as accurate publicity information. The federal government and the states all need to be on exactly the same page when it comes to the information we distribute. Different messages only tend to confuse people. We can't afford that right now. Misunderstandings and misinformation are going to cost lives."

"Thank you, Admiral," said Abel Adams "Ladies and gentlemen, we all have a hell of a lot to do. And as the admiral has made clear, every minute counts. We'll hold this call at five PM tomorrow for an update and reassessment."

Social media sites engaged at full throttle, despite having no evidence to support their information.

Underneath the image of two rough-looking Hispanic males, the following was posted: *A witness at the Bonaroo event in Tennessee took this picture of the men suspected of spreading anthrax to the crowd. If you see these men, contact law enforcement immediately.*

Health expert says infected people from Bonaroo can

spread anthrax to the rest of us. Why aren't all of us receiving antibiotics?

The previous post is false. Inhalational anthrax is not spread from person to person.

Shortage of Lifesaving Antibiotics! Federal government is trying to hide this information from the American people. Act quickly. Wherever you live, get your doctor to prescribe the antibiotic for you and your family in case anthrax comes to your city and the federal government's supply is exhausted.

Main stage at Bonaroo said to be the source of anthrax. One hundred percent of patients in Chattanooga hospital say they were in area of main stage.

Why was there no biological detection equipment at Bonaroo? Who decided it would be too much trouble? Or too expensive?

Government attempting to sterilize Bonaroo area. Worker says task is impossible. Environmental sampling reveals anthrax spread by wind into the next county.

Do the people of Chicago really want to take a chance on what happened in Memphis and Manchester, Tennessee coming to our area? Have we not learned anything from these two attacks? Why not be safe? Let's cancel the Lollapalooza Music Festival this year!

According to the organizers, there were 98,412 paid admissions to Bonaroo. Additionally, there were wristbands distributed to 960 exhibit booth workers and 668 entertainers, stage hands, and law enforcement personnel. So of a total of 100,070 people who were actually on the grounds of the festival, it was a mystery why the total number of patients seen at the twelve prophylaxis clinics were 138,764. Somehow, over 38,000 people decided they were also at risk for anthrax, despite not even being at the event.

After the attacks of September 11th and the establishment of the Department of Homeland Security, millions of dollars had flowed to state and local governments to improve their capability to respond to a variety of terrorist attacks. While the money lasted, it was very effective in helping local governments improve their responsiveness. However, as the years progressed, the funding stream dried to a trickle.

Most local governments no longer had the funds to train and exercise their personnel for chemical, biological, and other large scale attacks. Frankly, many municipalities no longer saw the necessity of training and exercising for things which never seemed to happen.

Given the lack of training for the last ten years or so, it was miraculous that the multi-state response to anthrax went fairly well. Other than over-crowding, parking difficulties, long waits in line, quite a few instances of pushing, shoving, and name calling, as well as a dozen fist fights, the intense job of prophylaxis was completed in 72 hours.

Thank goodness there were ten regional emergency coordinators from HHS under the direction of Captain Andy Chen, with one of them attached to each prophylaxis site. They all proved to be a great resource for standing up the locations. The over 600 men and women working in the clinics had all worked at least sixteen-hour days so that everybody could be processed and protected as quickly as possible.

For the most part, their work proved to be life-saving. However, for 1,102 individuals, the workers' efforts would be in vain. It represented the greatest loss of life in history due to a single act of bioterrorism.

⚛

In preparation for the next weekend's concert, Summer Jam, which was to be held in East Rutherford, New Jersey, directly across the Hudson River from the Bronx, the three men from Niger were all staying in a hotel room in Newark, New Jersey. A second identical shipping container for The Music Man would be waiting for them at their exhibit booth early Friday morning.

Assistant Secretary Abel Adams with DHS and Assistant Director Lynn Jones from the FBI were paying attention as Dr. Martinelli gave her report. "As I mentioned previously, three of the men who I dealt directly with in Vietnam, giving them translated materials regarding anthrax, and vaccinating them against anthrax, indicated they were from the African nation of Niger. They were all tall and thin, probably between six-two and six-five, and all had an extremely dark complexion.

"When I last saw them, all had shaved heads and smooth faces. The photographs taken at Bonaroo are not of the best quality, and many of them only caught side views or pieces of faces. However, I spent several days with these three men, and even with their hair and beard growth, I'm positive these are the same men who were sent here as part of the North Korean terrorism plot."

Jones looked at his DHS counterpart. "I think we should publicize these photos across all law enforcement. We have no idea when or where their next attack will occur, and there are just too many possibilities for our personnel to be in all the possible locations."

"Agreed. We should probably also include the name of the exhibit they set up at Bonaroo. Whether they use this Music Man moniker again or not, there's no way of knowing, but it could help."

"When I said I vaccinated these guys," Martinelli said, "that's not exactly true. I injected them with water. In all likelihood, they're going to end up as victims of their own actions."

"We can only hope."

The three men from Niger had not gone to a prophylaxis clinic, convincing each other that their vaccinations would protect them. When two of them died in their hotel beds, the third finally decided to go to a local hospital. His high fever obviously interfered with his driving skills, as he rear-ended a city bus at high speed on his way to the emergency room.

⚛

Feeling the pressure of his position, the fat man returned to Sep'o County, hoping for some measure of relief from his worries. Putin had contacted him again after the anthrax attack at Bonaroo. Although he couldn't be absolutely sure, it appeared Putin was about to disavow not only their trade relationship, but also their longstanding mutual defense treaty.

His advisers continued to say that Moscow and Beijing did not have a close working relationship, and counseled there was little risk that Putin might persuade the Chinese president that they should both divorce themselves from North Korea, but the Wonsu was no longer sure of that. For one thing, his advisers had not witnessed the insulting language used by Putin during their last two phone calls. For another, he was acutely aware that his so-called advisers told him what they thought he wanted to hear, rather than engaging in perhaps a more realistic appraisal.

More than one world leader suffered from this same lack of honest information and analysis. Having close confidants gloss over the truth, let alone not attempt to correct a misunderstanding or misinterpretation of factual information, did not help any leader or any country.

The Wonsu feared for his nation if he lost these two longtime allies. Worse, he was pessimistic about the longevity of his own reign. Without the support of China and Russia, whether via economic support or mutual defense, his current living standards could no longer continue.

Absent that external support, let alone those sources of outside funding, he believed his military would soon rise up and take over the country. He had pondered more than once what some of his generals might do if they ever took control of his nuclear weapons. He was fairly confident that a good third of them would happily start something. After all, they had over a million men in uniform and a million more in the reserves. It was undoubtedly a temptation for his military leadership to explore ways to take such a force to war. Frankly, he regarded himself as the only man who could prevent his country from going to war!

For not the first time, he considered the ramifications of selling Iran a handful of his launch-ready nuclear weapons. He was absolutely sure that such a transaction could easily net him in the neighborhood of ten billion dollars. His hesitation in doing so was simply based on the suspicion that such a sale would be compromised and disclosed to the Americans, and most assuredly to the Russians.

Putin had told him, point-blank, to discontinue the attacks against the U.S. Despite the fat man's attempts to explain that he had no way of knowing who these terrorists were, where they were, or what their timeline might be, Putin refused to take no for an answer. Per the information shared with him by Colonel-General Moo-sung, there were several more events yet to come, yet neither he nor the general could think of a way to stop them.

He finally decided that he needed to be seen as a man who still regarded the Americans as his enemy rather than a negotiating partner. He would back away from any attempt to placate the Americans. After all, he knew his solitary strategic value to Russia and China was to occupy the immediate strategic attention of the Americans. He prepared a note for his Minister of State Security to send to the American secretary of state.

The United States is still not ready to meet our expectations in terms of taking a step forward to sign a peace treaty. They must first show a good faith effort to reduce sanctions.

The response was swift in coming.

The Secretary of State will not be going on his planned trip to North Korea because the country is not making sufficient progress with respect to denuclearization.

North Korea's Foreign Minister advised the U.N.: *There is no way the DPRK would disarm first as long as the U.S. continues to push for ridiculous and unfair enforcement of sanctions against Pyongyang.*

He hoped drawing a new line in the sand would show his allies that he still possessed a winning hand. After all, he was doing their dirty work.

⚛

The Wonsu also decided to change his tactics where the girl was concerned. Apparently she had been forced to stay inside the cabin for the many months she had been in residence. Rather than start any romantic endeavors in his bedroom, perhaps he would ultimately get what he was after by giving her at least a small taste of freedom. Besides, her gratitude for such a gesture might be exceptionally satisfying.

His guards in Sep'o County had proposed that they accompany the two of them, but the Wonsu declined. "After all, she is only a girl." And so their afternoon began.

Although spring had turned into summer, a few surrounding mountaintops still held on to their crown of snow in mid-June. The fat man met the girl at the front door of the cabin. She wore black jeans, a white T-shirt, and a floppy white hat. He of course wore his "uniform" of black pants, black long-sleeved shirt, and a black fedora.

A basket containing cold sandwiches and a cooler were strapped onto the back end of the two-seat four-wheeler in anticipation of a leisurely lunch. They sped away from the cabin before one of the guards could ask, yet again, if he should not go along.

Although well maintained, the road away from the compound, across a large pasture, and up into the woods was dirt, covered lightly with gravel. In the flat areas, he drove too fast, trying to illicit a pleasurable response from the girl. As they rose further into the timber and the road became less

predictable, he slowed down, providing plenty of opportunity
for her to take full advantage of the view of distant mountains.

When they stopped for lunch far up on the mountainside,
he spread a valuable red-and-black patterned Persian rug on
the grass for their comfort. The only liquid refreshment he
had brought was Cristal champagne. It was new to the girl,
and she drank very sparingly. He, on the other hand, consumed a bottle and three-quarters.

The fat man eventually passed out, or rather fell pro-
foundly asleep. Hiroko had not thought about that particular
scenario, but she considered what might happen if she simply
took off in the four-wheeler. She had paid enough attention
on the way up the mountain that it had seemed fairly simple
to drive, but she had no idea where she was in relationship to
the rest of the country.

How far was the coast and the Sea of Japan? How difficult would it be to travel through these mountains? How
would she obtain food and water to sustain her? How much
gasoline would be needed to get to the coast? What would she
do when she reached it? What would the Wonsu do if his men
caught her? If—what a joke. Of course they would catch her.
And then what? Most assuredly, her life would not be better if
she tried to flee and was caught.

She sat there, puzzling on her decision for another fifteen
minutes. Hiroko then reloaded the four-wheeler with their
lunch and woke the fat man. He was quite disoriented, but
she got him and his Persian rug back into the four-wheeler,
then drove back down the mountain.

When she arrived at the cabin, he was again asleep. She
got out of the vehicle and knocked on the front door. His
guards rushed out to be sure their leader had not been the
victim of an attack by the crazy Japanese girl, then escorted
him inside. After speaking briefly to the auntie in the kitchen,
Hiroko went up to her room.

If she was honest, she had to admit that she had absolutely loved being outside for the afternoon. The weather had
been beautiful, the views were glorious, and the fat man had
been harmless. Perhaps it would be possible to enjoy herself
yet still control him. She would cautiously look forward to the
next time.

Chapter 35

The 1812 Overture
Washington, D.C. July 4, 2024

There is a man who plies his trade in the Russian city of Semipalatinsk. He has no store front, no cash register, no goods on a shelf, and no employees. The local banker would probably disclose that Aleksandr Kuznetsov was known to bounce a check from time to time, and although he always made it good, he was hardly a man of any substance.

His living quarters matched his meager bank account. He lived in a second story walk-up apartment in an area of town which was often the scene of police action. However, there was never anything obviously illegal going on in Aleksandr's home. Everything seemed to be above board. In fact, he had been faithful in his small, semi-annual donations to the police league, and every Christmas he reliably sent over four liters of Stolichnaya Elit vodka for the fellows. Law enforcement—on all continents had a tendency to remember these no-strings-attached kindnesses.

He was a fiftyish, thick-waisted fellow, with a disappointing hairline, who could always be spotted in a well-worn brown three-piece suit. He did not own a car, but rather was seen regularly on a bicycle. He had confided in the police lieutenant that he was afraid for his safety in the neighborhood, and asked if he might carry a concealed weapon. When he was asked what kind, he replied he'd like to carry his father's old Makarov .380 caliber automatic. The lieutenant revealed that he had one at home as well.

To his customers, the most endearing qualities Kuznetsov possessed were his reliability and his willingness to keep his mouth shut. So when he had been asked by a middleman to obtain four 82mm mortars, two dozen standard explosive shells, and six shells containing white phosphorous in addition to the explosive charge, his first comment had been, "Are you sure you don't want the 81mm mortars from NATO? The shells are more reliable than the old Soviet product, although the phosphorous would have to be added after the fact."

"My client was most specific—the 82mm, please."

"Of course. I am happy to accommodate the request. You understand there will be a quite significant addition to the bill for transportation and delivery charges."

"I have one more request. Along with this order, please include three Kalashnikov AK-12 fully automatic assault rifles, three sound suppressors, nine drum magazines which hold ninety-six cartridges apiece, and four thousand rounds of ammunition in the 5.45x39mm caliber."

"You do realize that is a very new rifle and is only now being supplied to the Russian military? It will be very expensive."

"I'm not interested in those problems. Please confirm that you can complete my entire order and give me the total price."

He would pick up most of the items himself at a military surplus warehouse in his own city. Semipalatinsk seemed to be the repository for Soviet-era infantry weaponry, with multiple government warehouses dotting the area. The new rifles and related items would have to come from a quartermaster friend of his at a nearby military base.

The entire order would be transported 3,824 kilometers via railroad, all the way to the port city of Rostov-on-Don. There they would be picked up by a Turkish-flagged freighter, which would first pass through the Black Sea into the Aegean, then cross the Mediterranean Sea, and eventually arrive on the far side of the Atlantic in Vera Cruz, Mexico.

From Vera Cruz, the package would be accepted by the vicious Gulf Cartel and concealed in two shipments of grapefruit on two separate trucks. The vehicles would then depart Mexico on consecutive days, each finally reaching the agent for Kuznetsov's customer in Charlottesville, Virginia on June 20th. Both shipments of grapefruit and their companion cargoes arrived unblemished and undetected.

The customer then electronically transmitted the second

half of Kuznetsov's bill for 28 Bitcoins to a trusted bank in the Caribbean. That transaction would improve his bank balance to something north of nine million dollars U.S. He looked forward, God willing, to a very enjoyable retirement in the not too distant future. He had already spent years dreaming of experiencing wonderful things he had thus far denied himself.

Yet another shipment had already been requested of Kuznetsov from the same middleman. He knew that particular merchandise would be far more difficult to obtain, as those systems were just off the assembly line and not mothballed somewhere in a poorly secured warehouse, or subject to the whims of an insufficiently salaried quartermaster. However, the payday promised to be far greater than any of his previous arms deals. He was already working on a source.

The Fourth of July celebration on the National Mall in Washington, D.C., features entertainment by the National Symphony Orchestra and a number of renowned popular soloists and actors. The program is broadcast on national television stations. Perhaps the most anticipated portion of the evening is the playing of *The 1812 Overture*, wherein the part mimicking the roar of cannons is actually duplicated by real artillery west of the Capitol Building. At that same time, dramatic fireworks are launched over the Mall.

It's a bit odd that Americans see the *Overture* as being "their" song, when in reality Tchaikovsky wrote it to commemorate Russia's defeat of Napoleon at the battle for Moscow in 1812; Andrew Jackson defeated the English outside New Orleans in 1815, a month after the War of 1812 concluded. Certainly the music is powerful and invigorating, but it was not composed for Americans.

People spend the day on the Mall, first watching the Independence Day parade in the early afternoon, then visiting a number of the museums, perhaps laying out a blanket to have a picnic supper while listening to the concert, and of course, watching the fireworks. It's not unusual for 700,000 people to crowd the Mall, spread from the Capitol steps all the way to the Lincoln Monument. Other people watch from the taller buildings surrounding the Mall, and some even anchor their boats out on the nearby Potomac River to enjoy the spectacle.

The individuals responsible for security at an event of that size and visibility refer to it as a National Special Security Event (NSSE). Several planning meetings are held in advance of an NSSE to ensure that all the players understand their roles in case of a mass casualty event. The planners include the FBI, the Secret Service, DHS, the National Capitol Police, the D.C. Police Department, the Office of the Attending Physician of the U.S. Congress, the Military District of Washington, the National Pharmaceutical Stockpile, the U.S. Public Health Service directed by the U.S. Surgeon General, and the National Disaster Medical System under the Assistant Secretary for Preparedness and Response at HHS.

Since the attacks of September 11, 2001, it has become far more common to declare large events, particularly those with high profile national or international politicians in attendance, as NSSEs. The men and women in charge of planning for these events are very knowledgeable, highly trained, and experienced in the extreme.

Access to the Mall is controlled for the entire day, and it's necessary to pass through metal detectors to attend. Ambulances and health care providers are on standby. A couple of medical decon teams are positioned in out-of-sight locations so they can rapidly decontaminate people in case of a biological or chemical attack. There are representatives of all the involved agencies in multiple linked command centers. Those centers remain active until the event is completely over and the crowd dispersed. In short, the nation is prepared, or at least as prepared as it can be in an open society.

A half block west of the intersection of K Street SW and Half Street SW is a dead-end road. It is not in a particularly attractive neighborhood, even though it's situated a mere 6,000 feet almost directly south of the steps of the U.S. Capitol. Looking down the length of the Mall, the dead-end street was just over two miles from the Washington Monument and almost three miles from the Lincoln Memorial.

The bob-truck with a 17-foot bed was parked at the end of the street, and had been sitting there all day long. So far, nobody had paid the least bit of attention to it. The vehicle had a special feature which was not visible from the street. The usual metal roof of the truck had been replaced by a sliding aluminum panel, which could be completely opened up so that someone inside the vehicle's rear could look straight up into the heavens.

Unfortunately, the four men in the back of the truck would not be star-gazing that evening. They had each practiced with their own 82mm mortar, but only with a single shot, as they lacked adequate ammunition to waste more than that. It was obvious to them that they lacked precision in their shooting, but it was possible to miss the exact target by many yards and still accomplish the mission. In fact, there was ten pounds of explosives in the head of each mortar, and it possessed the ability to kill people within a thirty yard radius of the landing spot. They had arrayed their individual mortars to hopefully spread the shots from one end of the Mall to the other.

To improve their accuracy, they had a spotter who was positioned in a seventh-floor room of the Hampton Inn on New York Avenue near Union Station. It was his responsibility to use a cell phone and call out the approximate landing area for each mortar round. With that information, they hoped they could adjust the trajectory of the next mortar for a more desirable spot on the next shot. Once they had a landing in the midst of the crowd, they were to use one of the internationally outlawed white phosphorus mortars on the following shot.

Early and Angela used the holiday and NSSE as an excuse to spend the evening together. For the first 45 minutes, they sat close to the orchestra, but then moved closer to the Washington Monument to get maximum exposure to the fireworks. Just negotiating their way through the packed audience was an ordeal. They could hear the first bars of Tchaikovsky's masterpiece just about the time they found an ideal spot some hundred yards west of Fourth Street.

The men in the back of the bob-truck each grappled with a mortar shell. Each shell was approximately 28-inches long, with three fins at the rear to stabilize flight and improve accuracy. The four mortar tubes were each affixed to a 25-pound base bolted to the truck bed, while at the bottom of the inner tube sat a firing pin. When the thirteen-pound mortar was dropped down the tube, the pin ignited the mortar and off it went. Depending on the loft, or angle of the launch, the weapon could travel up to three miles.

As the music on the Mall built to a crescendo, the people

enjoying the festivities began rising to their feet. The men in the bob-truck were on their feet as well, and the spotter at his hotel room window craned his neck in anticipation. When the sound from the firing of the first artillery piece reached the dead-end street, the fireworks began in earnest, and the man designated to go first dropped his mortar down the tube. It struck the firing pin, ignited, made a sound no more threatening than a loud cough, and was on its way. In twenty seconds, the response came from the spotter. "Re-target one hundred yards east. Mortar landed in the middle of the Capitol reflecting pool."

For the nearby onlookers, they simply thought one of the fireworks had misfired and had struck the water in front of them. While mortar number one's position was adjusted, number two coughed as its load launched.

"Shot was long, hit the roof of the Department of Labor. Shorten distance by two hundred yards... Direct hit in middle of Mall... Direct hit. Mortar malfunction. No explosion."

The third mortar shell struck less than one hundred yards from Early and Angela. They saw the explosion, at first believing that a fireworks shell had gone haywire and exploded in the crowd. The two of them moved forward to see if anyone required assistance, but as the people in the vicinity of the mortar's landing started fleeing, Early recognized the wounds he was seeing were not compatible with a firecracker. He called the command center, and was connected at the same time that a second shell landed nearby.

That explosion caused damage that he had never seen in combat, but only read about from studying the war in Vietnam, when the U.S. had used chemicals like napalm and white phosphorus against the VC and NVA. People were actually on fire. Some tried to douse the blaze on their clothes. Others screamed in pain from the deeply penetrating burn of the now-banned chemical.

The orchestra ground to discordance then stopped playing, the artillery stopped firing, and the fireworks ceased as additional mortar shells landed up and down the Mall in the middle of the crowd. Early looked around for Angela, panicking when he couldn't find her immediately, then finally spotting her kneeling and working with the injured.

There were so many people packed into the Mall that trying to flee was impossible. Per security preparations, the number of entrances and exits was limited, and people bunched up as they tried to funnel away from the carnage. At the same time, emergency medical personnel tried to get into the Mall, but were blocked by several hundred thousand panicked and stampeding people.

As quickly as they began, the explosions stopped. The attack had lasted less than three minutes. Although people still tried to escape the area, they finally realized the immediate danger was over. At the intersection of Half Street and K, an unused mortar shell was discarded at the side of the road. Taped to it was a set of instructions for firing the devices, written in Farsi. The bob-truck's sliding panel roof had been tugged back in place, avoiding any suspicion from the three helicopters which were lifting off from Andrews Air Force Base eight miles away.

The truck drove east innocently, turning right on South Capitol Street SW, crossing the Anacostia River, and finally entering the I-295 Interstate, headed south. By one AM, they would be back inside their warehouse outside Charlottesville, Virginia. Their directions had been specific. They were to save their modified bob-truck and mortar tubes for a second attack.

Back at the Mall, Early assisted emergency medical technicians and other responders attempting to take care of trauma and burn victims. Nearby, Angela remained on her hands and knees, stopping dangerous bleeding and stabilizing broken bones. Their date night continued in this manner until all the injured were finally evacuated to hospitals in D.C., Virginia, and Maryland.

The spotter simply enjoyed the luxury of spending the night in a nice hotel. The next morning, he departed with a pair of field glasses and a travel bag packed with plush hotel towels. His flip phone was deposited in a trash can in the lobby. Upon inspection later by investigators, the phone's sim card contained only one phone number in the address book. It was listed as belonging to *Marzban*, which, incidentally, translated as *Guardian of Persia*.

The authorities estimated a total of thirteen explosions, with three of them containing white phosphorous. Sixty-two people were pronounced dead upon arrival at area hospitals. Two hundred and forty-seven had significant injuries, with 25 of them designated as critical. Twenty-eight of the dead were children.

From the unexploded duds which landed on the Mall, it was learned that the mortars were originally constructed within the Soviet bloc. Of course, that did not mean these particular weapons originated in Russia, as they had been distributed en masse to every member of the Warsaw Pact from the 1950s through the late 1980s. The same weapons had also been sold to Russian allies, such as Iran, Syria, Cuba, Pakistan, North Vietnam, Venezuela, and North Korea, as well as a rather large number of Russia-sponsored guerrilla groups and terrorist cells around the world. American intelligence would play hell trying to figure out their origin, let alone who was responsible for the people who actually used them.

Once again, the social media titans seemed unwilling to interfere with posts designed to mislead and cause discord:

Over 1,000 Americans Dead in Washington, D.C.! Yet our government spins like a top in the wind. Who is responsible? Why don't we strike back? Is there a single reason not to believe it was ISIS? All evidence points directly at them.

How much money has been spent on the Department of Homeland Security's budget? And for what result? What happened to all of the government's BS about protecting the homeland? Do you feel safe yet?

MS-13 has taken credit for the attack on Fourth of July ceremonies in Washington, D.C. Take them on in El Salvador, in Guatemala, in Mexico, even in our own cities. But ACT! Our government should stop fiddling while Rome burns.

The sophisticated attack on Fourth of July celebrations in Washington, D.C., could only have been carried out by a government with sufficient resources. There's no way some group of El Salvadoran gang-bangers are responsible. Look toward Iran as the guilty party. The evidence is slapping us in the face!

Underneath a Photo-shopped picture of Hispanics burning the American flag, the text read: *MS-13 received the mortars from their fellow murderers in Venezuela and Cuba! Stop dealing with terrorist countries. Revoke travel visas to sponsors of terrorism. Stop spending American dollars in Havana and Caracas.*

Idiots! It was Iran that launched the Fourth of July attacks. The evidence is crystal clear. When will we act?

Every day for the past eleven years, Peter Knott had re-ported to his job on North Randolph Street in Arlington City, Virginia, like clockwork. He had never taken a sick day, and only rarely used his vacation time. As an electrical engineer who liked nothing better than immersing himself in highly technical work, his position at the Defense Advanced Re-search Projects Agency, or DARPA, was a perfect fit.

DARPA had been organized in 1958 as an independent arm of the Department of Defense, with a reporting line straight to the department's top. Early in its history, it had worked on satellite development, rocket systems, and ballistic missiles, but along the way had performed most of the early development of the Internet, the Global Positioning System, and artificial intelligence. Its unofficial mission was to develop "high risk, high gain, far out" research that looked well into the future in developing what the military would need one day to carry out its work. Its annual budget was just shy of three billion dollars.

As a GS-12 civil servant, Peter Knott was often described as an odd duck. After repeated unsuccessful attempts to hit on most of the females in the building, he no longer made any effort to socialize with his fellow workers. He brought a lunch to work and ate at his desk, while most of his 240 co-workers almost always took a full hour-long lunch break.

When he struck upon the vision for an entirely new weapons system, he began a labor of true passion. He arrived at his lab at seven AM and seldom departed before seven PM. His supervisor had no idea about his new work ethic. After all, the man was out the door at four PM every single day, and probably couldn't spell passion. For the last three years, that had been fine with Knott. He was convinced his personal pet project was going to change the world's battlefields for all time. He was probably correct.

He was combining the fields of GPS, laser guidance, and explosives. More specifically, his project was to use the con-ventional, very basic technology of a mortar and combine it with a guidance system so that it could land within one meter of a target up to six miles distant. That compared to a tradi-tional mortar which might land within fifty meters of the same target, even after multiple attempts by a spotter to zero it in.

To accomplish this, he put a laser receptor system on the nose of a mortar, electronically connected to the exact wavelength of a laser sighting mechanism. For this to work, either a soldier or a drone aircraft needed to actually see the desired target. The soldier or drone would aim a laser sighting system at the exact spot they wished the mortar to land. The mortar would be fired from a distant location, its laser receptor would lock onto the laser-sighted target, and boom, no more target, or anything else within thirty meters.

Knott had finally convinced three layers of supervisors to spend the money to actually build a prototype of his invention. The money was eventually allocated, the system was built, and it was test fired. It worked exactly as he'd projected it would. The Department of Defense was elated at the prospect of such a weapon. The Secret Service, however, viewed its development as a supremely complex threat to be dealt with.

The DOD spent $35 million with an armament manufacturer to create 2,000 laser-receptor mortar shells and fifty linked laser sights. Six months later, at a DARPA awards ceremony, Peter Knott received $5,000 as an award for his earth-shaking invention, which he had spent three years envisioning and developing. His annual salary was just over $92,000. When he saw the amount of the award, he almost tore the check up on the award podium. Instead, he got even.

Within three months, an agent at the Russian Embassy in Washington paid Knott $150,000 for an electronic copy of his plans. Within six more months, the Russian military possessed four times as many of the devices as the Americans. Everybody in the militaries of the free world knew that American forces possessed this new super-accurate weapon. Nobody had any idea the Russians were already ahead.

By the time the first copy of Knott's invention was manufactured in Sevastopol, the arms agent, Aleksandr Kuznetsov, knew all the specifications of the new weapon. Six months later, three hundred of the Russian-manufactured mortar shells and twenty laser sights were shipped to Crimea, while a similar number were sent to Syria. Before they reached their destinations, Kuznetsov had established a source.

In the mix-up of receiving the systems, apparently ten mortar shells and two sights were misplaced. In two days, the ten laser-directed shells and two laser sights miraculously showed up on a freighter, bound for Vera Cruz and the waiting hands of the Gulf Cartel.

Chapter 36

Friday Night Lights
Oklahoma and Texas September 18, 2024

The annual battle between the Tahlequah Tigers and the Claremore Zebras, which was the highlight of high school football in northeastern Oklahoma, was always scheduled for the third Friday in September. Claremore's claim to fame was as the home of humorist Will Rogers, while Tahlequah was celebrated as the National Capital of the Cherokee Nation and the United Keetoowah Band of the Cherokee. Both teams were well populated with Native American athletes, and more than a few regarded this contest as the Cherokee Bowl.

The Tigers and their cheerleaders traveled the 57 miles in two buses to Claremore for the game, and were accompanied by over two hundred fans in automobiles. Like most of their contests, the score was uncomfortably close as the game progressed. The stadium was full, the noise seemed to only get louder as the game marched toward a dramatic close, and the two Tahlequah bus drivers, who were required to stay with their vehicles during the entire game, listened closely to the action on the local radio station.

With just three minutes to go in the fourth quarter, Claremore was ahead, 21-20, but Tahlequah was moving the ball downfield. So who could blame the bus drivers if they paid no attention to the side of the bus facing away from the stadium? As time wound down on the game clock, a man crawled underneath one of the vehicles and attached a shaped charge of cyclotrimethylene trinitramene to the underside of the carriage, adjacent to the fuel tank. While the game's final seconds ticked away, he crawled out, left the parking lot, found his stolen Hyundai Sonata, and sat on the side of the road waiting for the bus to load up and head back home.

Just after ten PM, the buses were finally filled with joyous players and cheerleaders. The vehicles were literally swaying from side to side as the occupants celebrated their come-from-behind winning field goal. The rest of the parking lot had emptied out fifteen minutes earlier. The Sonata fell in behind the two buses, following them out of town until they reached U.S. Highway 412, headed east.

In the midst of the celebration on the players' bus, the team manager, student Jamie Sprague, finally wore himself out with his cheering and retreated to the rear, where he lay down on the long bench seat, using his football jacket as a pillow. By the time the buses were less than fifteen miles from home base, Jamie had nodded off to sleep.

Seeing no traffic in his rear view mirror, the Sonata accelerated ahead of the two buses, then the driver dialed a number. When the explosion went off in the bus undercarriage, it was instantaneously followed by an eruption from its fuel tank. The driver was thrown against the support stanchion to the rear of the side window, cracking his skull. The bus almost split in two, most of the windows were blown out, and a fire engulfed the front of the bus. Jamie's sleeping form slammed against the back of the seat in front of him, then slid onto the floor. Although dazed, he came to his senses almost immediately.

Jamie was maybe five feet two inches and couldn't have weighed more than 125 pounds, but like many of his teammates, he was a dedicated weightlifter. He forced open the damaged rear emergency door before hollering toward his players. There was no response. He had no choice. He began carrying and dragging boys through the heat and thick smoke down the aisle of the bus, then pulling them outside and depositing them several yards down the roadway. Some of them outweighed him by a hundred pounds, but that didn't stop him.

Before two cars finally arrived and stopped to help, the diminutive manager had rescued eleven young men. Or at least he had pulled eleven from the fire and wreckage. Only nine of them survived. The driver, three coaches, and eighteen other players had been killed.

The first highway patrolman on the scene took one look at Jamie, another at the much larger boys lying on the side of the road at the rear, and pronounced the young manager a hero. Jamie's hands and face were burned and blistered, his throat was raw, eyes watering, hair scorched, and he eventually realized the blood on his shirt was his own. He had a severe gash on the side of his head which would require eleven stitches to close, and probably was due to his banging into the seat-back in front of him.

The Sonata turned to the south at the next exit. The driver still had more to do on his task list.

Social media posts:

Has anyone noticed that all the terrorist attacks to date have occurred in cities with mayors who are all Democrats? Are they targeting those cities because they know those mayors are soft on crime, they don't support law enforcement, and they won't cooperate with ICE? Do you really want to attract terrorists to your city? Vote Republican instead!

Over half of the states where terrorist attacks have occurred are led by Republican governors with a majority of Republicans in the state legislature. Are the terrorists targeting those states because of the persecution minorities and foreigners suffer in those locations? Vote Democrat!

To the fools who want to politicize the locales struck by terrorists: it makes no difference to the terrorists what party holds sway in those areas. Terrorists are simply looking for weaknesses in our security. They seek opportunity to strike, escape, and strike again, sowing chaos. Stop politicizing. Unite with your neighbors, whatever their political persuasion, against this despicable group of people!

※

The entire state of Oklahoma focused on the threat to high school football. After all, the sport resembled a religious fervor as school opened every year. There was considerable security by local police, county sheriffs, and the state highway patrol at every game in the state the following weekend. However, the bomber was almost 500 miles away in a different state, driving a black Ford F-150 pickup in the lights of the next Friday night.

Another grudge football game, between the Goliad Tigers and the George West Longhorns, was being played near the site of the Goliad Massacre, a famous battle during the Texas Revolution. The opponents were both small schools, and George West could only muster one school bus, filled with players, coaches, and cheerleaders, as well as a handful of cars, for the 53 mile drive.

The game was not particularly close, with George West ahead by 21 points toward the end. The bus driver, Edgar Emanuel, was nonetheless very interested in the game, as his son, Ed Junior, was a star linebacker on the team, and his reputation was such that a scout from Texas A&M was reportedly in the stands. So there was no way Edgar was going to miss watching the last quarter. After all, he could still keep an eye on the bus from the edge of the parking lot.

His son delivered in a big way. For the third time in the game, he tackled the Tiger running back for a loss, then followed up two plays later with an interception on an attempted screen pass. Edgar was ecstatic when he saw a fellow from the grandstand come down on the field as soon as the game was over and spend a few minutes talking with the George West head coach. Not recognizing the man, he had to believe it was the A&M scout. From their gestures, he was sure they'd been talking about Ed Junior.

Approximately thirty minutes later, the Longhorns' bus was fully loaded. The coach stopped briefly and patted Edgar on the shoulder. "We need to talk."

Edgar nodded with a grin, then turned around for a quick look to be sure his passengers were seated, and saw his son sitting beside that same red-headed cheerleader, Wendye Horner—the one who kept saying she was going to be a nurse. He smiled. Ed and Wendye were quite the couple. Could life get any better than this?

The bus departed the stadium parking lot and headed west toward home on US Highway 59. Less than two miles from Goliad stood a highway bridge over the San Antonio River. A black pickup was parked on the side of the highway about four hundred yards beyond the bridge.

Just as the bus entered the overpass, the last digit of a phone number was dialed and the explosion caused the vehicle to go airborne. It came to earth, on fire and leaning precariously over the side of the bridge railing. It teetered back and forth, and within seconds tumbled over, landing upside down in the river below. On that night, no miracle would occur and no heroic trainer would pull victims to safety. Only one occupant, Edgar Emanuel, the bus driver, would survive. For the rest of his life, he would curse his Maker for allowing him to live rather than Ed Junior.

The bomber turned south at the next intersection, finding his way eventually to the town of Alice, Texas, where he stashed the black Ford pickup. A motel receipt was in the glove compartment, made out to a Hamid Hashemi. He then stole an older model Chevrolet sedan, drove it to McAllen, and crossed over the border to Reynosa on foot. After taking three different buses, he arrived in the port city of Tampico, where he retrieved his real passport and leftover counterfeit funds from a bank safety deposit box. He then purchased space on a freighter headed back to Venezuela. He looked forward to receiving a very lucrative fourth deposit in his Caribbean bank account for his final successful contribution. He would be disappointed.

After considerable investigation, there was general agreement between the ATF and the FBI that the characteristics of the two school bus explosions were not compatible with those from Maryland and New York. The bomb maker was undoubtedly a different person. They still had no real description of either suspect, but had been able to retrieve a perfect set of prints from the pickup. They were not in any available database.

From social media: *Now they're targeting our children! Two more attacks by ISIS terrorists. How can any patriotic American defend these people?*

Once again, evidence confirms that ISIS or al Qaeda is the responsible party. It certainly sounds like their modus operandi: cowards killing children, and using explosive devices to do it. Whether it's in the Middle East or in our own country, they're kid killers. It's past time to totally destroy these evil people.

Chapter 37

A Lifeline?
Fort Gordon, GA / Washington, DC October/15/2024

Vice Admiral Julie Mathis, commanding officer, U.S. Cyber Command, was speaking to representatives from the Joint Chiefs, the Department of State, the FBI, DHS, and CIA, the chairmen and ranking members of the House and Senate Intelligence Committees, the National Security Advisor, the Defense Intelligence Agency, the Cyber and Infrastructure Agency at DHS, the National Geospatial Intelligence Agency, the National Security Agency, the National Counter Terrorism Center, and the President's chief of staff. "Ladies and gentlemen, as you know, my office is responsible for the security of all DoD-related IT systems, websites, and communications. Our charge does not include protecting systems in the private sector. Nonetheless, as we track IT weaknesses and communications from our adversaries around the world, from time to time we discover threatening information which may not be directly targeted at our Department of Defense.

"All of you are aware of Russia's Internet Research Agency. This government-sponsored entity actually began operations as a tool to suppress individual Russians. They were the first targets after the downing of a Malaysia Airlines flight over Ukraine in 2014. This Russian troll factory immediately tripled their output to almost sixty thousand per day, all specifically blaming Ukraine for the downing of the airliner.

"Surprised with that demonstrated success under their belt, they, along with their Iranian allies, turned much of their efforts from that time forward against the United States. Troll farms directed by Russia and Iran, located in those two countries as well as in Syria and Cuba, created just under four thousand internet accounts and released approximately ten million tweets toward Americans. Russia was, by far, the largest contributor, with some ninety percent of messaging originating in that country. Additionally, the Iranian messaging was not nearly as sophisticated as we have seen from Russia. Iran's trolls seem almost entirely fixated on joint Israeli and American interests."

The undercurrent of private conversations in the room got louder, and Mathis held up her hands for quiet. "This information is not partisan. There is no Republican nor Democrat version of this information. And the sooner we accept it without blaming one side or another, the less effective the Russian strategy will be. Rest assured, we have concrete evidence of these numbers, and they have continued, almost unabated, from one administration to the next.

"Some of you know that in 2018, a presidential finding was issued. This gave us the authority to aggressively target Russia, China, Iran, and North Korea with all of the cyber operations at our disposal. Those four countries were included simply because each of them were fully participating in information warfare by 2018. Although their actions related to information warfare significantly increase in election years that is not to say that it goes away in off years.

"Even today, in this election year of 2024, these four nations continue to issue messages directed at our citizens on both sides of political issues, simply trying to inflame Americans, rather than consistently blaming a particular group or party. What I have to report is new evidence related to this social media dis-information campaign. In the last few months, four relatively new dis-information operations have joined forces with the Russians and Iranians to coordinate their messaging to further create discord and even chaos surrounding the recent attacks on our country."

"Admiral," said Assistant Secretary Abel Adams, "my office has information on this subject as well, but we lack corroboration on several important issues. We'd like very much to determine if we can marry up your information with ours."

Bob Williams waved his hand. "Admiral, the CIA also has information which we would be glad to share in this venue."

Mathis nodded. "As I mentioned, we see materials being

created and disseminated by Russia and Iran in particular, and to a much lesser degree by China and North Korea; oddly, we also have found the same kinds of campaigns located in Vietnam, Venezuela, Namibia, and Mexico."

"When did this start, Admiral?" demanded the ranking member of the Senate IC.

"Senator, those campaigns started some two months ago, but we find no evidence to link them to the governments of Vietnam, Venezuela, Namibia, and Mexico. Rather, we have good reason to believe those server operations are managed covertly by the Bio-Terrorism Directorate in Pyongyang, North Korea."

Both Adams and Williams rose for recognition. Williams won the race. "Our information substantiates that, with this additional evidence. One of our agents has direct knowledge that North Korea is responsible for hiring, training, and deploying twenty-three terrorists to our shores. Those individuals were Iranian, as well as other ISIS or al Qaeda fanatics, plus individuals from Eastern Europe, Mexico, Cuba, and Central America, to include MS-13 gang members. Although our agent cannot verify that the various fires, explosions, and the recent mortar attack on the Fourth of July were carried out by these people, she does have unimpeachable evidence that the anthrax attacks were part of their mission."

"Is your agent safe, Mr. Williams?" asked Assistant Secretary of State Daniel Beck.

"She is now, Secretary. However, we deployed a second agent to North Korea to get her out of the country, and we've heard nothing from him for over two months. We fear he has either been killed or imprisoned."

Beck shook his head. "Please see me after this meeting. Perhaps we can work on something regarding your agent."

"So are you telling us that not only has North Korea been waging information warfare against us," asked Marine Commandant General Tom Justice, "but they are responsible for biological attacks that have killed hundreds of Americans, and perhaps may be behind the fires, bombings, and mortar attacks which have killed almost a thousand more? And if this is so," he paused, glancing around the room, "just what do we intend to do about it? Apparently, up to this point our response has been to turn the other cheek!"

The president's National Security Advisor stood up, walking around the table until he stood next to General Justice. "I for one would appreciate hearing advice from this room along the lines of what measured steps we could take to stop these activities. In other words, when the chief of staff and I present this situation to the president, what specific actions could we recommend be taken, absent jumping into a shooting war?"

The chairman of the Senate Intelligence Committee laughed, his voice a harsh bark. "Just what are those hundreds of American lives worth, sir? Are you suggesting their families don't deserve a strong response from our government?"

"Those hundreds of lives are worth a great deal, Senator Dobbs, but once the shooting starts, I have to ask, what are an additional two million or perhaps twenty million American lives worth? What about millions of deaths among our allies in Japan and South Korea? I'm certainly not recommending we merely slap their hands by adding more sanctions, but how many more must die to satisfy our desire for revenge? Is there not a just punishment without the very real possibility of punishing ourselves?"

Robert Williams whispered to Abel Adams. "Nobody wants to discuss the scary issue here. The opposing party accuses the president of doing nothing about these terrorist attacks. But that's when I really get nervous. If the president's handlers decide something drastic has to be done before the election, there's no telling what that might be—let alone what it might lead to."

Adams held his hand in front of his mouth and whispered in response. "Nothing like taking some wild-ass action to win another term."

Vice Admiral Mathis stood up again. "Working closely with my friend, Assistant Secretary Chet Hollomon at the Cyber and Infrastructure Security Agency, we believe that perhaps there is another way, gentlemen and ladies."

※

They sat on a park bench near the Jefferson Memorial. It was isolated enough that they felt confident in having a conversation which couldn't be overheard. "Early, I had no idea their plans included a mortar attack. I heard nothing at all to indicate something like that was in the works."

"Is it possible the mortars were the idea of some other

group? Maybe some entity trying to take advantage of the opportunity to pull off a major attack and have it blamed on the ones who were already suspects from the previous events?"

"I'd tend to agree with you if it weren't for the obvious clue that was left behind to make us think it was an Iranian-sponsored attack. They've been leaving similar clues almost everywhere, hotel receipts in an Iranian name, threatening notes in Farsi, cell phones and notes in Spanish, all obviously trying to direct suspicion away from North Korea and toward entities which we would easily accept as candidates."

"Once again, you've got a point, Angie. I guess it's hard to think in such a convoluted way. Do you suppose there are any more attacks planned?"

"I'm thinking the North Koreans have convinced themselves that so far they've been successful in not drawing suspicion toward themselves. As long as they believe that, I'm afraid the attacks will go on."

"So when is the U.S. going to make a move which will convince them otherwise?"

"Bob Williams attended a principals only meeting the other day with our director. He says the push is on to do that very thing."

"Thank God for that."

"Something else is bothering me. As far as I could tell, Colonel Ho-young might have been the only one who had any real knowledge of the people he had recruited for this program. Now that he's dead, who knows what comes next, where it happens, or how to contact the terrorists? So even if we show North Korea that we know who's behind all this, how are they going to contact the people they sent over here so they'll stop the attacks?"

"Damn it! That sounds like information the principals need before they put any plans in motion."

⁂

Bob Williams received a phone call, inviting him to visit the State Department's assistant secretary. It wasn't the kind of invitation you ignored. Since parking was nonexistent in the area, he caught a cab for the short trip from Langley to the Harry S. Truman Building in the Foggy Bottom neighborhood of Washington, D.C.

"Good morning, Mr. Williams. Thank you for coming."

"Good to see you again, Secretary Beck."

"During our meeting the other day, you mentioned a situation that reminded me yet again of how agencies are not sharing information. Secrets are kept by every intelligence entity in American government—FBI, CIA, State, DOD, DHS, Justice—and it's so compartmentalized and protected that the result is it's seldom shared. It's no wonder we miss things like your agent who is lost in North Korea. All of us should have been working on the release of this man."

"Yes, sir. Daniel Won-shik was born and raised in South Korea, went to school at Stanford—degrees in political science. We recruited him right after graduation, about twelve years ago. Now he has dual citizenship. He's got a wife and two small children who live near here in Fairfax County. This is his third trip into North Korea in the last three years. We sent him in because we had another agent there who had communicated with us that she needed to come out."

"This is the agent who they recruited as a translator for the group of terrorists?"

"Right. About the time Won-shik entered North Korea, we found out the other agent had actually returned to the U.S. along with the terrorists."

"And she's the one who you were talking about at the principals meeting?"

"Yes. So we have to assume that Won-shik got into the country, as he hasn't responded to our attempts to contact him for almost two months. His strategy was to penetrate the Ryongsung Complex in Pyongyang, since that was where the other agent was located when we last heard from her."

"Isn't that where the so-called Central Palace is located? Good grief, I would have figured the place was impenetrable. So let's talk about a plan to get him out of there, at least if he's still alive."

"He was entering the country as Pak Dong-woo. He had used that alias before and possessed a believable back-story."

"Was the story that he was North Korean or South Korean?"

"North Korean. I guess it all depends on when they caught him. If it was when he was entering the country, he would likely be treated as a spy and executed. If it was inside the palace complex, he may have assumed the identity of a DPRK soldier, and they would probably charge him with assault, or murder, or whatever it took to get a soldier's uniform and identification. If they caught him on the way out of North Korea, hopefully with his Pak Dong-woo identity, then he'd likely go to prison."

"All right, let's assume the latter of the three options. If it's either of the first two, we probably won't be able to help him anyway. What if we came up with something plausible, like a mother or sister in South Korea who is ill? Something that gives him an understandable reason to leave the country is what we're looking for. Then we could use our friends in South Korea to plead for his release on behalf of their sick citizen."

"Isn't it likely the North Koreans are going to want some sort of quid pro quo?"

"That's always the case where the DPRK is concerned. It could be something as simple as fifty tons of rice, or if the request goes to the chairman, maybe a few cases of his favorite champagne."

"If Daniel is confined in the Kaechon Prison, he may not have much time left. Our intelligence is very specific about the kind of treatment that goes on there. If he's still alive, he could be in pretty bad shape."

"I'll call the South Korean Ambassador today."

"Thanks for being the kind of person who gives a damn, Secretary."

"I consider that a true compliment, Mr. Williams."

CHAPTER 38

I Hold You Responsible
Sep'o County, North Korea November 1, 2024

One of the Wonsu's favorite pleasures was to ride horses. He kept Arabians at his palaces in Pyongyang and Wonsan, as well as at his cabin retreat in Sep'o County. At the palaces, his riding was limited to a half-mile racetrack and a small pasture. However, at his cabin there were thousands of acres at his disposal and approximately twenty miles of trails, some leading well above the tree line in the surrounding mountains.

On his next expedition to penetrate the defenses of Hiroko, the fat man decided to stage another outdoor event which he thought might interest the girl. As a precursor, however, he had to make arrangements for her to receive lessons.

His elderly sheepherder, Yoo Ki-hong, was his resident horseman and farrier at the cabin, and was only too happy to spend two hours a day with the girl during the time before the fat man's next visit. Hiroko was a willing pupil, and Yoo was very knowledgeable. Yoo's age was a mystery. Much of his unlined face was covered by a grey beard and mustache, and he kept his head shaved. In truth, he colored his facial hair so that he might pass for a much older man than he actually was.

Yoo had watched Hiroko carefully since her arrival, and appreciated the respect with which he and the auntie were treated by the girl. He also enjoyed the way she disdained the attentions of the guards. Most pleasing of all, he was heart-

ened by the auntie's confidential information that the Wonsu
had so far been unsuccessful in his boudoir pursuits of Hiroko. Her actions were certainly far different than some of the
cheerleader-types who had been guests at the retreat in the
past.

Yet Yoo was concerned with the fat man's new strategy of
pursuing the girl. Roundabout methods were sometimes surprisingly successful with girls who would otherwise be re-
pelled by a direct or forceful approach. So he had mixed feelings about this new assignment. He looked forward to being
around the girl, but he had no desire to play a supporting role
in the Wonsu's illicit love-life.

He considered being truthful with Hiroko, but he had
avoided that disclosure to anyone for several years now. Not
only was he thirty-five years younger than he appeared, he
was also in deep cover for his country. His only contact with
his employer at the South Korean National Intelligence Service was once a year, when the auntie was given a vacation to
visit her family in Pyongyang. The remainder of the time, he
went dark.

His mission assignment was simple: Kill the chairman.
There had been multiple opportunities to accomplish this.
However, the part that wasn't so simple was getting away with
his own life. Although the retreat was a mere sixty-five kilometers from the border with South Korea, it might as well
have been sixty-five hundred.

Yoo was confident he could do away with the guards on
the property, but the terrain to the south was extremely rugged and nearly devoid of people. His escape would have been
spotted from the air before he was more than a kilometer or
two off the property. Even if he could avoid the aircraft, the
border was well patrolled, and the DPRK guards happily shot
anyone in the Demilitarized Zone between the two Koreas.

On their fourth day of riding together, Yoo tried a limited
approach. "Hiroko, you're doing very well. How do you like
horseback riding?"

"I love being outside, particularly up here in the mountains, Mr. Yoo. But my backside is having a hard time getting
used to riding."

He laughed. "That always takes some getting used to. I
remember having similar problems in my younger days."

Hiroko abruptly pulled up her horse and sat there waiting for him to rein in and come back to where her horse was standing. "Mr. Yoo, do you really think your masquerade is believable?"

Yoo looked at her for a long moment. "What do you mean?"

"I've seen you throwing a saddle on these horses as though it weighed nothing at all. When you think no one is looking, you don't hunch over. In fact, you stand straight as a tree. From my window, I can see you in the barn in the early morning, doing your calisthenics and martial arts exercises. Furthermore, you have no more wrinkles than I do."

"I think you have me mixed up with someone else."

She dismounted and led her horse over to a bush so she could tie off the reins. "Can we not be honest with one another, Mr. Yoo?"

He dismounted as well. "Honesty is sometimes a very dangerous thing."

"I agree. For two years, I have been evasive, and often untruthful. Being honest would probably have cost me my life on more than one occasion."

"Perhaps I have noticed things about you as well. That you are old beyond your years. That you are very intelligent. That you are not a coward. That you have so far been able to keep your good conscience, despite pressures from the most powerful man in North Korea."

It had been a very long time since she had heard praise for anything other than her appearance. She cast her eyes down. "Thank you for noticing those things, Mr. Yoo."

"Regarding my age, have you considered that suspicion is very seldom directed toward the elderly?"

"No, but I suppose that might be correct. How old are you, Mr. Yoo?"

"Twenty-seven. I have kept this secret for five years."

"Your secret is safe with me. I will not ask you why."

"The answer to why may not be something you want to hear, Hiroko. Thank you." He paused, not sure if he should bring up the subject, but it certainly was something she needed to know. "Did Kim tell you what happened to your new friend, the girl you had to rescue from one of the guards?"

"I know that Konomi was transported to a hospital. I have heard nothing since then."

"I'm so sorry to tell you this. One of the guards told me she died before reaching the hospital. I don't know if it was from the injuries she suffered in the attack, or perhaps they did away with her on the way."

Hiroko hung her head. "I asked the auntie about her, and she told me she didn't know anything. For some reason, I didn't believe her. Thank you for telling me." She wiped tears from her face. "I find myself in a difficult position, Mr. Yoo. Do you have any advice for me?"

"My first observation is that the chairman may be dangling this feeling of freedom in front of you, just waiting to see whether you will use the four-wheeler or the horse to try to escape. As someone who has thought a great deal about the subject, I would recommend you not try it. Although it's only sixty-five kilometers to the South Korean border, and seventy from the Sea of Japan, you would be discovered in a matter of minutes. The punishment would undoubtedly be beyond anything you could imagine.

"Secondly, I may be wrong regarding his motivation. In that case, he is trying to gain your affection by allowing you this tiny bit of freedom. Do not be fooled. I hope you realize that once you surrender to these advances, you lose all of your power."

"Why do you say that?"

"Because many times at least half of the attraction which one person feels for another is the excitement of the pursuit and the thrill of anticipation. Once the pursuit is no longer necessary, the relationship can change dramatically."

"I don't understand why I possess any power. I am only a Japanese girl from a poor village. My father is a fisherman."

"Take my word for it, Hiroko. You do have power, but where Kim is concerned, it only exists as long as you keep the upper hand."

She stared at him. "Are you sure that fleeing is such an impossible thing?" She briefly touched his shoulder. "What if we went together?"

Her touch sent an electric shock from his shoulder to his face. He struggled with his 'Oriental inscrutability.' "That would only make it more so, Hiroko, as I would be honor bound to protect your life no matter the cost."

※

Daniel Won-shik had very little to remind him of the passage of time, so he had begun to keep track of the days by counting when they came for him to administer his daily beating. However, he could swear there had been a lightening of the sky in the filthy window high up on the prison wall at least twice, and there had been no beating to follow. Had they finally decided he was no longer worth the trouble? Perhaps that was so. Then again, maybe they figured he was almost dead anyway. Whatever the reason, Daniel was grateful for the opportunity to allow his lacerations and bruises to heal a bit.

He received no help whatsoever from the other prisoners. Perhaps that was because they feared any association with a person who was the subject of such continuous abuse. They had no desire to hear his complaints, let alone share in his misery in case the guards decided they were somehow connected.

Although all of them were slowly starving to death, on no one was this more obvious than Won-shik. His former chubby exterior was only a gaunt shadow of its former self. He was about to lose three teeth, as they wobbled every time his tongue found them. His gums were raw and swollen. Diarrhea was his constant companion, and his hair could no longer be described merely as sparse, but simply had been snatched out of his head by the handful by his torturers.

From the little bit he understood about untreated gunshot wounds, his leg was no longer hot to the touch, but the entry and exit areas were surrounded by proud flesh. The muscles in his thigh had drawn up to the extent that he estimated his injured leg was at least two inches shorter than the other. So running was completely out of the question. In fact, hobbling was almost more than he could manage.

On the afternoon when a jailer, someone previously unknown to him, came to his cell, Won-shik decided that this man undoubtedly would be the escort for his final trip. Surely, it was the day they intended to kill him. He certainly had plenty of regrets, but the only thing that came to mind was his wife and two little boys. Not only would he never see them again, but he wouldn't even have the opportunity to tell them goodbye. Despite the CIA's non-disclosure policy for agents killed in the line of duty, he prayed someone at the Agency would have the good heart to at least tell his family something about where he had gone and what he had been doing for his country. He almost broke down in front of the guard, just thinking about his family.

The two of them finally arrived at an area in the prison where he had not been before. The guard unlocked a cell and unceremoniously pushed Daniel inside. The guard said something to him, but he was unable to hear or understand his words before the door was locked behind him. Unlike his former cell, with multiple piles of rags crawling with bed bugs, there was only a single cot in the room. But most amazing was the razor, bar of soap, towel, and change of clothes lying on the bed. Miracle of miracles, there was a flush toilet in the corner.

As he hobbled into the room, he also saw a shower head on the wall. What in the world was this about? Probably they were going to expose him to this, and then suddenly take it away, as some sadist's idea of having fun with his sanity.

Although the shower only had a cold water tap, he luxuriated in the feel of finally getting himself clean after months of accumulated filth. He spent long minutes soaping and re-soaping his multitude of bug bites and skin lesions. The pleasant odor of the soap was a dramatic change from the smells of his former cell. There was no mirror in the room, but he managed to shave fairly well in spite of that. When he emerged from the shower, he found that the filthy clothes which he had worn day and night for many weeks had been removed. That was unplanned, as he had a 50,000 won note rolled up and sewn inside the band of his underwear. Too bad; perhaps he could have used it as a bribe. Nevertheless, he tugged on the new clothes and settled down to wait on what might come next.

Less than an hour after his clean-up, he was presented with a meal, plus two tablets in a small cup. The guard pointed at the pills and simply said, "Worms"—or at least that was what Daniel thought he said by reading his lips. For the first time in two months, the amount of grain was almost adequate, with small pieces of shredded chicken on top. The water in his flask seemed to be clear, rather than the cloudy mixture to which he had become accustomed. So he polished off his meal with the two anthelmintics, which were specifically used for the treatment of tapeworms, pinworms, and hookworms.

He finally decided that some human rights organization,

like the International Red Cross, was probably going to make an inspection, hence the prison authorities were performing a quick about face for the inspectors' benefit. Even so, if they were going to take this all away tomorrow, at least he was going to enjoy himself today.

But nothing happened. Every day he expected the other shoe to drop. Every day he was surprised. Contrary to his guess, the Red Cross did not make an appearance. Finally, on the fifth day, they came for him. Two guards escorted him, the one on his right side having to support him because of his limp. They passed through several internal passageways, all blooming with black mold, before emerging into a large open compound where hundreds of inmates were milling around.

Daniel quickly identified his final destination, a wall with three wooden posts standing in front. All of the posts were splintered, the wall itself was pock-marked, and the ground below was stained a permanent rusty brown. Not a sprig of grass attempted to show itself. He steeled himself to be walked to the wall, tied to one of the posts, and shot before this large, uncaring audience. He told himself not to break down at the last minute. If there was nothing left, at least he should go out with his dignity intact. He said a silent prayer that he wouldn't embarrass himself, and hoped his two small sons would not forget him.

Instead of being tied to the post, he was shoved into the back of a panel truck and handcuffed to a bar on the side. One guard sat in the rear with him, two others in the front seat. None of them spoke. None of them would even look at him.

The vehicle started up, approached the sally port, which consisted of two separate locked gates, and stopped. The first gate was raised electronically and the truck drove through to the open space between fences. The first gate was then locked behind the vehicle, a guard looked at some paperwork, opened the rear of the truck to check on the accuracy of the document, then the second gate opened in front, and they passed through to the outside world.

Daniel looked back through the filthy rear window, for the first time seeing the prison's exterior. He estimated the concrete walls were twelve feet high, topped with multiple coils of razor wire. The vehicle continued on its journey, heading south. What in the world did it mean?

When the truck entered the outskirts of Pyongyang, he decided they were taking him back to the Ryongsong Complex to officially charge him with the murder of the corporal. However, they drove on into the heart of the city, eventually leaving the metropolis, still headed southward. It struck him that there had been very few people lounging on the streets. In every American city, there would have been a significant number of panhandlers hanging around. In Pyongyang there were none. He did not know the government forcibly removed those people to the countryside to avoid the capital city making a poor impression on its few, mostly Chinese, visitors.

Still it was likely he was simply being relocated. There were many prisons in the country, and he searched his memory for one this far south, but could not think of any. They continued away from the capital. The roads were much rougher the further they drove from Pyongyang. Potholes and deep ruts made for defensive driving challenges over the next hundred kilometers.

They eventually entered the Joint Security Area, and approached the 72-hour bridge, which had been quickly erected in 1976 after an incident at a former border crossing. The panel truck stopped at a guard house simply labeled KPA #4, the driver showed their paperwork to the North Korean guards, and the rear of the vehicle was then opened. While Daniel was quickly loaded into the front seat of a small truck, radio contact was made with opposing forces on the South Korean side of the bridge.

The border crossing post on the South Korean side had not been manned for years, as a result of North Korean soldiers snatching Republic of Korea guards in uniform and taking them back to North Korea as hostages or prisoners. The post had thereafter been deemed unsafe by South Korean officials. Only on rare occasions, like that day, was the post occupied.

The truck pulled forward, stopping at the exact center of the bridge. Just across the yellow Military Demarcation Line sat four small wooden crates. The North Korean driver left his vehicle and walked to the crates, opening each one to check on the contents. He then returned to the truck, removed Daniel's handcuffs, and gave him a last, unceremonious push toward the other side. Daniel briefly wondered what had been in the crates. He might have been surprised to learn he had been traded for two dozen pairs of collectible tennis shoes.

While he shuffled across the bridge, now supported by a South Korean army lieutenant, the driver loaded the crates on his truck and reversed back to solid ground, returning to North Korean soil. Both sides observed the progress of the truck, as the bridge had actually been declared unfit for travel several years previously. The Americans had volunteered to repair it, but the DPRK refused. So everybody was relieved that the loaded truck made it across, and both bridge and vehicle remained unscathed.

Standing beside a military ambulance on the South Korean side of the bridge was Angela Martinelli. She had insisted she be the one to welcome Daniel back home, as well as participate in his debriefing. When she saw his physical deterioration, her usually professional demeanor failed her, and she couldn't help but weep. When the realization struck her that he was also deaf, she was wracked with guilt for what the man had gone through in his heroic attempt to extricate her from North Korea and save her life. How in the world could she ever repay him?

When his military airlift reached Los Angeles five days later, Daniel was met by his wife Sarah and his boys, Sam and James. As the elder of the two, Sam, who was all of six years old, took his mother and little brother by the hand and led them to his father, who waited for them up the rear ramp of the aircraft in its small medical unit. James and Sarah were crying, but Sam was determined to show Daniel he had been the man of the house while his father was gone. While his lip was quivering, he simply brushed his eyes with his sleeve, then grabbed hold of his dad's neck with both arms and would not let go.

It fell to Angela to take Sarah aside and explain that her husband had been rendered deaf by his captors, but that he had been evaluated at the Allgood Army Hospital at Yongsan Garrison in Seoul, and the opinion was that there was likely treatment to help him recover. Likewise, they acknowledged that several surgeries on his leg were in his future, as well as months of physical therapy, but the expectation was the damage could be almost completely corrected. At any rate, he had survived, and he was home.

⚛

In Sep'o County, the fat man had returned to his retreat, and, as expected, his first order of business was to go horseback riding with Hiroko. She hesitated, pleading a lack of experience, but of course he prevailed and they struck out across the countryside.

In mid-fall, the temperature in the highlands was not yet extreme, but this happened to be an unusually mild day. As they rode higher, however, the thermometer began a slow descent, and the wind out of the north made Hiroko wish she had worn a heavier jacket. They stopped for lunch, but it was a hurried affair, as they couldn't seem to find a spot which was sheltered from the wind.

As they rode on, the Wonsu said, "Your riding is very good for a beginner. The shepherd has done well in his instruction."

"Old Mr. Yoo is an excellent teacher, but I am still not very good at this."

"It only takes practice. You'll be galloping your horse in no time."

"I can't imagine riding any faster than we are now in the mountains."

The fat man grabbed the opportunity to impress the girl with his skilled horsemanship. "Perhaps you are ready to attempt a canter." He spurred his horse forward at a rapid clip until he was some hundred meters ahead, then he pulled up and waited for her to catch up at her much slower pace.

Hiroko pushed his ego. "Was that a gallop?"

"Oh, no. A gallop is much faster." And with that he tore off up the inclined path at a frenzied pace. He then pulled his horse up, turned around with a rollback, and repeated the demonstration coming back down the hill. Perhaps he had overestimated his abilities, as it became necessary to focus his complete attention on keeping his seat while attempting to appear nonchalant.

Neither the animal nor the rider was accustomed to such a pace on a steep, rock-strewn path. The horse was due some sympathy, in that she was trying to endure the bouncing weight of a large fat man on her back, as well as retain her footing going downhill at a high speed. Something had to give.

The horse stumbled on a loosened rock, and the chairman of North Korea flew over his animal's head. He was able to twist to the side just before impact and instead of breaking his skull, he snapped his right clavicle, with a jagged bone protruding through the skin. The tumble further down the path almost tore off his jacket and left him bruised and bloodied on his side and shoulder, while his right ear was shredded in the rough gravel.

Hiroko slid down and hurried to him. "How badly are you hurt?"

The fat man moaned in pain, attempting to keep his arm stable while he rolled to his left. "That damned horse almost killed me." He finally pulled himself to his knees with his left arm and extracted a double-barreled derringer from a holster in his boot.

Seeing the gun, Hiroko backed away, thinking he was about to take out his wrath on her. Instead, he turned his attention to the bay mare, which limped back up the hill toward the two of them. He took quick aim and fired both barrels into her chest. The horse screamed, reared up on her hind legs, and fell when she attempted to land on her damaged front leg. She tried twice to regain her footing, and then lay back panting in agony before she died.

The Wonsu turned to the girl and spoke through gritted teeth. "You'll need to go back to the barn and bring me another horse." He took another look at his shoulder. "Maybe you'd better drive the four-wheeler up here." She turned to go and he called out again. "Leave me your jacket. The wind is very cold."

Hiroko and Yoo were back in 45 minutes, Yoo driving the dual-seated four-wheeler and leading a horse behind. The Wonsu noticed the girl had found a coat. Hiroko's small jacket had done little to warm him, and his teeth were chattering. "What took you so long? I'm freezing up here!"

"You're quite a distance away from the cabin," Yoo said, "and it's pretty rough going in spots for a four-wheeler, Chairman. Let's get you loaded. Hiroko can drive you. I'll follow along on her horse."

"That horse you trained is worthless, Yoo."

Keeping his anger invisible, Yoo looked over at the formerly beautiful animal. "I guess you're right."

"I hold you entirely responsible for this, Yoo."

Hiroko flashed a quick look in the shepherd's direction.

"Yes, Chairman."

After they returned to the cabin, the fat man's arm was

bound to his body with strips of cloth cut from a sheet, then he was carefully placed in the back seat of the helicopter, and per his orders, provided a bottle of brandy to consume during the two-hour journey. Within minutes, the bird was up, and he was whisked away to a waiting physician at a hospital in Pyongyang.

As the copter disappeared over the distant tree line, Hiroko walked back to the barn with the horse while Yoo stowed away the four-wheeler. They met briefly before her return to the cabin. "You do realize he was serious in his threat?"

"I have no illusions about that. My only wish is that I had been ready to flee when I went back up the mountain. However, with no water or provisions in hand, it would have been foolhardy."

"Why don't we leave tonight?"

He shook his head. "Two things. I have unfinished business to which I must attend, and I won't allow you to risk your life just so I can save mine. That is unacceptable."

"What unfinished business?"

"Again, Hiroko, it is better you did not know."

Social media posts: *Our country continues to accept Muslims, despite mounting evidence they are committing acts of terrorism against us. The handwriting is clearly on the wall. They want observance of Sharia law. Our flag, our national anthem, and our God offend them. So we bend over backward to kowtow to their demands. Many countries in Europe have already come to realize how damaging Muslim immigrants can be to their way of life and peace of mind. How many attacks will it take for us to stand and say enough is enough?*

America has always been a land of immigrants, and we are stronger for it. Some, however, would have us go back on our promise to the rest of the world, a promise that we are a nation which welcomes and values other people.

The message on the Statue of Liberty was written by the FRENCH, not Americans. I for one am sick of the stinking huddled masses coming to our shores, particularly when all they do is take our welfare, complain about our culture, disrespect our flag, and then attack us.

For the third time in a week, Early and Angela found themselves in totally unfamiliar territory. Sarah Won-shik was spending as much time as she could at her husband's bedside as he worked his way through multiple surgeries and physical therapy. In response, Angela had offered to help look after the two boys, Sam and James. Although he couldn't exactly identify how it had happened, Early had been recruited to assist.

Neither had been around small children before for any length of time, let alone where they were supposed to be the responsible adults. The first two evenings, they'd taken the boys out to eat, but weren't quite prepared for the typical appetite requirements, let alone the attention span, of a three-year-old.

So on this night, Angela had agreed to prepare spaghetti. It was quite a hit, as was the ice cream for dessert. Early then occupied the boys in the den while Angela tried to remove dried spaghetti sauce from her usually spotless table, chairs, and floor.

Thank goodness Sarah had provided entertainment for the evening, so Angela found them some fifteen minutes later laid out on the rug. The boys were draped all over Early. He was reading *The Cat in the Hat* for the second time, and using different voices for the characters.

She let him finish. "All right, you two, get in that bathtub and see if you can wash the spaghetti off your faces. Then we'll get you in your pajamas before your mom gets here."

They resisted to the tune of "Aw, do we have to?" But she was not to be challenged, so they retreated to the tub.

Early cocked an ear. "From all that splashing, it sounds like there'll be more water on the floor than in the tub."

She gave him an appraising look. "Why didn't you ever have kids, Early?"

"To the best of my recollection, I think you need a wife for that. Besides, I never had the time, too many deployments, and too many long work weeks in between. How about you, Angie? It looked like you knew what you were doing with them."

"As much as I've traveled, it would have been impossible."

"Yeah. Maybe so. Still, it looked sort of like it came naturally to you."

Angela sat on the couch beside him, a flood of thoughts passing through her head. All of a sudden, it was overwhelming. She didn't trust herself to say anything.

Chapter 39

At Last, A Response
Fort Meade, Maryland December 18, 2024

Russia refers to information warfare as 'spetzpropaganda', or special propaganda. They include all of an adversary's computer network operations which they can reach via electronic, psychological, and information operations to achieve political objectives without using military force. They are joined in this mindset by China, North Korea, and Iran in particular, and to some extent, by several other smaller players.

America had long convinced itself that cyber warfare was only to be used during wartime. During peacetime, the country occupied itself by finding weaknesses in security systems so that, when war came, they could initiate an attack on the enemy's information technology. Contrarily, Russia holds three very different beliefs.

The first is that the Cold War never ended. For sure, the United States emerged at the end of the 1980s and beginning of the 90s as the world's primary power. But there had been no surrender by the Russians, so their side of the Cold War simply became low key. However, it did not stop. In fact, they continuously tested the limits of America and its allies. Their continuous efforts to provoke America—either through spycraft, supporting terrorists, trading with pariah countries, information manipulation, and all manner of threatening activities, and even dangerous fly-bys by Russian aircraft— always came close to the edge of what could be tolerated.

Secondly, there is a quote from the Russian chess champion and dissident Gary Kasparov which reveals much of his homeland's motivation. *Every country has its own mafia, but in Russia, the mafia has its own country.* Almost every decision by Putin ensures that his oligarchs not only are protected, but also personally profit from his conniving. After all, he is one of them, and by some estimates, the richest of them all. There is much speculation that he is perhaps the richest man in the entire world, with literally his entire fortune obtained outside what normally is perceived by Western nations as the rule of law.

Finally, Russia believes there is very little difference between wartime and peacetime. They are constantly defending themselves in either circumstance, as well as continuing to mount offensives against the West. They have discovered that submarines, aircraft carriers, and missiles are very expensive and only serve to maintain the status quo. Moreover, it's almost impossible to outspend the United States on military hardware. So Russia has finally concluded that geeks and hackers are just as good as, and perhaps more effective, while certainly less expensive, than soldiers and spies.

If they can disrupt, deny, degrade, or distort the information their enemies rely on to keep their nations running, then so be it. If they can plant seeds of doubt or mistrust, if they can confuse, if they can polarize, if they can demoralize the mighty United States and its allies by merely launching an information warfare campaign, then they have successfully met many of their goals and by comparison, at very low cost.

Social media and the content published on it certainly has been proven to influence people, and there is ample evidence polarization has been created. Whether the issue is partisan politics, religion, race, respect for women, education, Confederate flags and statues, sexual orientation, gun control, abortion, police brutality versus police support, military spending, illegal voting, immigration, the influence of money on the political process, environmental protection, respect for the American flag, exports/imports, tariffs, social ills, the availability of an affordable college education, a higher minimum wage, income disparity, taxation methods, government spending, or relationships with other countries, it seems the American people are all too willing to take non-negotiable sides on almost everything.

One important strategy behind information warfare is

aimed squarely at people who have been identified via computer algorithms as believing strongly on either side of a given issue. Frankly, the Russians don't care which side the individual is on. The point is to flood social media with posts which inflame either or both sides on a given subject. The matter being discussed differs, but posts either supporting or demeaning the issue are guaranteed to be shared and spread like wildfire.

So there was ample evidence for the United States to engage in reciprocal activity. However, the straw which broke the proverbial camel's back was the finally proven linkages between Russia, North Korea, and Iran in the many physical attacks of terrorism which had struck the United States in the spring and summer of 2024.

After weeks of intricate planning, during which the United States secretly pre-inserted malware in hundreds of foreign information systems, as well as in collaboration and coordination with her most trusted allies, the U.S. Cyber Command, located at Fort Meade, Maryland, stood ready to launch a series of attacks to convince this triumvirate of enemies that they were going to pay a high price for their recent actions. There would be no last-minute negotiations, added economic sanctions, or back-and-forth snide remarks on social media.

At 8:30 AM Eastern time on the appointed day, four very high-level telephone calls were initiated from Washington, D.C. Assistant Secretary of State Daniel Beck contacted the Minister of Foreign Affairs in Moscow: "Minister, I do not require a response from you as to what I am about to say, but it is important you hear this information right now. During the last six months, the U.S. has been attacked in a variety of ways by agents of North Korea.

"Three of those attacks involved the distribution of anthrax among large numbers of our citizens. While we know that Russians did not directly participate in the attacks themselves, we have undeniable proof that you supplied North Korea with ten thousand doses of anthrax vaccine in late February of this year. Your country understood very well why the DPRK was obtaining that vaccine, and so you bear a significant measure of the responsibility. We also have a full confession from a North Korean agent who was captured after one of those anthrax attacks. You might be familiar with his name—

Colonel Ho-young. He was second in command in their Bio-Terrorism Directorate, and during questioning was quick to disclose your country's role.

"Additionally, at least three mortar tubes and a dozen mortar shells, some of which contained the United Nations-banned white phosphorus, were shipped from one of your military warehouses in Semipalatinsk to members of a Mexican cartel and then used against American citizens in Washington, D.C. Finally, since 2014, your country has operated a cyber-warfare program against our country, first just from St. Petersburg, and more recently via a number of other locations around the globe.

"We had hoped that shutting down your troll factory in St. Petersburg during the 2018 election cycle would convince you that your interference in our social media communications would no longer be tolerated. Apparently, your president and your government fail to learn.

"In 2020, your agents inserted malware in the computer systems of 87 of our federal agencies and private sector companies; all attempting to steal information or interfere with operations. Perhaps after today you will give pause to such behavior in the future.

"At this time, Russian troll groups are operating, not only from St. Petersburg, but from no less than six other locations, having targeted the United States with over ten million messages just in this year alone. Your country has attempted to use these troll groups to influence the last four U.S. elections, including those just last month. This will not stand.

"For these acts, as well as your endorsement of other heinous acts by your partners in other countries, you will be punished. Now listen very carefully. No armaments will be used in this punishment. No members of our military will enter, fly over, or sail near your country during the carrying out of this punishment. So you will not—repeat not—be under armed attack. You need to immediately advise your president of this message so that he will not overreact. If he miscalculates and responds in a knee-jerk fashion, the consequences could be a holocaust, after which your country will cease to exist.

"Also know that the proof for all of the items I have discussed will be presented to a full meeting of the U.N. General Assembly. Do you understand?"

"My government will not stand for—"

"I have given you our message. This conversation is over, Minister."

The first vice-president of Iran was contacted at the same time at his residence in the Sa'dabad Palace by the vice-president of the United States, with much the same message. The VP accused that country of supplying terrorists for the attacks on the U.S; their support of the fighting in Syria, Iraq, Yemen, Afghanistan, and the Palestinian Territories; violating U.N. sanctions against their country; building out a stockpile of weapons-grade uranium far in excess of any agreement; attacks on Israel through their proxies; supplying anthrax seed stock to North Korea; obtaining missile parts from North Korea; carrying out banned missile testing; intercepting ships carrying oil in the Persian Gulf; purposely downing a Ukrainian airliner over Iran; continuing cyberwarfare attacks against the United States and her close allies in the region: Israel, Jordan, United Arab Emirates, Bahrain, Qatar, Kuwait, and Saudi Arabia; and the wholesale murder of thirty of America's foreign agents and informants.

The Iranian vice president interrupted. "All these so-called facts have been manufactured by the Israelis. They are determined to bring our country to its knees. They want us to remain a pariah in the international community, but they can only accomplish that with lies. They provided your country with intelligence so that you could launch your drone strike against Major General Qasem Soleimani, commander of our Quds Force, thus murdering him in the desert. Then Israeli agents murdered our heroic nuclear scientist, Mohan Fakhrizadeh, outside Tehran."

"You mean the same Fakhrizadeh who you told UN inspectors was a scientific educator and academic, who had nothing to do with your military? And yet you buried him via a military funeral. Why is it that your government continues to think the rest of the world are fools?" The U.S. VP concluded by saying Iran was not being attacked militarily, but nevertheless, a heavy price was to be paid.

The president of South Korea had agreed to contact his

counterpart in North Korea, saying that he was providing the information at the request of the United States simply because the two Koreas had open communication channels, while the U.S. had less direct contact with the North on a short timeline. He began by listing the many attacks that representatives of the North had carried out against the United States, as well as the satellite cyberwarfare sites in Vietnam, Venezuela, and Mexico. "They have detailed information about your arms sales to Syria, Yemen, Namibia, and Libya, as well as missile sales to Iran. They have satellite proof of you violating trade embargoes by transferring oil and coal shipments at sea. Your use of counterfeit American currency and stolen cyber-securities to pay and be paid for these operations are well documented.

"They know all about the operations of your Bureau 121, Chairman. But most damning of all, the U.S. has undeniable, first-person evidence, provided by a Colonel Ho-young, who they captured in Memphis, and he has confessed that every incident—conventional, chemical, and biological—as well as all cyber-attacks, originated from your personal, direct orders.

"What is mystifying to me is your actions during one of your recent conferences with the American president."

"To what are you referring, Mr. President?"

"I wonder what you were thinking during such an important conference. Your cyberwarfare location in Namibia launched just over one hundred attacks—first against financial, petroleum, and utilities industries in New York City and Houston—then on organizations in London, Berlin, Tokyo, Tel Aviv, Rome, Madrid, Ankara, Bangkok, and Hong Kong, as well as banks here in Seoul. The American president knew about those attacks within minutes of their occurrence. Is it any wonder you have not been able to establish an agreement? The Americans will be providing all of these proofs to the United Nations General Assembly. They also caution that you should not overreact to the punishment."

"How dare they imply that my country uses biological weapons?"

"Chairman, I have seen the evidence to everything I mentioned with my own eyes and can affirm their proof will be very obvious to every nation on this earth which views it."

"It must have been the fault of the general in charge of my state security program. I will see that he is punished. Will that satisfy the Americans?"

"I am sorry, Chairman. The Americans will accept no excuse. Your own agent has implicated you personally. They have told me there is no longer another alternative." He glanced at his watch. "Within seconds, your country will be unable to carry on normal business." He hesitated. "I wish it were not so, Chairman. When this punishment is over, and if you have finally decided to make satisfactory amends in order to avoid prosecution for war crimes, we must speak again."

The U.S. president spoke to the president of the Peoples' Republic of China, advising him of the overwhelming evidence gathered against the three guilty parties, particularly as it related to biological and chemical incidents and mortar attacks using white phosphorus, as well as the steps the U.S. was taking as they spoke. He reiterated that China remained a valuable partner to the United States, but there was a limit to his tolerance. He mentioned the Chinese government's ongoing and complicit role in the shipment of tens of millions of doses of Fentanyl to the U.S. He also spoke about the continued violation of international law related to the theft of intellectual property by the Chinese government as well as Chinese businesses. He spoke about the disregard of trade agreements. He spoke about China's continued economic support of the North Korean dictatorship. He made sure to mention Chinese attempts to monopolize sea lanes in the South China Sea. He spoke about the Chinese failure to adhere to agreements made as to the independence of Hong Kong, and China's recent military incursions against India. Finally he added there might be a lesson to be learned related to launching information warfare against his country.

The Chinese president thanked him for the courtesy call, smirking as he hung up. When the completeness of the response against Russia, Iran, and North Korea became evident within a few hours, perhaps he had an entirely different level of appreciation for having avoided similar treatment.

At 8:35 AM Eastern on December 18, 2024, Vice-Admiral Julie Mathis at U.S. Cyber Command, in synchronized coordination with Chet Hollomon, Assistant Secretary for Cyber

and Infrastructure at DHS, gave the go-ahead. Simultaneously, aircraft, satellites, military bases in Japan, South Korea, Germany, Great Britain, France, Canada, Australia,
Guam, Bahrain, Afghanistan, Greenland, Iceland, the United
Arab Emirates, Hawaii, and Alaska, as well as ships and
submarines in the Atlantic, Pacific, Arctic, and Indian
Oceans, began their coordinated and overwhelming cyber-
attack. Every piece of disabling software was activated. Jam-
ming operations were switched to full activity mode. It began
without leaks, tweets, or any further warnings.

As a special recognition of the suffering he had endured
at the hands of North Korea, CIA Agent Daniel Won-shik had
positioned his wheelchair on the right-hand side of VADM
Mathis in the command center. Daniel's right leg and head
were still bandaged. It was appropriate to acknowledge that
he had earned the right to observe his government's revenge
in action. During the course of the morning's cyber-attack,
many people in the center, including the secretaries of Defense, State, and Homeland Security, came by to thank him
for his heroism and wish him well in his recovery.

No communication system was left as a functioning entity in Russia, Iran, or North Korea. No cable, telephone,
internet, nor intranet was working. No military facility and no
ship at sea possessed any ability to transmit or receive messages other than by mechanical means such as semaphore.
All public utility systems were breached. Computerized electricity, natural gas, water, sewer, and wastewater systems
were shut down. All local and international banking and
credit transactions came to a screeching halt. All traffic signals within the three countries were taken out of service.
Money ceased to move within, into, or out of the targeted
countries. The United States military did temporarily take
over air traffic control systems in order to get airborne planes
safely on the ground, but once that was accomplished, even
those modern communication systems stopped.

Also targeted were auxiliary cyber locations, such as
those launched by North Korea in Vietnam, Venezuela, Mexico, and Namibia; one in Syria sponsored by Iran; and a half-
dozen sites connected to Russia. Both Mexico and Vietnam
moved police forces to cordon off the North Korean sites and
took the occupants into custody for further investigation. Cy-
ber-operations in Namibia and Venezuela had been pene-

trated by U.S. Cyber Command and were taken out of service.

The Bank of the Caribbean also had its information systems taken down. Any deposit and payment transactions that could be traced to North Korea, including accounts linked to terrorists, were zeroed out, with those monies transferred to a holding fund at the International Court of Justice within the United Nations.

After receiving the insulting phone call from the president of South Korea, the Wonsu was just reaching for his call button when the lights blinked twice and then went out. Because he was averse to being in a room with window exposure, the darkness was overwhelming. He hollered at the top of his voice for his aide, inadvertently bumped his slowly mending right shoulder on the chair, and screamed at a significantly higher pitch.

The aide ran in, waving a large flashlight before him. "Yes, Great Leader?"

"What is going on?"

"It must be a power problem, Great Leader. It happens all the time outside the palace. May I escort you to a room with a window?"

"Yes, of course. Then tell my personal guards to report to me right now. Once they are here, contact Colonel-General Moo-sung and have him visit me immediately. Then ask my doctor to fetch me an injection for this unendurable pain."

"Yes, Great Leader."

When his palace guards reported, the Wonsu issued explicit orders. The guards then faded into the shadows of the room. When Moo-sung arrived, the chairman started in on him immediately. "The Americans have begun a cyber-attack on the Fatherland, and it is all due to your incompetence!"

"Wonsu, I simply—"

"Silence. You have carelessly left evidence that could be traced directly to our country. You had no authority to initiate these attacks on your own order! Your lackey, Ho-young, has been captured and spilled his guts to the Americans." The chairman grimaced in pain as he leaned over in his chair, withdrew the derringer from his boot, and pointed it at his general. "I think I'll shoot you right here." He glanced around the room, not failing to note the three layers of oriental rugs beneath Moo-sung's feet, which undoubtedly would be soiled with blood and gore. He shook his head in disgust and motioned to his concealed guards.

"Strip him of his rank and take the former general into custody. Place him under a triple guard. Killing him in private is far too good for him. If he resists, shoot him in both knees and both elbows. This requires a great audience so the people can witness what we do to traitors."

The effect was similar in Iran and Russia, with entire cities coming to a complete standstill. Actually, it was more severe, as Iran and Russia were more dependent on technology for normal life. In North Korea, most of the poor people in the countryside noticed very little difference in their lives. Those in the cities, however, suddenly began to appreciate the few luxuries they no longer had.

In Iran and Russia, except for face-to-face interchanges, there simply was no communication. Entire armies, navies, and air commands were incommunicado. Russia lost contact with its communication, weather, and spy satellites, its missile and radar defense systems, and even the International Space Station.

President Putin wanted to call a meeting of the Russian Federal Assembly, which was composed of the State Duma (lower house) and the Federation Council (upper house), intending to declare a state of emergency and introduce martial law until the situation could be corrected. But then, calling a meeting required being able to communicate in some way with his assembly members to notify them to report at a certain time and place. Likewise, many of them had to travel long distances, normally via train or airplane. To say that he was apoplectic was an understatement.

Chapter 40

Calling on Genghis Khan
Pyongyang, North Korea January 2, 2025

Despite the impact on infrastructure in his capital city, the chairman came to a decision. He put two dozen soldiers to work creating posters that were lettered by hand, then deployed two dozen more into the city to distribute the notices, which ordered the populace to assemble at Kim Il-sung Square at ten AM on the morrow.

The men who maintained his small herd of Quarter horses at the Central Palace were directed to polish every square millimeter of four sets of saddles and bridles. Four others were selected for the honor of riding those beautiful animals, and they set to pressing and polishing their dress uniforms, including ceremonial swords. In addition to their regular regalia, each would carry a twenty-meter length of hemp rope.

At the appointed hour, three thousand soldiers—almost the entire contingent from the Ryongsung Complex—goose-stepped down the highway, eventually reaching the square, where some hundred thousand men, women, and children had assembled. All shivered in the frigid temperature of the new year. Behind the soldiers came a small flat-bed truck. In the back, chained to an upright beam, stood former Colonel-General Moo-sung. His rank insignia had been ripped from his collar and epaulets.

Next in the parade came the four Quarter horses, all with matching tack, silver accouterments, and riders. As the jingling spectacle arrived in the square, some in the audience were undoubtedly reminded of glorious days gone by, when all the great wars in Asia were fought on horseback, and entire countries were won and lost because of their warriors' skills in the saddle.

Finally came the black Zil limousine, which had also been shined beyond brilliance. When the great vehicle reached the square, the chairman himself emerged and climbed the stairs to one of two hastily erected podiums. In the absence of electricity, a generator was started in the background to power the loudspeakers so that all might hear their fearless leader. Also, a heater had been included with the temporary power supply for the convenience of the chairman.

Moo-sung was escorted to the other of the wooden podiums and held there by two of his former soldiers. The Wonsu glared over. His right arm was still in a wrapped sling, concealed underneath a heavy jacket. He had always been self-conscious about revealing any injury or sickness which his subjects might interpret as a sign that their leader was merely human.

Finally deciding the crowd was ready, he approached the microphone. He first explained to the audience his version of what had happened, and that their mortal enemy, the United States, was behind it all. He explained that he had been advised there was evidence which showed beyond a doubt that former Colonel-General Moo-sung had, without his knowledge or the knowledge of the rest of the country's military leadership devised plans to attack their enemy.

He followed by admitting that, although the attacks had been successful, killing 'several millions' of Americans, Moo-sung had dishonored the Fatherland by using biological and chemical weapons, which were banned by the United Nations, and had drawn the disgust of the rest of the world. He raised his voice to a shout. "And so, fellow comrades, I come to you this morning with this undisputed evidence. I ask that you decide, what shall we do with a man who, as the Minister of State Security, we all entrusted with the safety of our nation? What shall we do with a man who betrays that trust? What shall we do with a man who caused our enemy to attack our communications and power grids? What shall we do with a man who brings shame and dishonor on the Fatherland?

"Reflect on our great history. Think of our great ancestor,

Genghis Khan, whose soldiers rode magnificent animals like these," he paused and gestured toward the horsemen, "and ruled over half of the known world eight hundred years ago. The blood of the great Khan still courses through our veins—yours and mine. In fact, it is to him that we owe our strength, our virility, our rightful place in the world." He pointed at Moo-sung. "What would the great Khan have done with a traitor such as this? Tell me, what is your verdict?"

Moo-sung was not the sort whose reputation engendered any positive emotion—let alone sympathy—among his own troops, let alone the citizenry. The response started within the ranks of the men and women standing at parade rest, and quickly was taken up by many of the crowd. "Justice! Guilty! Execute him!" It took no time at all for the chant to develop into a demanding roar which shook the square. "Execution!"

The Wonsu bent slightly at the waist and bowed his head, giving the impression that he was simply obeying the will of the people. "Then he will suffer like all condemned traitors suffered in the days of our ancestors." He nodded to the guards at either side of Moo-sung. They took up the ropes extended to them by the horsemen, wrapping and then tying one around the prisoner's upper right arm, a second to the opposite arm, and the last two ropes to each of his legs directly above the knee.

The convicted man was then pushed off the small podium, and each of the horsemen took one of the opposing four points of the compass. A very large bass drum began a slow beat over the loudspeaker. The horses were trained to respond to the drum. Every time the beat sounded, each animal raised one leg high above the concrete and took a half-step forward. This continued until they had taken up the slack in the ropes. The drum stopped. The horsemen then looked to the chairman for final instructions, and he made a cutting motion with his left hand.

As the drum began again, each horse took a half-step forward and the prisoner's upper body jerked, suspended a few inches above the ground in a spread-eagled position. The Wonsu suppressed a laugh as he noticed the sunlight reflected from the condemned man's bald head.

Another half-step in the four directions and the ropes grew so taut that some in the audience swore they hummed. They held that position for some thirty seconds before the drum struck again, followed by another half-step. Moo-sung's former look of belligerence dissolved into an otherworldly scream.

The drum sounded again, the horses took another half-step, and the body was now four feet off the ground, level with the horsemen's saddles. Many would say later that they saw the general's limbs stretching. Others said they could hear his shoulders and hips popping out of joint. The screaming continued, but the volume was much decreased, punctuated by panting and moaning.

Another drum beat, another half-step, and his left arm separated from his body. Blood gushed from the wound, spraying some in the nearby crowd, but the drum did not pause. Another beat and a half-step more, and the other arm separated, this time with less blood and no sound whatsoever from the general. A final drum beat, a half-step more, and the final ropes were no longer taut, as his right leg separated.

The riders removed the ropes from their saddles, and the separated remains were left for the street cleaners. The crowd moved off in silence, stunned into stupefaction by what they had seen, and convinced beyond any shadow of doubt that they would never commit a crime which required such punishment.

⚛

Early and Angela had just completed another evening taking care of Daniel and Sarah's two boys. This time they'd built a small charcoal fire in Angela's tiny back yard, letting Sam and James cook their own hot dogs. Nothing burned up and miraculously, nobody got burned. It was a success.

"Those two are starting to grow on me, Angie."

"Yeah, me too."

"Do you know anywhere we could rent a couple of kids?"

She laughed. "A lease would probably be too much of a long-term commitment. We'd have to throw in a clause to give them back when they reached fourteen."

He stretched in the lawn chair, looking up in the sky. "How long has it been since you've seen any stars?"

"Every night in North Korea, when they shut off the electricity."

He snorted. "Maybe there's an easier way than that. I'm going to see my mother in a couple of weeks. Why don't you go with me? On a clear night, you can see at least a million stars from her back yard."

"I'm afraid to leave town while this cyber-warfare is going on. I've got a feeling this won't be the end of the confrontation."

He nodded, "Probably true, but there's always going to be a reason to stay close to the office. Right now I'm looking for an opportunity to get away from the place."

"Why don't you ask me again next week? I'd like to meet your mom."

"Thanks. She's a good person. How long do you think our cyber-attack is going to continue? From what I'm hearing, those countries are already in pretty dire straits. Early winter in Russia and North Korea with no heat—that's enough to start a war right there."

"Nothing seems to be resolved on that yet. I'm betting they'll let up on Russia and Iran first. The allies are raising hell about the disruption in oil shipments all across Europe. The price at the pump is already up eighty cents a gallon here. So, if for no other reason, they'll get some relief. But North Korea is another matter. Nobody depends on them for anything, except maybe Iran buying their missile technology, and terrorists purchasing weaponry.

"Unfortunately, China is pressing for the DPRK's relief, although I'm not sure why. The Chinese president may want to be perceived as their benefactor and savior. My guess is the White House was hoping for a regime change, and are holding out in hopes there's a military coup. That's probably why China is trying to get things resolved right away."

"A military coup could be extremely dangerous. You never know what kind of substitute fool you might get after a coup."

"That's one reason why I'm vacillating about going out of town."

After the boys had been retrieved by their mother, and Early was on his way home, Angela lay awake for a very long time. She'd always thought of herself as a rational being, with the ability to think through complex problems which either life or her career threw her way. But the subject of Early Johnson was somehow not fitting into her common approach of a simple analysis of pros and cons.

If there was to be a life together, which might even include kids—after all, she was not yet forty—how could that possibly fit with her work? How in the world could she continue in this role of risking her life when she had someone or several someones waiting on her to come home?

She was unsure how to evaluate him on issues such as awakening feelings which she had previously found ways to suppress or ignore. Up to that point, she would have claimed to be generally satisfied with the status quo of her life. Early, however, was confusing the picture.

She found herself thinking about him even when he wasn't around, and that was very odd. It had always been a simple thing to keep portions of her life compartmentalized, but thoughts of the colonel were intruding in unexpected times and places—even in North Korea, for goodness' sake.

Was that acceptable? Angela acknowledged there were really only two options, chase or embrace. Chase him away, at least far enough away so that she could regain control over her thoughts, emotions and plans—or embrace what was happening and open herself up to a radically different life, with all sorts of unknowns.

Chase had always been her go-to option. Even during college, she had retreated from relationships which threatened to become meaningful. First, it was because she wanted to finish her education, and then had come the CIA, which had obviously left no room for any personal life. But now there was Early. Times change.

❀

Early's mother, Ruth Johnson, was not what Angela expected at all. "Grandmotherly" was probably not even in the woman's vocabulary. She was fit. Her clothes were every bit as up-to-date as Angela's, and her hair was cut stylishly short, with blond highlights throughout. Now retired, she had been the county prosecutor, then a circuit court judge. Thankfully, she had not yet directed her powers of interrogation toward her son's new romantic interest.

Early's description of Angela's job had simply been that she was employed by a sister government agency and couldn't talk about her work. Apparently, having heard a similar story about her son's job, Ruth understood and observed the restriction.

After what his mother described as Early's favorite

meal—roast beef, potatoes, carrots, onions, brown gravy, and homemade yeast rolls—she delivered an unbelievable cherry cobbler to the table. Too late, Angela realized she had not consumed so much food since she was in high school.

"Judge Johnson, that was a fantastic meal!"

Early's mother shot her a look that she undoubtedly had used numerous times from her judicial bench. "Now we could go on calling each other judge and doctor, but why don't we just go with Ruth and Angela?"

"Then Ruth that was a fantastic meal!"

"Do you happen to cook authentic Italian dishes?"

"My mother wouldn't have it any other way."

Ruth's eyes lit up. "Would you mind showing me how to prepare a real Italian meal, maybe tomorrow evening?"

Angela returned the enthusiastic grin. "I'd love to."

Early decided it might be a good time to make himself scarce, so he cleared the table and adjourned to the kitchen to stuff the dishwasher while they got to know one another. He emerged a bit later. "Mom, I promised Angie that you had more stars in your backyard than anywhere else I'd ever been. We're going outside to sit for a bit."

Ruth saw the two of them holding hands and gave them an obviously appraising look. "By the way, I forgot to mention that I promised to stay with your Aunt Becky tonight. Your cousin Gwen needs a night off now and then."

"Sure, Mom. How about breakfast at nine tomorrow? I'll do the cooking."

Ruth grinned at Angela. "I hope his cooking has drastically improved since the last attempt."

"I can only verify that he knows how to boil water for pasta."

The two of them went outside after Ruth hurriedly put an overnight bag together and left the house. Angela turned to Early. "Why do I get the idea her trip to Aunt Becky's was a last minute decision?"

"Maybe she's pretty smart."

They pulled two chairs off the porch and into the yard, away from the trees, so they had an uninterrupted view overhead. When Early turned off the porch light, the sight of the heavens left them both transfixed.

"This always reminds me of a few lines my father used to quote." Early said. "Do we not gaze at the same stars?

Breathe the same air, Bleed the same red blood, Worship the same God, and Drink of the same cup of Liberty?'"

Angela thought about that. "Maybe that needs to be printed in big letters in Washington these days."

"I believe looking at these stars is one of the main things I miss living in the city. Just think, probably billions of people live their whole lives without even knowing all this is right over their heads."

"It must be rejuvenating to come here to this."

"It's always had a deep effect on me." Early cleared his throat. "What are we going to do with one another, Angie?"

"I was hoping you might be able to answer that question for us."

Early left his seat and stood behind Angela's chair, the heels of his hands lightly touching the back of her neck. "Does your shoulder still bother you, Angie?"

"Not much." She leaned backward, pressing against his hands, surprised to feel a little surge of electricity at his touch. It had been a very long time. In fact, if asked, she wouldn't have been able to remember the last time.

He massaged the back of her neck, then her temples, and finally the lower lobes of her ears. She wondered just how rubbing the cartilage on her ears could make her tingle like that.

She finally stood up and faced him. They leaned forward tentatively and kissed, lightly at first, then with quite a bit of enthusiasm. Angela finally pushed herself away, and they stared at each other for long minutes. Making the decision she knew they both sought, she reached out and took his hands in hers.

※

Social media posts: *Do you realize how much the U.S. taxpayer contributes toward dealing with illegal immigration? Border wall/fence, Border Patrol, U.S. Marshals Service, federal detention centers, immigration courts, immigration attorneys, immigration judges, welfare, Medicaid, education, housing, sanctuary cities. This all amounts to 115 billion annually— Right out of your pocket! At the same time, American veterans are homeless. American children live in poverty. Our elderly are forced to choose between food and medicine. Many schools are failing. Our infrastructure is in disrepair. What are your priori-*

ties?

Legal immigration to the U.S. was limited to 500,000 people annually. How many actually came here—legally or illegally? Well over a million a year. How many did we deport? Anywhere from 150,000 to 250,000 annually. But now? I've heard we don't even know the numbers any more and just make them up. How long before this is simply not sustainable? If not, exactly why do we allow this to continue?

Would your own ancestors have been allowed to enter the United States if the current immigration regulations were in effect? Or would they have been put back on the boat, or perhaps locked up? Exactly where would you be if that had happened?

Chapter 41

The Inauguration of a President
Washington, DC January 20, 2025

After each presidential election, approximately 35% of the voting age population are thrilled with the results. Another 35% are disappointed or worse, while almost 30% apparently do not care one way or another, as they do not bother to vote.

Presidential inaugurations are attended by large numbers of private citizens. Depending on who does the counting, and who is the newly elected president, anywhere from 300,000 to almost a million people stand in often miserable January weather to witness history and the U.S. Constitution in action.

On the elevated stand erected on the steps of the U.S. Capitol Building are seated several hundred elected politicians, family members, political nominees, and favored donors of the elected president, as well as many members of the opposition party. The recently elected president sits approximately fifteen feet from the outgoing president. Seldom are so many of the nation's political, social, and economic powerhouses gathered in one place at one time.

For that reason, inaugurations are always designated as National Special Security Events and are planned down to the smallest detail for several weeks by the agencies that are either directly involved or might potentially become involved if a mass casualty event occurred. The day includes a religious service in the morning, if so desired by the incoming president; the motorcade from the White House to the Capitol; the actual list, seating, and order of escorted dignitaries on the reviewing stand; the swearing-in and following speech at the podium in front of the Capitol; the dignitary luncheon inside the Capitol Building; the Inaugural Parade with its own reviewing stand; and fifteen to twenty inaugural balls during the evening.

To say that the Secret Service is overburdened on inauguration day is an understatement. To date, the what-if planning sessions were certainly good exercises, but other than cold weather, rain, sleet, and snow, circumstances have never occurred which might bring the more drastic special planning forces in to play.

Complicating inauguration day security was the backlash over deployment of the National Guard after the 2020 election and how those troops were treated, with a number of governors declaring they would not order their state's guard force into Washington, D.C. But with large-scale terror once again rearing its head, the need was greater than ever. In the end, form trumped function and the National Guard stayed home.

The Charlottesville, Virginia warehouse which had previously been utilized by the Gulf Cartel to receive and store mortars and mortar shells was no longer in use, as the Cartel believed it had been compromised. In its place, a large townhouse had been rented in Olney, Maryland to not only hold weaponry, but also to house the remaining four members of the Hispanic special weapons team. The Olney location was some nineteen miles due north of the Capitol Building.

Very early on the morning of the inauguration, two mortar tubes, ten mortar shells with the new laser detection systems on the noses, two new laser direction systems (which had been fitted inside what appeared to be nothing more threatening than telescopic camera lenses), a driver, and three men loaded up the box truck with the sliding panel roof, and drove south down Georgia Avenue, through Silver Spring, and into the city, then found a small street just north of Q Street, between Marion Street NW and Seventh Street NW. They were 3.5 miles straight north of the Capitol steps.

Because traffic was always terrible in the city center on inauguration day, and many streets were blocked off, two of the Hispanics then walked the remaining distance with their 'cameras'. After going through security, just like the other 600,000 attendees, one positioned himself on the north side of the Mall, while the second man walked even further, circling the Capitol Building before finally finding a spot just southeast of the National Museum of the American Indian at the intersection of Fourth Street SW and Independence. They were each linked to the truck via disposable flip phones.

Of the mortar shells in the rear of the truck, five would be synced with the laser direction system carried by the man on the north side of the Mall, and five others synchronized with the man near the museum. The crowd was already building at eight AM and rapidly filling the grassy area west of Fourth Street. The two men in the truck had plenty of time, passing the next few hours playing poker, particularly since they had the proceeds of their upcoming Bitcoin payment to bet with.

All of them would look forward to a huge payday at the successful completion of the morning's events. After all, each had been the beneficiary of three Bitcoins after their July Fourth mortar attack, so it was logical to assume at least that much would be added to their individual accounts after the inauguration. After all, this would be an event no one would ever forget.

The crowd continued to build, eventually reaching the area around the Reflecting Pool and expanding further west. The temperature was a balmy 34 degrees. Since it had been just over six months since the terrible attack on the Fourth of July and months since any other terrorist attack, most attendees were comfortable with their decision to attend the ceremony. On this particular occasion, the assumption of the huge crowd of civilians on the mall was correct—*they* would not be the targets of a mortar attack.

At eleven AM, VIPs emerged from the doors of the Capitol in a pre-ordained order and made their way to their seats on the raised platform. The outgoing president and his spouse were seated in the front row, to the right of the speaker's podium. On the left, the incoming president and spouse were seated, also on the front row. It had been announced just a half-hour earlier that the newly elected vice-president would not attend, having come down with a severe intestinal complaint that very morning.

Finally, the band struck the first notes of *Hail to the Chief,* and the newly elected president and spouse descended the steps, shaking hands along the way, before finally reaching their seats.

An opening prayer was offered with a multitude of bowing heads, many of whom were not thinking about what was being said at all, but rather how they might position themselves, either in the new administration, or in the case of the outgoing administration, in a lucrative position in the private sector. Two men in the crowd quickly focused their telescopic camera lenses, one aiming a yard to the left of the priest, the other a yard to the right. The first two extremely accurate mortars would be launched before there was an amen.

Prior to the mortars even reaching the ground, two more shells were poised above the mortar tube, pausing only long enough for the laser pointers to be re-positioned at the exit ramp leading back into the Capitol. Explosions three and four cut off the main route of panicked escape for any surviving VIPs. Rounds five through ten took out different locations on the reviewing stand.

Within ninety seconds, it was over. Nine of the mortars struck within a yard of the laser dots. Very few of those on the podium would make it back into the Capitol Building.

While the Presidential Succession Act of 1947 clearly delineated the order in which the vice president, speaker of the House, president pro tempore of the Senate, and members of the cabinet succeed to the presidency in an orderly fashion, many of the individuals tapped in that line of succession did not survive the attack. In fact, only the vice-president survived. The leaders of both houses of Congress died, most of the Supreme Court justices died, most of the outgoing and incoming cabinet members died. Within hours, conspiracy theories flooded social media.

The two men on foot faded away into the crowd. The men in the truck closed the vehicle's roof and proceeded north on Georgia Avenue, connecting with the perimeter expressway and heading west, before switching to I-270 and driving north toward Pennsylvania. None of them would receive the anticipated additional Bitcoins.

Perhaps the primary remaining question for many Americans was not so much whether the vice-president-elect would become president. Rather, what sort of coincidence had occurred such that the VP-elect just happened to be the only person in the line of succession to have survived due to a self-reported illness?

Chapter 42

Fat Tuesday
New Orleans, Louisiana February 13, 2025

The two large shipping containers which had been off-loaded from the freighter *VNL Emerald* in Eureka, California, had been sitting in a Baton Rouge warehouse north of the city center, near the Louisiana Training Institute, off Samuels Road. Although the warehouse was a full three miles away, on most days with a wind out of the west, you could smell the dankness of the Mississippi River as it snaked its way around the city and on through the lowlands to the east toward New Orleans and the Gulf.

Storage charges had been paid like clockwork each month on the two containers for the last twelve months, but finally, two days before Ash Wednesday, a couple of flat-bed trucks arrived to pick up the 25-foot-long steel containers. The Hispanic drivers who called for them provided the shipping numbers, along with the name of the addressee—The King's Krewe. A final payment was made for the previous month's storage charges, this time with crisp twenty dollar bills, and the trucks departed.

Some two hours later, the vehicles backed up to a warehouse receiving dock on South Claiborne Street in New Orleans. Given the information at the warehouse, Container #6647 was moved into a locked storage compartment on the west wall within the warehouse, while Container #6648 was placed inside a separate locked compartment on the east wall.

That afternoon, the two purchasers of the containers, The Krewe of Zulu and The Krewe of Rex, took possession of them. Both organizations had been thrilled at the terrifically discounted price they had paid to a dealer in Vietnam. According to the shipping manifest inside the containers, there were five hundred thousand beaded plastic necklaces in each. They were conveniently bagged in lots of one thousand, all colored in a sparkly yellow, green, and blue.

Within the next six hours, twenty bags, or twenty thousand of the gaudy necklaces, were transferred to each of 25 parade floats for Zulu and 25 floats for Rex. The following morning, Fat Tuesday, the Zulu parade began at eight AM, proceeding from South Claiborne and Jackson Avenue, over to St. Charles Avenue, turning on Canal, then down Basin Street, before ending at Orleans and Broad. All along the route, well over a hundred thousand people screamed and pleaded with outstretched arms to be thrown yet another shiny bauble to add to their existing raiment. They were almost always rewarded by the costumed riders on the floats.

The Rex parade began at ten AM at South Claiborne and Napoleon, then headed down St. Charles, and ended at Canal and South Peters. Since this was usually the last parade that could be attended, the audience was even more determined to obtain more decorations.

Along the route, float riders flung every last one of the million necklaces to the quarter of a million parade watchers. The necklaces were immediately donned by the happy onlookers, who would undoubtedly wear them all day and half the night as the festivities and parties continued.

Unknown to all, the necklaces had all been exposed to a fine spray of powdered *Bacillus anthracis* before departing Vietnam. The anthrax was not bothered in the least that it had been confined in a closed environment for almost a year; in fact, it flourished in the anaerobic setting inside the plastic bags. But now the bacteria had much work to do. And no doubt its migration to the lower lobes of 250,000 sets of lungs would be aided by the wild screaming and singing, the constant motion, and the frequent handling of the necklaces by both the flingers and the wearers. Unlike all previous attacks, no North Korean agents were involved in the direct distribution of the biological agent. The attack was completely self-starting.

A Bio-Watch air filtration system, permanently stationed in New Orleans near the Super Dome, eventually alerted to the presence of a biological agent after dawn on Ash Wednesday, soon after the wind shifted from southerly to easterly. By the time the specific agent had been identified by a local laboratory, hundreds of thousands of Mardi Gras attendees were on their way home in 34 states and nine countries. Many thousands would not be alerted in time to save their lives.

The call was received in FBI headquarters and passed forward to the Assistant Director of Counter-Terrorism. "Director Jones, thank you for taking my call. This is Special Agent Avery Meyer in Kansas City. We have a court-approved FISA wiretap on a suspected Syrian terrorist by the name of Abbud Dweck, who apparently runs operations across the upper midwest. Our interpreter listened to one of his recordings from yesterday, and it seems to indicate that there were two nuclear devices being held in a warehouse in Duluth, Minnesota, and now, at least according to our analysis, we believe they've been picked up."

"You've got to be kidding me, Meyer. How long have you been monitoring this Syrian?"

"Three months, Director. But only in the last couple of days has there been any indication of one or more nuclear devices being in play."

"Are you talking a dirty bomb, or something bigger?"

"We suspect bigger, simply because they were apparently large enough to require a truck for shipment. Also, there was the alert we received six months ago, reporting the ISIS theft of a large quantity of high-grade uranium in Raqqah. I have no evidence to connect the two events, sir, but I'm assuming that uranium has not been recovered."

"Please tell me you know where these devices are at this time, Meyer."

"We have no idea, Director Jones."

"What about the Syrian? Can you pick him up?"

"That was our intention this morning, at least until we found him dead."

"Shit! Thanks, Meyer. I've obviously got some calls to make."

Chapter 43

The War on Bacon
Southwest of Topeka, Kansas March 3, 2025

Professor Tareq Shegemi, who worked at the Faculty of Agriculture within the University of Tripoli, received an unlikely visit at eight AM from Lupe Aristide, who said he was a graduate assistant at the Agrarian University of Havana. He was obviously aware of Doctor Shegemi's recent publication on his current research, and made him an offer which was impossible to refuse.

Aristide retrieved a cloth bag from his briefcase and poured the contents on the laboratory worktable in front of the professor. Shegemi spent less than fifteen seconds counting the twenty gold Canadian Maple Leafs in front of him, quickly converting that figure to Euros in his head. Aristide allowed him a full minute to pick up the coins and examine them.

"Professor, my country, and my university, are greatly concerned with the risk posed to the global food supply by the African swine flu virus." Shegemi nodded silently, although much of his attention was still focused on the riches on his table. "Even the Americans are afraid. Their Center for Food Security and Public Health believe that ASFV presents the greatest risk to worldwide starvation in a generation."

"Indeed, Mr. Aristide, this has been my area of concentration since the terrible outbreak in 2007. The Americans have been very lucky, but that hasn't been the case in much of Africa, Asia, some of Europe, and a bit of South America and the Caribbean.

"Because of this virus, the world has lost twenty-five percent of its pig population. Prices have skyrocketed, and many people can no longer afford meat in their diet. In 2017 and 2018, China culled an estimated forty million pigs in their efforts to wipe out the virus. This is particularly difficult for the Chinese, as pork represents some fifty percent of its supply of meat."

"Tell me, Professor, why does a Muslim country perform research on a disease of pigs? I would have thought that to be the last thing of interest to you."

"My research has proven very profitable for the university, Mr. Aristide." He once more allowed his eyes to caress the small pile of Maple Leafs.

"My country wishes to take your work and see if we can develop a vaccine, Professor. We also would like to take economic advantage of the virus, by selling such a vaccine to the rest of the world. However, we suspect that much of the economic gain from your research has been for the benefit of the university and not yourself." He looked expectantly at the professor.

"Isn't that the way it always is?"

"It doesn't have to be that way, Professor. According to your writing, you obviously keep quite a stock of the strains of ticks which transmit ASFV—the *Orthinodoros moubata* and *sonrai.* What if you sold me ten thousand of the *sonrai* strain for the thirty-two thousand US dollars of gold you see before you?"

"What would you do with such a stock, Mr. Aristide?"

"I trust you have a method of keeping them alive in a blood-based medium of some kind. I'll transport them via jet to Havana immediately, then place them in a bio-secure laboratory to begin our research."

By ten AM, the 'graduate student' had boarded a Bombardier Global Express private jet, and the plane was wheels up and on its way. Not, however, to Havana, but to link up with representatives of the Gulf Cartel in Vera Cruz, Mexico. The thirsty ticks were immediately placed on two produce trucks, filled with crates of cantelopes, except for a convenient false back wall in the trailer, and the vehicles crossed the Texas border, headed for a rendezvous with Jose Gorgas near Wichita, Kansas.

Driving a double-cab Ford pickup and pulling a stock

trailer, Gorgas rendezvoused with the cartel's produce at a truck stop off I-35, just south of Wichita Wednesday morning. In the trailer were a dozen feeder pigs. Gorgas donned a pair of gloves and spread a handful of the *sonrai* ticks in the straw of the trailer. The trick was not to expose the pigs too soon, as they could possibly begin to exhibit symptoms of the infection within 24 to 48 hours of the ticks beginning to feast on them.

Just after four PM, Gorgas and his hungry charges arrived at the Wildcat Livestock Sale Barn halfway between Topeka and Salina, Kansas. He made arrangements to sell his twelve pigs via the sale barn, herded them into a small pen, fed and watered them, then began his tour of the twenty or so pens, looking over the competition. He was apparently very curious, as he walked through the pork section at least three times. He unobtrusively dropped thirty to a couple of hundred ticks in each pen, depending on how many feeder pigs were in a particular unit.

The sale began early the next morning, and by eleven AM, 2,800 pigs had been purchased and were being loaded up by nine other farm operators, ready to head back home to their feeder pig operations across central Kansas and southern Nebraska. Even Gorgas had made a purchase of his own, paying in brand new twenties for a dozen more pigs. He didn't wait to collect the earnings for the sale of his own trailer-load of animals.

The next morning, Gorgas repeated his actions at the Corn Husker Livestock Sales south of Lincoln. The animals from that sale were destined for farms in eastern Nebraska, western Iowa, and northwestern Missouri. His purchases on this occasion miraculously escaped from his stock trailer late that evening near the small town of Jefferson, Iowa. The animals immediately fled into the dense undergrowth along the North Raccoon River, where they made contact with several hundred wild hogs.

One of the buyers back at the Wildcat Sale Barn unloaded two large trucks full of pigs from the sale at his own feeder operation twenty miles southwest of Topeka. Bina Bacon, Inc. was owned by Chris Bina, who grew up on his father's farm and had taken over the operation four years previously when his father's knees gave out on him. Of course, this affliction did not stop the old man from giving plenty of advice.

Bina Bacon fed 1,000 pigs at a time, with a quarter of

them being brand new purchases, a quarter having been on the farm for four weeks, another quarter for eight weeks, and the remainder for twelve weeks. The four groups were separated in the huge hog confinement barn by strong, solid steel piping, which was necessary due to the pounding the separators received from a thousand rambunctious pigs.

The hog confinement barn was an impressive structure, with over half a football field under cover. The manufacturer claimed it could withstand winds of 105 miles per hour—an appropriate capability when considering Kansas storms. It looked like a huge, brilliant white metal barn, with two large steel feed tanks located on the east side. A huge propane tank served as the power source, powering heating and air conditioning, six large fans, and an auger system which transported feed from the tanks to concrete enclosed, raised circular feeders inside.

The building was very well insulated, and the floor was composed of concrete, angled at about a 10% grade. This was interspersed with slanted steel panels, which allowed manure to be forced through narrow openings in the panels, then easily washed into a ten-foot-deep manure pit.

The pigs began their residency at Bina Bacon as fifty-pound animals, but with intense feeding efforts consisting of milo, corn, a protein and carbohydrate supplement from the local co-op, vitamins, Lincomycin every now and then, and lots of water, they were ready to go to slaughter in four months as 250-pound animals. It would seem a business created to manufacture money—buying fifty-pound pigs for 45 or so, then selling the market-ready animals four months later for approximately 200 apiece. However, the business was not without risks, with market price fluctuations, bad weather, increasing feed prices, and a variety of diseases being the main threats.

Bina kept an eagle eye on his pigs and was in the barn at least twice daily. His most hated day was Saturday, when he drove the honey wagon up to the large pit at the foot of the four hog pens. This pit contained approximately 4,000 pounds of pig waste each week. He rigged up a suction hose attached to a large tank, pulled at least 90% of the material out of the pit, then spent the remainder of the day spreading it on his farm as fertilizer.

When Bina finally returned to the barn, he gave his ani-

mals a bit of an inspection as he observed the feed mixture being injected into their feeders. They were all of the American
Yorkshire variety, which possessed the ability to rapidly put on
weight, yet much of it was described as lean. The animals were
white in color, with ears that always seemed to stand on end.

As he reached the final pen—the one containing his most
recent purchases—he noted that five or six of them were
standing off by themselves, making no effort to compete with
the others for their late afternoon feeding. With his curiosity
immediately on alert, Bina entered the pen for a closer look.
Each of them had a runny nose, three pigs were exhibiting
what had to be described as a cough, and they all possessed a
dull look about their eyes.

These symptoms alone would probably not have been
much cause for alarm. Bina's usual response would commonly have been to make sure they received an antibiotic,
and then watch them closely for any changes. However, as he
moved among the symptomatic animals, he noticed red sores
on their lower legs. This was new enough that he picked up
his phone.

He phoned his veterinarian, Dr. Gary Chaney, who he
had on retainer. This relationship was now necessary due to
recommendations by the state that high-density animal feeding operations should have an agreement with a veterinarian
to provide on-site services. "Doc—I don't know what I've got
here but I bought two truckloads of feeder pigs on Thursday
at the Wildcat Sales Barn west of Topeka. I'm looking at six of
them, and they've got a runny nose, a cough, they're not eating, and I'm seeing a red rash or sores on their legs. One of
them has the same problem on his snout."

"Any of the other animals showing any sign of sickness?"

"Not that I can tell, but I'm separating these six from the
rest."

"Sounds like the flu from your description. Why don't you
put on a mask when you're around them, and maybe change
boots when you go from their pen to where the others are. I've
got to check on a sick horse, but I'll be out your way by
seven-thirty or so this evening."

⚛

"Chris, they've all got a fever, and I see what you mean
about the skin ulcerations on the inside of their front legs and

their nose and mouth. I looked at the other animals you bought Thursday, and it looks like at least a dozen have similar problems."

"What does that mean, Doc?"

"There's no point jumping to conclusions at this point, but these areas on the skin look a whole lot like some of the pictures that USDA has been distributing for the last couple of years." He pulled up a recent communication from the extension service at Kansas State University Ag School on his phone and showed the enclosed images to Bina.

"I see what you mean. Is this some new kind of flu, or something different?"

"First off, it seems impossible, because there's never been a case of this in the entire U.S. It's been in epidemic status in Asia and Africa, but not here."

"Then what could it be?"

"Well, you've heard about some of the disease outbreaks this year among beef cattle and the food supply. Since then, we've gotten several warnings from USDA and the state of Kansas to be on the lookout for what they call agricultural terrorists. Apparently somebody, or several somebodies, are responsible for those outbreaks."

"So you think this is more of that?"

"I hope not, Chris. You saw the same pictures I did. It looks like the symptoms for African swine flu."

"How do you treat it?"

"That's the thing. There is no treatment. The only thing you can do is destroy your animals and quarantine your farm."

"Do you mean destroy the ones that are sick, or the whole operation?"

Doctor Chaney hated to tell Bina what he was thinking. "We're getting ahead of ourselves. We'll have to submit tissue samples to Plum Island in New York. I'll overnight them, but I'm thinking we won't have any results back until midweek. If it's positive, I think you're looking at a mass kill, disposing of the carcasses in a plastic-lined pit, and making sure you and your family, or anyone who visits the farm, as well as any vehicle, doesn't spread this to another farm."

Bina held onto a steel support post, wondering if his legs were going to fail him. "That's at least one hundred and fifty thousand dollars' worth of animals, and no telling how much to bury them. I've got death-loss insurance on them, but there's some kind of clause in there about it not being valid in case of war or terrorism."

Chaney said, "Just don't jump to that conclusion yet. I may be wrong. After all, I've never seen a case of this ASF before. If it's what I think it is, the USDA has the authority to help with the money situation. However, I'll need to contact that Wildcat Sale Barn as soon as possible. Surely they'll have a good record of who bought pigs at the sale. Every one of them will need to be called immediately to take their own set of precautions."

"There were about a dozen of us bidding on feeder pigs."

"Were there any market pigs being sold? We'll need to check on them also."

"Not that I noticed."

"I'll be back out here first thing in the morning to check on the rest of your animals. I've got a pump sprayer in my truck, so I'll spray my tires, the underside of my vehicle, and my boots with Clorox before I leave your farm. You need to do the same for your truck and your wife's car, as well as anybody who comes on your property."

The teleconference was opened by Willis Ames, assistant secretary of the Department of Agriculture. "Good morning, ladies and gentlemen. I'm joined by my colleagues, Rear Admiral William Harrison, Assistant Secretary for Preparedness and Response at HHS, and Lynn Jones, Assistant Director of Counterterrorism from the FBI, as well as USDA Chief Scientist Dr. Patty Sullivan. On the phone, we have Governors Gunnar Grey from Nebraska, Wilson Redmon from Iowa, Mark Hayes from Kansas, and Bill Shiveley from Missouri, as well as Dr. Sean Waterman from Kansas State's School of Veterinary Medicine. I'll let the FBI Special Agents introduce themselves as they enter the call. Dr. Sullivan, the floor is yours."

"The news from our laboratory at Plum Island confirms our worst expectations. To date, we've received positive results for African swine flu virus from eight farms in your four states, with samples from another fourteen farms still pending, but highly probable for the virus. The farms which made pig and hog purchases from the Wildcat and Corn Husker

Sale Barns last week are all apparently affected, as are the sale barns themselves.

"Not only must all of the purchased animals be destroyed, but all other swine on those farms, plus those within five miles of each of the affected farms. Although the USDA has emergency funding allocated for these kinds of events, this year's funds were exhausted in a recent outbreak of foot and mouth disease."

"Governor Grey in Lincoln here. Are you saying my farmers will not be made whole?"

"We hope that's not the case, Governor. We ask that each of you governors immediately submit a request for emergency funding via a Presidential Stafford Act Declaration. At the same time, you might consider advising your senators and representatives that Stafford Act funding has been exhausted, as Congress will have to allocate additional funds to that program. On the phone with us is FEMA Regional Director Chris Kates. His region encompasses each of your four states. Director Kates, the floor is yours."

"Thanks, Dr. Sullivan. We have knowledgeable folks standing by to work with each of the governors' staff to draft those requests as soon as possible. I think those requests should include a cost breakdown for assistance to disaster survivors—that would be each individual farm or feed lot for the actual cost of their pigs—as well as a separate line item for hazard mitigation, which would include the costs for destroying and burying the animals on site, as well as clean-up of properties and vehicles."

"Thank you, Director Kates. We'll get right on it."

"Avery Meyer, Special Agent in Charge, Kansas City Office. The sales barn west of Topeka possesses two security cameras which are directed at the sales pen area. After review of about sixteen hours of tape, we're convinced we have a suspect. We've designated him as Popcorn Man, because as he walked back and forth among the animal pens last Thursday, he carried a container which appeared to be a box of popcorn. As he leaned over each of the feeder pig pens, supposedly to inspect the animals, Popcorn Man dropped a handful of what we thought was popcorn inside the pens. We now believe he was distributing ticks.

"When our friends at USDA advised us that ticks and blood-sucking flies were the vectors for African swine flu, we went back and examined the straw which littered each pen. There were numerous ticks still remaining in each cubicle."

"David Baker, Special Agent in Charge, Omaha. We were asked to check for evidence at the Corn Husker Sales Barn. Although that facility has security cameras on the exterior of the building, there are no cameras inside the barn. Once we were advised by Special Agent Meyer about the tick infestation, we discovered the same situation in the pens at the Nebraska site.

"According to the staff at the Corn Husker facility, they also pointed out Popcorn Man as having been on site at their facility last week. So apparently the perpetrator was one and the same."

"Lynn Jones, Assistant Director for Counterterrorism at the FBI. Thank you, Special Agents Baker and Meyer. We've circulated the best of the security camera photos to law enforcement and state government across the country for distribution to every sales barn, veterinarian, and swine farmer. If this Popcorn Man tries again, we hope to be ready to pick him up before he acts."

"Patty Sullivan from USDA again with one last word of warning. If you have wild hogs anywhere near your farms, it is possible that this virus could have been transmitted to them. When your farmers finally get past this event and repopulate with a new stock of feeder pigs, those wild hogs could transmit the virus right back to your animals."

"Kates here at FEMA. Dr. Sullivan, I thought only specific ticks could transmit the disease."

"I wish that was so, Mr. Kates. Our testing has shown that four different ticks, all common in the U.S., can accomplish the same thing.

"That's how the disease has remained endemic in Africa—by passing the disease back and forth between tame and wild animals. We've furnished this information to your state Departments of Fish and Game, and encouraged them to aggressively move toward eradicating any nearby herds of wild hogs. Perhaps your farmers will have a new, good reason to get rid of those wild animals themselves."

As the call ended at the FBI's central office in Washington, Jones turned to Angela Martinelli. "Do those photographs remind you of one of your terrorists?"

"Director Jones, I can't be sure, as I think the beard and

mustache are recent additions, but as it is, I believe he's one of the men I was with on the ship. If he's caught, I'd like to be involved in his interrogation."

CHAPTER 44

Venezuela's Contribution
Caracas, Venezuela March 25, 2025

The *Anopheles* mosquito is one of the most deadly life forms on the planet. The female of the species is responsible for transmitting malaria. We don't have recent figures, but in 2020 there were approximately 228 million cases reported worldwide and over 405,000 deaths.

Venezuela was one of the very first Latin American countries to declare their nation free of malaria infections. Alas, with the gradual economic collapse of the country came an extreme reduction in the budget devoted to public health. One of the first programs to go was mosquito control and eradication. Within a short span of years, Venezuela experienced a huge increase in malaria, with over one million cases estimated in every year since 2018. Unfortunately, Venezuela no longer reports its health statistics to the World Health Organization, but it's believed those numbers are still increasing. The great majority of those patients involved species which were deemed to be multi-drug resistant. Unfortunately, those cases weren't just confined to rural areas, as even Caracas has its share.

When the phone rang in his lab at the Institute of Tropical Medicine within the Central University of Venezuela, Dr. Diego Obregon was somewhat surprised to note the call apparently originated in Cuba. "Dr. Obregon? This is Leopoldo Hernandez in Havana. We have mutual friends who have recently advised me of the huge reduction in your budget these last several years."

"May I ask who those friends are, sir?"

"They wish to remain anonymous, but I can assure you they have nothing but your best interests at heart. They tell me everything seems to be falling apart in Venezuela. I was shocked to learn that food is so scarce throughout your country that malnutrition is now common. I'm told that the availability of medicine is almost nonexistent. I also understand that some days Caracas has no electricity or running water, and the police and the military are abandoning their responsibilities. I even hear you have pirates now off your coast attempting to steal your oil."

"Much of that is true, Señor Hernandez. Even good people have become desperate."

"At any rate, I have a colleague here at the Escuela Latinoamericana de Medicina who is in great need of perhaps five hundred thousand malaria-carrying *Anopheles* females."

"What would be your colleague's use of those mosquitoes, Señor Hernandez?"

"As you know, Cuba experiences very few cases of malaria. It is Dr. Santos' desire to experiment with the DNA of the *Anopheles*, more specifically, to work with gene editing. His plan is to actually render the species sterile. Can you imagine what it might do for your country if the *Anopheles* mosquito becomes unable to reproduce?"

"That would indeed be wonderful. I've heard of research efforts to alter their DNA to reduce the length of their proboscis, thus preventing their ability to easily reach blood vessels in humans, but nothing as drastic as eradicating the species."

"Our Dr. Santos is particularly interested in working on mosquitoes which carry two of the plasmodium species—*falciparum* and *vivax*."

"We've gone to considerable trouble here in the Institute to maintain our *Anopheles* stock in pure strains, with most of our efforts toward *falciparum*, and perhaps twenty percent of resources involving *vivax*."

"We appreciate those achievements, Dr. Obregon. Perhaps the lot you prepare for us could replicate that ratio. In light of your budget problems, Dr. Santos is prepared to bring you personally twenty of Mexico's gold fifty peso coins if you will facilitate his request."

There was hesitation on the other end of the line as Obregon performed some quick mental calculations. At the current price, that would translate to over 45,000 U.S. Given the rampant inflation in Venezuela and his current, pitiful salary during their depression, that amount represented just over nine years of income. It also would provide enough funds for him and his wife to leave Venezuela for good. He attempted to hide his enthusiasm when he replied, "Dr. Hernandez, it would be my pleasure to assist in Dr. Santos' research."

Two days later, he was met at his laboratory door by his fellow scientist, who was carrying two rather cumbersome duffel bags. To say that Dr. Santos was vague when Obregon attempted to talk about his proposed research would be an understatement. In fact, the man was almost careless in his observance of standard laboratory safety protocols. However, the telephone promise was fulfilled within the first ten minutes of his visit when he emptied the small pocket on the side of one of the bags and dumped twenty of the gold fifty peso coins on Obregon's desk. It was all the professor could do to keep from touching the gold.

The plan for shipping his half-million females and a thousand males was unorthodox, to say the least. Santos opened the duffels, which contained ten sections of six-inch-diameter PVC pipe, painted a mottled green, and cut into four-foot lengths. Each pipe held an interior oxygen source, water supply, and food source, as well as the capability of having the two ends temporarily sealed once each pipe was occupied.

Within four hours of his arrival on campus, Santos departed the university. His next stop was the docks, where he and his charges were loaded onto a container ship, with a destination, not to Havana, but to the deep water port of Texas City, on the eastern boundary of Houston.

In Texas, Santos was met by Raymondo Torres, who was driving a rented blue van. It took less than fifteen minutes for Santos to provide marching orders. "You will make a total of ten stops, beginning with Lake Conroe outside Houston, and ending with Rock Creek in Washington, D.C. All the stops are carefully marked on this map. Each of these pipes has a GPS device attached. Every time you place one of the pipes at a prescribed location, one-half Bitcoin will be wired to your bank account."

Torres looked at the map. "You expect me to do all this

traveling, expose myself to malaria, plus put my neck at risk for a long prison sentence for only five Bitcoins?"

"Please don't interrupt me. Once we receive reports of malaria, we will wire another half Bitcoin to your bank account for each location where cases are reported."

"What if no cases are reported?"

"That will only be because you didn't perform your responsibilities correctly."

"Just exactly what do I have to do?"

"It's very simple. You find a site near a large number of houses, or a marina, or a public campground. Then you place one of the pipes in shallow water, being careful to submerge only half of the pipe. You camouflage the pipe with a few branches, and finally you remove the end plugs from the pipe."

"What's to keep me from catching malaria?"

"Have you already started taking doxycycline?"

"No, what's that?"

Santos handed him two plastic vials. "Here are enough pills in the first container to last throughout your trip. The second vial is to be taken at the conclusion of your trip, and continued for four weeks afterward. You need to start taking the first one right now, and continue that twice a day until completed." Santos looked hard at the fellow. "Do not disappoint us."

Torres placed his first pipe right after dark near a highly populated area of Lake Conroe. Over the next week, he headed northeast, stopping at Lake Ouachita outside of Little Rock, then Hyde Lake in Shelby Farms Park north of Germantown, Tennessee, a large marina at Pickwick Lake as it entered Mississippi, Guntersville Lake in Alabama, Lake Lanier outside Atlanta, Lake Seminole in southwestern Georgia, then down to a well-known golf club in West Palm Beach. Here, he stopped his vehicle at Lake Lytal Park at one AM off Gun Club Road and found a spot to conceal a pipe in the lake. There was a family aquatic center and soccer fields less than a hundred yards distant. His ninth stop was at Lake Norman, adjacent to the small city of Westport, North Carolina.

Finally, he drove north to Rock Creek, depositing his last pipe in the small waterway directly behind the rear fence of the panda exhibit at the National Zoo. Less than a quarter of a mile away were the expensive row houses of the Adams Morgan neighborhood, plus the popular bars and restaurants along 18th Street in a high-end area of Washington, D.C. He could hear the echoes of children laughing in the zoo as he placed the tenth and final device.

Torres had been pleased to note the first five deposits of Bitcoins in his Caribbean account as he made his scheduled stops, then he settled back to wait on those future Bitcoin deposits. It took a month of waiting before he realized he'd been had. By then, his aching, dizziness, and fever had led him to suspect the medication he had been given in the second container was not effective.

The malaria parasite is deposited in the skin of a victim via the bite of an infected female *Anopheles* mosquito. The parasite quickly enters the liver, undergoes rapid multiplication, and then begins to destroy red blood cells. It is only during and after the red blood cell stage that the person shows signs of illness.

Sometime within eight to thirty days after being bitten, the victim begins to experience symptoms like headache, bone aching, dizziness, fever, and diarrhea. Unfortunately, those symptoms are vague, and would often not immediately lead to a doctor's visit, let alone to a rapid diagnosis of malaria, particularly in a geographic area where doctors never encounter the disease. If the patient sees a physician, and the symptoms are accurately interpreted as malaria, then treatment is started, and the patient, although feeling terrible for perhaps weeks, will survive, generally without any permanent damage.

However, if left untreated, or if that particular strain of malaria is drug resistant, the patient's early symptoms may progress to kidney failure, seizures, coma, and even death. Because malaria is almost never seen in the U.S. except in people returning from a trip abroad to a country where the disease is present, it's reasonable to assume many early cases would be missed and treatment delayed until at least some damage was done.

Within twelve days of Torres' first deposit of mosquitoes outside Houston, the first patient was diagnosed, and by the four-week mark, the Centers for Disease Control and Prevention confirmed 12,000 cases and outbreaks in eighteen states and Washington, D.C. The United States medical system was forced to acknowledge and confront an entirely new threat within its boundaries.

Many more cases were finally diagnosed after people experienced more severe symptoms. As malaria cases cropped up across almost every southern and eastern state, public health authorities realized it would take a great deal of time and money to get the genie back in the bottle.

※

At eleven AM, Kim Yo-jong sat in her brother's office, waiting for him to finally get out of bed and get dressed. She knew exactly why he couldn't awaken at a reasonable time, but realized pointing that out would not be helpful to the conversation she needed to have.

Finally, he entered, still disheveled, but that would have to do. "Good morning, brother. Have you heard anything in the last few days from the Chinese president?"

He shook his head to clear it. "Should I? What day is it anyhow?"

"April fifth, brother. Something strange is going on in the American financial markets. You probably remember that the Chinese hold just over a trillion and a quarter dollars' worth of American Treasuries, as well as another trillion in foreign currencies—with the majority of that in English pound-sterling, and Euros."

"I believe you've mentioned that before."

"Here's the interesting part, brother. In the last week, the Chinese have almost completely sold off their U.S. Treasury bills, and are trading in their new wealth to buy gold all over the world. Also, as of last night, their foreign currency consisted of less than five hundred billion in Euros remaining. Our reports indicate the Chinese were willing to take quite a loss on those transactions. In fact, they gave up at least eighty billion dollars just so they could sell off."

"Apparently they're losing their faith in the imperialists. It's about time!"

"Yes, brother. But the question is, why? Why do it now, particularly after the Americans displayed their power by shutting down Russia, Iran, and the DPRK? You would think the value of the dollar would rise. In fact, it did in the week or so afterward, but as soon as the Chinese started selling, it's dropped by almost ten percent against the Euro. This is unheard of, brother."

"What is your analysis, dear sister?"

"What if they know something—something very bad that's about to happen to the Americans? Something that would cause the rest of the world to also want to get out of dollars."

"Are you suggesting we should buy American dollars since they're so depressed?"

"Absolutely not. Not if we believe the Chinese know something catastrophic is about to happen. What about our terror attacks? You previously mentioned the nuclear weapons which might be utilized."

"I never received any verification from Ho-young. He was the one who was supposed to set those attacks in motion. As far as I know, he was captured before that could happen."

"Ah, but brother—what if he completed that mission beforehand?"

Kim stared at his sister, realization dawning. "If the Chinese do know something, that could mean steps are already being taken. If that is so, it can't be stopped, sister dear."

"What do you plan to do to protect our country from the Russian president if it really does happen, brother?"

Chapter 45

An Unexpected Travel Companion
Sep'o County, North Korea April 07, 2025

The fat man had thought a great deal about his last visit to the Sep'o County retreat. The girl, Hiroko, had been given every opportunity to attempt an escape. There had been the unfortunate picnic incident where he drank too much. It would have been a simple thing for her to use the four-wheeler to flee, and yet she hadn't. In fact, she had apparently loaded him into the vehicle by herself, then returned to the compound. Frankly, he remembered very little of that day.

The most recent visit had also been telling. He was injured and had no way of alerting his guards. She could have been halfway to the DMZ on horseback before his plight would even have been discovered. Yet she had not failed him. He could only conclude that he had established at least some level of affection with the girl. Perhaps it was time for him to finally make a stronger move.

Damn it! He'd almost forgotten the shepherd. He would have to deal with him during his visit on the morrow. He doubted if it would be difficult to find a farmer in the area who would be glad to take Yoo's place and make some extra money. He shook his head. He was so weary of having to discipline those who failed him.

Thankfully, some of the communications controls had finally been lifted by the Americans, which made it possible by ten AM the next morning for a radio message to be transmitted from the capital and received by one of the guards at the retreat, informing them that the Wonsu had just lifted off from Pyongyang and would arrive in time for lunch. Yoo found out from the auntie, who was scurrying around in an attempt to prepare the kind of meal the chairman always expected.

Yoo surreptitiously swiped some food from the pantry and a few necessary items from the barn, before going to his quarters and preparing for an attempted escape. He then spent time isolating each of the four guards on the estate, killing them one by one with his knife and concealing their bodies in the barn. He went about his task with great skill and without being observed, or at least so he thought.

Standing in her second-floor bedroom, Hiroko saw Yoo dragging two of the guards across the barn. She said not a word, but rather prepared her own cache of food and spare clothing, as she knew exactly what his next move would have to be.

Yoo saved the guard stationed at the radio for last. In fact, he was loitering in the room when the helicopter radioed that it would be landing in a few minutes. He wasn't surprised to also hear a question from the aircraft as to the shepherd's whereabouts. At the conclusion of the message, Yoo relieved the guard of his rifle and his life, then quickly stripped off the man's uniform and donned it himself.

When the helicopter set down on the concrete landing pad, Yoo was standing to the rear of the aircraft with his cap pulled low and the guard's rifle slung over his shoulder. When the two pilots stepped out, straightening to attention for the Wonsu as he exited, Yoo shot them both with double taps to the chest.

He then pulled his rifle down to the port arms position and called out to the Wonsu. "Step over here, Kim."

The chairman had never been addressed in such a familiar manner in his entire adult life. "What do you think you're doing, Yoo?"

"Getting rid of one of the world's problems, Kim."

A voice rang out behind Yoo. "Be careful. He's got a pistol in his boot."

At that, Yoo jerked his head around to be sure Hiroko was out of the way.

She screamed, "Watch out!"

Yoo stepped sideways at the same time he pointed his rifle at the fat man. A shot rang out, the bullet taking the hat off his head. "Drop it or you're dead, Kim."

The Wonsu reassessed the situation, staring at the business end of a Type 58 assault rifle, derived from the old Soviet AK-47. He dropped his derringer, then turned his venom toward Hiroko. "Traitorous bitch! Do you really think you can escape with this old man? You'll be cut to pieces by the guards before you can turn around."

"I wouldn't hold my breath, Kim. They're all piled up in the barn." He turned to Hiroko. "Would you ask the auntie to come out here, please?"

When the old lady exited the cabin, she was in a panic. "Chairman, I didn't know anything about this. Please believe me."

Yoo looked at the fat man, "She's telling you the truth, Kim. If you happen to survive, leave her alone."

"You are the one who should worry about survival."

"Let's put it this way. If I survive, then you might survive, Kim." Yoo glanced at Hiroko, realizing that, because of her warning, she could no longer remain there. "I've got a small backpack behind my pillow. Would you get that, and also get enough food to last a couple of days, as well as a couple of four-liter jugs of water. You'll need warm clothes, as we'll be traveling on horseback." He pointed at the fat man. "Either you're coming with us, or I'll kill you right now."

Before they departed, Yoo put three slugs into the ignition and radio on the helicopter, then as an afterthought, fired two into the radio transmitter in the barn, just in case the auntie decided it was in her best interest to report what had happened. He then turned to the woman. "When they don't hear anything for a day or so, they'll send a helicopter to investigate. Tell them I have their chairman, and if they interfere with my escape, he will be the first to die."

"What about Hiroko?"

"I'm taking her hostage as well."

"Why not take me also?"

"After Kim killed the mare, we only have three horses left, Auntie. You have truly been a good friend."

The three of them rode off to the south, hoping to temporarily confuse a search. Hiroko led the way with the fat man behind her. Kim said his shoulder was killing him and they needed to stop. Yoo laughed out loud.

Within three miles, they changed direction and rode almost straight east until dusk, stopping at a mountain stream east of the village of Chujon. Yoo could tell the girl was tiring, but it couldn't be helped. He fed the horses a sufficient amount of grain, then the three of them ate a quick supper of cheese, hard bread, and apples. The fat man had undoubtedly never eaten such a poor man's meal in his life.

"Mount up. We've got a long way to go before we stop."

Hiroko resignedly did as she was told, but the fat man folded his arms. "It is dark. We need to rest."

"There's plenty of moonlight. Either get on your horse voluntarily, or I'll tie you on, laid across the saddle on that big belly of yours."

"I need a cigarette."

Yoo grabbed the pack and dumped the cigarettes in high grass. "Let's see how you do going cold-turkey, Kim."

Just before sunup, they passed an ever-increasing number of small farms to the east. Yoo realized they were close to the small town of Kwirak, and resolved to find a place to conceal themselves during the daylight hours. Within thirty minutes, they arrived at an abandoned farmhouse which was very near collapse. Yoo was happy with it, as they could bring the horses inside with them, and no search aircraft could spot them while they ate and rested.

The fat man's nicotine withdrawal was exerting its effect. He was exceedingly nervous and would not stop talking. When Yoo confronted the Wonsu with a wadded-up rag and told him to open his mouth, the man clamped his jaws shut. Yoo simply forced him to the ground and pinched his nose closed. Within twenty seconds, the fat man opened his mouth, gasping for air.

He spent the remainder of the day with the gag in his mouth and hands tied to a wooden support beam in the middle of the one-room home. The strong, fresh result of horse biology permeated the space. Hiroko slept soundly, her head laid across Yoo's shoulder. He, on the other hand, slept in fits and starts, his previously developed strategy requiring significant alteration due to the presence of Hiroko and his hostage.

A new plan gradually formed in his mind. Why not depart along the same path he had taken when he entered the country five years ago? Yes, there were patrols and guard posts, but the same could be said for the length of the entire DMZ. However, the concentration of forces was much diminished this far to the east. The country was just too rugged and remote to maintain troops in any number. Nonetheless, Yoo remembered that the DPRK had no less than 200,000 special forces commandos located near a few large towns throughout the southern region of the country.

❦

It was just after nine PM in Pyongyang when there was a tentative knock on the door at Kim Yo-jong's residence. An aide answered the door and was surprised to see a young lieutenant standing there with a very unhappy look on his face. As the duty officer for the evening, it fell to him to provide some new information to the Wonsu's sister.

The aide tried to dissuade him from interrupting her at this hour, but the lieutenant insisted, and he was finally admitted and directed to the library. It was empty, so he had no choice but to sit and wait. Sister dear finally entered twenty minutes later, apparently after very little effort to make herself presentable. "Speak, Lieutenant."

"Madame Director—please forgive this intrusion. You may know that the Wonsu departed this morning for his retreat in Sep'o County. There have been numerous efforts to contact both his helicopter and the retreat over the last four hours, but without success."

She knew her brother's habits related to entertaining members of the pleasure squad. "Does this mean that there has been no answer whatsoever, or that the chairman is just not available?"

"Madame Director, neither radio is being answered at all—neither by the pilots nor the guard staff. We checked for some sort of bad weather event in Sep'o County, but nothing of the sort has happened."

"What has been done in the past when this has occurred?"

"To my knowledge, this has never happened before, Madame Director."

"I suggest you try again in the morning. Perhaps there is a simple explanation. If there is still no answer, then contact me again. I'll speak to the army base in Wonsan and send one of their choppers to find out what's going on."

As soon as the lieutenant departed, sister dear contacted Colonel-General Go to get his impression, and also to let him know that he was her first choice to request advice and counsel.

✻

At nightfall, the three travelers entered a small fishing village on the extreme northwest side of the large lake created by the Bukhan River Dam. Yoo gagged and securely tied the fat man to a tree, then went to look for a boatman with a gasoline motor.

With very little persuasion, Yoo traded the three thoroughbred Arabians and their saddles for an all-night boat ride to the southernmost end of the Bukhan. The horses and tack were worth perhaps a hundred times the cost of a boat ride, but Yoo could have cared less about the chairman's valuable property.

The Wonsu retained his gag, and Hiroko covered the top of his head and some of his face with a wrapping of cloth. The pompadour was a dead giveaway, and Yoo did not want the boatman to be so terrified of the consequences that he would back out of their agreement. The wooden boat certainly would not have borne up well under western-style inspection, but the few leaks were minimal, and the small ten-horsepower motor propelled them to the south at five kilometers per hour.

Just before daylight, they arrived at the south end of the lake, making landfall at the mouth of a feeder stream which had its source five kilometers further to the south inside the DMZ. As the three of them departed the lake, the boatman busied himself with changing out gas cans, and then puttered away, thrilled with his newfound wealth.

The terrain was more rigorous than Yoo remembered, but perhaps he was seeing it this time knowing Hiroko would have a difficult time with the remainder of the journey. They pushed on to higher ground, staying in dense woods to hide them from above. There was also a concern about DPRK border patrols, so out came the gag again to make sure the fat man didn't raise the alarm.

Yoo noticed that the Wonsu was more nervous than ever, and despite the cold, he was perspiring heavily. "How about a cigarette, Kim?" The fat man's eyes lit up in anticipation, and Yoo laughed. "Sorry, we're out."

CHAPTER 46

The Search
The DMZ, North Korea April 08, 2025

The call came a bit earlier than expected. At ten AM, Colonel-General Go contacted Kim Yo-jong via her private line. "Madame, you won't believe what my air crew discovered at the Wonsu's retreat. The only person there was the cook. Kim's helicopter crew and the four guards were all dead. The radios in both the chopper and the guard shack had been destroyed."

"What about my brother, General?"

"The cook says the elderly shepherd who managed the livestock took the Wonsu hostage, along with a girl who lived there. The three of them departed on horseback, headed south toward the DMZ."

"A girl living there? Leave it to my brother. No wonder he went to this particular cabin every couple of weeks. When did all this happen, General?"

"Yesterday, right after the Wonsu arrived at the compound around noon."

"So they've been gone almost an entire day!"

"Yes, madame. I sent the chopper in as we discussed. When they discovered what had happened, they lifted off almost immediately and flew straight to the south. They made two passes over the territory between the cabin and the border before having to return to base in Wonsan for refueling. They and two other crews are preparing to leave again within the next few minutes. In fact, I'm here at the airfield to observe."

"With a full day's head start, they could easily be at the border by this time, if that's where they were heading."

"I can't imagine they would try to remain in North Korea, madame, after what they've done. I'm also sending four of my special forces personnel in each of the three choppers. They'll be dispersed over a fairly large area, hoping to find some sign of three people on horseback. There are very few small towns in the area. About half of the men will be dropped off near those towns in case they decided to find a place to spend the night."

"As we discussed last night, General, contact me directly when you have anything to report. Make sure the base commander understands he must keep the whole thing quiet until the picture is clearer. And even then, all information must be cleared through me."

By midday, they had reached a spot where they could see the DMZ up ahead through the woods. In fact, the land flattened somewhat ahead of them, forming a rather wide valley. Once again, Yoo had them stop to rest. He and Hiroko ate the last of their food and drank the remaining bottle of water. When the Wonsu motioned for water, Yoo simply shook his head. If he removed the gag, what would prevent his prisoner from screaming his head off? He was fairly sure that border guards could not be too far away.

Even though his deep-cover assignment was simple and explicit—*kill the chairman*—Yoo found himself reluctant to actually pull the trigger, although he'd had multiple opportunities to do just that over the past few days. Worse yet, he didn't understand that reluctance. He suspected it had something to do with Hiroko's presence, though.

It was only when night had fallen that Yoo got them both up and moving. From that point forward, they would travel up the middle of the feeder creek. According to his previous experience when he'd entered North Korea, the creek bed and a few feet either side of the water had been a safe place. However, when they actually entered the four kilometer-wide DMZ, he was painfully aware that North Korea had planted three million land mines on their side of the demarcation line. Additionally, there were many large tank traps which had been dug across the landscape, apparently to interfere with any attempt at a land invasion by South Korea and her allies.

Surely there was a decreased concentration of mines this far from any population centers, in such hostile, mountainous terrain, but Yoo knew there were still hundreds of mines between them and freedom. After all, it only took one. So the three of them stayed in the creek bed in the dark, slipping and sliding on the slick rocks, wading almost up to their knees in some spots, but at least remaining in one piece. As a result of the wading, all three of them were miserably cold. The water in the creek bed began to peter out as they arrived in an area which was extremely flat.

Although it was still dark, Hiroko got the impression that the flat space went on for some distance. "How close are we to the DMZ?" she whispered to Yoo.

"We're right in the middle of it. This creek bed runs about three-quarters of the way across. We should be safe until that point. Once we leave the creek, we go very, very slowly."

"Don't we need to get across before daybreak?"

"Yes, but in one piece. This flat space on the North Korea side of the border is full of mines."

When the threesome reached the end of the creek bed's safety, Yoo withdrew a compass from his pack, held it level in front of him, and took a reading. He then pointed ahead into the dark. "We stay on a bearing of two hundred degrees." He showed her the compass. "If something happens to me, stay on this heading. When this area was being mined, the South Koreans observed very carefully, and they believe this is a safe pathway to the demarcation line. I used it myself five years ago."

The fat man stood at the end of the creek bed, gesticulating. When the gag was partially removed, he choked out, "You go first, Yoo. We'll see if you know what you're talking about."

The gag was stuffed back in his mouth. "There's no way I'm turning my back on you with the girl. You're going first, Kim."

The answer was simply a shake of the head, and then the fat man sat down in the high grass. Yoo's response was quick and direct. He struck the Wonsu's right collar bone, where it was still knitting together, with a rapid downward chop of the heel of his hand.

Even with the gag in, the fat man squalled like a freshly castrated bull calf. Finally, with Yoo's hand positioned above his shoulder again, he dragged himself to his feet, gingerly holding his right elbow against his chest while beginning a slow, cautious walk across the mine field. Yoo and Hiroko followed behind at a respectful distance.

They inched across the remaining mile of the North Korean portion of the DMZ, the fat man sliding one foot along the ground, feeling his way for the tell-tale protruding peg of a buried mine. Behind him, Yoo kept a constant eye on his compass, regularly correcting the Wonsu's direction. "To the left one meter" or "A half-meter to the right."

Yoo also began to watch the eastern horizon for any sign of dawn approaching. He had no desire to be caught out in the wide open DMZ by the DPRK border guards, who were positioned in elevated guard towers every thousand meters along the perimeter to their rear. He foresaw a situation where they would simply fire sniper rounds at them once they were spotted, not knowing that they were shooting at their Fearless Leader alongside two escapees.

With scarcely two hundred meters to go before reaching the ten-foot steel fence, topped by coiled strands of razor wire, which ran along the demarcation line between the two Koreas, the sky began to lighten on their left. He noted Hiroko's white jacket, and removed his own green military jacket for her to wear so she wouldn't be as easily seen by the border guards. Unfortunately, that meant his pale bare back would instead provide an alternative target.

Noticing the coming dawn, the fat man slowed his pace to an even greater degree. Yoo called out, "Kim, you fool, you've delayed us until it's almost daylight! Do you think your guards will hold their shots because of you? All they will see is three people trying to escape. The three of us simply represent three targets for their practice. Don't you realize you have no chance out here in the DMZ? Your soldiers have been trained well to shoot first and ask questions later. Your only chance to survive is to come with us to South Korea."

The Wonsu picked up his speed appreciably. They were now a mere fifty meters from the fence. A shot rang out. The guard obviously had not been sighted in for a target well over two and a half kilometers distant. As far as Yoo could tell, the bullet had not come close to any of them. But precaution took over, and he ordered both the fat man and Hiroko to crawl the rest of the way on their bellies.

Because of his injured shoulder, Kim was unable to make any appreciable progress in that position. Yoo told him to get up on his knees and proceed in that manner. But when he did, the report of two rifles trailed off around them. One of the bullets whizzed close enough that all three of them involuntarily ducked. Kim went back on his belly.

✦

"I apologize for this rude phone call at such an early hour, madame, but I have further news."

"What is it, General?"

"My men discovered a boatman in Kimhwa County who was trying to sell three Arabian horses."

"My brother's?"

"Undoubtedly. They still wore their silver-trimmed tack. The boatman required very little encouragement. He swears he had no idea that the Wonsu was one of the three people he transported to the south end of Bukhan River near the Imnam Dam. He claims there was an old man, a girl, and a very fat person who had something pulled over his head."

"What did you do with him, General?"

"As soon as he ran out of information, he was eliminated, madame."

She said nothing to this, simply smiling to herself. "Did they mention where they were headed, General?"

"Not according to the boatman, madame, but the DMZ is only a few hours' walk from the dam."

"What is your next step?"

"Put together a contingent of my Lightning Commandos, along with search dogs, to pursue them. We'll need to hurry, as the dogs are most effective within about six hours of a trail being created."

"And what if this shepherd is able to get my brother safely across into South Korea?"

The general paused. "Unless you direct otherwise, my men will only know they are pursuing three escapees, Madame."

"Excellent. I'm grateful that we understand one another. Thank you for your report, General Go."

✦

Despite Yoo's threats, the fat man would not move forward. In desperation, Yoo considered knifing him in the back, but he'd have to waste time wriggling around to reach his knife, beneath him in the minefield. He glanced aside and met Hiroko's trusting glance. Yoo made his decision. He and the girl crawled past the Wonsu, still adhering to the same compass bearing. The North Korean guards continued their firing, but only sporadically and without a visible target. Yoo figured it was simply to keep the three of them pinned down until a helicopter could be called in from the military base in Wonsan, no more than a hundred kilometers away. He imagined the guards had radioed for assistance as soon as they spotted them in the DMZ. Yoo figured a helicopter would make quick work of them within the next thirty minutes unless they could get clear.

Between the green vegetation of the minefield and the demarcation fence was five meters of bare dirt. Yoo was worried about crawling into this area, but they had no choice if they were to reach South Korean soil. When he reached the dirt, he scooped up handfuls of it and applied it to his upper body, head, and pants. Although it left much to be desired as camouflage, it was all he had.

Before he crawled into the open space, he also liberally applied dirt to Hiroko's green military jacket, reducing the clear outline of her back. "Once I get an opening cut in the fence, crawl forward and cross through. If something happens to me, crawl away from the fence and then stay absolutely still. I think a North Korean helicopter will be here in just a few minutes, and it won't hesitate to shoot somebody on the South Korean side if they can see you."

He pointed to the southwest. "After the helicopter is gone, go straight toward that cell tower you see in the hills. You'll find a town just beyond the tower—Imnam-myeon. Go to the police station and tell them what happened. Tell them that you were working with a South Korean intelligence agent." He noticed her eyes went wide at this admission, but he plugged on. "They'll probably want you to tell your story to someone in the government. But within a day or so, they'll eventually find someone to get you to the coast so you can contact your father."

"You mean it's actually possible that I can see my family again?"

"If you can get across the DMZ without being seen, then yes, you'll be with your family in just a couple of days."

"Thank you, dear Yoo. Now don't let anything happen to you either. I know my family will want to thank you." She looked away. "As will I."

Hiroko remained prone in the weeds while Yoo crawled forward across the dirt. He pulled a bolt cutter from his pack and lay on his back, starting the arduous process of making at least a dozen cuts through the heavy-duty links.

A shout came from the fat man, still lying in the minefield. "What do you intend to do with me, Yoo?"

Yoo wondered how he had removed the gag. "I could shoot you, but I think I'd rather see you choose between recrossing that minefield without my compass, and taking your chances with the helicopter gunship which ought to be here in about ten minutes." Yoo resumed cutting.

He was through nine links, but that still hadn't provided enough space for him to wiggle underneath. He reached higher with the bolt cutters and kept cutting. The next bullet was not well-aimed, but it unfortunately struck pay dirt.

The bolt cutters flew out of Yoo's grasp, and he gasped at the bloody stump where his left thumb and index finger had been. He concealed his wound and called to Hiroko. "Hurry up. Crawl over here and get through the fence while I hold it for you."

She did as he asked, while two more sniper bullets whined over their heads. It was only when she was finally lying on the South Korean side of the fence that she realized Yoo was injured. He couldn't seem to get enough grip with one hand to pull himself through the hole he had created.

Two more bullets barely missed. She reached through the fence and pulled, but only could move Yoo a half meter or so. She then raised herself to her knees to improve her leverage. A bullet ripped through the sleeve in her coat, miraculously missing her arm.

"You've got to get flat," Yoo yelled. "They have the range on us now!"

"We must get you through the fence, Yoo."

"Don't worry about me. I have room to pull myself through now. Conceal yourself in the high grass, and by the way, there are no mines on the South Korean side of the fence. It's only the North that does such things to their own people."

Hiroko leaned forward and kissed him on the forehead.

"Please hurry, Yoo." She then backed away on her belly and concealed herself in the weeds.

"Get further away from the fence," he yelled. "Cover yourself with weeds, then lie still. A helicopter may show up at any minute."

Yoo rolled over on his back, then began inching under the fence. The wire sliced into his chest. He was sweating profusely, despite having given up his jacket. Perhaps it was because he suddenly did not want to die. He grabbed the bolt cutters, thinking if he could just cut one more link he could make it. He braced one handle of the tool in his armpit and grabbed the other with his undamaged right hand. He finally made the additional cut, laid the cutter down, and inched again. There was finally enough space for him, and he painfully maneuvered his shoulders and upper body through the fence.

Yoo did not hear the next shot. The sniper's bullet caught Yoo under the chin, exited the top of his skull, and killed him instantly.

Whumpa-whumpa-whumpa from the east rapidly increased in volume.

"I hear the helicopter coming, Yoo! Is the fence open?" The fat man paused, waiting for a response. "Yoo, come back here and get me."

The MD 500E gunship streaked down the length of the DMZ. Originally a civilian helicopter, it and 86 others had been modified since being smuggled into the country from West Germany during the 1980s. The small gunship had been equipped with side-mounted Soviet AT-3 anti-tank missiles and two mini-machine guns. On the first pass, it directed machine-gun fire at someone attempting a fence crossing, as the person's head and shoulders were already on the South Korean side. It then began a looping turn and came over the spot where they had seen a person all dressed in black, lying some thirty meters from the fence. On that pass, they failed to see anyone, but fired three missiles in that general direction. The concussion from one of the rockets caused a land mine to trip. It detonated with a huge thump, the explosion raining down dirt and weeds. The helicopter made two more passes, firing both thirty-caliber machine guns blindly each time in the same area. They made one more pass, but seeing nothing, finally turned back toward the military airfield in Wonsan.

As the sounds of the helicopter receded, Hiroko peered through the grass. "Yoo, please tell me you're safe." She crawled back toward the fence, but the extent of his injuries was obvious from ten meters away. "Yoo, dear Yoo. You've saved my life and lost your own." Her breath caught in her throat, and she wondered for a full minute if she was going to breathe again.

She was forced to weep at a distance, knowing the snipers would like nothing better than to finish their practice on her if she revealed herself. She reflected on something Yoo had said—*honor bound to protect your life no matter the cost.* How true that had been! She realized Yoo was someone she would never forget. It was so painful to see him lying there. She would be grateful to him for the rest of her life. As to the status of the Wonsu, he didn't even enter her mind.

Finally she crawled on her belly in the two-foot-high grass, then on hands and knees for two hundred meters in the direction of the distant cell tower before rising up and running as fast as she could. She heard shots fired, but kept running. She tried to ignore all thoughts of Yoo as she kept the cell tower in her sights. Hiroko Arita would finally regain her freedom and her family.

Chapter 47

Karma
Wonsan, North Korea April 09, 2025

"Madame, Colonel-General Go again. I've just gotten a remarkable update from the airfield. They received a call at six AM from a border guard post, saying that two or perhaps three individuals were in the DMZ and apparently trying to cross over into South Korea. Because the guards were unsuccessfully shooting at targets three kilometers distant, they called in a helicopter gunship from Wonsan Air Base. The gunship arrived as requested at six thirty-six and sighted two individuals. One was in the midst of crossing thru the border fence into South Korea. The other was lying in the weeds and undergrowth within the minefield, approximately twenty-five to thirty meters from the first person."

"Was either of them my brother, General?"

"That is unknown, madame, although one, according to the pilot, may have been wearing black or at least dark clothing. He indicated the light was still poor at that hour and he couldn't be sure. The gunship fired at both individuals. They are, to quote the pilot, 'confident' that they were successful in immobilizing the individual at the fence. The other escapee took steps to hide in the undergrowth so the gunship could no longer clearly see that person when they fired in his vicinity. However, one of their shells struck a mine in that area, which was triggered. The chopper made two other passes, but did not see the second escapee again."

"Did they see a third party, General?"

"The chopper pilot did not. However the border guards

believe there were three people, madame."

"How soon can they land a contingent at the site to see exactly what the situation is, General?"

"Apparently it will be a dangerous landing site, as the second individual is—or perhaps was—inside the minefield. I'm getting on a chopper myself as I speak. If I understand you correctly, I think it's important for me to know exactly what has happened as soon as possible."

"Agreed, General. I'll head to Wonsan myself on my brother's special train. That way I can keep out of sight from any prying eyes, but still be close by."

"Madame, this is only a possibility, of course, but what if the Wonsu is actually on the South Korean side of the border?"

"That possibility carries with it all sorts of concerns. I should arrive in about three and a half hours, but call me just as soon as you have eyes on the situation, General."

※

"This is Park Chung-so, assistant director of the National Intelligence Service in Seoul. To whom am I speaking?"

"Director, thank you for taking my call. This is Lee Kyo-ahn, police chief in Gimhwa in Yanggu County. My small city is five kilometers south of the DMZ."

"Yes, I know your jurisdiction. What is the nature of your emergency?"

"Director, I have here before me a Japanese girl who tells an incredible story. She claims to have just escaped from the DPRK, aided by one of your agents. She also says they were accompanied by Kim Jong-un."

"Is this some sort of prank, Chief Lee—or whatever your name is?"

"Not as far as I can tell, Director. The girl tells quite a tale."

"All right. This is easily debunked. Just who does she claim was my agent?"

"The girl says his name was Yoo Ki-hong, Director. She states he was twenty-seven years old."

There was a short pause as the Assistant Director digested this, particularly the use of the past tense in referring to Yoo. "Chief Lee, you must not discuss this matter with anyone! Not anyone! Hold the girl there. Do not let her speak to anyone else, either personally or by phone. My chopper should arrive in two hours. Make arrangements for you and the girl to meet me."

"Madame, I'm over the location as we speak. We put two men on the ground via a harness, but we are unable to set down because of the minefield. The men on the ground confirm there is a body entangled in the DMZ fence on the border with South Korea."

"Is there any evidence that my brother passed through to South Korea, General Go?"

"Let me confirm with my men on the ground, madame... They state that the breach cut in the fence is barely large enough to accommodate the body they found. My men believe someone weighing over a hundred and twenty kilos could not possibly have passed through the opening into the South."

"What of the second subject the chopper shot at this morning, General? I believe you said he was not visible in the undergrowth."

"We spent some time hovering over the weeds and cover near the fence opening but were unable to spot anything. As I mentioned, the area is heavily mined, and so we can't put the chopper on the ground."

"Can your two men carefully walk over the area, General?"

"I'm afraid we'll need a portable minesweeper, madame. I can't ask my men to take the risk without one. We're running low on fuel just hovering here, so we'll return to base, refuel, and come back with the tools we need."

"How long will that take, General Go?"

"The pilot estimates about an hour and a half, madame."

"Please keep me posted."

When Park Chung-so's helicopter touched down on the edge of town, he was surprised at the small size of it. As he disembarked, the door to an older model Hyundai Sonata opened, and a uniformed law enforcement officer stepped out. From the passenger door, a girl, a young teenager, rounded the front of the car.

After introductions, Hiroko told her story to an incredulous assistant director of the South Korean National Intelligence Service. Park stopped her several times to clarify a point, but otherwise listened intently for ten minutes. "Hiroko, do you think you could take us back to the spot where you crossed into South Korea this morning?"

"I think so, Director Park. At least, I can get to the general area. Then it's a matter of finding dear Mister Yoo at the fence."

The three of them boarded the large Airbus H225 Super Puma helicopter, commonly used for both military and civilian functions. There were six intelligence agents dressed in SWAT-type gear in the vehicle's rear. The director had come prepared.

Although the break in the border fence was less than six kilometers from Gimhwa, it took fifteen minutes to reach the general vicinity due to Hiroko's uncertain directions. What they saw below as they passed over the final wood line with a clear line of sight to the DMZ was enough for Assistant Director Park to contact his boss.

"Sir, we're within sight of the border where the Japanese civilian indicated agent Yoo was killed. In fact, a body is visible within the fence. But sir, the DPRK has what appears to be one of their MD 500E gunships directly over the site. What seems to be happening is that they have two soldiers inside the DMZ, and their chopper is raising a rescue gurney carrying either a live patient or a body. This is very near the location where Hiroko Arita says Chairman Kim was when the gunship fired on him at daylight this morning."

"Is there any way to intercept the gunship, Park?"

"Negative, Director. They've got air-to-air and air-to-ground missile capability. Any fight would be over in ten seconds. Also, they're hovering over the DMZ. Even if we took their bird down, it would be in the middle of a minefield."

"Is there any sign of life from the gurney?"

"We've been watching for any movement, Director. So far there's nothing. Sir—they're lowering the gurney again to pick up the two soldiers on the ground."

"Have the North Koreans seen you yet, Park?"

"No indication, sir, but we'd be hard to miss. So far they're carrying out their mission and ignoring us ... Sir, they're heading to the northeast—probably to their air base in Wonsan."

"All right, Park. I'll share what we know with the intelligence services of our strategic partners." The senior agent paused for a deep breath. It was possible that Yoo had actually achieved the impossible. They wouldn't know for a while, though. "Will you pick up Agent Yoo's body for transport back to Seoul? At least we can give him the kind of honorable burial he deserves."

⁂

"Madame, Colonel-General Go here. We have located the Wonsu."

She tried not to sound hopeful. "Is he dead, General?"

"Our medic says he is barely alive, madame. He has multiple lacerations, probably from the mine explosion, his blood pressure barely registers, his heart rate is erratic, and our medic says he's in shock. We have him on the chopper and are heading back to base."

"Why don't you deliver him straight to the rail head, General? There is a fully staffed medical unit on board the chairman's private train. At least if he's on the train we can take control of the flow of information—whatever that turns out to be. If he ends up in the hospital, those issues become much more difficult to control."

"Madame, I suggest you warn the medical staff we have a critical patient on board with multiple challenges and will arrive in approximately twenty minutes."

Later that day, after South Korea's National Intelligence Service communicated with Japan's Public Security Intelligence Agency, and Hiroko Arita's family was contacted at their home on Sado Island. The Aritas were advised that their daughter was alive and well, and arrangements were made to reunite their family. Her parents were ecstatic and wanted to know when they might see their daughter. They were surprised that the answer depended on how long Hiroko's interviews with the National Intelligence Service in South Korea would take. Of course, it was all a shock, but perhaps not so much as the next condition. They were also told that certain portions of her story could not be shared in Japan under any circumstances—not with friends, not with family, and certainly not with members of the media.

The message was soon shared with the U.S. Department of State and the Central Intelligence Agency. Within an hour of receiving the information, Dr. Angela Martinelli was wheels-up on an agency jet, headed to Seoul.

Martinelli could not help but be impressed by the quiet calm of the young girl sitting before her and an officer of South Korea's National Intelligence Service. The only language they had in common was Korean, although neither was entirely proficient in it. The telling took the better part of two hours, but Angela made no attempt to hurry her. Her main interest was in trying to determine whether or not Kim was alive or dead, but obviously the girl did not have that information.

Much of the conversation involved the girl's gratitude to Yoo Ki-hong, and she made no attempt to hide her admiration and affection for the South Korean agent. "Mister Yoo only died because he was protecting me. Had he been looking out only for himself, he could have easily gotten through the fence at the DMZ. Instead, he delayed his own escape and made sure I was safe. Before this happened, I did not know such courage existed."

"In the last month, I have met two people like that, Hiroko. The first was a man who entered North Korea in order to rescue someone else. He was captured, imprisoned, starved, and beaten every day for months—so badly that he lost his hearing. Yet he told them nothing. When he was finally released, I heard his story."

"Who was the second, Dr. Martinelli?" Hiroko asked.

"Why, the second is you, Hiroko. You resisted perhaps the most powerful murderer in the world for over a year, and managed to hold on to those things most important to you. You may be the most courageous person I have ever met. I am honored to know you."

The girl lowered her eyes. "I would have had no courage if not for Mister Yoo."

"Perhaps Mr. Yoo would have had no courage if not for you, Hiroko."

※

As soon as the Wonsu was carried aboard the train's medical unit, Kim Yo-jong contacted the Central Palace, inquiring as to his scheduled responsibilities over the next few weeks. For any appearance which she deemed critical or self-serving, she either rescheduled or agreed to appear herself to represent the Wonsu. She realized it was dangerous, because

she didn't want anyone to know that the chairman was in
critical condition. But she also wanted to send the message
that she was capable of carrying out any and all responsibilities normally expected of her brother.

When specifically asked about the whereabouts of the
Wonsu, she diplomatically replied that he had decided to take
a short vacation, and had asked her to stand in for him when
necessary. Sometimes there was discussion after she had departed a particular meeting or event. That was when Colonel-
General Go Lak-chol was able to verify her previous statements related to the Wonsu. So far, so good.

Back at the train, among the many surgeries, tests, and
procedures which the Wonsu underwent, perhaps the most
embarrassing injury was repairing a severe wound to his right
buttocks. The cheek had almost been torn completely away by
a nasty piece of shrapnel from the exploded mine. Eighty
stitches were required externally, and some forty more in the
musculature beneath, thus making it necessary for him to lie
on his stomach for a week afterward. There were a half dozen
similar injuries, mostly on his back and legs, but not requiring so many stitches. He would then have to endure removal
of each one of those external stitches seven days later. His
almost continuous screams of protest could be heard from
one end of his train to the other.

The Wonsu had symptoms of withdrawal from not only
nicotine and alcohol, but also from the narcotic he had been
given for "unbearable agony". He cursed every person he encountered in a white coat. He threatened his primary physician with execution if he wouldn't provide him with his cigarettes and alcohol. With good reason, the doctor was petrified.
For several days, Kim lay, furious, in medical restraints to
prevent his stitches being torn loose during his ranting and
raving.

In the course of several in-depth examinations, it was
also discovered that he had two significant blockages in critical cardiac vessels. Each required placement of a stent. It was
actually quite serious, as the health of his heart muscle was
affected by the dramatic weight gain which had occurred over
the last ten years, a lack of exercise, extreme tobacco use,
type II diabetes, uncontrolled hypertension, and evidence of
alcohol induced steato-hepatitis.

Complicating his treatment, the Wonsu began having

spells of night terrors, where he dreamed over and over again that he was trying to crawl across the entire width of his country's demilitarized zone, with each move threatening to encounter another mine, thus blowing him up again. His physician began to administer a potent sleep aid and a twice daily dose of an anti-depressant so he could cope with his PTSD. Perhaps an added benefit was that his physician could then finally get a decent night's sleep himself.

Kim Yo-jong was hopeful when she first saw her brother brought aboard the train, hooked up to multiple IVs, with a skin tone about the color of paste. Her anticipation strengthened as the additional co-morbidities were discovered. However, the longer he survived, the more she began to lose that hope as she realized he might possibly recover.

Actually, if the nuclear devices were activated in the United States, she desperately needed her brother alive so that *he* could be the target of blame. The transition to her leadership might be very easy indeed if he was blamed, and she of course professed to have no prior knowledge of such attacks.

She and Colonel-General Go had several private conversations on that subject. These conversations invariably ended with the whispered statement, "When I'm in charge, and you are the Minister of State Security..." Perhaps during this portion of their discussion, the whisper was not adequately guarded. Colonel-General Go took the liberty of placing a finger across his lips to quiet her. One couldn't be too careful when the conversation had to do with treason.

⚛

The world's media began to wonder out loud.

In America: *Chairman Kim Jong-un has not been seen in public now for almost two weeks. Is he ill? Is he dead? Has he been deposed?*

In Japan: *The chairman of North Korea has neither been seen nor heard for some weeks.*

In South Korea: *South Korea has no evidence whatsoever that Chairman Kim Jong-un is dead. His personal train has been sighted near one of his mansions in Wonsan Province. He undoubtedly traveled there via his train and is utilizing it to stay out of the public eye.*

In North Korea: *Our chairman is recovering on board his private train near Wonsan from a minor heart procedure.*

❋

Several days after the incident at the border, and under orders from Kim Yo-jong, acting chairman in the absence of her brother, the DPRK blew up the Inter-Korean Liaison Office, established several years ago as a point of contact between North and South Korea. The office was located very near the Demilitarized Zone, just inside DPRK territory, and was now no more than a smoldering pile of rubble.

Kim Yo-jong followed up by issuing a public statement: *Our enraged people are determined to force the human scum (North Korean defectors) and those who have sheltered the scum to pay dearly for their crimes. I will leave to the DPRK's mighty military the right to take the next step of retaliation against South Korea.*

The president of South Korea urged the DPRK to stop raising animosities and return to talks. Foreign observers were once again on alert for what might happen next on the Korean Peninsula, let alone what the timeline might be.

Over the next 24 hours, Kim Yo-jong was heartened to receive a handful of congratulatory messages from her country's senior military leaders. She hoped to be hearing more of the same as other officers realized just how much authority she had suddenly granted them. She smiled in anticipation of soon replacing her brother and leading her country to greatness not seen since her grandfather had been chairman.

Then unexpectedly, 26 days after the Wonsu disappeared, he issued an invitation to his sister, as well as 67 senior officers from his army, air corps, marines, and navy, to report in dress uniform to the Wonsan Air Base on the following Tuesday. He made no reference as to what he had in mind.

That morning, the Wonsu stood on a podium with his sister on his left. In front of them waited the invited senior officers, arranged in seniority from major-general to lieutenant-general to colonel-general, and finally to those two men of four star general rank. The chairman made no reference to his public absence, but instead gave a long, rambling address about the formidable power of his military, the many progresses which had been achieved since he began serving as his nation's leader, and his gratitude for the great sacrifices and contributions of the men standing before him.

The day was unseasonably warm, but the Wonsu had the

benefit of standing in front of a cooling fan, while the officers before him perspired heavily in their dress uniforms. However, the heat was the last thing on their minds when they realized what was about to happen.

The Wonsu read out a name from among the one-star major-generals in the first row and asked him to step to the podium. An aide handed over the shoulder boards of a two-star lieutenant-general, the officer was promoted, and the next man in line's name was called.

The Wonsu progressed through 27 one-stars, promoting each of them to two-star rank, then called the names of 20 current lieutenant-generals, promoting them to three-star rank. It did not go without notice that two of the men standing in the ranks were not called forward. Kim Yo-jong realized with a sudden sense of foreboding that the two who had been ignored were among those who had contacted her with notes of appreciation just three days earlier.

The chairman promoted thirteen three-star colonel-generals to full army-general rank, this time not calling three men forward. Kim Yo-jong was now in silent panic mode, as two of the men not promoted had also contacted her. Even worse, the third man was none other than Colonel-General Go. The only officers who had not been promoted were the ones she had counted as being in her corner.

Her brother glanced at her. There was no mistaking the message behind his chilling grin. She began to shake in spite of a conscious effort to control herself.

Of the two men remaining, General Ri Pyong-chol was promoted to Vice Chairman of the Central Military Commission, while General Pak Jong-chun was named Vice Marshal for all DPRK military forces. These promotions carried with them the added benefit of living in one of the mansions inside the Ryongsung Compound.

⚛

A note was delivered by military courier to the residence of Kim Yo-jong and her husband within the Ryongsung Compound shortly after eleven PM that evening. The courier refused to provide the note to the house servant who answered the door. "For Madame Kim's eyes only," he said.

Sister dear met the courier at her door, dismissing him with nothing more than a sullen look. She took the note into her dressing room before opening it, recognizing Go's hand-writing immediately.

"Madame—The chairman has just purchased the loyalty of 62 flag officers of consequence. I do not know how, but have no doubt that the chairman knows. I suggest making your peace with him immediately. For me, there is no escape. It's too late."

CHAPTER 48

A Female?
Washington, DC April 13, 2025

Deep inside the Pentagon, in a room guarded by armed sentries as the first of four levels of security, a single outdated computer sat in an out-of-the-way corner among new machines and a vast room filled with servers. The computer served no known function, but neither did it interfere with any of the other programming. Truth be told, nobody remembered it existed.

The original purpose had been to monitor all government databases and communications networks that dealt with credible threats, and, when such a threat cropped up, to alert a variety of assets as to the nature of the threat. It was, as the coders who programmed it joked, their own version of Skynet from the *Terminator* movies, or *Colossus, The Forbin Project*. Except the program fell victim to budget cuts soon after being initiated and was quickly forgotten.

Canceled less than a week after having been setup, only one small military component had been tied into the system as a test. Now, unknown to anyone currently in the military or government hierarchy, it still monitored all of those channels, and an hour before sunrise the algorithm picked up a credible threat warning that fell within its programming parameters. It issued an action order to the only asset to which it had access, a top-secret black ops team called Task Force Zombie.

The Washington, D.C. Metro transports some 600,000 to 800,000 people daily during the work week, among them civil servants, members of the uniformed services, tourists, and all sorts of folks just trying to live their lives. Much of the Metro is underground, particularly as it enters the city from outlying areas in Virginia and Maryland. It's composed of six separate subway lines, 91 stations, and a total of 117 miles of track. The system is designed to move people from the suburbs into, thru, and out of the city, beginning operation in 1976 and expanding several times since.

The Red Line has its first station in Gaithersburg, Maryland, north of Rockville, travels south through Bethesda and Chevy Chase, and then into the heart of the city, before heading back through Union Station and then north through Silver Spring and Wheaton, in the direction of Olney, Maryland. During the rush hours, the trains are all standing room only, and people are often packed so close together you dare not scratch yourself, for fear of scratching your neighbor by mistake.

The Yellow Line originates well to the south, near Huntington, Virginia, stops at the Ronald Reagan National Airport, the Pentagon, and Alexandria, before arriving at Gallery Place in the city. From there it heads northeast to Howard University, Hyattsville, and the University of Maryland.

These two very busy lines intersect at Gallery Place Metro Station, adjacent to Chinatown and only a couple of blocks from the city's convention center in one direction and D.C. government buildings in another. During rush hours, hundreds of people are simultaneously loading and unloading on both lines with trains traveling in both directions. As many as four separate trains can be stopped at Gallery Place at one time, with people heading to work, trying to get home, or going to and from the airport.

At half past seven on Tuesday, at the peak of the morning rush hour, a woman dressed in the full regalia of a conservative Sunni Muslim, including the niqab, which covered all but her eyes, stood near the edge of the passenger loading area of the east-bound Red Line track at Gallery Place. She was surrounded by over a hundred others, all maneuvering to get close to where they thought the arriving train would open one of its ten entry doors. When the first car of the oncoming train began to emerge from the tunnel, applying its brakes as it drew closer to the platform, the crowd of waiting passengers surged even further forward.

As the train began to brake, the Muslim woman appeared to attempt to move toward the opening doorway, but the mix of off-loading passengers and those pushing and shoving to get on board was too great. She studied the crowd for a few seconds and moved closer to three young women whose faces were buried in their phones. She seemed to lose her grip on the briefcase she was carrying, and it slipped from her fingers at the feet of the threesome. As the rest of the crowd maneuvered to get aboard in the minute or so before the electric doors closed, she retreated rapidly toward the exit along with the unloaded passengers.

After using the first set of escalators, she stepped behind a large concrete stanchion, produced her phone, and dialed a number. As the phone completed its electronic connection, the C-4 in her briefcase exploded with all the power of an improvised electronic device. The train was blown completely off the rail, which carried 750 volts of direct current, and its electric connection broke loose, popping and snapping about in the crowd like a great wounded snake.

The three subway cars closest to the explosion were ripped apart, as were most of the occupants. People still standing on the walkway who had been unable to board, positioned within a hundred feet of the blast, were inundated with large staples of the sort commonly used to attach barbed wire to fence posts. The terrorist had tightly packed twenty pounds of the staples around the C-4 for maximum damage. Along with approximately two hundred other survivors, the Muslim woman fled the subway, emerging onto the street at the site of the elaborate Chinatown sign overhanging H Street NW at the intersection with Seventh Street.

Black smoke with a harsh, metallic taste billowed out of the escalator behind her. A small number of people heroically ran toward the danger. With a gloved hand, she dropped her flip phone in a trash can. There were two witnesses who took note of this odd action, and would later swear to it.

She stepped to the curb, flagged down a cab, and headed north. By the time it had traveled five miles, the Muslim garb had been discarded underneath the front passenger seat, and a man who would later be described by the cabbie as Hispanic, exited the cab dressed in a pair of blue jeans, a

Georgetown University sweatshirt, and a black ball cap pulled down low. Paco Batista strode away from the cab toward the Georgia Avenue Metro Station with a broad smile on his face. He was satisfied that his morning's work had only targeted adults.

Back at Gallery Place, there was pandemonium. The entire Metro system had to be shut down in case there were other actors involved in other locations. The morning commute came to a screeching halt for hundreds of thousands of people. Those already at work would have one devil of a time getting back home that evening. The Red Line rail tracks in both directions at Gallery Place were twisted into pretzels. The Yellow Line, running on a different level, survived the explosion, although the resulting fire from the blast had ruined its electronics.

EMS personnel rapidly triaged the victims by separating them into groups according to the time which might be required to save their lives. Immediate attention was given to those who might possibly be saved, stabilizing and transporting them to area emergency rooms. Those in need of urgent attention who might deteriorate rapidly were taken care of immediately after the first group. Those who were injured but their needs were not urgent and the walking wounded would be cared for later. Then there was the ever growing group of remains with black tags attached, which were placed in an area encircled in crime scene tape.

Despite heroic efforts from the D.C. fire department, the three most damaged subway cars still smoldered, with several passengers dead from the heat and smoke inhalation. Other bodies were literally destroyed by the blast. Limbs and still warm internal organs littered a large area. As the morning wore on, those body parts were placed in individual body bags and moved over with the dead. Reunification of body parts might never be fully achieved. Identification of many would have to depend on dental records and genetic studies.

Metro police and the D.C. police interviewed potential witnesses inside a restaurant near the exit escalator on H Street. Only a tiny percentage claimed to have seen anything. However, a growing public clamor in the crowd had begun to draw the same conclusion, that the entire incident was the fault of a Muslim woman.

❄

Assistant Secretary Campbell from the ATF co-chaired the meeting with Lynn Jones, assistant director of the FBI's Counter-Terrorism Division, and Abel Adams, assistant secretary of DHS.

"At this point," Campbell said, "it appears that the Metro explosive device was prepared by the same set of hands which built the bombs that went off in Baltimore and in New York."

"How do you come to that conclusion?"

"Mr. Mayor, our explosives experts look closely for a bomb-maker's signature—the way the components are connected, the products used, soldering techniques, triggering, you name it, they analyzed everything about this device, and then compared it to what we know from the previous two bombs. They collaborated with their counterparts in the FBI and told me they have little doubt this is from the same terrorist."

"Let me call on D.C. Police Chief Katherine Ash regarding what we've discovered about the Gallery Place bomber," said Assistant Secretary Adams.

"We have three different cameras which captured the perpetrator as she, or rather he, as I'll explain in a moment, entered the metro station with a briefcase, stood on the platform waiting for the train, and then exited the station some four minutes later without a briefcase. Because the individual was completely covered in Muslim dress, we can't make out any distinguishing characteristics, other than estimating that he was between five feet six and eight.

"We have two witnesses who saw him discard a cell phone in a trash can at the Metro exit. Although we don't know the phone number of the bomb device, by triangulating cell tower records, we know he made a call to a number in that immediate vicinity at seven-thirty-two AM. There were no other calls made on that phone. It was apparently purchased solely for detonating the bomb. The seven-thirty-two call coincides with the time on several phones found on the dead and injured which cut off at that exact moment.

"This Muslim female was seen entering a Yellow Cab at the Chinatown entrance immediately after the bombing. We tracked down the driver, who said he distinctly remembered the fare. He explained that he was ordered to stop near the Georgia Avenue Metro Station, and he was shocked when a hand from the back seat dropped three twenty dollar bills on the front seat console and said no change. So he wasn't paying strict attention to his passenger, as he was scrambling to use his counterfeit identity pen on the currency. However, he did confirm that a woman did not exit his cab. He described the individual as a Hispanic male."

"Did the cab driver look at any mug shots that might possibly match the suspect?"

"Yes, sir. But apparently the man was wearing a cap which partially obscured his face, and the driver complained he didn't get a good look at the fellow. He also reported that he found the individual's discarded clothing under the seat."

"Did he get a close enough look to believe the individual actually was a man, and not simply a woman dressed as a man?"

"He swears it was a man, but we certainly must keep your question in mind as we pursue this."

"Were any prints recovered from the cab, Chief Ash?"

"Many, Mr. Secretary. We've submitted what we have to the FBI."

"Did the cabbie see whether the man caught the Yellow or Blue Line train at the stop?"

"He said he lost sight of him almost immediately and couldn't tell whether he even entered the metro station. He also was very unhappy that all of the bills he received were counterfeit."

"Are there cameras at the Georgia Avenue Metro Station, Chief Ash?"

"Yes, sir. We had the cabbie review the Tuesday morning video taken from eight AM until eight-twenty, and he saw no one who resembled our suspect."

"You're saying the bomber may not have even entered the station at all?"

"Yes, Mr. Mayor. He may have simply used that location to draw attention away from his true escape venue."

"Was there any video from the Gallery Place Station which would provide a clue as to the identity of the bomber?"

"The individual was completely covered in the dress of a conservative Muslim female, so the video revealed nothing."

"So here we are," said Lynn Jones, "back with the vague description of a Hispanic perpetrator. Mr. Mayor, I don't want to put you on the spot, but do you have any idea as to how many Hispanics live in your city?"

"Actually, I do know, Mr. Secretary. Almost sixty thousand self-declare as Hispanic residents. But that's far from the whole story. Another three hundred fifty thousand declare as black, and three hundred forty thousand declare as white, but some of both groups are undoubtedly part or wholly Hispanic, and your witness might decide that some of those persons fit the general description of a Hispanic. To complicate things, six million people live in the D.C. Metro Area, and by seven-thirty on a weekday, at least three hundred thousand of them will have traveled into the city via the Metro for their employment. As to how many of those are Hispanic, I have no idea.

"At any given time, there are also seventy-four thousand foreign immigrants in the city, which may or may not be included in our census. Those numbers are not necessarily broken down by race or appearance. All this to say the number of people which might be described as Hispanic in the city last Tuesday at seven-thirty AM was probably closer to eighty thousand. I have no desire to see a situation develop where the rest of this city starts demonizing eighty thousand people because of the acts of one bomber, who may not live here, might no longer be anywhere close to our city, and might not even be Hispanic."

A clerk entered and handed Adams a sheet of paper. Lifting an eyebrow, he scanned the others to get their attention.

"I just got this from the Secretary of Homeland Security, who got it from the Secretary of Defense. Have any of you ever heard of something called Task Force Zombie, or someone named Green Ghost?"

"Sounds like a comic book," Ash said.

"No," Jones said, "not a comic book, a code name. Why do you ask, Secretary?"

"Because whoever they are, they're on our side and they're tracking the terrorists, and the Secretary of Defense says we are to help them in any way possible."

※

Social media posts reached levels not seen since the last presidential election cycle. Under mug-shot photographs of three anonymous Hispanic men inked with obvious MS-13 tattoos ran the following text:

If You Have Seen Tattoos like These in Your City, Report it to the Police! *Witness after witness has come forward, stating that the guilty parties of the bombings in Washington, New York, and Maryland were Hispanic men. Other witnesses of food poisonings not only identified Hispanics, but also saw the tattoos as pictured. When is the government going to ACT to protect us? Arrest them! Deport them! Stop them at the border! Clean up this mess!*

Can any of us say we now feel safe in the United States? Where is our government? Rome is burning. Tell Nero to stop fiddling!

In contrast:

Ambassadors of Mexico and four Central American countries call upon the president to speak to the American people, telling them that people of Hispanic heritage wish them no ill will. Also, that Hispanic people residing in the United States are peaceful, law-abiding members of society. Vilifying them as a people, just because one or two have committed heinous crimes, does not represent the spirit of American justice.

In another message:

We love the Hispanic people. But ICE must remove every MS-13 gang member from our country. This gang represents everything that is evil. Drug Smuggling, Sex-Slavery, Child Pornography, and now Mass Murder!

Chapter 49

The End of the Beginning
Northwestern Tennessee April 15, 2025

Bijan Al-Hawi, Naveed Somom, and Darius Dabiri had been warned by the Syrian, Abbud Dweck, that they were at risk of being discovered. He claimed to have excellent intel that a mysterious black-ops group, led by some character called Green Ghost, was running them to ground. Assuming the intel was real, that is; in their shadow world, disinformation was more common than the real thing.

The Syrian's suggestion had been to pick up their two packages a day or two early from the Western Kentucky Warehouse in Paducah, Kentucky and in Hackensack, New Jersey. If this so-called Ghost had information as to the Iranians' schedule, perhaps the black-ops outfit would make assumptions about the time and pick-up of their shipment, so why not confuse the issue?

Naveed had questioned the risk posed by an extra day or two of exposure to the package. The Syrian had responded that the units had been sitting in the two warehouses for five months, and no problems had been reported by any warehouse workers. Perhaps the Syrian had forgotten to mention a couple of recent events, but who knew?

On April 13th, the three Iranian agents arrived at the designated address in Paducah and loaded their two-thousand-kilogram package into the back of their truck, which they had appropriated in Union City, Tennessee the day before. Since seizing it, they had made several adaptations to the black GMC dually. They added a matching camper top and altered the truck bed so that a section five feet long and eighteen inches wide was completely removed from the floor of the bed, leaving an open slot which reached from the back of the cab to the tailgate. Also, they affixed padding on either side of the missing bed section so that their package could be transported without any risk of movement.

They took the extra precaution of relocating across the river to the small town of Caruthersville, Missouri. Naveed and Darius followed the GMC in a white Ford Escape, which they had purchased with two hundred brand new twenty dollar bills from the previous owner in Dyersburg, Tennessee. While they were waiting on the calendar, Al-Hawi paid a man in Caruthersville to allow him to park his truck in the man's barn for two nights while he went fishing with friends.

At five AM on Income Tax Day—April 15th—Al-Hawi retrieved the truck, and the three of them enjoyed a big breakfast before crossing back over the river and heading north. At seven AM, they filled up the tank on their Ford Escape at a wide spot in the road called Cates, Tennessee. This was in preparation for a long day's drive ahead.

The Iranians parked the Escape on the farm road, then Naveed drove the pickup across a bean field to a set of GPS coordinates, which were adjacent to a narrow ditch. He parked, donned a white protective jumpsuit, a hood, boots, and gloves, then slashed all the tires so the vehicle could not be easily removed. He next retreated to the rear of the truck, removed a small panel on the end of the steel canister, then, per his specific directions, set a timer and turned a switch.

Naveed quickly shed his protective clothing, tossed it inside the truck, locked it, ran back across the farmer's field, and jumped in the car with his compatriots. They wound their way to the south until they hit US Highway 412, then southeast before striking US Highway 64. The men then drove east toward the Tennessee-North Carolina border before they headed northeast. Their next warehouse stop was in Hackensack, New Jersey. They hoped to retrieve a second steel cylinder from there before depositing it in a parking garage off 42nd Street in New York City, within three blocks of the United Nations building, the Queens Midtown Tunnel, a Con-Edison substation, and many hotels.

Whoever had tipped off the Syrian, his information was accurate. Naveed and the others couldn't know it, but the mysterious American black ops team called Task Force Zombie was not only real, but had tracked them halfway across the world, and at 0500 hours, Green Ghost and his team were in Paducah, Kentucky, waiting in hiding for a certain warehouse to open for business. Ghost soon discovered through the warehouse manager that his targets were a step ahead.

It didn't take long for him to realize the terrorists had slipped away, or maybe he'd been fed bad intel. Not knowing the ultimate destination of the men he pursued, Green Ghost and his eleven commandos split up into four vehicles and struck out in four directions on a search and destroy mission. While he didn't know the location, the intel was adamant that today would be the day. Per the warehouse worker, Green Ghost now also knew that the bad guys were driving a black GMC pickup with a black camper top.

As the morning ticked away, Green Ghost could almost feel the radiation burns on his skin; they knew a nuclear device was involved, and the longer they delayed stopping their target, the more likely they would be inside the danger zone when it eventually went off. Vaporizing in a nuclear fireball didn't worry him if it meant stopping the attack, but dying slowly of radiation poisoning scared the hell out of him. Finally, patched into a live feed from the NSA, he saw via an overhead satellite that a similar vehicle to their target had been spotted in Hayti, Missouri, headed west. Then the satellite disappeared over the horizon and lost contact with the suspect vehicle, but Ghost Ghost *knew*, he just knew it was the one. With the FBI live on the same feed, he requested they contact the Missouri and Arkansas highway patrols for a roadblock on all possible roadways departing Hayti. Three minutes later, he received word the orders had been issued. Now all he could do was wait.

An hour later, Missouri authorities let him know they were holding a man and wife—both in their seventies—in Poplar Bluff, Missouri, as their truck fit the description of the one provided. The misunderstanding was quickly resolved and the elderly driver got a law enforcement escort to the local regional medical center so he could make it to his chemotherapy session in time.

There was nothing to do except for the Zombies' four vehicles to press on, each one taking a point on the compass along a major roadway and praying for a miracle. At half past four that afternoon, they received another satellite spotting, this time very near the Mississippi River on the Tennessee side, approximately seven miles from Reelfoot Lake. The satellite indicated the vehicle was parked in a farmer's field and had not moved during their ten-minute pass overhead. The NSA provided GPS coordinates.

The Zombies were all over two hundred miles away, except for Green Ghost and his crew, who had headed back toward the east. However, even they were eighty miles distant. Green Ghost called the NSA, asking that they contact the 101st Airborne Command at Fort Campbell, Kentucky, but even with the NSA's clout, it took fifteen minutes to reach the base commander. Green Ghost's recommendation was to launch a jet aircraft which would get close enough to fire a missile to hopefully take out the bomb without detonating it.

Fifteen more painful minutes and Green Ghost was finally on a direct line with the Air Ops Chief for the Combat Aviation Brigade, who promised at the very least a fly-by of the GPS coordinates from the satellite. Pending no nearby buildings or people, they would consider taking out the black truck via a Lockheed Martin F35A Lightning II fighter jet with an air-to-ground missile, as no combat drones were available.

There was nothing more to do except wait. If the Zombies converged on the truck and it wasn't the right one, they'd be stuck in the middle of nowhere. It was better for the unit to reassemble somewhere west of the Mississippi in case the truck was a decoy or simply the wrong one. So once again, tapping into the clout of the NSA, he ordered his other three teams to drive west to Whiteman Air Force Base in Knob Noster, Missouri, where a flight would be waiting to transport them to McConnell Air Force Base in Wichita. They were directed to wait there for the rest of the team.

The F-35 was just passing thru three thousand feet in altitude, headed west at 1700 hours Central time. Unfortunately, the pilot was only 25 miles from his target, and facing in exactly that direction, when the bomb detonated.

As the three terrorists in the white Ford Escort approached the border between Tennessee and Virginia, even at a distance of almost five hundred miles from the black pickup, the horizon in their rear view mirror suddenly brightened as though the sun had risen twice in one day. The United States of America would never be the same.

Glancing through the SUV's back window, Zeus, one of the three Zombies with Green Ghost, turned his face and shielded his eyes as a blinding flash filled the far horizon. Seconds later, all of them turned and gaped at the mushroom cloud climbing skyward.

"Tell me this is a movie, boss."

Even the taciturn Green Ghost gaped at the sight. As always, though, he recovered faster than anybody else. "That mission's a washout. On to the next."

His team didn't ask how he could be so calm, because they already knew the answer; he wasn't calm, he was focused. Emotions didn't win battles, and the fight wasn't over yet.

With the realization that what had just happened in rural Tennessee could happen in the nation's largest city, Green Ghost quickly contacted the Fort Campbell Air Ops Chief and requested an immediate flight from Fort Campbell to New York City, or as close as they could get. He was convinced the only way to head off another attack was to intercept the terrorists at the warehouse in Hackensack, New Jersey. After the base commander's protests that he didn't take orders from some unidentified person on the phone, particularly one named Green Ghost while the country was under attack. That call was followed by a twenty-second communication from the NSA, immediately after which the base commander called to inform the Zombie leader that air transport was on its way.

"Who are you people?" he asked.

"We don't exist, Colonel."

With the stubbornness of a bureaucrat who didn't like being out of the loop, the colonel refused to take the hint. "You sound like you exist."

Green Ghost had never been one to suffer fools gladly, especially with a terrorist nuke in the mix. "And you sound like you want to be a major again, or maybe a captain. Now focus—your career is the least of my worries right now."

The colonel's hostility filled the noisy breaths coming through the phone, but he said nothing more.

Because of the chaos following the nuclear detonation, no fixed-wing aircraft were available, so within an hour, Green Ghost and his men were wheels-up in one of the Blackhawk helicopters belonging to the 101st Airborne's Air Assault Wing. The aircraft had a maximum speed of 174 mph, and with a distance of 821 air miles between Fort Campbell and Fort Houston in Brooklyn, New York, their forecasted arrival time was 0300 hours Eastern.

Green Ghost briefed his team in the bird's noisy passenger compartment. Despite each man listening through the intersquad helmet communications, he still had to shout to be heard. "We'll have a vehicle and driver waiting on touchdown in Brooklyn, and that should put us at the warehouse before zero four hundred hours. If there's a night guard, we'll go inside and set up. Otherwise we wait until somebody shows."

"That's a long way from the target, GG," said First Squad's second in command, the man called Vapor. "Gotta be something closer."

"We're under nuclear attack and everything is a shit sandwich. Best we can do."

"Speaking of nuclear attack," Vapor said, "what if this second nuke goes boom and we're in the warehouse with it?"

"No worries about that. You'll be vaporized before you know it went off."

"Why does that not make me feel better?"

"It's also not armed yet."

"How do we know that?"

"That's what they told me," Green Ghost said.

"Oh, *they* said it. Well, if *they* said it, it's gotta be straight up. And are *they* gonna be in there with us?"

"It's not armed, dammit. It can't go off."

"What about a dirty bomb?"

"Stopping that is easy—just don't blow it up. Look, the only reason the damned thing is still in there is because grabbing the terrorists is deemed worth the risk. New York City is within the immediate blast zone, so if it detonates, bye-bye Big Apple."

"You say that like it's a bad thing."

"Any word on the Bible thumpers?" asked Wingnut. That was the team's nickname for Third Squad, which contained members named Judge, Isaiah, Ruth, and Rev, short for Revelations. It surprised the team because Wingnut rarely spoke, but his crush on Ruth was well known, even if never mentioned.

"Nada," Green Ghost said. "Comms are down over most of the country. Last I heard they were inbound from Iceland, destination Shaw or Langley. No worries, though. Judge is grade A and you know it."

"Any chance they meet us in Jersey?"

"Not impossible."

As promised, the Blackhawk set down at Fort Houston. To Wingnut's disappointment there was no word on Third Squad. By 0310 hours they were on their way out of the city and headed to Hackensack. If there was a guard on site at the warehouse, he didn't show himself when they banged on the door, so they settled down to wait a block away.

Green Ghost said, "Two of you—Vapor and One-Eye—you change into warehouse uniforms and stand by. Remember, eyes up. We don't know if the employees are part of the plan or not, so take no chances. Zeus, you and I are backup. We can assume at least one tango stays outside as wheel man. Wingnut, you open the overhead door and stand by. Once they're all inside, move in. The NSA wants prisoners to interrogate, but the priority is stopping them. Do whatever it takes."

"Alive's the priority?"

"Alive's the *preference*."

At 0701 hours, two men dressed in grey coveralls made their appearance, and one unlocked the street-side door. Before he could turn around and lock it from the inside, Vapor stuck his foot in the doorjamb and his pistol in the man's ear. One Eye repeated the maneuver with the second man.

"Akrhus," Vapor whispered. (Shut up)

Instead, the men started to scream, until two heavy wrenches struck the base of their skulls, just hard enough to debilitate, not kill.

The four of them settled down to wait, as they didn't know when the terrorists might arrive. Vapor and Zeus were soon outfitted in coveralls, but the actual warehouse workers were a bit chilly on April sixteenth, sitting on the concrete floor in a closet in just their tidy-whiteys and a gag in their mouths.

Green Ghost set out to find the package which the terrorists might be seeking. However, it was not difficult, as the only carton in the entire warehouse space possessed an attached bill of lading which originated in Duluth, Minnesota. The rest of the warehouse—from wall to wall—was completely empty. At least they wouldn't be bothered by other customers.

Finally, at 0900 hours, there was a knock on the door.

Green Ghost and Zeus faded into positions that were out of sight, and Vapor cracked the door. Only one man stood there. The Iranian looked at Vapor, Vapor looked at him, then the man peeked around the doorway and spotted One Eye standing there.

Finally Vapor spoke, using his limited Arabic. "Did you come for a shipment?"

"Yes."

"Where was it shipped from?"

The Iranian paused at that, and turned his head to ask a question of someone out of sight. He turned back around. "San Francisco."

Vapor shook his head. "We don't have anything for you."

The Iranian squinted, turned his head again, then back. "Duluth."

"Where's your truck?"

He gestured in the direction of the overhead door on the loading dock. Vapor motioned that the man should come inside, and the two of them walked over to the dock, where Zeus opened the big steel door. Two other men entered, both of them armed—one with a .45 automatic pistol in his belt, the other pulling an AR-15 from under his jacket.

"Where is my package?" asked Naveed.

"Why are you waving that gun around? All you have to do is ask. My boss says you're supposed to pay the shipping costs."

Naveed pulled the muzzle of his pistol up so that there was no doubt where it was being directed. "Then tell your boss to come down here and collect his money."

Vapor nodded, switching to English and hoping the Iranian followed suit. "This thing is heavy as hell. Me and my buddy can't handle it by ourselves. You guys are gonna have to help."

"The other warehouse had it at the dock door," came the reply in heavily accented English.

"Sorry. It's back here out of sight in case somebody unexpected showed up."

Naveed grunted, then nodded. "How much it weigh?"

"The bill of lading says five thousand two hundred pounds."

"You got forklift?"

"Yeah, but the bill also says it's fragile."

"Just put on forklift and strap it down."

"Like I say, we're gonna need some help."

Out of the corner of his eye, Vapor saw Green Ghost signal that everything was okay outside on the street. Without even a nod or change of expression, Vapor called to One Eye. "Help us out over here. Everything is A-okay."

Naveed refused to put his AR-15 down and help, but called to his two companions to come and assist. Vapor sat in the forklift, maneuvered it to connect with the crate's wooden base, then handed straps to the two terrorists to affix around the crate, securing it to the forklift.

While they were occupied, Zeus stepped behind them with his own weapon, while One Eye grabbed Naveed's AR-15 from behind and pressed it against his throat. The man pulled the trigger several times, trying to jerk himself loose, but all he accomplished was to have One Eye very nearly crush his larynx with the barrel of his own weapon. Naveed stopped struggling about the time Green Ghost re-entered the warehouse, his own weapon on display.

With the three men appropriately detained, Green Ghost again contacted NSA, and within five minutes all of the Iranians were cuffed and in the back of a black SUV with FBI escorts. A couple of military nuclear weapons specialists were quickly on the scene, along with a platoon of heavily armed guards as they awaited the Nuclear Response Team.

In another two hours, the team was back on board the Blackhawk. With the mission completed, reality had time to sink in as early reports indicated unbelievable damage along the Mississippi River. Green Ghost and his Zombies were able to return to Fort Campbell, but they were forgotten as the magnitude of the crisis deepened.

Given their nebulous status on base and their quasi-military appearance, the base commander assigned them to the Bachelor Enlisted Quarters. Green Ghost didn't argue; they'd stayed in worse places. Most of them collapsed into their bunks, and within minutes filled the barracks with snoring. But Green Ghost couldn't shut off his mind.

Lying beside him, Vapor noticed. "We got one of them, GG. Bat five hundred in the majors and they open the vault."

"Yeah." Green Ghost's tone was flat. "It's gone, you know, all of it, everything we grew up with. Voodoo Village, the Pyramid, that little barbeque shack down on Jackson. They said Memphis is under fifty feet of water."

Vapor didn't respond for a while. "I can't think about it yet. It's too soon. We saved a lot of lives, though, and those three chumps will talk, just you watch."

"They said the designated detonation spot was three blocks from the U.N. Building, during a meeting of the General Assembly. The representatives from a hundred nations would have been vaporized, along with millions in New York City and New Jersey."

"If I'd known about the U.N. part, I might not have stopped them. So what happens now, GG?"

"Now? Now the world goes to hell."

The End

If you were thoroughly engaged in this novel, please leave a review on the book's page at www.amazon.com or on www.goodreads.com.

If you'd like advance information about my next novel, please sign in at www.johnbabbauthor.com or connect with me on Facebook.

I suggest you read William Alan Webb's series on The Last Brigade Universe *to see what happens next to the remains of the United States of America.*

Also, see my own coming books in that series sometime in 2021, Hell's Hip Pocket *and* A Reservation in Hell. *For a look at the FIRST CHAPTER of* Hell's Hip Pocket, *turn to the end of this book.*

Appendix: Alphabet Soup

ATF—Alcohol, Tobacco, and Firearms Agency
ATSDR—Agency for Toxic Substances and Disease Registry
Bowibue—North Korean Secret Police
CDC—Centers for Disease Control and Prevention
CIA—Central Intelligence Agency
DARPA—Defense Advanced Research Projects Agency (DoD)
DHS—Department of Homeland Security
DMAT—Disaster Medical Assistance Team
DMZ —Demilitarized Zone between North and South Korea
DPRK—Democratic People's Republic of Korea (North Korea)
EPA—Environmental Protection Agency
FDA—Food and Drug Administration
FEMA—Federal Emergency Management Agency
G-2—Intelligence staff of a military unit, or the intelligence
    being collected
HHS—Department of Health and Human Services
LD-50—Lethal dose of a substance required to kill 50% of test
    subjects
NPS—National Pharmaceutical Stockpile
NSA—National Security Agency
NSSE—National Special Security Event
NTSB—National Transportation Safety Board
Reconnaissance General Bureau—DPRK Intelligence Service
ROK—Republic of Korea (South Korea)
RPG—Rocket propelled grenade
Ryongsung—Principal palace of the Wonsu within North Ko-
    rean Capitol City
SAIC—Special Agent in Charge (FBI)

Savama—Iranian Ministry of Intelligence and National Security

SCIF—Secure Communications Information Facility

Taewonsu—Highest possible rank in North Korea, previously held only by Kim Jung Il and Kim Il-Sung

The Agency—CIA

USDA—U.S. Department of Agriculture

USPHS—U.S. Public Health Service

VMAT—Veterinary Medical Assistance Team

Wonsu—North Korean military rank, held only by the chairman

Acknowledgments

Gunnar Grey, publisher at Greyweaver Press, for her many excellent editorial suggestions, which served to make this a better story.

William Alan Webb, fellow author, for his advice, counsel, and editorial recommendations, as well as his work in making sure this story meshes with his series The Last Brigade.

CAPT Angela Martinelli, USPHS (ret), whose experience as an operating room nurse, PhD nurse educator, an emergency planner, and an international responder, served to make her an exceptional role model for the heroine of this book. To date, she has deployed to domestic and international medical missions **48** times, both in uniform and as a civilian. She deserves to be a heroine!

CAPT Hugh Mainzer, USPHS (ret), whose comments as a veterinarian and public health professional were extremely insightful regarding animal diseases and outbreak control, and were critical in making this book more accurate.

Eugene McKenzie, MD, who, as an internal medicine physician, was kind enough to review and correct all of the medical components of this book, thus making me look like I knew what I was talking about. Also, as a 21st century Renaissance man, and celebrated musician, he corrected my mistaken assumptions about the *1812 Overture.*

RADM Robert Williams, USPHS (ret), whose long experience with the Agency for Toxic Substances and Disease Registry, made him the perfect subject matter expert to comment on all issues related to civil and environmental engineering, thus making those segments of the story accurate and believable. His habit of reading at least one political thriller a week for the past several years also helped illuminate shortcomings in the text.

RADM Chris Bina, USPHS, whose early experience in raising feeder hogs in rural Kansas gave him the needed background to advise on issues related to pork sale barns and feedlots.

Lieutenant Carl Schweers, Shelby County, TN Fire Department Supervisor, whose recommendations regarding the actions and training of first responders were extremely helpful in many scenarios of the story.

About the Author

John Babb is a former Assistant Surgeon General and retired Rear Admiral in the U.S. Public Health Service. Since his retirement from the practice of pharmacy, emergency preparedness, and public health, he spends much of his time writing historical fiction.

BONUS CHAPTER

Hell's Hip Pocket
John Babb

Chapter 1 The Leftovers
Smoky Mountains, North Carolina Oct. 25, 2076 AD

It would be generous to refer to the two horseback riders as getting on in years. In truth, Jase and Pard were well aware that they weren't the robust men they once had been, but they weren't about to acknowledge that fact to anyone, and particularly not to each other.

At least once a month, they made an all-day trip out of it, riding out of the Smokies and down into lower elevations to check on their holdings. After a quick stop for lunch, they topped a rise, and both spied the long narrow valley down below. The land was well watered, being the beneficiary of a fine creek which originated some 3,000 feet above them between two of the higher peaks in North Carolina.

Of course, the States had ceased to exist since The Collapse, and now meant no more than sketched outlines on a useless map. While they realized that was an accurate statement, it was difficult for them to accept, still thinking of themselves as not only North Carolinians, but Americans. As they rode down into the valley, their recently harvested field of forty acres of tobacco spread below them. That was one of their tasks for the trip—checking on their tobacco crop, currently drying in their tobacco sheds.

When they neared a narrow, rocky ravine on the north side of the valley, they turned their horses toward it. A casual observer would never realize what lay beyond such an inauspicious entryway. A barely visible trail wound through a narrow path, surrounded on either side by sheer rock cliffs. The rough track extended just over a hundred yards before suddenly opening up into a broad, lush pasture.

"How many times have we been up here to Hell's Hip Pocket, Jase?"

"Too many to count, Pard. We've had many a good time here. All my boys love this place, and I think it looks exactly like it did the first time my father showed it to me. This place might be the only thing in our lives that hasn't changed in the last fifty years."

"What about us? We haven't changed either. It's like you and I are a couple of leftovers from the way things used to be."

Jase nodded. "Leftovers—that's a pretty accurate description! Come on, let's check on those cattle while we're here."

Jase and Pard had been friends for forty years, and during that entire span, Padraig McMaster had never been called anything but Pard, not only by Jase, but also by everybody within hearing distance. Pard was not a large man, but was the owner of an outsized set of shoulders matched with a pair of forearms and fists which had been directly responsible for rearranging the noses and front teeth on many a mountaineer—some who were asking for it, and others who were merely in the wrong place at the wrong time.

Pard's roots originated from what many referred to as the Black Irish, giving him coal black hair, green eyes, and a somewhat swarthy complexion, rumored to have been inherited from Spanish ancestors. Many Spanish sailors had appeared along the eastern and northern coastlines of Ireland after the overwhelming defeat of the Armada in 1588 by England's naval forces and bad luck.

Pard's family had worked fields of tobacco in North Carolina since the potato famine had finally run his barely surviving Irish ancestors out of County Donegal in 1846. His fourth great-grandfather had brought those indelible memories of hard times with him as he became an indentured servant to a gentleman farmer from Asheville by the name of Winston Burdette.

Burdette had raised his crop on eighteen small fields perched just beyond the lower eastern flanks of the Smokies. Before the elder McMaster had satisfied the seven years of indebtedness which had reimbursed Burdette for the cost of his passage to America, he knew every bit as much about planting, cultivating, harvesting, curing, and preparing tobacco for market as did his sponsor. He had judiciously passed on his expertise to following generations, and finally to Pard.

Jase Calhoun claimed to be the fourth great-grandson of John C. Calhoun himself. But in reality, Jase's last name wasn't actually Calhoun, let alone possessing any blood relation whatsoever to the former South Carolina segregationist, congressman, senator, secretary of state, secretary of war, and vice-president. In fact, his mother had finally confided that she had no idea what his last name should be.

However, there had been times in the distant past when his claiming kinship to Calhoun had been beneficial, both to him and to his family. Besides, he even looked the part. Like his purported ancestor, Jase exhibited a flowing, snow-white pompadour combed straight back and draped over his collar—hair his wife managed to cut perhaps twice a year, if she could catch him. His blue eyes had been known to drill a hole in a concrete block, while his square jaw seemed to work in unison with that glare, as he had a habit of clenching his teeth when appropriately agitated.

Both men carried matching Colt Anaconda .44 Magnum revolvers tied high on their right legs. On those occasions when a broken nose or a damaged set of front teeth was not adequate to convince an antagonist they meant business, neither Jase nor Pard hesitated for very long about drawing their big pistols. So when the two of them spied the destroyed section of fence just inside the Pocket that afternoon, it wasn't surprising that their right hands instinctively felt for the worn-smooth hand grips protruding from their holsters.

They dismounted, tying their horses' reins to one of the few fence posts still standing near the loading gate. Pard squinted into the distance, looking for any sign of someone hiding up in the timber. It would be a simple thing to bushwhack them from a hundred yards away.

At the same time, Jase knelt over a couple of spots on the ground, studying the tracks in the dirt to see if they would tell him a story. "Probably yesterday morning—maybe the evening before. Five horses—one of them carrying a heavy load."

"You figure it was that damned Simple Samples? He's bound to weigh two hundred seventy-five if he weighs an ounce."

"One thing about The Collapse—there's hardly any fat

people left any more. My daddy used to say that at least half
the people in the old times were fat as corn-fed hogs. Nowadays, everybody struggles just to put enough food on the table
to get by, and if you don't have a horse, you're walkin'. So
most folks have got hardly any excess."

"Yeah, that kind of narrows it down to Samples. I passed
up two opportunities to shoot that SOB a couple of years
back. I guess I let my gentle nature override my judgment. I
knew good and well when I let him ride off that I'd made a big
mistake." Pard gazed off in the distance. "I suppose there's
not much point checking this whole eighty-acre pasture. I figure they got the entire thirty head without too much trouble.
It's not like the cattle were gonna fight back."

"This herd was supposed to feed our whole community,
at least long enough to get us through the worst of the winter.
Now we'll be hunting deer and wild hogs, maybe a sugar bear
or two, if we get a taste for fresh meat." Jase remounted his
horse. "Come on, let's ride up in the woods and hope they
missed a few stragglers."

A thirty-minute search of the timber revealed that the
rustlers had been thorough, so Jase considered their next
move. "It shouldn't be hard to follow their trail. Thirty cows
and five horses tend to advertise where they've been."

"A couple of things are bothering me here." Pard stared
off into the distance as if his elderly eyes could see through
the trees. "There's five of them and two of us, and we've only
got a couple of handguns with us. What's to stop one of them
with a decent rifle waiting out there on their back trail for us
to catch up? It would be a piece of cake to pick us off. The
other thing—what if this is more of a coordinated attack than
a one-shot deal?"

"Meaning what?"

"What if they went after our tobacco sheds at the same
time? We've harvested three times already, and all four sheds
up here are packed full of drying tobacco."

"You really think they're wantin' to start a war?"

"Hell, Pard—Samples has got as many guns as we do,
maybe more. He probably figures it wouldn't be that difficult."

"That might be, but he doesn't have the resources necessary to do anything for very long."

"If he's got our tobacco crop, then all of a sudden he has
all the resources he needs to fund a good long war. He'll have

all the help he wants, too. There's plenty of men who'll swap the shirts off their backs for a supply of burley tobacco."

"Say, Jase—isn't Junior and that brother-in-law of his supposed to be at the tobacco sheds?"

"Yeah. I hope to hell my oldest son is watching his back. Come on, let's get going."

It was a rough fifteen-minute ride up the Pocket to the sheds and the old cabin, just over a mile beyond the cattle pasture and over the hills from the little community of Green Valley, located in once-upon-a-time North Carolina. The late October weather started getting chilly at sundown.

They didn't notice the advancing chill, though. When they were still a half-mile distant, the acrid taste of burned tobacco was carried to them on the light wind, and the two men spurred their horses. The view ahead told at least part of the story.

All four tobacco drying sheds were burned to the ground, with little but still-smoldering oak posts to announce the location of where they'd housed what, for them, had been a small fortune in tobacco. Another hundred yards beyond the sheds sat the similar smoking remains of their cabin. Upon closer inspection, Jase discovered multiple wagon tracks along with what he deciphered as mule sign.

"How did you know they'd be coming here, Jase?"

"Just a feeling I had. I hope to hell they don't know about our other sheds, not to mention our stash of cigarette rolling papers up by Rock Creek." He looked at his friend. "It looks like they loaded every leaf they could onto maybe two or three wagons, then set everything else afire. Not only were they stealing—it looks like they were trying to wipe us out."

Pard nodded. "You stay here, Jase. I'll take a look around."

"If you see Junior, or that damned Wilson, tell them to get on back down here. Of course, they might be following those wagons so they can report where they went."

Within a few minutes, Jase discovered four sets of hoof prints, as well as the deeply depressed horse track he was seeking. Proof enough, as far as he was concerned, that Samples had led not only the stealing of his cattle, but this operation as well. Since The Collapse, there had been little attempt to have any formal law enforcement system away from the few remaining knots of people who'd gotten together for mutual safety, and at least attempted to control lawlessness. That was where men like Jase and Pard were forced to step into the vacuum. After all, there had to be a reckoning for what had happened. That was the only way men like Samples could be taught what was acceptable in these hard times.

As he digested the tracks, he gradually became aware of Pard sitting on his horse some twenty feet away. When the two friends' eyes met, Jase gave an involuntary shudder. "What is it, Pard?"

The message came out in a rush. "You can't go back there, Jase. It's bad—real bad."

"Just tell me. Tell me all of it."

"I don't want you to see, Jase. I'll take care of your boy. I'll treat him just like you would. But don't go see, Jase." At that point, wet tracks trickled down Pard's cheeks.

Jase mounted his horse, snapped the reins hard, and galloped by his friend as fast as his horse could go. He needn't have been in a hurry.

The tulip poplar stood sixty or seventy feet tall and almost as straight as an arrow two hundred yards beyond the destroyed cabin. Even on normal days, the solitary tree could not be missed. It almost insisted that it be noticed. Today, it didn't just insist—it demanded attention.

A figure dangled from the tree. Although completely unrecognizable at that point, Jase identified Junior by the silver belt buckle he'd given him one Christmas. Absent that evidence, he wouldn't have known his own son.

Junior hung upside down, his body gently swaying in the evening breeze by a rope tied to both ankles. He'd been there long enough that the blood had pooled in his head, and his face was a purplish, black mass, at least half again larger than it had been in life. His son had first been rendered defenseless, having been shot at close range in both knees and both elbows by a large caliber weapon. His belly had then been cut open, and someone had pulled several feet of intestines out of the wound. A multitude of flies lifted from the body as Jase finally managed to cut him down.

Sickened though he was, Jase forced himself to look at each individual wound. He wanted to be able to immediately call these visions to mind when he confronted the man who was undoubtedly responsible for such a cowardly, depraved act. His heart was heavy, but his mind was already preparing for a war of total destruction.

With only two horses and a fifteen-mile ride back up into the mountains, there was no way to take his son's body home. Besides, Jase would have died before allowing his wife to see her eldest son that way.

Pard rode a couple miles to a neighbor's place and fetched a pick and shovel while Jase did his best to get Junior cleaned up and ready for burial. It was all he could do to concentrate on the job at hand rather than fixate on the kind of agony his son must have endured while he hung in that tree—for no telling how long—waiting to die.

Some two hours after dark, the deed was finally done, and the two men stood over the fresh grave, hats in their hands. The words just wouldn't come. Finally, Jase managed to get out a sentence without breaking down. "He was a fine, God-fearin' man. I guess in the end, that's all there is to say. I only wish I could trade places with him."

As they started their journey back home, Jase's thoughts turned to what faced him. He had no idea how he was going to tell his own wife, let alone Junior's young wife, Tess. Not only had he cleaned up his son's destroyed body, he would now have to clean up the telling of his death to the rest of the family.

After thirty minutes of riding, Jase finally trusted his voice enough to ask a question. "Did you see any sign of his brother-in-law?"

"It looked to me like Webb Wilson wasn't even there when it happened. Either that, or he took off at the first sign of Samples and his bunch."

"Did you find any empty cartridges where Wilson might have at least got off a few shots?"

"No, but I found where Junior had been. It looked like he'd used up two clips before they got to him. Knowing Junior, I'd bet he took out several of Samples' boys first."

Jase nodded. "Let's go by Wilson's place—see what he's got to say for himself."

"Maybe he wasn't even there when it happened, Jase. You can't kill a man if he didn't even know about it."

Even in the dark, Pard could tell that his friend's jaw was clenched like a vise. "Let's just drop by and have ourselves a little conversation."

Thanks for reading! Dingbat Publishing strives to bring you quality entertainment that doesn't take itself too seriously. I mean honestly, with a name like that, our books have to be good or we're going to be laughed at. Or maybe both.

If you enjoyed this book, the best thing you can do is buy a million more copies and give them to all your friends... erm, leave a review on the readers' website of your preference. All authors love feedback and we take reviews from readers like you seriously.

Oh, and c'mon over to our website:
www.DingbatPublishing.ninja

Who knows what other books you'll find there?

Cheers,

Gunnar Grey,
publisher, author, and Chief Dingbat

δ

Made in the USA
Middletown, DE
05 August 2023

36228515R00229